Cold Warfare

A Compact History

Dr. Patrick J. Pacalo, Capt., Phd

PublishAmerica
Baltimore

First printing

ISBN: 1-4137-1925-2
PUBLISHED BY PUBLISHAMERICA, LLLP
www.publishamerica.com
Baltimore

Printed in the United States of America

This book is dedicated to my parents:
Capt. Nicholas Pacalo (USN-ret), and
Rose B. Pacalo

Table of Contents

Preface

This is essentially a book about ideology and the Cold War. In much of the course of this writing the US/Soviet relationship is the focus. Two chapters are concerned with material related to the time before the USSR was founded. These chapters on pre-Cold War developments are included since they relate directly to the reasons the Cold War happened.

Extensive use of quotes from public domain documents, many formerly classified and obtained from the Central Intelligence Agency under the Freedom Of Information Act (FOIA) are made in this work. All of these many quotes are footnoted, so the readers may see the sources and judge their validity accordingly. I realize that just because the CIA said it was so, does not make it fact. This being said, however, the documents are primary source material and evidence of what the US government was thinking at the time in each case. Also used extensively in this work are other primary sources such as collections of presidential papers and documents obtained from the private National Security Archive (housed at George Washington University). Additionally, microfilm of documents related to the US involvement in the Russian Civil War was obtained from the National Archives and used in chapter 2.

Perhaps here it would be best to give a brief explanation of how this book came to be. My interest in the Cold War dates to high school in the late 70s and early 80s. My first significant research on the topic came in the later part of 1983, as an undergraduate Political Science intern at the US Army War College (in the Strategic Studies Institute). I completed 4 months of full-time work as a research assistant for the Director of Military Strategy (the late Colonel William Staudenmaier) and a paper entitled "The Broken Promise of Sandinism: A Case Against US Aid to Nicaragua." A sanitized narrative of that experience is included in chapter 8 of this book. This sanitized version was cleared through the security office of the War College, and had to be so because I worked with and around a significant amount of classified material and attended classified lectures.

The reader will note that two sections of the work are redacted (the redacted portion marked with asterisks *) due to objections made by the War College. I submitted the narrative of the internship to the authorities for review because I was charged with safeguarding classified information during the course of my duties, and upon leaving the service signed an agreement that I would continue to do so under possible civil and criminal penalties. In addition, I do not want to do anything that may endanger national security or the lives of any members of the armed forces, intelligence services, diplomatic corps, or other government agencies.

This compromise being made, it should be noted that the remainder of this book was in no way censored by the US government. The balance of the information obtained for the book was found in public libraries and, with the cooperation of the CIA, through the Freedom of Information Act (FOIA). The law charges the CIA with compliance with the FOIA, and in my experience they were cooperative, consistent with the act. Some of the material the CIA provided demonstrates a "not too flattering" record of events for the agency. Additionally, some of the source material for *Cold Warfare* was found at the private National Security Archive at George Washington University and a few other documents were found at the public National Archives in Washington, DC. The bulk of this manuscript has not been submitted for security review, nor is that warranted because it is not based upon classified material to which I was exposed in the course of my duties. This book represents the free exercise of the free press.

The next significant watershed in the development of this book came in 1987-88, when as a Political Science senior at Indiana University of Pennsylvania, I completed an independent study on Iran-Contra entitled, "Democracy Divided: The Case of Covert Paramilitary Assistance to the Nicaraguan Resistance" under the direction of Dr. Ed Platt (formerly of the Army Security Agency). In the course of completing this study I developed the spectrum of conflict found in chapter 1 of this book. It is, I believe, a workable model of the range of action during the Cold War, along which most of the events of the conflict can be plotted.

Chapter 5, on John F. Kennedy and Cuba, was largely written in late 1992 as a part of a Historical Research Methods course taken for my Masters and taught by Dr. Saul Friedman at Youngstown State University. It was then that I thought for the first time of writing an encyclopedia of the Cold War. The idea of an encyclopedia mutated into the concept of a one volume compact history. The paper written for Dr. Friedman was entitled "The Cuban Missile Crisis in the Context of the Cold War." It won the Marion Blum award for best graduate paper in the history department, for that effort. Portions of the paper were presented at conferences at Duquesne University and the State University of New York (SUNY) in Buffalo in 1993.

Some of the rest of the raw data for chapters 1-4 and 6 were gathered as part of an independent study for my MA in 1993-94 and a seminar on Vietnam during that time period. Use of the FOIA was also begun at this time. I obtained my MA in 1995. For most of the next four years work on the book was very on again off again. Then in 1999 I found the motivation that led to finishing. For three and a half years I made FOIA requests and processed thousands of pages of formerly classified documents. Chapters 1-6 took their final form, and Chapters 7-8 were written. A web site was erected. And the book was finished.

According to the noted Columbia University historian, Henry Steele Commager, history is "subjective, fragmentary, and inconclusive—like almost everything in life … ."[1] We can, therefore, go into our examination of the Cold War with the notion that history is in many cases an inexact discipline. But with this in mind, we must go forward to do the work of history. Perhaps the contemporary saying "*easy does it... but do it*" applies. In this vein, I try to avoid drawing too many conclusions from the documents available, but to present the evidence and allow the reader to judge by quoting what I see as significant passages from the record.

There are several major schools of historical thought on the Cold War. Perhaps the most influential are what I like to call the dominant school, "initial contemporary" or "post World War II" historians. These people state that the Cold War was geopolitical at base and it began at the close of WWII. To understand its origins, they say, we must study Yalta, Potsdam, and the map of Europe.

I say that the Cold War was ideological at base and was well underway by the close of WWI, at the latest. To best understand the origins of the conflict, I say, study the U.S. Constitution, Marx, Lenin, and Woodrow Wilson.

In terms of sustainment of the conflict most Cold War histories pay far too little attention to the bureaucracies involved. The foundation of the CIA is a case in point. I spend much of a chapter on this watershed.

Another common characteristic of the initial contemporary historians is the emphasis on drama, as opposed to political process or bureaucratic momentum. The drama of the various crises was but mere symptoms, not the essence, of a conflict that was at its base bureaucratic and ideological. The roots of that conflict date to even before the Russian Revolution of 1917. Crises and drama are a part of this history, but far from its center.

A note on some things left out of this book: Not much coverage is given to China and Korea. In my judgment there was just not room for extensive coverage of these topics in a compact history. To the flow of US/Soviet relations, events in Korea and China were largely peripheral. This assertion is not to say they were unimportant, just that understanding them does not give much light to understanding the larger US/Soviet contest. I hope this position is not in any way taken as ignorance of the service of US diplomats in China, or soldiers in Korea. Their contributions to American security were significant.

In terms of historical school of thought, I am an *eclectic.* I say take what works and use it. I take this approach throughout this work, rather than subscribing to a single set of ultimate truths that explain all action. I hope you will enjoy this book.

Chapter 1

Concepts, The American Revolution, and The Constitution

Key Concepts

This work is an examination of the events and circumstances of how America opposed Soviet Marxism and won the Cold War. It also explains why the Soviets were seen as a grave threat to American interests. It is not an expose about the intelligence community; it is not even primarily about the broad topic of intelligence. This book presents what this author sees as the most important events and concepts in Cold War history based upon original research. The interpretations in this work will differ from many standard interpretations.

No one book can hope to tell the whole story of every aspect of the Cold War; this one explains the major policy watersheds and some of the important events of the conflict. First and foremost among means employed by America was covert paramilitary action, a large portion of this work is devoted to this type of warfare. It is covert paramilitary and political action combined with brinkmanship over a spectrum of conflict that this author calls "cold warfare." This type of warfare was semi-secret, on the margins, in the gray areas between diplomacy and total war. It involved subterfuge, threats, and quasi-legal or down right illegal activity at times. References to overt actions add descriptive detail to the context that made cold warfare necessary or desirable. The intent here is not to provide excuses, but to understand the events of the Cold War. It is of necessity, in this first chapter, to discuss some terms and concepts, American's earliest covert paramilitary action experiences, and the Constitution as related to the means used in the Cold

War.

A few definitions are key to this work. They may seem to have obvious meaning, but there can be more complexity than first appears. Take for example, the term "covert" action. What do we mean when we say an action is covert? It does not mean secret in the sense of clandestine intelligence gathering activity. When intelligence gathering is done correctly, the target never knows it was the subject of espionage. If on the other hand, for example, a covert sabotage campaign is launched against a given state, the target knows something is going on, though it may not be able to identify who is responsible. Rather than secret, covert means partially obscured, or unable to be attributed to a specific source. For the meaning of paramilitary we can take that it is almost military action, or the organizing of civilians to fight in low intensity combat operations.

Covert action in general, and specifically a refined form of covert paramilitary action, fit a niche for America during the Cold War. American leadership (presidents and the National Security Council [NSC]) sought to oppose the spread of Soviet Marxism, but they did not always have the desire or ability to call forth the standing military. Thus, they called on the secret operatives of the Central Intelligence Agency (CIA) to raise armies of indigenous civilians to fight the nation's battles against Soviet Marxism.

During WWII the Office of Strategic Services (OSS) was used to deal with the Axis powers behind the lines and in remote areas. Though it was quite effective in gathering intelligence and conducting sabotage against the axis powers, it was not the type of true covert paramilitary action agency capable of operating in peacetime. For one, the OSS reported to the joint military staff, not the president, as the CIA would in later years (through the National Security Council).

Clearly, by 1948-49, when the CIA was invested with its covert action capability and the Soviets had detonated an atomic device, a spectrum of conflict, which included covert paramilitary action, had evolved. Covert action was not new with the establishment of the CIA, but it was institutionalized with that act. The spectrum of conflict, or possible responses to a crisis, looked something like this:

Figure 1-1, The Spectrum of Conflict

Soft Policy Options--Hard Policy Options

Take No Action
Diplomatic Initiatives
Economic Sanctions
Covert Paramilitary Action
Direct U.S. Military Involvement
U.S. Soviet Confrontation
Nuclear War

Those options on the left of the spectrum are referred to as "soft" because they have fewer of the unpleasant side effects (mass casualties for example) than those on the right or "hard" end of the spectrum of conflict. The spectrum is not exclusive, that is to say that more than one option was often in use at one time, measures in actual fact tended to be on-going and over-lapping. It is illustrative of the fact that as a crisis progressed, over time, options selected tended to gravitate toward the right side of the spectrum. Direct use of US forces in Vietnam, for example, only happened after diplomatic efforts and covert action had failed to produce the results desired.

In 1831 a Frenchman, Alexis de Tocqueville, came to America to do research, which resulted in the popularly titled *Democracy in America*. Tocqueville said American democracy was inferior in foreign affairs, and from his remarks one could have concluded it would be impossible to win a conflict, like the Cold War, which spanned most of the 20th century. In Chapter 13, the section entitled "Conduct of Foreign Affairs, by the American Democracy" Tocqueville said in part:

> It is most especially in the conduct of foreign relations, that democratic governments appear to me to be decidedly inferior to governments carried on upon different principles ... Foreign politics demand scarcely any of those qualities which democracy possess; and they require, on the contrary, the perfect use of almost all those faculties in which it is deficient ... a democracy is unable to regulate the details of an important undertaking, to persevere in a design, and to work out its execution in the presence of serious obstacles. It cannot combine its measures with secrecy, and it will not await their consequences with

> patience. These are the qualities which more especially belong to an individual or to an aristocracy; and they are precisely the means by which an individual people attains a predominant position.[2]

Was Tocqueville correct? Clearly America was able to stay the course over the Cold War. On deeper examination, though, it becomes clear that only by sacrificing some of the democratic principles in the Constitution, about which the Frenchman wrote, was America able to win the Cold War. One thing Tocqueville seems to have overlooked in his examination was the secret diplomacy and covert paramilitary action involved in bringing France to America's aid during the revolution. In fact the Continental Congress waged a secret campaign to bring France into the war for a number of years. As a way of looking at the context that the Cold War was waged, we next take a brief look into America's early covert experience.

The American Revolution

From its earliest beginnings as a nation, America was involved in sponsoring covert action, including paramilitary action by privateers. One of the earliest secret programs was the diplomatic effort to enlist the support of France in the war with Great Britain. The entire scope of the effort involved a network of agents supervised by the Committee on Secret Correspondence of the Continental Congress. The initial success of the effort brought six-million dollars in secret aid from France in July 1775, a full year prior to the declaration of independence. Covert activities of the committee also included gunrunning and powder purchases from England, British colonies, and Holland. The Revolutionary War could not have been won without the efforts of the secret committee.

In September of 1775 the committee was given formal authority of Congress to expend funds and make contracts for the delivery of war material.[3] The committee was also empowered to arrange for the export of produce in exchange for war material. Distribution of the war material to the colonies, the continental army, and the selling of powder to privateers were also within the committee's realm.

A letter from General Washington to James Mease on May 20, 1777 reveals the motivation behind some of the almost mundane efforts of the Secret Committee to obtain proper clothing for US soldiers. From the letter we read:

> Sir: I am favoured with yours of the 12th Instant. I am informed, that Colo. Moylan has provided frocks for his men, with which they cover their Red Coats occasionally; it so, it takes off the objection which I had to their uniform. But this cannot be done by the foot, as they cannot carry a coat and frock, you must therefore contrive to have their coats dyed, as quick as possible.
>
> Colo. Mason's regiment must have brown and buff clothing. I imagine the troops from North Carolina will want every kind of necessary, you will therefore make preparation for them. I am informed there are about two thousand of them. I beg of you, every now and then, call upon the Secret Committee and know what accounts they have from abroad; if they are not frequently put in mind of our wants, they will, perhaps, forget or overlook them. I am, etc.[3]

Benjamin Franklin was the chief correspondent for the committee, which was a forerunner of the modern State Department. Since the American government was operating without a chief executive, the Continental Congress conducted the executive functions. The committee also had members like the prominent businessman, Robert Morris, who personally profited from some of the business deals the committee made.

The committee, through a combination of diplomacy and subterfuge, sought to get the French to enter the war against Great Britain; the secret aid was not enough. In turn the French urged the Americans to separate formally and finally from Great Britain, as the declaration of independence had not been issued yet. Silas Deane was one of the agents America employed in Paris in the effort to bring France to war with Britain. Dean had to constantly deal with the problem of British agents on his trail. He lived in Paris under an assumed identity.

In April 1776, the secret committee was empowered to arm and man vessels in France for attacks on British shipping.[5] This was America's first covert paramilitary action campaign. The privateers were to capture British prizes and bring them to French ports. It was hoped that the missions operating from French ports would lead to war between Britain and France. The Ships also had some Frenchmen in their crews as a further provocation against Britain. There was even the bold suggestion of raids on the British cities of Glasgow and Liverpool in Franklin's correspondence on the matter.

Contained in the committee's correspondence was the clear statement of intent, "it is our business to force on a war ... for which I see nothing as likely as fitting our privateers from the ports and islands of France."[6] If the French King had read this correspondence, it would have seriously soured relations between France and America. As it was, the raids were having an effect of British/French relations, British Lord Rochford attacked France publicly on the matter.

The privateers were successful in that they increased the tension level between France and Britain. The French acted to stop the raids by holding the American ships in port and taking the French members of their crews to prison. The feelings of glee over the friction between the two European powers, which the American rebels experienced, were expressed in one of Washington's letters in November of 1777, which states in part:

> We have an account, indeed, which seems to gain credit, that (Captain) Weeks, with a squadron of ships fitted out of French ports, under continental colors, had taken fifty-three homeward bound West Indiamen (chiefly from Jamaica) in the English channel; and war expected every moment between France and Britain. God send it.[7]

The diplomatic goal of the secret committee was an alliance with France. In this they enjoyed a large measure of success after the defeat of the British forces at the battle of Saratoga on October 17, 1777. Believing America had a chance for victory in the war, the French entered into a secret agreement to form an offensive and defensive alliance with America in December 1777. In early 1778 France publicly entered the war against the Britain. The American victory at Yorktown, the most decisive of the war, would not have been possible was it not for the presence of the friendly French fleet.

Subsequent to America's victory in her war for independence, the Constitution was approved to replace the immediate post war Articles of Confederation. The new federal Constitution contained some pitfalls that would literally dog United States policy formulators, particularly in the post Vietnam/Watergate era of the 1980s when events precipitated that caused the Iran-Contra scandal to burst on the political scene.

The Constitution

The framers of the Constitution developed the American government in such a way that power was fragmented. They put together a system of coordinate responsibilities so no part of the government could act in a tyrannical way. This fragmentation of power and these coordinate responsibilities are part of what led to the evolution of the spectrum of conflict responses in figure 1-1.

Let's look at Article I, section 8. Congress is given the following powers ... *to provide for the common defense ... to declare war ... to raise and support armies ... to provide for and maintain a Navy ... to make public laws which shall be necessary and proper for the carrying into execution the foregoing powers, and all other powers vested by this constitution in the government of the United States, or any department or officer thereof.*

Then in Article II, section 1 and 2, the president is given his share of power as follows: *The executive power shall be vested in the President of the United States ... the president shall be the commander in chief of the army and the navy of the United States, and of the militia of the several states, when called into the actual service of the United States ... and with the advice and consent of the Senate, shall appoint ambassadors, other public ministers and consuls, judges of the Supreme Court, and all other officers of the United States ...*

So, the Constitution complicates matters in foreign affairs, and deliberately so that too much power is not concentrated in any one particular's hands. It takes the powers of both the legislature and the executive to fight a war. Later we shall see how the Congress and the office of the president sought to uncomplicate it in the face of Soviet Marxism/ Leninism and thus ceded away some of the protection in the Constitution.

Conclusions to Chapter 1

From America's early experience we can conclude that the nation had a cunning ability to use covert warfare. Tocqueville was incorrect when he said democracy could not employ secrecy, in the revolution it had with the Committee on Secret Correspondence. However, Tocqueville had identified points of friction—it would be difficult for America to employ secret means because her form of government required openness. In the years following the revolution, when the Constitution was adopted, there were no provisions for an intelligence bureaucracy. In fact, article I, section 9 required all expenditures to be a matter of public record, thus making it ever more difficult to establish an intelligence operations agency.

George Washington seems to have been an advocate of there being no secret bureaucracy in the government. He hinted at the idea that an organization like the CIA with its military heritage might prove counter to democratic government. In fact, though he employed a network of secret agents during the war for independence, he stated in his farewell address:

> Avoid the necessity of overgrown military establishments, which, under any form of government, are inauspicious to liberty, and are regarded as particularly hostile to republican liberty...[8]

And further:

> The spirit of encroachment tends to consolidate the power of all the departments in one, and thus to create, whatever the form of government, a real despotism.[9]

Another former general turned chief executive, President Eisenhower, sounded essentially these same warnings as he left the oval office after the 1960 elections and in his own words warned of a "military industrial complex."

Thomas Jefferson was even more specific when he approached the issue of an intelligence operations agency. In Jefferson's day, the term "secret service" was often applied to what we would today call covert action or intelligence gathering, not only the specific protecting of the president as the term implies now. In a letter to James Madison in 1804 Jefferson addressed the issue as follows:

> Every person who undertakes to expend money for secret service, must take on themselves the risk of being approved or not by the government, on view of the nature of the service, which can only be judged by knowledge of what it was. This kind of expenditure is susceptible of such abuse, that a strict eye should be kept on it.[10]

Jefferson hit on roughly the same concepts as Tocqueville. Though America had engaged in covert operations during the war for independence, her government was not well-constituted to handle such operations on a routine basis, and such activities were to be suspect in a democratic society. Jeffersonian-Madisonian democracy[11] with its emphasis on the consent of the governed and checks and balances would be the moral underpinning for US actions during the Cold War and may have seemed originally to have been viewed as the antithesis of maintaining a covert bureaucracy.

Jefferson's and by implication Washington's suspicion of any secret bureaucracy was accepted by American policy makers. This position of the founders that secret service was unnecessary was also a result of the practical fact that two huge oceans protected the country from foreign threats. The nuclear Inter-Continental Ballistic Missile (ICBM) had not been invented yet. The forces that caused the spectrum of conflict in figure 1-1 to come into effect in the 20th century were not yet present. So, America opted out of forming an intelligence community until 1882 when the Office of Naval Intelligence (ONI) was formed. Even the Civil War had not been much of an affair as far as the use of covert action was concerned. ONI is the first permanent covert agency, though primarily concerned with information versus operations (such as covert paramilitary actions), that still exists today, and it was formed 106 years after independence.

In the next chapter we examine Marxism-Leninism, the force that would cause America to adopt covert paramilitary means in a fight for survival. By 1948 the US would have a full-fledged covert action agency, and the perception of a Marxist-Leninist threat was the reason this agency was brought into existence. Now for a look at the force we call Marxism-Leninism, as it evolved from the 1840s.

Chapter 2

The Roots of Conflict

Marx and the Manifesto

Why, throughout the Cold War period, would the mighty United States be obsessed with the affairs of small, poor nations who could do her little direct harm (like Guatemala, Afghanistan, Cuba, and Nicaragua)? At first glance it appears absurd. In reality, the US was reacting to an ideological threat, not the relative strength of these nations. American policy makers were concerned with the spread of Communism throughout the globe; in these regions she chose to draw the line against Soviet expansionism. These efforts often resulted in support of equally undemocratic right-wing governments. Understanding of why the US acted this way begins with a complete understanding of Marxism/Leninism and the life of Karl Marx.

Marx was born in the city of Trier in 1818. In the 1830s he studied law and philosophy at the universities of Bonn and Berlin. In the fall of 1841, he received a doctorate in philosophy. From 1842-43, Marx edited the liberal newspaper *Rheinishe Zeitung*. A government censor put an end to Marx's tenure with the newspaper after Marx began to call for complete democratization in Prussian politics.

In 1844 Marx entered self-imposed exile in Paris, where he began publishing socialist literature and started a life-long collaboration with the wealthy Frederich Engles (1820-1895). Marx's writings again resulted in a tangle with the government and he was expelled from Paris. He took up residence in Belgium and continued to publish his work. In 1848, he published his most famous and influential work, *The Manifesto of the Communist Party.*

The Manifesto begins with the statement that, "the history of all hitherto existing society is the history of class struggles."[12] In the thesis, Marx proceeded to outline how history had evolved to the point where the bourgeoisie (owners of capital and land) held the average workers down in an oppressed state of being. As Marx put it, "these laborers (the proletariat), who must sell themselves piecemeal, are a commodity, like every other article of commerce, and are consequently exposed to all the vicissitudes of competition, to all the fluctuations of the market."[13]

Marx continued, stating that the proletariat must organize to end the oppression by the capitalists. He noted that, "all previous movements were the movements of minorities, or the interest of minorities. The proletarian movement is the self-conscious movement of the immense majority.[14] The proletarian class in one country, Marx held, had more in common with other proletarians in other countries than with the bourgeoisie in their own country. Marx proclaimed that, "the working man has no country." Thus, a "self-conscious" (or class-conscious) organization of proletarians worldwide should be developed. The Communist Party is the name Marx gave to this new and global proletarian organization.

Marx explained that, "the immediate aim of the Communists is the same as that of other proletarian parties: the formation of the proletariat into a class, overthrow of bourgeois supremacy, (and) conquest of political power by the proletariat."[15] This process would yield to the formation of a "dictatorship of the proletariat" in which committees of workers would rule by decree. During this period the dictatorship would do away with private property on the way to building communism. When that stage of the revolution was completed, all property would be held communally and a utopian state would be established. Marx concluded the Manifesto with the famous call to action, "workers of the world unite, you have nothing to lose but your chains."

After publication of the Manifesto, Marx continued to agitate in favor of a general worldwide workers' rebellion. In 1850, he made a speech before the Central Committee of the Communist League. He predicted violence and stated, "in the coming bloody conflicts, as in earlier ones, it is the workers who, in the main, will have to win victory through their courage, determination, and self sacrifice."[16] He also outlined the tactics Communists should use when operating in an emerging democracy:

> Alongside new official governments they must establish simultaneously their own revolutionary workers' governments, whether in the form of workers' clubs or workers committees,

> so that the bourgeois/democratic governments not only immediately lose their backing by the workers from the outset, but see themselves supervised and threatened by authorities who are backed by the whole mass of workers ... In order to be able energetically and threateningly to oppose this party whose treachery to the workers will begin from the first hour of victory, the workers must be armed and organized. The arming of the whole proletariat with rifles, muskets, cannons, and munitions must be put through at once.[17]

Marx did not see his revolutionary theories put into practice in his lifetime. In 1848, the Manifesto played a minor role in uprisings that took place in Europe, after which there were no significant developments. He published the first volume of his comprehensive study of capitalism, *Capital,* in 1867. He died in 1883 with the work unfinished. Frederich Engles, his longtime sponsor, edited and published the final volume of *Capital* in 1894.

Lenin

Lenin (Vladimir Ilich Ulyanov, 1870-1924) and his revolutionary cohorts were the first to fully attempt to put Marx's teachings into action. Lenin's stealing of the popular 1917 Russian revolution against the autocratic Czar was the product of a lifetime of writing, publishing, and socialist organizing. Born in a small town on the Volga on April 23, 1870, Lenin became a radical after his brother Alexander was executed for plotting to assassinate the Czar in 1887. He was once expelled from Kazan University for demonstrating, but obtained a law degree from St. Petersburg University in 1891.

Arrested twice in 1895-96 while organizing the "Union of Struggle for the Emancipation of the Working Class," Lenin was exiled to Siberia from 1897-1900. He published his first major work, *The Development of Capitalism in Russia* and married while in exile. After his exile he worked on the Communist newspaper *The Spark*. He founded the paper *Forward* in 1905 after he failed in an attempt to take complete control of *The Spark*. At the time of the outbreak of fighting in the First World War, Lenin was to be found in Austrian Galicia near the Russian border in an attempt to foment revolution there. From Galicia he was exiled to Switzerland, where he remained until the downfall of the Czar in 1917.

In his 1901 work, *Where to Begin* Lenin had added significantly to Marx's works. Marx never called directly for the use of terror in the course of the revolution against the bourgeois; Lenin did. His view of terror was that it was a useful tool, but not a substitute for more conventional use of force, like more "regular" operations conducted by a standing Communist army. He wrote in part:

> We have never rejected terror on principle, nor can we do so. Terror is a form of military operation that may be usefully applied, or may even be essential in certain moments of the battle, under certain conditions, and when troops are in a certain condition ... But it is our duty to utter strong warning against devoting all attention to terror, against regarding it as the primary method of struggle, as so many of the present time are inclined to do. Terror can never become the regular means of warfare; at best it can only be of use as one of the methods of final onslaught.[18]

Lenin's chance to implement the dogma he had both studied and developed came in October 1917. The events of the Russian Revolution are well-documented and will not be repeated here. Briefly, the Czar was overthrown by a popular revolt in March of 1917 and a government under an attorney named Alexander Kerensky was formed. Shortly after the Kerensky government was formed, Lenin arrived on the scene. He had returned to Russia on a train from Switzerland that had been provided by the Germans (who hoped Lenin would get Russia out of the war). Kerensky failed to get popular support because he kept Russia in the war, and by October 1917, Lenin and his Bolshevik party were able to take control in Russia. The Bolshevik slogan of "peace, bread, and land" played well with many of the Russian people.

On the ouster of Kerensky, Lenin argued before his party that a dictatorship of the proletariat should be set up with Lenin as dictator. This was done. A secret police force, called the Cheka, was also set up in order to be able to employ terror to opponents of the Bolsheviks. When Lenin unleashed the Cheka, after an attempt to assassinate him failed, more than 50,000 Russians were shot in the four-year-long "red terror." Another 2-3 million were forcibly starved to death when the Red Army cut their food supply.

In late 1917, Lenin called upon the Allies to end the fighting in the First World War. The Allies rejected this proposal and, in fact, President

Woodrow Wilson sent emissaries to Russia to try and convince Lenin to stay in the war until Germany was defeated. With Lenin's proposal for a total cease-fire rejected by the Allies, Russia entered into negotiations with Germany to establish a separate peace. The negotiations were initially unsuccessful, as the Bolsheviks were not prepared to accept the harsh terms insisted upon by the Germans. In February of 1918, the talks broke down and the Germans responded to the stalled talks with an offensive at the front. The Russian army literally melted before the advancing Germans. Lenin called upon the Bolshevik central committee to make peace at any cost. On March 3, the Bolsheviks and the Germans signed the treaty of Brest-Litovsk and the fighting on the eastern front ended. Lenin had given up Poland, the Baltic States, and Ukraine to gain the peace with Germany. A consequence of the loss of territory was that the Bolshevik capital had to be moved from Petrograd to Moscow, so as to be a safe distance from the border.

Woodrow Wilson and the Russian Civil War

Just as the Bolsheviks (who changed their official name to Communists in March of 1918) were ending one war by signing a peace treaty with Germany, another fight was beginning. The Russian Civil War would rage from early 1918 until March 1921. In the conflict, Lenin's Communists would be fighting both their own countrymen, and forces from nine different countries. Well over a million soldiers[19] from France, Romania, Poland, Japan, Britain, Italy, Serbia, Greece, and America entered the war against the Red Army.

In the beginning, the Allies (with the exception of America) wanted to intervene in the Russian Civil War for four reasons. First, they wanted to prevent the large amounts of military supplies provided to the Russians from falling into German hands. Second, the British, in particular, had the notion that the eastern front could be reconstituted with Russian volunteers, thus keeping up two fronts against Germany. Third, there was a strong anti-Communist feeling in most of the Allied nations. Winston Churchill expressed this reason for intervention when he said it was necessary to "kill the snake in its own nest."[20] The fourth Allied rationale for intervention was the gain of territory; this was a strong motivator for the Polish and Japanese.

In the summer of 1918 the British and French, who had already sent troops to fight the Red Army, were encouraging U.S. President Woodrow Wilson to do the same. Within the American government there was sufficient anti-Communist sentiment to support intervention. The American Counsel-General in Moscow, who had met with opponents to the Communists (called

"White Russians") urged Wilson to send troops. Wilson initially refused the proposition. However, in July of 1918, the president approved the sending of some 5,710 American troops to north Russia "to guard military stores."[21] Similarly, some 10,000 U.S. troops were sent to Siberia to secure ports and railroads. When the north Russia contingent arrived in the country in September of 1918, they were placed under the command of British General Frederick Poole. General Poole immediately sent the Americans into offensive combat operations against the Red Army. Over the course of their stay in the country over 200 U.S. soldiers died in north Russia.

As a result of Poole's ineptitude, Wilson almost immediately began consideration of withdrawal of American forces from north Russia. It had taken much convincing on the part of French Prime Minister, Clemenceau, to get Wilson to send the troops in the first place. Wilson had hesitated to do so because he felt that any U.S. involvement in the Russian Civil War would only make matters worse for the average Russian. He also was doubtlessly concerned with sending doughboys to such a remote area in a time when reinforcing them or even communicating over the great distance was a slow process.

The troops were on the verge of being ordered out of north Russia when Wilson got word of Poole's actions. As well as sending the Americans into combat with the Reds, Poole had appointed a French officer as military governor of the city of Archangel. Wilson was infuriated, as he was dead-set against political involvement concerning the government in Russia. Wilson had initially believed that the overthrow of the Czar was a good thing, and that the Russian people would eventually come up with a working form of democracy on their own. He believed the action Poole took only made matters worse.

All of the president's frustration over British action in north Russia was put aside when he received word that Lenin's Red Terror was sweeping across Russia. On receiving notice from Secretary of State Lansing that the Communists were on a mass killing spree, he put the removal of troops from north Russia on hold and issued an anti-Communist directive to all U.S. diplomatic stations throughout the world. The directive was the first coordinated effort on the part of America to fight Marxism-Leninism. In large respect, this dispatch represents the real beginning of the U.S./Soviet Cold War, or at least the ideological underpinning, in that it outlines why America would oppose Soviet Marxism for the next seven decades. The text of the dispatch was as follows:

> This government is in receipt of information from reliable sources revealing that the peaceable Russian citizens of Moscow, Petrograd, and other cities are suffering from an openly avowed campaign of mass terrorism, and are subject to wholesale executions. Thousands of persons have been shot without even a form of trial; ill administered prisons are filled beyond capacity and every night scores of Russian citizens are recklessly put to death; and irresponsible bands are venting their passions in the daily massacre of untold innocents.
>
> In view of the earnest desire of the people of the United States to befriend the Russian people, and lend them all possible assistance in their struggle to reconstruct their nation upon principles of democracy and self-government and acting, therefore, solely in the interest of the Russian people themselves, this government feels that it cannot be silent or refrain from expressing its horror at the existing state of terrorism. Furthermore it believes that in order, successfully, to check the further increase of the indiscriminate slaughter of Russian citizens, all the civilized nations should register their abhorrence of such barbarism.You will inquire, therefore, whether the government to which you are accredited will be disposed to take some immediate action, which is entirely divorced from the atmosphere of belligerency and the conduct of the war, to impress upon the perpetrators of these crimes the aversion with which civilization regards their present wanton acts.[22]

Probably because he did not want to send a mixed message on the Red Terror, the president left the troops in north Russia and Siberia for the time being.

Wilson did not, however, wait an inordinate amount of time before withdrawing troops from north Russia. In November 1918 an armistice was signed between France, Britain, America, and Germany; this made the guarding of war stocks no longer a valid rationale for having American troops in Russia. A letter sent by General Pershing in Washington, to the Chief of Staff and the heads of the Army intelligence and operations sections, demonstrates the low morale of the American Expeditionary Force in North Russia in November of 1918. Part of the letter reads as follows (the style of the letter is preserved so as not to alter any meaning):

> For Chief of Staff. Following cable received repeated for your information Archangel 173 November 27th 7:00 P.M. The following report concerning American and Allied troops in northern Russia for your information. The morale of our troops has been low since the signing of the armistice with Germany. The men and some of the officers seem unable to understand why they should be kept in Russia after fighting has stopped with Germany, the profess to believe that American troops are being used to further selfish designs of England upon Russian territory and resources. Our troops are split up into small detachments covering numerous portions of a wide front with the chief command invariable in British hands, frequently a "local" rank being given to retain seniority. Several of these British officers have been grossly inefficient. The attitude of the others toward the Americans has been such as to cause great irritation and exasperation. As a result there has been much friction and bad feeling between our troops and the British. This seems to increase rather than diminish with time. At a time grave doubts were expressed by many of our officers that orders for aggressive operations would be obeyed. Some of my assistants and myself have visited the front, talked with officers and men, and found this feeling quite general. Many thought our troops now here should be replaced by regulars or volunteers.[23]

The above letter was kept classified in the War Department archives until 1958. All of the records from the expeditions to Russia were classified, the first of them were declassified in 1947 and the last of them were made public in 1973 (full 65 years after the events). Official Washington probably wanted to keep the lid on the disharmony with the British and the story of direct American combat with the Reds so as to be able to manage public opinion and foreign relations.

Lenin took advantage of Germany's defeat to reclaim Ukraine and other lands lost in the treaty of Brest-Litovsk. His position as Soviet leader grew stronger throughout 1919. On June 7, 1919, no longer having a reason to be there, the last of the Americans left Archangel in north Russia. It was, however, not until almost a year later, on April 1, 1920, that American troops were withdrawn from Siberia. America's experiment with fighting Communists directly on their home territory had failed. U.S. troops departed with nothing to show for their efforts but a bloodied nose.

For a time the White Russian forces held much of the country and the Communists had been in a tough position. This changed abruptly and permanently in October 1919, when the Red Army launched a counter offensive against the overextended White front of over 1000 miles in length. Key to the red victory in the civil war was the efforts of Leon Trotsky (Lev Davidovich Bronstein, 1879 – 1940). Trotsky's leadership of the Army brought a total Red victory by 1922.Trotsky's association with Lenin went back to 1905.

As Commissar of War and President of the Supreme War Council, he was personally responsible for the increase in strength of the Red Army from less than a million men to over 5 million. Trotsky believed in permanent revolution; that is to say that he believed there should be no pause to consolidate a Communist state in Russia. He favored the revolutionary efforts of the Communists to continue until the entire world was under Communist control. He would enter into a rivalry with Joseph Stalin (Iosif Vissarionovich Dzhugashvili, 1879 – 1953), the Communist Party Secretary General, for control of the Soviet state after Lenin's death.

A Red Scare and its Consequences

The Red rise of power in the former Russian Empire brought immediate consequences in the American body politic. Fear of possible worldwide Communist revolution ignited and peaked in 1920. Some in the Wilson administration looked at the activities of Russian nationals in this country and saw a conspiracy to destroy America. In January of 1920, a nationwide sweep of arrests under the authority of Attorney General, Mitchell Palmer, netted some 4,000 arrests of suspected Communist revolutionaries. Palmer stated, "like a prairie fire, the blaze of revolution was sweeping over every American institution of law and order."[24] On the state level, the Illinois States Attorney announced that conspirators were going to "seize businesses, the industries, and the natural resources of the country by direct action" and set up a Soviet government.[25] The intent of the raids was to deport as many of those arrested, as they were Soviet citizens. In actuality fewer than 700 of those arrested were deported.

While the Marxist-Leninist ideology of the emerging Soviet state was indeed internationalist in character, it is highly unlikely that the Soviets gave much material support to the revolutionaries in the US, outside of advice and propaganda. The Soviets were in the midst of a war for their very survival, and they could spare little in terms of resources for the cause of world revolution. What American policy makers were in large part reacting to was Communist rhetoric directed at democracies and the reports of Red Terror in Russia. Fear of Red Terror spreading globally would be a key motivator for the United States during the Cold War.

Let's look at some of Lenin's statements concerning the need to spread revolution. In 1917, he stated:

> There is one, and only one kind of internationalism indeed; working wholeheartedly for the development of the revolutionary movement and the revolutionary struggle in one's own country, and supporting (by propaganda, sympathy, and material aid) such, and only such struggle and such a line in every country without exception, everything else is deception."[24]

And further, the Soviet leader proclaimed, "the substitution of the proletarian state for the bourgeois state is impossible without violent revolution."[27]

At the second congress of the Communist International in July 1920, Lenin said in part:

> If our international comrades help us to organize a single army, then no defects will prevent us from accomplishing this task. The task is the task of world proletarian revolution, the task of creation of a world Soviet republic."[26]

Even though Lenin did not have the resources to see his dream of world revolution come true, statements like these, combined with some criminal activity by revolutionaries in this country, constituted a threat in the eyes of US policy makers. The Communist International, at which Lenin spoke in 1920, had been set up with the express purpose of coordinating Communist revolution worldwide.

In this atmosphere of charged rhetoric and hostility between the two nations, America refused to recognize the new Soviet government. Secretary of State, Colby, wrote in August of 1920:

> We cannot recognize, hold official relations with, or give friendly reception to the agents of a government that is bound and determined to conspire against out institutions; whose diplomats will be agitators of dangerous revolt; whose spokesmen say that they sign agreements with no intention of keeping them.[29]

In his memoirs, Herbert Hoover (president from 1929-33) dealt with the problem of recognizing the Soviet government in stark terms. He wrote:

> The question of recognizing the Soviet government arose periodically. It was pressed by pseudo "liberals" and at times by business organizations that believed a lucrative trade could be established with the Communists. Secretaries Hughes and Kellogg and I were in complete agreement that we should have none of it. So were Presidents Harding and Coolidge. I likened the problem to having a wicked and disgraceful neighbor. We did not attack him, but we did not give him a certificate of character by inviting him into our homes.We were well aware that the Communists were carrying on underground organization and propaganda for the overthrow of our government by violence. But denial of recognition kept their potency from being serious.[30]

It was not until 1933, when Japanese militarism was on the rise and Hitler was in power in Germany, that the newly seated administration of Franklin Roosevelt decided to recognize the Soviets as a counterbalance.

Stalin and Lend-Lease

In 1924, Lenin died and a power struggle developed between Stalin and Trotsky. Trotsky called for the immediate global spread of the Soviet revolution; he claimed the USSR would only be safe when the rest of the world was under Communist control. Stalin, on the other hand, tended to advocate the strengthening of Communism within the USSR before attempting to spread the revolution.

Trotsky lost the struggle to succeed Lenin after he was removed from his official posts and exiled by Stalin in 1925. A Stalinist agent murdered Trotsky at his residence in Mexico in 1940. After ousting his opponent, Stalin consolidated his power in the Soviet Union until he was in firm control in the late 1920s.

During his consolidation of power, Stalin identified the slowly brewing Cold War; he predicted a collision of interests with the West. In 1927, speaking to a delegation of American workers visiting the USSR, he said:

> In the course of further development of international revolution there will emerge two centers of world significance: a socialist center, drawing to itself the countries which tend toward socialism, and a capitalist center, drawing to itself the countries which tend toward capitalism. Battle between these two centers for command of the world economy will decide the fate of capitalism and communism in the entire world."[31]

The above statement, when viewed combined with one made in 1939 that "the state would not whither away even after the transition from socialism to communism, unless the capitalist encirclement is replaced by socialist encirclement" shows a continuity of thought from Lenin and Trotsky to Stalin. While Stalin was more conservative than the other two ideological figureheads were, he still believed that communism must eventually span the entire globe, and the USSR must do what it could to see this happen.

Another continuity from Lenin to Stalin was on the use of terror. Stalin extended Lenin's terror policy when in 1934 he launched the "Great Terror." Stalin's terror was much greater in scope then Lenin's had been, though. Tens of millions of Soviet citizens were imprisoned, exiled, and perhaps 20 million were killed from 1934-40.

In spite of the diplomatic opening of relations with the Soviets by Roosevelt, in 1939 the Soviets entered into a non-aggression pact with the Nazis in Germany. The pact pledged both sides to neutrality in the event one of the parties became involved in a war. The Germans were prepared to launch their invasion of Poland that year. They knew war was likely with the French and British; they did not want to repeat the trauma of WWI with its two fronts. The Soviets reaped benefits from secret portions of the pact pertaining to the invasion of Poland; they gained about 1/3 of Polish territory. Also, Stalin gained parts of Romania and all of Latvia and Estonia (and later Lithuania).

At the start of the Second World War, with Germany opposed by an alliance of Britain and France, the Soviets adopted a policy of not provoking the Germans. In spite of Stalin's docility toward Germany, the Nazis invaded the USSR with 180 divisions on the morning of June 22, 1941. Having knocked France out of the war in 1940 the western front was secure. The German Army was free to advance deep into the Soviet nation in a bid for conquest of their ideological opponent.

Once Germany attacked the USSR, the beleaguered British welcomed Stalin as a new ally. Churchill put his willingness to enter into an alliance with the communists he so hated this way, "if Hitler invaded hell, I would make at least a favorable reference to the devil in the House of Commons."[32]

In October 1941, more than two months prior to Pearl Harbor brought America formally into the war, the US began sending vast amounts of aid to the Soviets. The aid, began because of American fear of Hitler conquering the entire Eurasian land mass, was continued after America entered the war on her own account. The reason for the aid was not because of any newfound American trust of the Soviets, it was sent out of a desire to see Germany defeated, it was a temporary and expedient measure. The total dollar value of the aid was some $11 Billion. The list of items provided by America included: 427,000 trucks, 13,000 Tanks and Combat Vehicles, 35,000 Motorcycles, 2,000 Locomotives, and 11,000 Rail Cars. Though Stalin wanted the flow of aid continued after the war, it was stopped when Germany surrendered.

Conclusions to Chapter 2

Marx called for world revolution by the working class in 1848, not much happened. In 1901, Lenin added the work done by Marx in that he allowed for the use of terror as a revolutionary tool. Revolutionary Marxism-Leninism was the cause for friction between the US and USSR even before the post WWII period. The actual roots of the Cold War lie in the end of WWI.

The Russian revolution of 1917 brought leadership to the fore in Russia that came into direct conflict with America's leadership. President Woodrow Wilson, who was initially slow to anger at the Soviets, eventually became a chief and vocal opponent of the Soviets and their Marxist-based doctrines. Wilson, a political science professor prior to becoming the 28th president, had tested his students on Marxism, in an unbiased way as a part of his course on advanced political economy at Princeton, in 1891. In 1922, after dealing with the Soviets for a number of years as president, he said of Marx, "I know of no man who has more perverted the thinking of the world."[33]

One misinterpretation of history has often been that the Soviets became a problem for US foreign relations only after WWII, when the Red Army occupied Eastern Europe. There was disharmony with the Soviets from the beginning of their revolution and even “hot” war between the two countries in 1918-1920. After that, it was some 14 years before America recognized the Soviet government. It was then that there was temporary tolerance of the Soviets with Lend-Lease (1941-45) because of US war aims concerning Nazi Germany. This was followed by a return to the status quo of hostile relations in the closing stages of WWII.

Chapter 3

The Emergence of The Central Intelligence Agency and Containment

Donovan and the OSS

After WWI America demobilized her intelligence services, as with every war up to that time. By 1922, the Army's Military Intelligence Division (MID) had its budget cut from its wartime high of $2.5 million per year to just $225,000 for the year. Reductions also occurred at the Navy's ONI, where the staff of analysts was slashed from 300 to 24 over a similar time period.

It was not until the flames of war appeared in Europe for the second time in a half-century that significant interest in intelligence resurfaced in the American government. Several projects for a centralized intelligence office were proposed and rejected throughout 1940 and the first half of1941. Finally, with the war in Europe almost two years old, President Roosevelt appointed Colonel William J. ("Wild Bill") Donovan to the post of "Coordinator of Information." Donovan would be the leading figure in intelligence throughout the war years. His task was to coordinate and correlate defense information, but not to direct the existing intelligence agencies. MID and ONI would still function under the direction of the Generals of the Army staff and the Admirals of the Navy staff.

Donovan was a man of humble origins. He was born to Irish Catholic immigrants in Buffalo on January 1, 1883. Being studious, he obtained a BA and a law degree from Columbia by 1907. After his studies he practiced law and, in 1911, became involved with the military.

Donovan helped to organize Troop I of the National Guard's "First New York Cavalry." Within a few months he was appointed as troop commander. In 1916, Troop I was called to active federal service to fight Poncho Villa on the Mexican border. By the time the US entered WWI, Donovan was a Major. Donovan's unit was sent overseas to fight the Germans, with Donovan now as a Lieutenant Colonel and squadron commander. He was in extensive combat in Europe and was wounded several times. Donovan not only won the Medal of Honor for his performance, he was also awarded the Distinguished Service Cross and the Distinguished Service Medal. By the end of WWI he was a full Colonel.[34]

After the war Donovan entered into politics and was defeated in a run for Lieutenant Governor of New York in 1922. In that same year, he was made US Attorney for the western district of New York. By 1929, he had been Assistant Attorney General of the US for five years under Presidents Harding and Coolidge. He remained active in politics throughout the 30s and was considered for the position of Secretary of War by FDR. At the behest of the Secretary of the Navy, on July 14, 1940, he made a secret trip to find out about fifth column activity in Britain. A year later he was in the position of Coordinator of Information (COI). The COI had a small staff; it was not a true intelligence agency, hardly even a beginning.[35]

By 1942, a new intelligence and operations organization had been developed, which would have far reaching impact. The office of COI had become the Office of Strategic Services (OSS) and was integrated into the military staff under the newly formed Joint Chiefs of Staff (JCS). In spite of his failure to predict the Japanese attack at Pearl Harbor the year prior, Donovan was retained as head of the intelligence effort by being placed at the head of the OSS. In addition to intelligence gathering, the OSS was heavily involved in psychological warfare, support of guerrillas, and sabotage operations. This combination of intelligence gathering and operations into one organization set the pattern for the post war development of the CIA into an intelligence gathering and operations agency in one organization. Typical of OSS operations behind enemy lines was the effort to support the French underground prior to the D-Day invasion. In the words of one OSS officer, who later became the head of the CIA, the OSS operatives assigned to the underground forces behind German lines were to,

> arrange for weapons and supplies to be parachuted into it, and coordinate its activities with that of Patton's Third Army,

> blowing up bridges, ambushing patrols, attacking depots, sabotaging communications, blocking road and rail lines, in a ceaseless series of hit-and-run harassing raids.[36]

The establishment of the OSS was not without its critics. The head of the Army's Intelligence effort (called G-2), Major General Strong, blasted the OSS and its procedures as "devoid of all reference to moral considerations or standards," and he called the OSS "a hydra-headed organization" that was setting itself up as a "central intelligence and planning agency."[37] Strong and others believed the centralization of intelligence functions had sinister implications for the future.

During the war, Donovan began contemplating the type of organization the country would need to perform intelligence functions after the allies were victorious. The plan he developed had several key objectives. Among these were that intelligence would be placed under civilian control (instead of JCS) and that the head of the new agency would be the chief of intelligence for the American government.

The functions of Donovan's proposed agency included the coordination of all intelligence agencies within the government (military and civilian), and the direct collection of information. Donovan included a function in his proposal that was a hold over from the wartime OSS. He gave his new unnamed agency the responsibility for the conduct of covert paramilitary action and subversion abroad.[38]

When Harry Truman assumed the presidency after Roosevelt's death in 1945, he rejected Donovan's plan. Further, when the war ended, Truman saw no need for a centralized intelligence and operations agency, and he disbanded the OSS on September 20, 1945. The disbanding of the OSS was a result of pressure from multiple quarters. In addition, the president had said, "this country wanted no Gestapo under any guise for any reason," the idea of a peacetime OSS had many enemies.[39]

Among the enemies of centralized civilian intelligence were the jealous generals and admirals, who had only grudgingly given wartime consent to the formation of the OSS after Donovan had agreed that it would report to the JCS. In addition, the State Department was not about to surrender any of its responsibility in foreign affairs. Further, the powerful J. Edgar Hoover, Director of the FBI, wanted to protect his own turf. At the time FBI turf included responsibility for espionage and counterespionage in Latin America. Finally, and not the least of the forces against the formation of a new intelligence agency, was the media. The press saw Donovan's plan as the creation of a new and "all powerful intelligence service to spy on the post war world and pry into the lives of citizens at home."[40]

Enter the Central Intelligence Group

For a short while, it seemed like America would have no permanent intelligence bureaucracy after the war outside of the military units involved in intelligence. This course seemed to follow the one set after all previous wars, with intelligence on the wane once peace was established. The OSS was carved up into three separate parts. Most of the analysts and researchers were transferred over to the State Department, where they were scattered throughout the organization rather than being kept together. The spies and counterspies were transferred to the War Department, where they were kept together as a unit. The third group, the paramilitary types who were responsible for covert paramilitary action, were "given the choice of making our careers in the regular military or going home," according to William Colby (former OSS man and later director of the CIA).[41]

In the post war world, it seemed like there might not be any threats to US interests. The Soviets had been a former ally (if only for a short time) and with no threats evidently replacing Germany and Japan, disbanding the OSS seemed to some a prudent move. Almost immediately after the end of hostilities in WWII, the terms of US posture toward the Soviets could be described as a "quid pro quo" approach. President Truman and his cabinet initially believed that if we respected the Soviets' interests, they would respect ours.

The quid pro quo approach ran into some problems almost from the start. After the London Conference of September 1945 US Secretary of State James F. Byrnes stated privately that, "the Russians were welching on all the agreements reached at Potsdam and Yalta."[42] The London Conference had been convened to establish formal peace treaties with Finland, Hungary, Romania, and Bulgaria (who had been allied with Nazi Germany). At the conference the United States representatives noted the failure of the Soviets to allow the free movement of persons in Romania and Bulgaria. The Soviets were clearly in the beginning stages of setting up Communist dictatorships in Eastern Europe in violation with agreements reached earlier. Stalin was acting on the basic communist doctrine of expansion of the ideology (or spread of the revolution).

In January of 1946, when difficulties with the intelligence gathering system had become apparent, and trouble with the Soviets was looming on the horizon, Truman did an about face and established the Central Intelligence Group (CIG). In his directive, Truman stated that, "it is my desire, and I hereby direct, that all federal foreign intelligence activities be planned, developed, and coordinated centrally so as to assure the most effective accomplishment of the intelligence mission related to the national security."[43]

Initially, the primary duties of the CIG were similar to that of the OSS forerunner, the COI. These responsibilities involved the evaluation of intelligence material and the coordination of existing intelligence agencies. Unlike the agency envisioned in the Donovan plan, there were no provisions for the CIG to conduct covert paramilitary activities. In the directive creating the CIG, President Truman specifically stated that, "no police, law enforcement, or internal security functions shall be exercised under this directive."[44] The director of the CIG was part of a newly created "National Intelligence Authority." This part of the provisions creating the CIG was more in line with the Donovan plan in that it called for the authority to consist of the highest level of presidential advisors who would be reporting directly to the president.

The CIG was a relatively small and weak agency. It had no budget of its own and a staff of only 80 personnel. Initially the CIG had no intelligence gathering capability of its own; it merely analyzed information for the Army, Navy, and State Department. In time it did acquire this capability when the former OSS spies and counterspies were transferred to the CIG from the War Department. In addition, the CIG was allowed to expand its scope to include espionage in Latin America (formerly the exclusive turf of J. Edgar Hoover's FBI).

The years 1946 and 1947 were ones of increasing friction with the Soviet Union. They would also determine the fate of US intelligence until the present time. We can get a good view of attitudes in the American government at the time from a 1946 telegram written by George F. Kennan, the Charge d'Affairs of the Moscow embassy. The 8,000-word "long telegram" was drafted in response to a query from Washington. In part Kennan stated:

> [The] USSR still lives in [an] antagonistic "capitalist encirclement" with which in the long run there can be no permanent peaceful coexistence...We have here a political force

> committed fanatically to the belief that with the US there can be no permanent accommodation, that it is desirable and necessary that the internal harmony of our society be disrupted, our traditional way of life destroyed, the international authority of our state broken, if Soviet power is to be secure.[45]

In terms of counter action, at the time, Kennan recommended only that the US study the Soviets with the same "detachment [and] objectivity with which [a] doctor studies [an] unruly individual."[46]

Secretary of the Navy, James V. Forrestal, expressed similar sentiments to Kennan in early 1946 when he wrote:

> We are trying to preserve a world in which a capitalistic-democratic method can continue, whereas if Russian adherence to truly Marxian dialectics continues, their interest lies in the collapse of this system.[47]

Clearly, important US policy makers were coming to the conclusion that the US and the USSR were bound to clash in the near future in some way. Kennan and Forrestal had identified the same ideological points of contention as Wilsonian policy makers had a generation earlier. In fact, the Soviets themselves had identified the points of contention between capitalist democracy and Communism some three decades earlier. Communism had to expand to survive; it could not coexist with capitalist democracy.

Patience and Firmness

In early 1946, the quid pro quo approach toward the Soviets gave way to a state of affairs known as "patience and firmness." As outlined by Secretary of State, Byrnes, patience and firmness was broken down into four elements. They were: 1) there would be no further concealment of differences with the Soviets; 2) there would be no further concessions to Soviet expansion; 3) US military strength would be reconstituted and the allies assisted in resisting the Soviets; 4) negotiations with the Soviets would continue.[48] Patience and firmness represented a more forceful approach to US-Soviet relations and events would demonstrate this forcefulness over the ensuing months.

Byrnes' recommendation that US military strength be reconstituted was largely a result of America's rapid demobilization at the end of WWII. At the end of the war with Germany the US armed forces stood at 12 million men.

In July of 1946 that figure was reduced to 3 million, and by 1947 the figure dropped further to 1.6 million men under arms. The defense budget took a similar plunge from $81.6 billion in 1945 to $44.7 billion in 1946; it further plunged to $13.1 billion in 1947.[49] In 1946 and 1947 the US was not preparing to fight a major war with anyone; she was cutting back from WWII and depending on her nuclear arms for protection.

Early in 1946 the US was faced with a crisis in Iran. The Soviets had occupied part of the country during WWII and were refusing to leave. Iran was the first real test of patience and firmness. By a combination of US diplomatic initiatives and Iranian appeals to the United Nations, the Soviets were forced to leave Iran by May. More information on the Iranian situation is provided in the next chapter.

On March 5, 1946, Winston Churchill sounded the theme of the American policy of patience and firmness in a speech at Westminster College in Fulton, Missouri. The speech crystallized the view that the struggle between the USSR and the west was real and a pressing problem. Churchill said in part:

> From Stettin in the Baltic to Triest in the Adriatic, an iron curtain has descended across the continent. Behind that line lie all the capitals of the ancient states of Central and Eastern Europe. Warsaw, Berlin, Prague, Vienna, Budapest, Belgrade, Bucharest, and Sofia—all of these famous cities and the populations around them lie in the Soviet sphere and are subject, in one form or another, not only to Soviet influence, but to a very increasing measure of control from Moscow... From what I have seen of our Russian friends... I am convinced that there is nothing they admire so much as strength, and there is nothing for which they have less respect than for military weakness.[50]

A year after Churchill's speech came the speech in which President Truman declared the policy that became known as the Truman Doctrine. The policy was the most forceful expression of patience and firmness. Moscow-supported Communist guerrillas who were besieging the Greek government in 1947 set the stage for Truman's proclamation. On March 12 of that year Truman went before Congress to ask for aid to Greece (aid for Turkey was also included in the plan). When Truman spoke he noted that an ideological conflict between east and west was underway. He said in part:

> The gravity of the situation, which confronts the world today, necessitates my appearance before a joint session of Congress.The foreign policy and the national security of the nation are involved... At the present moment in world history, nearly every nation must choose between alternative ways of life. The choice is too often not a free one. One way of life is based upon the will of the majority, and is distinguished by free institutions, representative government, free elections, guarantees of individual liberty, freedom of speech and religion, and freedom from political oppression.The second way of life is based upon the will of a minority, forcibly imposed upon the majority. It relies upon terror and oppression, a controlled press and radio, fixed elections, and the suppression of personal freedoms.
>
> I believe that it must be the policy of the United States to support free people who are resisting attempted subjugation by armed minorities or by outside pressures.[51]

The Truman Doctrine of assistance to free people resisting communism was the ultimate expression of Byrnes' patience and firmness policy, and it hinted at the next step in the process of development of policy toward the USSR.

Containment and the CIA Emerge

Five months after the proclamation of the Truman Doctrine, a new policy entered the scene in the form of an essay printed in *Foreign Affairs* magazine. This essay had unequaled impact on the shaping of American foreign policy for the remainder of the Cold War. The essay would lay to rest the policy of patience and firmness and replace it with a policy of "containment" of Soviet ambitions.

George Kennan wrote the essay entitled "The Sources of Soviet Conduct," under the pen name of Mr. X. He wrote under a pseudonym because he wanted to protect his career in the Foreign Service by keeping his name out of public controversy. In the article, Kennan outlined what he felt were the irreconcilable differences in US and Soviet society and he made some recommendations for US policy makers. In the article Kennan noted the importance of ideology as a cause of Soviet Conduct. Kennan's motivation for writing the article was simply that the Soviets had pressed their own designs for a totalitarian world order by expanding communism wherever possible. He recommended,

> the United States entering with reasonable confidence upon a policy of firm containment, designed to confront the Russians with unalterable counter-force at every point they show signs of encroaching upon the interests of the peaceful and stable world...
>
> ...The United States has in its power to increase enormously the strains under which Soviet policy must operate, to force upon the Kremlin a far greater degree of moderation and circumspection than it has had to observe in recent years, and in this way to promote tendencies which must eventually find their outlet in either the break-up or the gradual mellowing of Soviet power.[52]

Kennan called for the containment of Soviet style communism within its then present boundaries (which included Eastern Europe), not the rollback of Soviet influence (as some would later call for). This policy of containment, with rare exception, was the rule in US foreign affairs for four and a half decades.

In the atmosphere of increasing tension with the Soviets, the small and weak CIG did not survive long; in fact, it was doomed in the same month as Kennan's influential article was written. In July of 1947, the Congress passed the National Security Act of 1947 (which had been debated for much of 1946). The act created the Central Intelligence Agency, with the Director of Central Intelligence as its head (and the chief adviser to the NSC on intelligence matters). The functions of the new agency, as outlined in the act, were five fold. They are:

> 1) To advise the National Security Council in matters concerning such intelligence activities of the government departments and agencies as related to national security.
>
> 2) To make recommendations to the president through the National Security Council for the coordination of such intelligence activities of the departments and agencies of the government as relate to national security.
>
> 3) To correlate and evaluate intelligence relating to the national

> security, and provide for the dissemination of such intelligence within the government using where appropriate existing agencies and facilities, provided that the agency shall have no police, subpoena, law enforcement powers, or internal security functions...
>
> 4) To perform, for the benefit of existing intelligence agencies, such additional services of common concern, and that the National Security Council determines to be more effectively accomplished centrally.
>
> 5) To perform other functions and duties related to intelligence affecting the national security as the National Security Council may from time to time direct.

Now the intelligence community had the full force of law in its establishment. Whereas the COI, OSS, and CIG had been creations of the executive, the existence of the CIA had been debated and approved by both houses of Congress and then signed into law by the chief executive. America now had, for the first time, an independent civilian intelligence bureaucracy in peacetime. The CIA had a direct channel to the president through the top level of the NSC (the OSS did not have this). In the words of one director of the CIA years later, "the various competing intelligence services of the departments could [not]...control the agency's activities."[53]

The first four functions of the new agency, as outlined by the act, were classic information gathering and analysis functions; they also had to do with the coordination of information flow. The fifth, "to perform other functions," clause of the act left the door wide open for the CIA to follow the OSS and become involved in covert paramilitary operations.

Many of the original OSS operatives came into the CIA through the CIG; still, others took several years to return to intelligence work after leaving the service initially. This is why the CIA traces its heritage to the OSS, and the OSS had a deep paramilitary tradition. A good example of this carry over from the OSS to the CIA was the career of William Colby. Colby joined the OSS in 1943 as a 24-year-old major and paratrooper of the Army field artillery. Shortly before D-Day, Colby parachuted into occupied France to aid the underground resistance. His mission was a success and Colby survived the war.

When peace came and the OSS was disbanded, the paramilitary officers were given the choice of returning to the conventional military or pursuing civilian life. Colby chose to leave the service under these conditions. He went to law school and then went to work in Wild Bill Donovan's law firm. After a time working with his former OSS commander, Colby went to work for the National Labor Relations Board in Washington, DC.

In 1950, a former OSS associate, who was part of the CIA, recruited Colby to the agency. At first Colby agreed only to part-time intelligence work. In June of 1950, when the Korean Conflict broke out, Colby agreed to work for the CIA full-time. Colby would rise through a number of positions of responsibility in the agency to the position of Director of Central Intelligence in 1975. His rise through the ranks of the CIA demonstrates the esteem in which experience with covert action was held by the agency.

While Colby's career illustrates the point that many CIA men of the Cold War era had come from an OSS background, there was one notable face missing from the ranks of the CIA. Donovan remained out of the intelligence business after the war. He was involved in the debate around the creation of the CIA for a time, but then lapsed into relative obscurity. He would practice law until his death in 1959. Donovan, with his heroic military background, had given a military and paramilitary character to the OSS (which was, in essence, an arm of the military staff). When the OSS veterans moved into the CIA, they imparted this same military and paramilitary character to the agency.

Covert Action Capability

Containment called for opposition to Soviet thrusts; however, when it was founded in July of 1947 the CIA did not have the covert paramilitary action capability required to meet the threat. Kennan, who was by 1948 directing US foreign policy through his position as director of the State Department's Policy Planning Staff, was concerned about this lack of capability to intervene in areas threatened by the Soviets. In the top secret Policy Planning Staff memorandum #23 (PPS #23) of February 1948 (entitled "Review of Current Trends: US Foreign Policy"), Kennan and his staff stated:

> It cannot be too often reiterated that this government does not possess the weapons, which would be needed to enable it to meet head-on the threat to national independence presented by the communist elements in foreign countries. This poses an extremely difficult problem as to the measures, which our government can take to prevent the communists from achieving

> success in the countries where resistance is the lowest.The planning staff has given more attention to this than any single problem, which has come under examination. Its conclusions may be summed up as follows:
>
> 1) The use of US regular armed forces to oppose the efforts of indigenous communist elements within foreign countries must generally be considered a risky and profitless undertaking, apt to do more harm than good.
>
> 2) If, however, it can be shown that the continuation of communist activities has a tendency to attract US armed power to the vicinity of affected areas, and if these areas are ones from which the Kremlin would definitely wish US power excluded, there is a possibility that this may bring into play the defensive security interests of the Soviet Union and cause the Russians to exert a restraining influence on local communist forces.[54]
>
> The PPS concluded with a recommendation on what the US should do in response to the communist threat in the Mediterranean:
>
> The staff has therefore felt that the wisest policy for us to follow would be to make it evident to the Russians by our actions that the farther the communists go into Greece and Italy, the more surely will this government be forced to extend the deployment of its peacetime military in the Mediterranean area.[55]

Since the US did not have at its disposal the covert means to oppose the Soviets within the threatened areas, and US military forces were not suited for internal intervention (as the OSS had been); Kennan was recommending the visible deployment of US forces to the general area in order to force the Soviets to back down.

In the same month that PPS #23 came out, the Soviets cemented their hold on another East European country. The Czechoslovakian Communist party had held the premiership of the country and forty percent of the seats in the parliament. The Communists, with the aid of Soviet secret agents, took advantage of a crisis in parliament to exclude anti-Communists from the government. The Czech-Communist Party had established one party rule, with the aid of Moscow.

At this time, Kennan began to believe that some capability to resist moves like the Czech coup was needed in the US government. Kennan stated in his

Memoirs that, at this time:

> Some of us in the United States government, including myself, my friend, the late Allen Dulles, later deputy director and director of the Central Intelligence Agency, and certain members of our respective staffs, came to the conclusion that the government had need of some sort of facilities through which there could be conducted, from time to time as the need arose, operations in the international field for which it would not be proper for any regular departments or agencies of the government to take responsibility, or for which the regular procedures of government were too cumbersome. We needed, in other words, an agency for secret operations.[56]

Kennan's thoughts continued:

> The thought was entirely sound. It was not a question of establishing what became referred to as "a department of dirty tricks." It was a question of creating a facility designed to give greater flexibility to the operations of government, now involved in a global Cold War, whose traditional arrangements for the appropriation and use of public funds were wholly unsuited to such a role in world affairs.[57]

Under pressure from Kennan, the capabilities of the CIA were to be enhanced to include the ability to undertake covert paramilitary operations. On June 18, 1948, in the centennial year of the Communist Manifesto, the National Security Council authorized the CIA to create the "Office of Special Projects" to undertake covert actions. National security directive 10/2 reads as follows:

> The National Security Council, taking cognizance of the vicious covert activities of the USSR, its satellite countries and Communist groups to discredit and defeat the aims and activities of the United States and other western powers, has determined that, in the interest of world peace and US national security, the overt foreign activities of the US government must be supplemented by covert operations.[58]

With this step, the NSC now widened the options of the president in response to crisis. The president would now be able to take hard measures, short of full-scale war, against the Soviets and their allies. Further, the president would not have to go through the "cumbersome" (as Kennan called it) procedure of consulting Congress on each operation. The NSC and its small staff would do planning and debate on missions that would play out in secret. There was no public debate what-so-ever in the Congress over NSC memorandum 10/2. The Congress had already thrown away its constitutional rights on the issue when it approved the National Security Act of 1947 (which allowed the CIA "to perform other functions and duties related to intelligence affecting the national security as the National Security Council may from time to time direct"). This move taken by the NSC would involve the US in peacetime conflict that had some similarities to war but lacked the formality and intensity of full-scale war. It is this extended conflict that became known as the Cold War. The newly formed CIA would occupy the front lines in this Cold War.

William Colby put the rationale behind the CIA having covert operations capabilities this way:

> With the rising intensity of the Cold War and the clear use by the Communist world of infiltration, subversion, and guerrilla techniques—in Greece, in Western Europe, and in the Philippines—an increasing number of voices argued that the United States had to have not only the intelligence collecting and analysis capability to report on the Cold War, but also the political and paramilitary capability with which to fight.[59]

NSC directive 10/2 gave the president and the NSC permission to fight using the following methods:

> Propaganda; economic warfare; preventative direct action, including sabotage, anti-sabotage, demolition, and evacuation measures; subversion against hostile states, including assistance to underground resistance movements, guerrilla and refugee assistance groups, and the support of indigenous anti-Communist elements in threatened countries of the free world. Such operations shall not include armed conflict by recognized [US] armed forces.[60]

Directive 10/2 also stated the purpose of such covert operations was that they be "so planned and executed that any US government responsibility for them is not evident to unauthorized persons and that if uncovered the US government can plausibly disclaim any responsibility for them."[61]

Containment called for all Soviet thrusts to be met with equal counter-force. In the coming struggle, which would include much of the globe, these thrusts often took the form of covert paramilitary and political actions on the part of the Soviets. Soviet expansion in the third world also took the form of direct military action and direct military aid programs. The CIA, as constituted in 1948 with its covert action capability, would seem to be the perfect weapon for use in containing the Soviets and their allies.

The Cold War Comes of Age

By the end of 1948, Stalin had ended the capitalist encirclement that he and Lenin, before him, so despised. Romania, Bulgaria, Hungary, Poland, Czechoslovakia, and East Germany were all safely under Soviet control. In June of 1948, Stalin attempted to consolidate control of East Germany. He tried to force the western allies out of their occupation sectors of Berlin by blockading the routes into the city from West Germany (a distance of 110 miles away). The US resisted the blockade through an air resupply of West Berlin. In May of 1949 the Soviets lifted their blockade, having been unsuccessful in their attempt to force the allies out of the city.

Cold War fears and tensions were heightened by two events in 1949. First, in the early part of the year, Communist forces took control of China. The second blow to the west was when the Soviets detonated their first atomic bomb at the end of August (which was announced to the public on September 23 by President Truman). Communism had leaped forward in its quest for world domination. It had seized control of more of the global population, and it now had the most powerful weapons known to mankind. It should be noted here that the US intelligence community was not completely surprised by the Soviet's first atomic blast. In a Central Intelligence Group summary entitled "Soviet Foreign and Military Policy," dated July 23, 1946 the intelligence community took the position that, "the Soviets will make a maximum effort to develop as quickly as possible such special weapons as guided missiles and the atomic bomb." The report concluded that, "Some reports suggest that the Soviets may already have an atomic bomb of sorts, or at least the capability to produce a large atomic explosion."[62]

On June 25, 1950, the Cold War turned hot. The North Korean Communists, who had been trained and equipped by Moscow, invaded South Korea. The invasion took the American government, including the CIA, by surprise. Just five days before, the US Assistant Secretary of State for Far Eastern Affairs, Dean Rusk, had told a congressional committee, "we see no present intention that the people across the border have any intention of fighting a major war."

As a result of the CIA's failure to predict the North Korean onslaught, President Truman fired the Director of Central Intelligence, Admiral Roscoe H. Hillenkoetter. Truman replaced him with another military man, General Walter Bedell Smith. The fighting in the undeclared war raged until an armistice took effect on July 27, 1953. During the conflict, US troops would fight both North Korean Communist troops and their Communist Chinese supporters. When the fighting was over, there were 54,246 US dead and over 100,000 wounded. During the fighting the CIA played a role in sponsoring covert raids against North Korea and China.[63]

In April of 1950, the NSC reaffirmed its belief that covert actions were a proper means of pursuing foreign policy objectives. The formerly Top Secret "Strategic Reassessment of 1950" (NSC Memorandum #68) reads in part:

> The Soviet Union, unlike previous aspirants to hegemony, is animated by a new fanatic faith antithetical to our own, and seeks to impose absolute authority over the rest of the world...
>
> The integrity of our system will not be jeopardized by any measures, covert or overt, violent or non-violent, which will serve the purpose of frustrating the Kremlin design.[64]

With the issuance of NSC #68, the highest levels of the executive branch reasserted the position that the president had the power to undertake war-like action without congressional consent. Further, the NSC had gone to some lengths to state that these operations would not compromise the integrity of the American constitutional system.

Conclusions to Chapter 3

The Office of Strategic Services proceeded the CIA by six full years. It was not an independent civilian intelligence agency; it was primarily an operations arm of the joint military staff. The character of the OSS was determined by its leader, Colonel William "Wild Bill" Donovan, who was a WWI National Guard veteran and Medal of Honor winner. When the CIA finally was formed, using many veterans of the OSS as its base, the veterans imparted a military/paramilitary character to the CIA.

Donovan had proposed an agency to take the place of the OSS after WWII. The proposal was ignored and the OSS was taken apart after the war; there was initially no replacement for the OSS planned. Finally, in the year following the disbanding of the OSS, a small, weak agency called the Central Intelligence Group (CIG) was formed.

At the same time as these decisions were being made about the fate of US intelligence, several moderate policies toward the Soviets were tried (quid pro quo, and patience and firmness). Basic ideological differences with the Soviets were finally recognized and these policies gave way to an aggressive policy known as containment (the same differences with Soviet Marxism-Leninism were noted in the Wilsonian period, but were ignored for a time by Roosevelt and Truman era decision-makers). Containment, a creation of State Department bureaucrat, George F. Kennan, called for every expansionist move made by the Soviets to be met by equal counter-force.

In large part, due to these rising tensions with the Soviets, the CIA was created by the National Security Act of 1947. It was an independent agency, with its own classified budget, and a director who would be the president's primary intelligence adviser. Many OSS veterans, minus the heroic Donovan, made the transition to the CIA.

Initially, the CIA had no covert paramilitary capability. There was, however, a clause in the CIA charter, which allowed for the National Security Council to direct the agency to perform "other functions" related to national security and intelligence. In 1948, the NSC used this clause to create a covert action office within the CIA with the issuance of the memorandum number 10/2. By 1948 the CIA was a covert action agency as well as an intelligence agency.

The Cold War came of age in the years 1948 – 1950. Crises in Iran, Berlin, and China all brought the conflict with Soviet Marxism-Leninism to a head. The detonation of a Soviet atomic bomb in 1949 also raised the steaks and brought forth the specter of global Armageddon. In 1950 the Korean conflict brought the US regular military into direct combat with Communist forces.

By 1950, the use of covert paramilitary action as a policy tool had been twice ratified by the NSC, but never debated by the Congress. The reason was these anti-democratic measures were approved was because of Soviet,

Marxist-based doctrines that called for global domination, as opposed to any specific move by the Soviets. The US was now ready, willing, and able to fight the Cold War through the full spectrum of conflict on a global scale.

Chapter 4

The Eisenhower Era: Iran, Guatemala, and Hungary

Iran

Operation Ajax, the 1953 CIA inspired pro-Shah coup in Iran, is one of the first agency operations of which there is an extensive record. Much of what we know today comes from a 1979 book written by Kermit Roosevelt entitled, *Countercoup: The Struggle for Control of Iran*. Roosevelt was an OSS veteran who had first traveled to Iran in 1944. Operation Ajax was conducted under his leadership. Additional information on the climate in which the operation unfolded can be gleaned from declassified CIA files.

The confrontation unfolding in Iran in 1953, over who would govern, was viewed by the Eisenhower administration as an extension of the Cold War between the United States and the Soviets. As to politics within Iran, it was secretly the Eisenhower administration position that the Soviets were backing the Prime Minister, Dr. Mohammed Mossadegh, against the monarchy of the Shah (and his allies in the west). The administration's assumption of Soviet influence is all that it would take to bring the CIA into action in Iran.

As mentioned in the previous chapter, the incidents in 1953 were not the first occasion that the specter of east-west conflict over Iran was raised. In September 1941, the British and the Soviets, who were allied in the war against Nazi Germany, jointly occupied Iran to forestall German control of the area. As a result, on September 16, 1941, Shah Reza Pahlavi abdicated his throne to his son Mohammed Reza Pahlavi when an Angelo-Soviet force occupied the capital city of Teheran.

The control of Iran ended up being vital to the Allied war effort, in particular the provision of allied material support to the Soviets. An amount of Lend-Lease support was reaching the Soviets via the North Sea convoy route. However, the shipping losses over that route were high due to German U-boats. Much of the aid that the Soviets were to receive came through the Persian Gulf and then via overland rail through Iran to the USSR. This proved to be a vital link in supporting Soviet forces throughout the war.

When the war ended, the Soviets did not immediately end their occupation of Iran (as the British had). In fact, in early 1946 a crisis developed when the Soviets threatened to seize control of Teheran and at the same time maintain their occupation forces in northern and eastern Iran. On March 21, 1946 Iran made the second of two protests before the UN Security Council and the US took simultaneous diplomatic initiatives to encourage the Soviets to leave Iran. Five days later, the Soviets agreed to leave. By May 9, the Soviets were out and the crisis was over.

Soviet control of Iran would have accomplished two objectives. First, it would have given the Soviets access to a long coveted warm water port on the Persian Gulf. Second, it would have allowed them to control the Iranian oil fields, and thus deny them to the west.

Iran remained unstable after the Soviets pulled out of the country. In February 1949, a lone gunman who had ties to the Tudeh Party attempted to kill the Shah. The Shah survived the attack with only minor wounds. The royal bodyguards shot the assassin dead at the scene. The Tudeh Party was described in a CIA intelligence report this way:

> Despite its pretense of being only a national reform movement, the Tudeh Party is, for all practical purposes, the Iranian Communist Party and is unmistakably under Soviet influence.[65]

The Iranian government responded to the crisis by outlawing the Tudeh Party. In addition, on May 8, 1949, a constitutional convention gave the Shah the power to dissolve both houses of the Majlis (the Iranian parliament). This was not, however, the end for the Tudeh; the party remained an effective force in Iranian politics.[66]

In 1951, an issue that was to set off a chain reaction in Iranian politics was to come to the fore. In March the Majlis voted to nationalize the Anglo-Iranian Oil Company (AIOC), which until then had been a joint holding of the British and Iranian governments. Talks on the AOIC had been going on between the Iranians and the British for two years with little result. The same forces that brought about the vote on nationalization brought Mossadegh into the Prime Minister's office in April of 1951. A popular ground swell behind Mossadegh, who had favored nationalization, forced the Shah to appoint him to the position.

In July 1951, Averell Harriman of the US State Department (the former chief of mission to the USSR) was sent to Teheran by President Truman to attempt to facilitate an agreement between the British and Iranians as to the disposition of the AIOC. On arrival in Teheran, Harriman was met by an anti-American demonstration. According to Kermit Roosevelt,

> the Iranian Communist party, Tudeh, which was controlled and financed by Moscow, had now thrown its weight and money behind Mossadegh, and provided him with a street army of well-trained thugs ... Harriman, all prepared to smile and wave in acknowledgment to the cheering crowd he expected to meet on his way from the airport, instead ran into an ugly demonstration from a column of Tudeh demonstrators armed with sticks and screaming anti-American slogans.[67]

Harriman's mission did not play out as the Truman administration wanted it to. No agreement on the AIOC was reached. Harriman returned to Washington disillusioned. Official Washington began to see an inevitable conflict on the horizon between Mossadegh backed by the Russians, and the Shah backed by the British and Americans.[68]

In August 1951, the British Labor government tried its own negotiations with the Iranians over the disposition of the AIOC. The overtures were unsuccessful. The breakdown in the talks came over the British having a managerial executive in the new hierarchy of the Iranian Oil Company (the proposed replacement for the AIOC).[69]

Relations between the British and the Iranians took a decided downturn in September 1951, when Mossadegh ordered all British AIOC employees out of the country and sent troops to occupy the refinery at Abadan. In January 1952, Mossadegh went a step further and closed all British consulates in Iran. At this juncture the Americans again tried unsuccessfully to mediate the situation. The final blow came in September 1952, when the Iranian Prime Minister broke diplomatic relations with Great Britain and ordered all remaining British diplomats out of the country.[70]

In February of 1952, a secret CIA National Intelligence Estimate, entitled "Probable Developments in Iran in 1952 in the Absence of an Oil Settlement," had this to say about the situation:

> Prime Minister Mossadegh and the National Front movement continue to dominate the political scene in Iran. They have retained the enthusiastic support, particularly in Teheran, of the urban workers, shopkeepers, teachers, students, government employees, and religious zealots who, under Mossadegh's leadership, have seized the political initiative from the traditional ruling groups of wealthy merchants and landlords. Although his followers in the National Front do not form a firmly knit party, and some are ambitious, self-seeking politicians ... Mossadegh will most likely be able to prevent a split in the National Front in the near future.[71]

The above report also included extensive discussion on the future of the Tudeh. It stated as follows:

> The Communist-dominated Tudeh Party has bettered its position considerably during Mossadegh's tenure in office. Although Mossadegh is basically hostile to Soviet imperialism the government has failed to take a clear-cut stand against the Tudeh Party, primarily because Mossadegh is unwilling to take drastic action against an organization that he believes can be kept under control and that supports the government on the nationalization issue. In addition, some National Front leaders and government officials appear to be Tudeh sympathizers. As a result, Tudeh has been able to carry on a program of agitation and demonstrations and has gained increased support, notably among students, industrial workers, and civil servants. While the size of the Tudeh Party cannot be accurately determined, we believe its present strength is much lower than the several hundred thousand supporters claimed by Tudeh during its heyday in 1946. Recent US and British field estimates give a total of about 8,000 actual members in the Teheran area (with perhaps three or four times as many sympathizers) and a total of some 5,000 members in the oil field area, Azerbaijan, and

> along the Caspian coast. The Tudeh has succeeded in penetrating several departments of the government (notably Education and Justice), although not to the extent of seriously influencing government policy or operations. Available evidence indicates that the Tudeh has had less success in penetrating the army and security forces.[72]

In November 1952, the British approached Kermit Roosevelt with the idea of a joint US-British covert operation to overthrow Mossadegh. The British motivation was simple; they wanted their interest in the AIOC back. According to Roosevelt, he and others in the US government were in sympathy with the British, but their reason was communist influence. However, those favoring an operation in Iran would have to wait until the Eisenhower administration took office because, "Truman... had been charmed by Mossadegh on his visit to the US in October 1951." Roosevelt explained to the British that the proposed operation would "require considerable clearance from my government" and that he "was not entirely sure what the results would be."[73]

In the meantime the US government, more specifically the CIA and NSC, were becoming convinced that, while not imminent, conditions could come about that would lead to a Tudeh takeover in Iran. In an agency report dated January 9, 1953, we may read the following:

> The Communist Tudeh Party is not likely to develop the strength to overthrow the National Front by constitutional means or by force during the period of this estimate. Although the danger of serious Tudeh infiltration of the National Front and the bureaucracy continues, Tudeh is also unlikely to gain control by this means in 1953. Nevertheless, unexpected events, such as serious crop failure or a split in the National Front as a result of rivalry among its leaders, would increase Tudeh capabilities greatly. And if present trends in Iran continue unchecked beyond the end of 1953 rising internal tensions and continued deterioration of the economy and of the budgetary position of the government are likely to lead to a breakdown of governmental authority and open the way for at least a gradual assumption by Tudeh.[74]

On involvement of the USSR in Iran the position was stated as follows:

> The USSR appears to believe that the Iranian situation is developing favorably to its objectives. We do not believe that the USSR will take drastic action in Iran during 1953 unless there is a far more serious deterioration of Iranian internal stability than is foreseen in this estimate. However, the USSR has the capability for greatly increasing its overt and covert interference in Iran at any time, to the detriment of US security interests.[75]

A final conclusion in the January 1953 estimate was that, *a negotiated oil settlement during the period of this estimate is unlikely.*[76] By this time the intelligence professionals had clearly built a case for intervention in Iran. Now it was necessary for the White House to make the political decision to go forward with an operation.

In July of 1953 not much had changed in Iran and the British were still backing a coup against Mossadegh. The Prime Minister had been ruling by decree for a year under authority granted him by the Majlis. Mossadegh tried to put pressure on the Shah to leave Iran, but demonstrations by the monarch's supporters convinced him he had the backing he needed to stay on the throne.

Roosevelt stated in his book that, at the time, Mossadegh was "increasingly allied with the Tudeh and, at one remove through them the Soviets."[77] This is a bit more extreme a position than is outlined in the intelligence estimates noted above. One might surmise that, from agency estimates, Mossadegh was in as much danger from the Tudeh as the Shah was.

In mid-1953, the Eisenhower administration turned down Prime Minister Mossadegh's requests for increased American aid money. This was the beginning of the American turn against Mossadegh. By July of 1953 the White House had approved Operation Ajax and planning for the action was underway.

Roosevelt attended a planning meeting with Allen Dulles (the Director of Central Intelligence) and representatives from the departments of State and Defense. He then departed for Teheran. In July and August Roosevelt had a series of secret meetings with the Shah to plan strategy for the coup. General Fazlollah Zahedi was chosen to replace Mossadegh as Prime Minister.

Zahedi was, like most of the Iranian officer corps, a supporter of the Shah and was anti-Soviet. He had been interned by the British during WWII for being pro-Nazi. Now the British thought he would be a useful conservative tool.

The plan called for the Shah to move out of sight to a retreat on the Caspian Sea in the beginning of August. He would give Roosevelt two decrees, one removed Mossadegh as from office and the other appointed Zahedi Prime Minister. Roosevelt would see that officers loyal to the Shah delivered these decrees to the public and the individuals concerned. It was believed that the bulk of the Army would remain loyal to the Shah through any subsequent confusion. At this point the Shah was to fly safely out of Iran while Roosevelt orchestrated demonstrations of support for the Shah. The Shah would then return to Iran in triumph. By August 9, the Shah was at his retreat on the Caspian.

The coup began prematurely on August 15 when a young officer involved in the plot defected to Mossadegh's side. The officer in question went to the house of General Riahi (the pro-Mossadegh head of the army) and reported the plot to him. Riahi ordered Mossadegh's house surrounded by tanks in order to protect him from the coup plotters.[78]

At this point, Colonel Nassiry, one of the coup plotters, took a small force of tanks and brought the decree relieving Mossadegh to the Prime Minister's residence. The troops guarding Mossadegh let Nassiry pass through and he delivered the decree personally. General Riahi then had Nassiry arrested and prevented him from delivering the decree to General Zahedi, which named him as the new Prime Minister. Zahedi, meanwhile, was spirited to safety at the house of a CIA operative.[79]

On August 16, Mossadegh came on the air on Teheran radio. He announced that foreign elements were attempting to control the Shah, and that as a result he was obliged to take all of the powers of the state for himself. On August 16 and 17 there was some rioting by Tudeh supporters. Also on the 16th the Shah flew out of Iran to Baghdad, Iraq and awaited the next move in the plot.

During this time, Roosevelt and his team of agents were working to orchestrate pro-Shah demonstrations. On August 19, forces friendly to the Shah took over the main radio station in Teheran and broadcast "Zindabad Shah!" (Long Live the Shah!). The forces in control of the radio station also made the premature announcement that, "the Shah's instruction that Mossadegh be dismissed has been carried out. The new Prime Minister, Fazlollah Zahedi, is now in office. And his Imperial Majesty is on his way home."[80] In reality Zahedi was still in hiding in the CIA safe house and the Shah was still in Baghdad. On the same day events climaxed when Roosevelt's pro-Shah demonstrators marched on Mossadegh's house and there was scattered street fighting.

Once the streets were fully controlled by pro-Shah forces, Zahedi was able to come out of hiding and assume the position of Prime Minister. On August 22 the Shah was able to return to Teheran. The pre-arranged crowds of supporters met him at the airport and lined the streets on the route to the palace.

On his return to the United States Kermit Roosevelt briefed the Secretary of State (John Foster Dulles) on the apparent success of Operation Ajax. Roosevelt later wrote about the briefing in his book.

> If we, the CIA, are ever going to try something like this again, we must be absolutely sure that the people and the army want what we want. If not you had better give the job to the Marines… But Foster Dulles did not want to hear what I was saying. He was still leaning back with a catlike grin on his face. Within weeks I was offered command of a Guatemalan undertaking already in preparation. A quick check suggested that my requirements were not likely to be met. I declined the offer. Later I resigned from the CIA—before the Bay of Pigs disaster underlined the validity of my warning.[81]

The CIA at once claimed Iran was now stable, but the stated that the seeds of even greater trouble were as present as ever. A November 1953 report read in part:

> The overthrow of the Mossadegh government on 19 August 1953 checked the drift in Iran toward Communism and isolation from the West. The authority of the Shah has been reasserted, and a moderate government under General Zahedi is in power. This government is committed to maintaining the constitutional position of the monarchy and the parliament, suppressing the Communist Tudeh Party, and launching an economic development program predicated on settlement of the oil dispute. The accession of Zahedi to power has eliminated neither the economic and social problems, which have long plagued Iran,

> nor the weakness and inadequacies of the Iranian political system.[82]

Operation Ajax established a pattern for future covert operations. They were all directed against regimes that were Marxist or at least perceived as such. Mossadegh's government was doomed as soon as the Eisenhower administration determined to its satisfaction that the Soviets were involved in Iran. There is some evidence, outside the CIA estimates and Roosevelt's word, that the Soviets had their hand in the pie in Iran. Premier Nikita Khrushchev stated in his memoirs that, *the Shah knew perfectly well not only that we had sympathized with the rebellion but we had armed the rebels.*[83]

Guatemala

Half a world away, Guatemala would become the next focal point for CIA activity. In 1954, Guatemala was an impoverished country of only 2,500,000 people (70% of who were involved in agriculture). Malnutrition was widespread. It was also a top-heavy society in terms of distribution of wealth; 2% of the landowners held 72% of the land. The native Indian people, who were on the lowest rung of Guatemalan society, had a life expectancy of less than 40 years. Illiteracy ran at 70% in the overall society and 90% among the Indian population.[84]

The Spanish had first colonized Guatemala in 1524. The country gained its independence in 1821. The government consisted of rule by a secession of dictators until armed students and workers overthrew President Jorge Ubico in June of 1944. After the coup, two army officers, Francisco Arana and Jacobo Arbenz, and the civilian, Jorge Toriello, ran the country until elections could be held. On March 15, 1945, Juan Jose Arevalo became president; he had received 85% of the (literate male) vote. Guatemala had its first democratically elected government.[85]

Arevalo's rule (1945-51) was one of democratic reforms. He expanded voting rights, and freedom of the press and speech were guaranteed. All political parties, except the Communists, were allowed to organize.[86]

The difficulty of the situation Arevalo faced was that Guatemalan society was largely under the control of the United States. The American owned United Fruit Company was both the nation's largest employer and landowner. In addition the IRCA, a subsidiary of United Fruit, monopolized the nation's rail and port facilities. If that were not enough, the American owned Electric Bond and Share Company (EBS) produced over 80% of the underdeveloped nation's electricity. United Fruit was a good investment for its American shareholders. One estimate made in 1936 showed an annual rate of return of %17.75 for the years 1899 to 1935.[87]

Arevalo devoted 1/3 of state expenditures to social welfare programs with an emphasis on the construction of schools, hospitals, and housing. One of Arevalo's much need programs was a twenty-year plan to build 67 hospitals throughout the country. In addition, in 1947 a liberalized labor code was developed which allowed for broader worker organization.

Also in 1947, the government unsuccessfully attempted to gain a measure of control over the foreign companies operating in Guatemala. The government required that the United Fruit Company submit to arbitration on the issue of wages. The company successfully employed lockouts and suspended shipping operations to carry the day.[88]

In 1949, the campaign for the 1950 elections began. Shortly thereafter, a right wing opposition candidate, Francisco Arana, was assassinated. Supporters of Arana began a violent uprising. Then serving as defense minister, Jocobo Arbenz quickly distributed arms to students and workers who were friendly to the government. The Arana supporters were defeated in short order and calm was restored.[89]

Arbenz won the December 1950 general election with the backing of peasants, organized labor, two revolutionary parties, and the small but illegal Communist party. He received a total of 63 percent of the vote. Upon taking power Arbenz stated the objective of transforming Guatemala's economy from "feudalism" to independent capitalism.[90]

In 1951 Arbenz legalized the Guatemalan Communist Party. The party was known as the PGT, from its Spanish initials. The PGT subsequently held 4 seats out of 56 in the Congress. In addition, while they were by no means a majority, some PGT members held influential positions in the Arbenz regime. After legalization of the PGT, the US suspended aid to Guatemala.[91]

In facing the three US monopolies operating in Guatemala, Arbenz sought to limit their power. His was not a strategy of nationalization but rather one of competition. Soon, the government undertook three major construction projects. The Arbenz administration began construction of a government-run hydroelectric plant, which would provide cheaper power than the EBS. At the same time, construction of a highway to the Atlantic coast was begun (in order to compete with the IRCA's rail line). Finally the Guatemalan government began construction of a new Atlantic coast port at Santo Thomas, to compete with the United Fruit dominate Puerto Barrios.

Arbenz also sought to undertake a program of agrarian reform. In June of 1952 a law was approved by the Guatemalan Congress that provided for the confiscation of unused land plots of 223 acres or more. The confiscated land was to be distributed to recipients the government deemed qualified. Under the terms established by the government, peasants would receive land in a use-for-life arrangement or be granted direct ownership. Those working the land would pay for it at the rate of 3-5% of annual production. Government compensation for the original owners was in the form of government bonds, which were equal in value to the owners' 1952 valuation for tax purposes.[92]

The confiscation of land began in 1952. Land was taken from over a thousand large properties, which averaged over 4,300 acres in size. In total 1,500,000 acres were distributed to over 100,000 peasants. Among the confiscated lands were 1,700 acres owned by President Arbenz.

The most significant and by far the largest single confiscation of land was that which was held by United Fruit. In 1952 the company held over 550,000 acres in Guatemala. Only 15 percent of the land was under cultivation at any one time. United Fruit claimed that its large holdings were to offset the effects of banana disease. In a series of decrees the government confiscated about 400,000 acres from the company. The offer for the land was $600,000, the value United Fruit had placed on the land for tax purposes.[93]

United Fruit, backed by the US State Department, claimed its damages were $16 million. This was the first time the US government came into direct conflict with the Arbenz regime. It is significant to note here that Allen Welsh Dulles, the Director of Central Intelligence had worked for the law firm that represented United Fruit before he came to the CIA (the firm was Sullivan and Cromwell). Several other Eisenhower administration officials were stockholders in United Fruit or had other ties to the company. We may never know for sure how much this influenced decision-making on the issues at hand in Guatemala. It can be taken almost for certain that these relationships to United Fruit did not make the Eisenhower administration any more favorably disposed to the Arbenz regime.[94]

In his memoirs, President Eisenhower noted that upon his inauguration in January 1953, "Communism was striving to establish its first beachhead in the Americas by gaining control of Guatemala."[95] His official decision to move against Arbenz came in August 1953 at a secret meeting of the NSC's 54/12 committee (created to manage covert operations). The committee recommended Arbenz be overthrown and Eisenhower approved. Thus, was launched, the project whose goal was to liberate Guatemala from latent communism. The name of the operation was PB Success.[96]

When a CIA inspired attempt to bribe Arbenz into resigning failed, the plan for armed intervention started to take shape. Guatemalan exiles had been organizing their own liberation movement since early 1952. In 1953 the CIA made contact with them and appointed Carlos Castillio Armas as the leader. Armas was a graduate of US military training at Ft. Leavenworth, Kansas. The CIA provided the exiles with funds for training, equipment, and arms. Also provided was the cash necessary to hire a small mercenary army. The United Fruit Company contributed $65,000 to the effort. With the blessing of Nicaragua's dictator, Anistasio Somoza, military training camps for the rebel band were set up in his country.

During the training and the coup operations that were to follow, Armas had no more than 400 men under his command at any one time.[97] Since there were too few exiles to mount a serious invasion, the CIA opted for a strategy of psychological warfare against Arbenz. The campaign that was mounted was targeted at subverting the loyalty of the Guatemalan army. Arbenz had too much popular support to count on massive demonstrations by the public. As for Arbenz's supporters in the unions, the objective was to convince them that there was no hope for the president. The CIA even planned for sending US Marines into the country, under the guise of protecting Americans, if it became necessary to use direct US military involvement to topple Arbenz.[98]

One of the keys to Operation PB Success was the airpower with which the CIA supplied Armas' forces. This support consisted of about a half dozen WWII fighter planes[99] and 3 B-26 bombers. Various cargo and transport aircraft were also provided by the agency.

All of the aircraft were supplied to Armas through CIA front companies. They included planes from US southern National Guard units that were leased to Nicaragua for the sum of $1 a piece. While a few of the pilots were Guatemalans, most were US citizens and veterans of the US armed forces. The mission of the air force, which far outclassed anything Arbenz possessed, was not to destroy Guatemalan military forces, but to spread fear. The planes were to undertake widely scattered raids, in concert with short-wave radio propaganda broadcasts that would make it seem like the whole country was under attack.[100]

Almost from the beginning additional measures were considered to spread fear and reduce the effectiveness of the Guatemalan Communist Party. In September 1952 the CIA drew up an assassination list of 58 individual Communists. In March of 1954 the list of those to be killed was reduced to 34.[101] While the agency claims that none of the killings were conducted, a number of the members of the Communist party were mailed death threats as a part of PB Success.

Throughout 1953 and the early part of 1954, the Eisenhower administration marshaled its forces in readiness for PB Success. In October 1953, a new US Ambassador was sent to Guatemala. The proven anti-Communist, John Peurifoy, was chosen for the post because of his experience in combating communism in Greece. Peurifoy, who was known to carry a pistol (very uncharacteristic for a diplomat), would play a key role in the upcoming coup.

In March of 1954, the Organization of American States (OAS) met in Caracas, Venezuela. Secretary of State, Dulles, attended and sponsored a resolution that was directed against the Arbenz government. The resolution said in part:

> The domination or control of the political institution of any American state by the internationalist Communist movement...would constitute a threat to the sovereignty and political independence of the American states, endangering the peace of America.[102]

Nicaragua, the Dominican Republic, El Salvador, Peru, and Venezuela (all of which were under dictatorships) gave Dulles unconditional support. When the vote came, Guatemala, naturally, opposed the measure. Mexico and Argentina abstained. The revolution had passed, giving the Eisenhower administration the permission it desired before launching PB Success.

Even while Dulles was getting his approval from the OAS, PB Success was developing further. David Atlee Phillips was approached to run the propaganda effort being mounted against Arbenz. Phillips had worked for the CIA before, and he had some reservations about PB Success. When he was told Arbenz was the target he stated, "but Arbenz became elected in a free election." His recruiter was Tracy Barnes, a lawyer and an OSS veteran who had been behind German lines twice during WWII. Barns held the rank of GS-18 and that gave him authority similar to a general officer.

Barns worked on convincing Philips that it was not a matter of legitimacy. The facts as Barnes saw them were that

> we have solid intelligence that the Soviets intend to throw

> substantial support to Arbenz. There are 6,000 soldiers in the Guatemalan army, twenty-five hundred [in the] constabulary, and several government organized paramilitary units. Given Soviet backing that spells trouble in all of Central America. An easily expandable beachhead, if you want to use that term.[103]

As Phillips himself tells the story, he was still not convinced. He said to Barnes, "I'm still not sure that gives us the right to intervene ... why does the CIA get the job?"

Barnes countered that, "our marching orders on this operation come from President Eisenhower. He has asked us to assist the Guatemalans who are opposed to Arbenz."

Phillips said, "There could be a civil war [and] a lot of people might get killed."

"Yes," replied Barnes, "we will try to do it without bloodshed, if that's possible."[104]

Phillips was convinced. He would accept assignment as the director of a clandestine radio station that would broadcast anti-Arbenz propaganda. One of Phillips' co-workers would be E. Howard Hunt. An Ivy League veteran of the OSS in China, Hunt would later play a role in illegal domestic covert operations during the Nixon administration.

Phillips set about his task of recruiting broadcasters for the radio station he was to set up. Candidates were recruited in Guatemala City, right under Arbenz's nose. They were then brought together in Miami where the CIA trained them. In April 1954, the team was moved to a secret location in Central America to begin its deceptive broadcasts. The first broadcast of "radio liberation" was on May 1. Its time and frequency had been advertised by the CIA in Guatemala City newspapers. The station pretended to be broadcasting from inside Guatemala.[105]

In addition to the anti-Arbenz broadcasts, the mercenary air force dropped leaflets around the country, which called for the ouster of Arbenz. The US Information Agency also assisted by distributing 100,000 copies of an anti-Arbenz booklet called the "Chronology of Communism in Guatemala."

A defecting Panamanian diplomat had informed Arbenz of the plot against him in January. Once the propaganda drive was underway, Arbenz overreacted (as the CIA hoped he would) by obtaining congressional permission to suspend the constitution. The suspension of rights took place on June 8. It was quickly followed by the arrest of over 100 anti-Arbenz activists and some unexplained deaths. Restrictions were placed on the press. The result of all this turmoil was, according to Phillips, "in five weeks what had been a placid country was in turmoil."[106]

The "invasion" by Castillo Armas' rag tag band of mercenaries was now less than two weeks away. The US National Security Council decided to proceed with the plan when a shipment of Czechoslovakian arms was discovered at Puerto Barrios in May. Secretary of State, Dulles, announced the docking of the ship carrying the arms (the Alfhem) to the press on May 17. According to President Eisenhower:

> We learned that the cargo contained two thousand tons of small arms, ammunition, and light artillery pieces manufactured at the Skoda arms factory in Czechoslovakia. This quantity far exceeded the legitimate normal requirements for the Guatemalan armed forces.[107]

Eisenhower had the smoking gun he needed to launch PB Success. The presence of the large quantity of Communist Bloc arms was enough to confirm to Ike that Arbenz was planning to spread communism throughout Central America. As a result of the announcement of the presence of the Alfhem, Nicaragua broke diplomatic ties with Guatemala on May 19. Five days later the US announced that it was shipping quantities of arms to Honduras and Nicaragua to offset the Czech shipment.[108]

On May 24, Eisenhower informed the Congress that he was going to prevent further shipments of arms from going to Guatemala and that he was going to convene another meeting of the OAS in order to decide what to do next. He did not tip his hand about the ongoing coup plot to the Congress or the public. His plan to stop future shipments of arms never amounted to much, no ships were stopped and no blockade was implemented. During this time Armas' force moved from its training bases in Nicaragua to its staging area in Honduras.

On June 18, Radio Liberation announced that Colonel Armas had invaded Guatemala with 5,000 men under arms. In reality Armas had crossed the border with about 50 men, several trucks, and a battered station wagon.[109] Instead of deploying deep inside Guatemala for battle with Arbenz's forces, Armas' troops stopped not far from the border town of Esquipulas. The world's newspapers were unable to get a true picture of events because Armas cut the phone lines and barred news reporters from his area. In addition, the reporters located in Guatemala City were also unable to get the full story because Arbenz had them under a virtual state of house arrest.

At the same time as Armas and his men were occupying Esquipulas, the B-26s and WWII fighters were staging bombing and strafing attacks at widely scattered locations including Guatemala City. One attack seriously damaged the oil depot at Puerto Barrios. Another pilot bombed and sank a ship that he thought was the Alfhem. The ship turned out to be a freighter full of cotton that was insured by Lloyd's of London. The CIA later quietly paid Lloyd's one million dollars in damages.[110]

In the meantime the CIA propaganda machine kept up the broadcasts and announced that rebel columns were moving freely through the countryside. Another recurring theme of the broadcasts was that Arbenz was about to disband the army and form a people's militia. This effort, in concert with bribes paid to Guatemalan officers by the CIA and Ambassador Peurifoy, was working to undermine Arbenz's authority with the army. Due to the propaganda barrage, Arbenz grounded his inferior air force for fear the pilots would defect.

On June 20 and 21, the Guatemalan foreign minister appealed to the United Nations to stop the aggression. American diplomats made every effort to defeat a resolution that called for a discussion of the Guatemalan situation in the Security Council. On June 25, the council voted 5 to 4 against the discussion and referred the matter to the US dominated OAS.

The intensity of the bombing peaked on June 25 when aircraft again bombed Guatemala City. The aircraft attacked the military parade ground, the airport, and oil storage facilities. During one nighttime attack the US embassy played a recorded bombing attack from rooftop loud speakers. Believing the radio reports that the city was about to be occupied by Armas, many people fled to outlying areas.[111]

The end came for Arbenz on June 25. The Army sent him a directive to resign or they would come to an agreement with the rebels on their own. Arbenz made a last unsuccessful attempt to distribute arms to his supporters in the labor unions. When this failed he agreed to resign. Guatemalan Army Colonel, Carlos Enrique Diaz, then set about the task of putting together a group of military men that would run the country. Colonel Diaz was in contact with US Ambassador Peurifoy, who encouraged him to round up the leading Communists. Diaz agreed and in a short time the Communist leadership was being taken into custody by the military police.

At 9:15 am on Sunday June 27th Arbenz went on nationwide radio to announce his resignation. He said in part:

> The United Fruit Company, in collaboration with the governing circles of the United States, is what is responsible for what is happening to us.
>
> I have made a sad and cruel judgment. After reflecting with a clear revolutionary conscience, I have made a decision of great importance for our country in the hope of containing this aggression and bringing peace back to Guatemala. I have decided to step down and place the nation's executive power in the hands of my friend, Colonel Carlos Enrique Diaz, chief of the armed forces of the republic.
>
> I took the presidency with great faith in the democratic system, in liberty, and in the possibility of achieving economic independence for Guatemala. I continue to believe that this program is just. I have not violated my faith in democratic liberties, the independence of Guatemala and in all the good which is the future of humanity.
>
> I say goodbye to you, my friends.[112]

On June 28, Ambassador Peurfoy met with Colonel Diaz. The Ambassador expressed his displeasure that Diaz allowed Arbenz to condemn the United States. Peurfoy suggested Diaz consider stepping down in favor of Colonel Monzon (a proven anti-Communist). Diaz responded that he was going to proclaim a general amnesty for all including the Communists.

Peurfoy left the meeting enraged. He returned to the embassy and sent a telegram to the PB Success nerve center in Opa Locka, Florida. He stated that he had been double-crossed and that bombing should be resumed. Within hours the CIA's air force bombed the military barracks in Guatemala City and destroyed a government radio station.[113]

Under threat of assassination, Colonel Diaz and his deputy resigned. With Colonel Monzon safely running the country, Peurfoy set up a summit between Monzon and Armas for June 30. It was to take place in neighboring El Salvador.

As the meeting got underway, the Colonels could not come to any agreement. Peurfoy arrived shortly and facilitated an agreement that included the following provisions: a new constitution would be written, there would be a cease fire, all communists would be arrested and tried, Armas' troops could join the regular Guatemalan Army, and the government of the country would be run by a 5-man junta that would choose its own leader. One week later Peurfoy secured the resignation of two of the junta. A newly formed 3-man junta elected Armas as president on July 8. On July 13 the US recognized the Armas government.

On September 1, 1954 the junta resigned, leaving Armas in full control. On October 10 he held an election. The only question on the ballot was whether Armas should remain president. Ninety percent of the voters said yes.

In November, Armas restored the former dictator Ubico's chief of the secret police to his former position. A wave of book burnings, political arrests, and murders followed. By some estimates there were 9,000 imprisoned and many tortured under the governments unlimited power of arrest. In addition, approximately 8,000 peasants were murdered in the first months of the Armas regime as the landowners took their revenge.[114]

The Armas government canceled the registration of 533 unions and changed the labor code so as to limit the workers' right to strike. The United Fruit and IRCA unions were totally defunct after this action. The climate became so unfriendly for organized labor that union membership dropped from 100,000 under Arbenz to just 16,000. In addition the PGT and other parties were outlawed and press censorship was implemented. The government saw to it that most of the land confiscated under Arbenz's policies was returned, including that of United Fruit.[115]

Immediately following operation PB Success, US policy makers went out of their way to state that this country had no role in unseating Arbenz. On June 30, 1954, Secretary of State, John Foster Dulles, went on nationwide radio and said:

> If world communism captures any American state, however small, a new perilous front is established which will increase the danger to the entire free world and require even greater sacrifices from the American people...
>
> Throughout the period I have outlined, the Guatemalan government and Communist agents throughout the world have persistently attempted to obscure the real issue—that of Communist imperialism—by claiming that the United States is only interested in protecting American business.
>
> Led by Colonel Castillo Armas, patriots arose in Guatemala

> to challenge Communist leadership—and to change it. Thus the situation has been cured by the Guatemalans themselves...
>
> Now the future of Guatemala lies at the disposal of the Guatemalan people themselves.[116]

In October, Ambassador Peurifoy testified before a subcommittee of the House Select Committee on Communist Aggression. He stated in part:

> Mr. Chairman, let me say that the menace of Communism in Guatemala was courageously fought by the Guatemalan people themselves.... Communist power was broken by the Guatemalans alone.... They fought the battle, which is the common battle of all free nations against Communist oppression, and they won the victory themselves.[117]

In 1963 President Eisenhower published his memoir entitled *Mandate for Change*. He denied all but the most insignificant involvement in the coup when he wrote:

> One June 18 [1954] armed forces under Carlos Castillo Armas, an exiled former Colonel in the Guatemalan army, crossed the border from Honduras to Guatemala, initially with a mere handful of men—reportedly about two hundred. As he progressed, he picked up recruits. Simultaneously three obsolete bombers, presumably under his direction, buzzed Guatemala City and bombed the ordinance depot. Things seemed to be going well for Castillo's small band until June 22. On that date Allen Dulles (Director of the CIA) reported to me that Castillo had lost two of the three old bombers with which he was supporting his "invasion."
>
> ...our proper course of action—indeed my duty—was clear to me. We would replace the airplanes.[118]

Eisenhower concluded his remarks on the coup when he wrote:

> By the middle of 1954 Latin America was free, for the time being at least, of any fixed outpost of communism.[119]

On June, 18, 1948, the National Security Council had directed that covert operations be,

> so planned and executed that any US government responsibility for them is not evident to unauthorized persons, and that if uncovered the US government can plausibly deny responsibility for them.

Those in the Republican Eisenhower administration who denied major US involvement in Guatemala in 1954 were following a script written for them six years prior by a Democratic administration. Covert action had bi-partisan support.

Castillo Armas was assassinated in 1957 and was succeeded by an army general with reported ties to the CIA. A Communist inspired guerrilla army, the "MR-13" gained strength in the countryside throughout the 60s and 70s. Right wing repression caused the death of many thousands of Guatemalans during this period. The government's behavior on human rights was so poor that in the 1970s the US Congress suspended all military aid to the country. In 1981, under President Reagan, the US again began delivery of "non-lethal" military equipment and had the embargo fully lifted by 1983. The civil war ended in 1989, with the Guerrillas defeated. Some estimates of civilians killed by the government in the years following PB Success range up to 140,000.[120] The destabilization of Guatemalan society through the use of covert paramilitary action had had tragic results.

Hungary: Still Classified

In October 1956, a revolt occurred in the Soviet satellite nation of Hungary. The contest between the people and their oppressors began as peaceful demonstrations on the afternoon of the 23rd and erupted into large-scale, armed violence by nightfall. Throughout the 24th, 25th, and 26th fighting against the Hungarian secret police (the AVO) and the combined Soviet/ Hungarian armies continued in Budapest and spread into the provinces. By the 29th the moderate Imre Nagy was in control of the government and was negotiating a cease-fire and withdrawal of Soviet forces from the country.[121] The fighting stopped and US President Eisenhower's administration called for the introduction of UN peacekeepers into Hungary.

In spite of their initial withdrawal the Soviets would return to Hungary with a vengeance. By November 4th they had surrounded Budapest with

200,000 troops and 2,500 tanks. As many as 30,000 of the city's residents perished when the Soviet military retook the city. In the process of the Soviets re-conquering Hungary more than 150,000 people became refugees. Imre Nagy was arrested and later executed.

Some of the CIA's documentation on the Hungarian revolt was declassified in 1997. However, the portions of their documentation that the CIA is willing to release to the public on this matter are severely redacted (large portions of the documents are "blacked out"). Why? In 1989, Nathan Miller's *Spying for America: The Hidden History of US Intelligence* claimed that a massive covert paramilitary effort by the CIA was the cause of the tragic and failed revolt of '56. Miller provides little supporting evidence for his claim and further investigation is necessary.

This author decided to use the Freedom of Information Act to see what could be uncovered from the CIA databases on subject matter related to the revolt. Knowing that some OSS records were transferred over to the CIA when the National Security Act of 1947 gave birth to the new agency, and further suspecting that WWII era documents might betray some valuable information, the investigation was begun. First, a general search of CIA databases for previously declassified documents on Hungary from 1943 to 1958 was requested. Some valuable information, that has yet to be published elsewhere, was gleaned from this search and it will be discussed below.

However, it should first be noted that a specific search for information on CIA covert paramilitary action in Hungary was requested. The response to this request was a denial of the "existence or non-existence" of the records in question. The basis for the denial was that the request "applies to material which is properly classified pursuant to an Executive order in the interest of national defense or foreign policy," and, "applies to the Director's statutory obligations to protect from disclosure intelligence sources and methods, as well as organization, functions, names, official titles, salaries, or numbers of personnel employed by the Agency, in accord with the National Security Act of 1947 and the CIA Act of 1949, respectively."

Obviously Miller was on the right track and there is something the CIA has yet to hide about the stillborn Hungarian revolution. This author believes that by fitting together the pieces of the puzzle that we do have, we can determine the shape of those that are missing, thus understand the events of October-November 1956 more fully.

OSS and Eastern Europe

Throughout 1944-45 the OSS operated behind German lines in Czechoslovakia, Romania, Bulgaria, and Hungary. The precursor agency of the CIA also operated in those countries after the Russians moved in and expelled the Germans.[122] Over time the Russians exerted various types of pressure, which forced the withdrawal of the overt OSS presence in the Soviet sphere of influence. The earliest withdrawal of OSS personnel under Soviet pressure appears to have been the departure of a team, under the direction of a Lieutenant Harper, from Sophia, Bulgaria on December 25, 1944.[123]

As a result of increasing pressure from the Soviets, OSS Senior Staff Officer for Rear Zone Intelligence, Robert P. Joyce submitted a report on the prospects of continuing OSS activity in the Soviet sphere. The report, dated January 3, 1945, began with the following paragraph:

> The following represents an endeavor to analyze the present problems confronting us in the Southeastern European area as a consequence of military developments in this region, the result of which has been the dominating position of the Soviet Union in this part of Europe. The analysis will be undertaken by an exposition of the OSS position in five Balkan countries in which we are now operating (or have recently operated—in the case of Bulgaria), in addition to an analysis of the possibilities of operation in countries such as Hungary which will soon come under Soviet military and political control.[124]

The somewhat lengthy report summarized the situation as follows:

> Rumania, the Soviets were contesting attachment of OSS operatives to the Allied Control Commission; Bulgaria, the Soviets had insisted in the removal of OSS personnel from Sofia; Albania, it was questionable if the Soviets would allow entry of an OSS team; Yugoslavia, Marshall Tito was allowing some OSS activity in the country; Hungary, the OSS was waiting for Soviet permission to enter Budapest when the city fell to the Soviets, it was doubtful this would be forth coming. In short, overt OSS activity in the Soviet sphere was under pressure.

Joyce summarized this Russian position as follows:

> The Russians do not desire OSS activities in areas controlled by them or under their influence and they are prepared to prevent such activities.[125]

As well the report recognized that relations between the State Department and the OSS were becoming strained, as a result of Soviet pressures and the nature of the State Department mission. Citing a Mr. Barnes of the State Department mission to Bulgaria, Joyce characterized the interdepartmental relationship as follows:

> Mr. Barnes in Sofia, however, has recently indicated that he considers it his primary function to maintain good relations with the Russians in Bulgaria and that if the presence of overt OSS representatives in Sofia in any way operates to prejudice such relations he will oppose their presence. In general, I think it may be said that while State Department representatives find extremely valuable and useful the information obtained by OSS and, on this basis, desire OSS to continue operation, nevertheless State Department representatives at present in the Balkans have shown a tendency toward uneasiness and nervousness.[126]

In January of 1945, the OSS was under pressure from the Russians and the State Department to withdraw from the Soviet sphere of influence. Instead of withdrawal, Joyce proposed the agency employ the covert means it had been using against the Germans, only now that it employ them to hide its operations from the Soviets. In the concluding "recommendations" section of the report, Joyce stated that,

> arrangements should be undertaken in Washington at the earliest possible moment for clandestine OSS activities in areas now under Russian control…on a sound permanent basis.[127]

One interesting facet of Joyce's recommendations is that here we have a view of foreign affairs where Soviet and American interests are opposed. This statement juxtaposing interests is clearly before the Soviets installed

Communist governments firmly in Eastern Europe and well before the Churchill's "Iron Curtain" speech, the Berlin Airlift Crisis, or any of the other events that are often seen as precipitating the Cold War. The statement was in fact made while lend-lease aid was still flowing to the Soviet ally. Joyce was, no doubt, well aware of Soviet ideology, and correctly assumed that relations with the Soviets in the post war world would be hostile. He knew the much-touted alliance with the Soviets was a temporary convention.

One item in question related to the study of events in Hungary is whether the OSS went under cover in Eastern Europe (in accordance with Joyce's recommendations). It would be safe to assume that, if the OSS did begin clandestine operations in the Soviet sphere, when the OSS disbanded the operations Eastern Europe were handed over to the War Department. From there, jurisdiction over the operations would have gone to the CIA (when it was created some 2 years after OSS clandestine operations would have commenced). Thus, in 1956, when violence erupted in Hungary, it is likely that the CIA had a network of covert operatives that had been functioning behind Soviet lines for some 11 years.

The record on the suggestion of covert activities in Hungary that the CIA is willing to release dries up in 1945. However, there are indicators that the OSS was in contact with the resistance to Soviet occupation in Poland in June of 1945 (well over a month after the Nazi unconditional surrender). A memorandum to President Truman, by no less than William Donovan himself, states that the OSS had been in contact with "important industrialists, [text redacted] government office workers, and Soviet Polish military personnel"[128] behind Soviet military lines inside Poland. It may be significant to note that it has been 54 years and the intelligence community still insists on redacting this document. A likely candidate for redaction would be direct evidence of covert American paramilitary involvement in the satellite nations.

The memorandum goes into detail on the subject of resistance to Soviet occupation. It states:

> Polish underground groups, which many Poles believe to be still directed by the Polish government in London, have continued armed resistance to Soviet forces and are fostering a belief that the Western Allies will soon fight the Soviet Union. Large, well-equipped bands are reported to be operating in the vicinity of Lublin. The underground also appears to be well

> organized in Warsaw, where a clandestine newspaper appears and there are numerous daily acts of sabotage.[129]

It is only a small step from observing resistance inside Poland to becoming involved in such activity. The act of having active sources inside the satellite countries is a level of involvement; the use of these sources in the conduct of covert paramilitary action is, at this point, unconfirmed by the US intelligence community, but remains a real possibility.

We have then, in 1945, several sources that indicate OSS activity behind Soviet lines, well prior to the time many traditional histories place the start of the Cold War. It is quite possible that the OSS and its successors were developing networks of agents and saboteurs for later use; the OSS was at its core a paramilitary agency, with many of its members holding military rank. Later development of these networks would have been conducted as the National Security Act of 1947 (amended by NSC memorandum 10/2 in 1948) directly allowed.

In the "for what it's worth department" Soviet leader Nikita Khrushchev directly accused the US of supporting resistance movements behind the Iron Curtain in his memoirs, which was published in 1974. Khrushchev stated:

> Flare-ups, which sometimes amounted to war, were instigated by Ukrainian nationalists, not Poles; and the flames were fueled by the Americans, who parachuted arms, machinery, communications equipment, and other supplies to the insurgents... The Ukrainian nationalist activity within Poland became so serious that the Polish armed forces had to conduct full-scale military operations in the frontier areas of the republic near the Carpathian Mountains.[130]

Clearly Khrushchev may have had some ulterior motive, in trying to "blame" America for Cold War tensions. However, his observation tends to be confirmed by the available source material that shows a tendency for paramilitary activity in the satellite nations.

Allen Dulles, the Committee for a Free Europe, and the CIA

Key to the understanding of the events in Hungary in 1956 is the understanding of the Director of Central Intelligence at the time, Allen Welsh Dulles. Dulles was a blue blood in the world of American diplomacy; his grandfather had been Secretary of State under Benjamin Harrison and his Great Uncle was minister to London from 1877-79. His brother, John Foster Dulles, would become the Secretary of State under President Eisenhower.

By the age of 23, in 1916, Allen Dulles had achieved a Bachelors, Masters, and Law degree from Princeton and Brown universities. He went to work for the State Department until 1926 at which time he reverted to the practice of law at the firm of Sullivan and Cromwell. In 1942, after WWII had embroiled America, Allen Dulles became caught up in the action; he went to work for the OSS in Europe fighting the Nazis. In 1946 he reverted to the practice of law at Sullivan and Cromwell and was named president of the independent "Council on Foreign Relations."

In 1948, Allen Dulles, who had never hidden the fact that he was a Republican, assisted in the unsuccessful presidential campaign of Thomas Dewy. Dulles was very much opposed to the containment foreign policy of Harry Truman and was interested in developing networks of operatives in the satellite nations. He kept the company of like-minded individuals.

Arthur Bliss Lane, in a letter to Dulles in July of 1948, states that US policy toward the Soviets was "a sell-out in 1944."[131] Further, Lane tells Dulles that, "the Tehran, Yalta, and Potsdam agreements—in that they violate Articles I, II and III of the Atlantic Charter—should be repudiated by the United States government."[132] Lane continued:

> The other matter on which I touched very little over the phone the other day has to do with the desirability of our maintaining, unofficially, contact with various underground movements in Europe. Some friends and I have a skeleton organization, which receives valuable information from various undergrounds... Clandestine contact such as we have established is in my opinion highly desirable. We have been furnishing the information on a strictly confidential basis to certain officials in the government on the understanding, however, that the sources of the information are under no condition to be disclosed.[133]

This Dulles-Lane network resulted in the formation of the "National Committee for a Free Europe, Inc." (CFE) in 1949. With its headquarters on the third floor of the prestigious Empire State Building, the committee included no less than General of the Army, Dwight Eisenhower, and publishing mogul, Henry Luce, on its board of trustees (in addition to Dulles and Lane). Its purpose was, as its name stated, the liberation of Communist occupied Europe by whatever means available. From the committee's original bid to new members and potential supporters one can read:

> Arms and economic aid are indispensable but by themselves are not enough. Only in the field of ideas and spiritual values can victory be lasting.
>
> A new operation begins in the American defense and counter-attack against the Communist assault. Money is needed to finance the fight.
>
> We call on all Americans to join us by sending an urgently needed contribution. As the Communists like to remind us: "It is later than you think."

Many of the committee's records made their way onto CIA archives (from which they were in fact retrieved in order to write this book). The reasons CFE archives merged with that of the CIA are simply that the CIA played an active role in running the CFE, using it as a front. In March of 1950, the CFE began operations aimed at the radio broadcasting of propaganda into the satellite countries. The project called "Radio Free Europe" (RFE) included broadcasts by refugees into their former homelands. As well, General Eisenhower made a broadcast into the satellite countries on September 4, 1950 over RFE.

Soon enough the CIA took over RFE, part and parcel. This fact did not become public knowledge until 1975, when a 12-year veteran CIA operations officer published his memoir of CIA activity. From Philip Agee's *Inside the Company: CIA Diary,* we read:

> There are obviously hosts of...uses to which propaganda, both black and gray, can be put, using books, magazines, radio, television, wall-painting, handbills, decals, religious sermons, and political speeches as well as the daily press. In countries where handbills or wall paintings are important media, [CIA headquarters] stations are expected to maintain clandestine printing and distribution facilities as well as teams of agents who paint slogans on walls. Radio Free Europe and Radio Liberty are the best-known gray propaganda operations conducted by the CIA against the Soviet bloc.[134]

During this time, William Donovan continued to exert influence on Dulles and his activities. There are two rather vague letters between the two in the CIA file dating from 1950 and 1951. On November 6th, 1950 Donovan writes to Allen Dulles:

Dear Allen:
Here is something sent to me on the same topic I wrote you about the other day.
Sincerely yours,
Bill[135]

Whatever this letter covered is still withheld by the agency, but, we can tell that a regular correspondence between the two lawyers and former OSS men was ongoing into the next year when Dulles took a responsible position in the CIA as Deputy Director of Plans (DDP).

On January 8, 1951, six days after Allen Dulles took the DDP position, he writes to Donovan:

Dear Bill,
Many thanks for your letter of January 2, 1951. I realize the force of your comments and I shall certainly keep them in mind. [Redacted] and I had a good talk together before he left, and we are planning to get together immediately upon his return.
Please tell [Redacted] that I am looking forward to hearing from him and to be sure and see me if he comes to Washington.
[Paragraph Redacted]
Sincerely,
Allen W. Dulles[136]

These two documents were classified until 1992 when they were released to the public and portions of them remain classified today. We can surmise, from the paramilitary nature of Bill Donovan's background, and the other evidence available that they had something to do with paramilitary activity in the satellite countries. Donovan publicly stated that the US should "harass Stalin" with guerrilla forces inside the Communist countries in December 1952 in a speech to government students at Barnard College.[137]

One tip off to the CIA/CFE connection is contained in the CIA narrative concerning Allen Dulles' coming to work for the agency. Chapter 7 states:

> A.W.D. [Allen Dulles] will resign as Chairman of the Executive Committee and Director of the National Committee for Free Europe, since in his work at DDP [CIA Deputy Director of Plans] he will have...a responsibility for the conduct of NCFE operations.[138]

This narrative states that the same DDP had responsibility for controlling the CFE. The implications that the CFE was responsible for paramilitary operations inside the satellite nations are obvious.

In a letter to Allen Dulles dated January 19, 1951, which has the author's identity redacted, we see that Dulles was involved in discussions for operations behind the Iron Curtain. It is not clear if this letter was addressed to Dulles in his capacity as CIA DDP or as the CFE Executive Director (which was supposed to be resigned by this point). The reason it is unclear is that the letter is addressed to Dulles at Sullivan and Cromwell in his capacity as a private attorney (and this position was supposed to have been resigned as of January 2, 1951 with his ascendance to the position of CIA DDP). From the letter we read:

> *Dear Allen:*
> *Thanks very much for your letter in reply to mine. Of course, the West Germans will have to do a lot of work, which we can't do. On the other hand, there are things which they cannot accommodate. It seems to me very important not to leave the care and support of the fight against tyranny and for freedom in the Soviet Zone of Germany entirely to the Germans. As I indicated before I feel that, in that case, it becomes too much an issue with nationalist overtones.*
> *There is also the matter of creating a sense of comradeship among all those behind the iron curtain whom we want to cooperate in the common struggle. This is particularly important in view of the past. I believe some very real jobs can be done apart from radio, and they need not be very expensive.*
> *With warm regard.*
> *Sincerely,*
> *[Signature Redacted]*[139]

Just what the "jobs apart from radio" were we can only speculate. It is quite possible that these jobs included covert paramilitary action.

Allen Dulles rose quickly once a part of the CIA. In August 1951 he was promoted to the number two position in the agency (that of Deputy Director). In February of 1953, with his fellow Republican and CFE member, Dwight Eisenhower, in the White House, he was promoted to Director of Central Intelligence. The confirmation hearing in the Senate Armed Services Committee took about ten minutes in secret. By contrast confirmation hearings take days and are mostly public (as a result of the 70s revelations on intelligence abuses).

Thus, three years prior to the Hungarian uprising, an avid supporter of fostering such unrest was directing the CIA. This was plenty of time to have had an impact in Hungary and the popular support for the policy of "liberation" (as opposed to containment) may be yet another indicator that the American government was supporting paramilitary groups in the satellite countries by 1956.

The Policy of "Liberation"

In January of 1952, more than 100 Republican members of Congress signed a letter to Secretary of State, Dean Acheson, charging the Soviets with genocide. The Republicans who had opposed Yalta and Potsdam were now opposing containment, stating that it left millions as slaves behind the Iron Curtain.

The policy of liberation took another apparent leap forward when on January 18, 1952 the New York Times reported the Truman administration was sponsoring anti-Communist activity behind the Iron Curtain. The Times reported, in an article with the headline "U.S. Making Use of 'Escapee' Fund," the following:

> The government indicated today it had already begun to use secretly part of the $100,000,000 appropriated to aid the escape of men from behind the Iron Curtain who wished to join combat units for the ultimate liberation of their homelands.[140]

The leak of this information to the press may have been a calculated response among the Truman administration to appear strong on communism.

One of the most vocal advocates of liberation was Representative Charles

J. Kersten, a Milwaukee Republican. As early as February 1952 Kersten was calling for tough psychological warfare operations against the satellite nations. Allied with Kersten on this was no less than the future president, then a member of the House of Representatives, John F. Kennedy. The policy of liberation had supporters in both parties.[141]

On August 13, presidential candidate Eisenhower met with Kersten. The Congressman stated after the meeting with the general:

> It would be immoral and unchristian to negotiate a permanent agreement with forces which by every religious creed and moral precept are evil. It abandons nearly one-half of humanity and the once free nations or Poland, Czechoslovakia, Hungary, Romania, Bulgaria, Albania, Lithuania, Latvia, Estonia, and China to enslavement of the communist police state.
>
> It is un-American because it violates the principle of the American Declaration of Independence, which proclaims the rights of all people to freedom and their right to throw off tyranny.[142]

Eisenhower made a statement after their meeting with Kersten that he favored "peaceful" liberation of the satellite nations.

Ten days after the meeting with Eisenhower Kersten and four other members of Congress endorsed a private effort to raise forces to fight behind the Iron Curtain. Headed by Robert A. Vogeler, an American businessman who had been held in Hungary for 17 months, the group promised to raise enough money to arm 45,000 exiles from the satellite countries. The new group was known as "The American Liberation Center."[143]

In a speech to the American Legion National Convention on August 25, 1952 Eisenhower outlined his views on the liberation of Eastern Europe. On the subject of east-west conflict and the people trapped behind the Iron Curtain, he stated in part:

> How many people today live in great fear that never again shall they hear from a mother, a grandfather, a brother, or a cousin? Dare we rest while these millions of our kinsmen remain in slavery? I can almost hear your answer.
>
> The American conscience can never know peace until these people are restored again to being masters of their own fate.

> A hundred and fifty-five million united Americans are still the greatest temporal force in the world. We must have a policy that we can understand and support with confidence. And we must not abate our efforts until we have banished from the free world that last probability of Communist aggression."[144]

Two days later, Eisenhower's foreign policy advisor got more specific on plans for Eastern Europe. John Foster Dulles, brother of Allen Welsh Dulles, stated before the 48th annual meeting of the American Political Science Association that an Eisenhower administration would take the offensive against the Communists.

John Foster Dulles would become the Secretary of State after the election of Eisenhower to the White House. He stated that the plan for Eastern Europe would be carried out in this order. First, an announcement would be made by the president that the U.S. would never recognize Soviet domination of Eastern Europe. Then the Voice of America radio network would assure the captive peoples that they had the support of the United States government. Finally, he said that indigenous resistance movements would spring up and these freedom fighters would be supplied by "airdrops" from private organizations (like the Committee for a Free Europe and the American Liberation Center).

Further, Dulles Stated that the containment policy of the Truman administration must be abandoned. "That policy has not contained Soviet communism." He continued, in support of liberation:

> It is nonsense to say that General Eisenhower's liberation policy is a trap, and would lead to premature uprisings and more massacres... The only trap I see is that in the Democratic platform which says, *they look forward to the liberation of all peoples, but aren't willing to do anything about it.* That's a trap to get votes.[145]

President Truman responded to the Eisenhower camp's call for liberation on September 2, 1952. He said, in part:

> Nothing could be worse than to raise false hopes of this in Eastern Europe. Nothing could be worse than to incite uprisings that can only end by giving a new crop of victims to the Soviet

> executioners. All Europeans know quite well that insurrection in the Soviet borderlands these days could only be successful with armed support from the outside world.
>
> If the Republicans don't mean to give armed support—and I feel sure they don't—then they are trying to deceive their fellow-citizens at home and are playing cruel, gutter politics with the lives of countless good men and women behind the Iron Curtain.[146]

The Hungarian language press in the U.S. (which was being monitored by the CIA) was equally damning of the policy of liberation. On September 18, the paper *Magyar Banaszlap* commented that,

> anybody who has the slightest idea of the situation behind the Iron Curtain, knows that such resistance on the part of those nations would result in blood-baths and even more terrible terror.[147]

Given the opportunity to deny the CIA was fomenting revolution in the satellite countries, intelligence director Allen Dulles was illusive. In a 1954 interview he left the door wide open. The interview in US News and World Report reads in part:

> (Q) Since you can't tell us what you do, could you tell us some of the things you don't do? For instance, it is often reported in the papers that you send in provocateurs to stir up revolutions in the satellite countries. What truth is there in that?
>
> (A) I only wish we had accomplished all that the Soviets attribute to us. I am not going to deny all the compliments they give us in reporting our activities. I think it's better for them to be left a little in the dark as to how much they say is true and how much is false.[148]

In December 1955, an address by Secretary of State John Foster Dulles was reprinted in the State Department Bulletin. The text included part of a speech the secretary had made five years prior and repeated in 1955. He drove home the point that the US must take the offensive against the Soviets, and that this offensive could take any form available (presumably including covert paramilitary action in the satellite countries). He said, in part:

> With more than 20 nations strung along the 20,000 miles of iron curtain, it is not possible to build up static defensive forces, which could make each nation impregnable to such a major unpredictable assault as Russia could launch. To attempt this would be to have strength nowhere and bankruptcy everywhere. That, however, does not mean that we should abandon the whole idea of collective security and merely build our own defense area... Fortunately, we do not have to choose between two disastrous alternatives. It is not necessary either to spread our strength all around the world in futile attempts to create everywhere a static defense, nor need we crawl back into our own hole in the vain hope of defending ourselves against all of the rest of the world... As against the possibility of full-scale attack by the Soviet Union itself, there is only one effective defense, for us and for others. That is the ultimate deterrent... The arsenal of retaliation should include all forms of counter-attack with maximum flexibility... In such ways, the idea of collective security can be given sensible and effective content.[149]

Today we are expected to believe that the uprising in Hungary was the result of spontaneous combustion, with no help from the Eisenhower administration. Statements like this one, made by the president himself, may not have been so benign as they first appeared. He was definitely giving vocal support to the idea of taking up arms against the Soviets by the people behind the Iron Curtain. These remarks coincided with the opening of hostilities in Hungary on October 23. He said:

> The day of liberation may be postponed where armed forces for a time make protest suicidal. But all history testifies that the memory of freedom is not erased by the fear of guns, and freedom is more enduring than the power of tyrants. But it is necessary that the inspiration of freedom and the benefits enjoyed by those who possess it are known to those oppressed.[150]

One November 4, with the Soviets making a full force military drive to control the situation in Hungary, US Ambassador to the United Nations,

Henry Cabot Lodge, Jr., stated to the General Assembly:

> At dawn this morning Soviet troops in Hungary opened fire in Budapest and throughout the country. We learn from Vienna that the Soviet artillery were firing incendiary phosphorous shells at centers of civilian population. These are the shells which set fire to buildings and which burn the flesh of women and children and other civilian noncombatants whom they encounter. Prime Minster Nagy has appealed to the United Nations for help, and I must say we can understand it.[151]

Also on November 4, the UN general assembly passed a US backed resolution calling for the government of the Union of Soviet Socialist Republics to desist forthwith from all armed attack on the peoples of Hungary and from any form of intervention, in particular armed intervention, in the internal affairs of Hungary.[152] The resolution further called for the introduction of UN observers into Hungary. On November 9, a further US supported resolution was passed stating:

> Free elections should be held in Hungary under the United Nations' auspices, as soon as law and order have been restored, to enable the people of Hungary to determine for themselves the form of government they wish to establish in their country.[153]

Clearly, a US diplomatic power play was underway to roll back the Iron Curtain from Hungary. This was the policy of liberation at work.

As to whether any of the comments by John Foster Dulles and President Eisenhower in any way incited or otherwise supported the revolt in Hungary, Ambassador Lodge had this to say to the UN:

> Now, as regards the statement that we sought to give the impression that there would be United States military help in Hungary, I assert on the very highest authority—and this has been gone into very thoroughly—that no one has ever been incited to rebellion by the United States in any way—by radio broadcast or any other way.[154]

As for what the CIA will admit to today, they treat the records of the revolt as if protecting the highest order of national secrets. In a search of records of the then director, Allen Dulles, there are only 9 documents declassified to or from the director for October and November of 1956. One might think that there would have been a flurry of reports and letters to and from the director's office while the revolt was underway. This would be true even if the CIA was not involved fomenting the surge of anti-Soviet activity in Hungary and was simply monitoring developments. Clearly there is something being suppressed.

In the course of researching and writing this book, this author made several requests, under the Freedom of Information Act, for records specifically concerning CIA support of the revolt. After an initial denial and appeal to the "Agency Release Panel," the following reply was received:

> Your appeal has been presented to the appropriate member of the Agency Release Panel, the Information Review Officer for the Directorate of Operations. Pursuant to the authority delegated under paragraph 1900.43 of Chapter XIX, Title 32 of the Code of Federal Regulations (C.F.R.), it has been determined that the fact of the existence or nonexistence of any documents that would be responsive to your request is classified pursuant to Executive Order 12958. Further, the fact of existence or nonexistence of such documents would relate directly to information concerning intelligence sources and methods that the Director of Central Intelligence has the responsibility to protect from unauthorized disclosure in accordance with Subsection 103(c)(6) of the National Security Act of 1947, as amended, and Section 6 of the Central Intelligence Agency Act of 1949, as amended. Accordingly, pursuant to the Freedom of Information Act exemptions (b)(1) and (b)(3), your appeal is denied. By this statement, we are neither confirming nor denying that any such documents exist.[155]

The fact remains that the CIA refuses to deny that it was involved in the revolt.

Conclusions to Chapter 4

The Eisenhower administration was activist in terms of foreign policy and the use of covert action. In three instances (Iran, Guatemala, and probably Hungary) the warlike powers granted to the executive branch of government by the Congress in the National Security Act of 1947 were used to the maximum extent possible. Even taking into account the direct US military involvement in Korea during the early part of the decade, the 50s were a time of rigorous confrontation of perceived communist expansion at the middle of the spectrum of conflict.

The basic tenant of Eisenhower's foreign policy was anti-communism. In two out of the three cases discussed in this chapter (Iran and Guatemala), Eisenhower's action supported authoritarian rulers in order to vanquish perceived communists. In all cases the security interests of the United States were put ahead of human rights issues in the immediate sense. However, vigorous opposition of communism could be considered, in the long term, a pro-human rights stance since the communists were known for their use of red terror once in power.

Former OSS officer, Allen Dulles, commanded all three of these operations from the position of Director of Central Intelligence. In their own right, all three could have been considered victories. The operations in Iran and Guatemala resulted in hand picked rulers running those countries after the coups. They also resulted in the exclusion of the communist elements in those countries from power. In Hungary, the Soviets and Hungarian communists lost face before the world, and the US role in the action there remained undiscovered and is yet unconfirmed.

Confident of his power to shape foreign policy through covert means as a result of successes in the 50s, the Director of Central Intelligence would remain in his position and an advocate of covert action into the 60s. Allen Dulles would, however, meet his professional undoing in Cuba in 1961 with the Bay of Pigs. This is covered in the next chapter.

Chapter 5

Cuba and John F. Kennedy

Balance and Correlation

On October 22, 1962, the President of the United States, John F. Kennedy, went on national television to announce to the world that Soviet nuclear missiles and long-range bombers had been discovered in Cuba. The president also stated that the presence of these "offensive" weapons was unacceptable and that a naval blockade (or "quarantine") was being instituted to stop further shipments of similar weapons to the island. The president stated:

> The urgent transformation of Cuba into an important strategic base—by the presence of these large, long-range, and clearly offensive weapons of sudden mass destruction—constitutes an explicit threat to all of the Americas.[156]

Within a few days the crisis had been resolved; the Soviets had agreed to remove their missiles and bombers under UN supervision. In the process of reaching the settlement the US also made some concessions.

This conflict between the US and the Soviets was known as the Cuban missile crisis in the West and the Caribbean crisis in the Soviet Union. It was the superpowers' first direct confrontation since acquiring the capacity to destroy each other. More than being the first conflict in which nuclear annihilation was possible; the Cuban missile crisis of 1962 was an integral part of the Cold War. Far from being an isolated series of events in October of 1962, the crisis was more comparable to a battle in a campaign than a separate conflict.

The Soviet method of measuring relative strength during the Cold War was one of a "correlation of forces." In the West, the term "balance of power" was often used to describe the relative strength or weakness of countries involved. However, the term balance of power usually refers only to the military strength of each side (and perhaps some consideration is given to political factors such as alliances). The term correlation of forces, on the other hand, is a much more all-encompassing expression. The use of such a term reflected the view the Soviets held that capitalists and Communists were locked in a struggle that involved all aspects of both societies. To the Soviets, especially under Nikita Khrushchev's rule, the Cold War was a total war of each society against the other.

The calculations involved in determining the correlation of forces utilized four factors: economy, military, politics, and international movement. Economy refers to the gross national product and productivity of the work force. Military refers to the number and quality of each nation's arms and soldiers. Politics refers to the stability of each government and the relative support it enjoys from its people. International movement refers to the strength of a nation's foreign policy and its allies. International movement also includes an estimate of whether a nation's world influence is increasing or decreasing. Soviet theory held that each of these four factors could be measured with a high degree of precision. Once the factors were calculated, a determination could be made as to whether a correlation of forces was favorable to the Soviets or to their opponents.

The addition of Cuba to the Communist camp in 1959-60 (when Castro took control of the country and established relations with the USSR) promised the Soviets progress in all four areas of the correlation of forces. In consideration of economic factors, the opening of Cuban markets to the Soviets held the promise of an increase in trade. (In reality Cuba became a client of the Soviets costing them billions of dollars each year.) In the area of military power, Communist control of Cuba gave the Soviets a valuable strategic base only 90 miles from the United States. In regard to politics and international movement, Communist control in Cuba was seen by the Soviets as part of a trend toward eventual Communist domination of the Americas. Cuba gave the Soviets a base from which they could attempt to support Communist movements in Central and South America.

Prior to the crisis, Chairman Khrushchev had often stated that the Soviet Union and its allies were about to surpass the West. If this were a true assessment of the correlation of forces, then one might wonder why the Soviets would put missiles in Cuba. Such a move would risk the provocation of the United States. Any conflict over the missiles would take place far from the Soviet Union, in an area that was a traditional US sphere of influence.

At about the same time as the addition of Cuba to the Communist camp, the Soviets made apparent gains in space rocketry. The launch of the Sputnik satellite only a few years before Castro came to power led the Soviets to claim superiority in missile development. If the Soviets were indeed ahead in missile development, then such a provocation as the placement of nuclear missiles and long-range bombers in Cuba would seem unnecessary.

In reality the Soviets were far behind America in the development of long-range nuclear delivery systems. In addition, Khrushchev's proclamations and predictions concerning Soviet world revolutionary success appeared to represent wishful thinking rather than the world situation. The Soviet attempt to place nuclear weapons in Cuba was an effort to compensate for their lagging behind in the correlation of forces calculation.

By October of 1962, when the missile crisis came to a head, the United States had the clear advantage in long-range nuclear weaponry. US land-based nuclear rockets included 261 missiles: 156 were intercontinental missiles (ICBMs) based in North America, and the remaining 105 were intermediate-range missiles able to reach the USSR from Western Europe. In addition there were about 80 US submarine-based ballistic missiles in the naval inventory.[157] All of these missiles were capable of reaching targets within the Soviet Union. The inventory of US bomber aircraft capable of reaching strategic targets inside the Soviet Union included 1,700 planes. Of these, 1,550 were the modern heavy B-47, B-52, and B-58 aircraft. The remaining 150 planes were part of the Navy's "V-force" of carrier-based nuclear bombers (See Table 5-1).[158] With these aircraft and missiles, the total destructive force of nuclear weapons that could be dropped on the Soviet Union was equivalent to over thirty billion tons of TNT.

The Soviet strategic nuclear forces that were deployed at the time were much smaller than those of the US. The total number of Soviet long-range missiles that could reach the US from the USSR was only between 35-50 missiles. The Soviets also possessed between 200-300 medium and intermediate-range missiles which were only capable of reaching targets in Western Europe (they would be useless against the continental US from their bases inside the USSR). In addition, the Soviets had between 200-300 long-range bombers able to make the two-way flight to targets inside the US and back. To this total force the Soviets could add about 90 submarine-based missiles which could strike America.[159]

If one uses the median numbers for the Soviet forces and leaves the unreliable submarine-launched missiles out of the calculation, the ratio of delivery platforms (missiles and bombers) available to carry nuclear weapons was 2,041 platforms for the US to 790 platforms for the USSR. These figures, when reduced, show a 2.6 to 1 ratio in favor of the US. Further, when one considers only the Soviet weapons capable of reaching the US mainland (eliminating the medium and intermediate-range Soviet missiles targeted at Europe from consideration), the final ratio changes to an overwhelming 5 to 1 in favor of the United States.

US strategic nuclear forces also enjoyed a qualitative advantage over the Soviet nuclear forces. According to then Secretary of Defense Robert McNamara, the Soviet long-range intercontinental missiles represented "only a limited threat to the nuclear strike-force based in the United States or deployed at sea."[160] This is because Soviet missiles were known to be inaccurate and unreliable. The Soviet missiles were also in unprotected open-air launch sites (US missiles of the time were in sheltered underground silos). In addition the location of all, or most, of the Soviet launchers was known to US intelligence. According to one observer, "the whole Soviet ICBM system was suddenly obsolete"[161] because their unprotected launcher locations were discovered. The size of the nuclear forces facing each other at this time were: ICBMs: US 156, Soviets 35-55; medium range missiles: US 105, Soviets 300-500; Submarine Launched Ballistic Missiles (SLBMs): US 80, Soviets 90; intercontinental bombers: US 1700, Soviets 200-300; total nuclear delivery platforms: US 2041, Soviets 625-1045.

Khrushchev vs. Kennedy

In addition to being a conflict between the two great nuclear powers of the time, the Cuban Missile Crisis was a personal confrontation between two leaders. The missile crisis was a test of will between Soviet Party Chairman, Nikita Khrushchev, and President of the United States, John F. Kennedy. It was a matter of record that Kennedy had spoken out against Kremlin expansionism during his successful campaign of 1960.

Khrushchev was the successor to one of the most notorious dictators of the 20th century (Joseph Stalin). A veteran of the Russian Civil War, Khrushchev was only the third leader of the Soviet Union since the Communists came to power. He ruled the Soviet Union and was de facto leader of the East Bloc from 1956-1964. (After Stalin's death in 1953, it took Khrushchev several years to consolidate power.) Khrushchev often stated a belief in peaceful coexistence with the United States. However, his approach to US-Soviet relations was often one of confrontation.

Khrushchev stated his understanding of peaceful coexistence in a 1957 speech over Prague radio. He said in part:

> Indeed it happens that people do not get married for love, but despite that they live their whole lives together. And that is what we want. We live on one planet and therefore we want peaceful competition.[162]

All that peaceful coexistence meant to Khrushchev was that there would be no large nuclear war between the super powers, not that the two would be fast friends. After his forced retirement Khrushchev wrote:

> The struggle will end only when Marxism-Leninism triumphs everywhere and when the class enemy vanishes from the face of the earth. Gradually in some places, suddenly in others, the political conditions will change for the better; the people will have the final say, and the existing relationship between exploiters and exploited will dissolve.
>
> We Communists must hasten this process by any means at our disposal, excluding war.[163]

John F. Kennedy had been born on May 29, 1917. He was the son of a wealthy Boston family. His father, Joseph Kennedy Sr., was involved in politics and in the 1930s became the US ambassador to Great Britain under FDR. John Kennedy was plagued by childhood illnesses; yet, he struggled to overcome these maladies. He participated in football and tennis while a student at Harvard. He was a superlative student and his senior thesis, "Why England Slept," was published as a book in 1940.

"Why England Slept" dealt with the reasons democracies are inferior in their ability to prepare for war. During his studies of history, Kennedy had noticed that totalitarian systems, like Hitler's Germany, were able to mobilize their nations for war quicker than democracies. The attitude the young Kennedy developed was to influence him later in life, during his Cold War struggle with Khrushchev (and the totalitarian Soviet system). As the president, Kennedy stated repeatedly that he was determined to see the forces of totalitarianism not gain the upper hand over the nations of the free world.

Most famous of the addresses in which he expressed these sentiments is Kennedy's inaugural address of 1961. In the address he espoused the view that the Cold War between the US and the USSR was an ongoing struggle. He also stated his belief that the Soviet adversary must be met with determined resolve. Kennedy was determined that the democratic West would not sell out to the totalitarian Soviets, as Chamberlain had sold out to Hitler at Munich. From Kennedy's inaugural address we read:

> Let every nation know, whether it wishes us well or ill, that we shall pay any price, bear any burden, meet any hardship, support any friend, oppose any foe, to assure the survival and success of liberty. This much we pledge—and more...
>
> In the long history of the world, only a few generations have been granted the role of defending freedom in its hour of maximum danger. I do not shrink from this responsibility—I welcome it.[164]

It is clear that the "hour of maximum danger" that Kennedy referred to was the Cold War and the nuclear dilemma on the horizon. Kennedy had embraced his role as leader in that struggle. The stance he had taken in his inauguration was probably an influence on Kennedy as he chose from options in the missile crisis a year and a half later. Having taken such a strong position against the Soviet expansionism, a major Soviet advance (such as the successful placement of nuclear weapons in Cuba) would amount to a tremendous loss of face for the young president.

As a candidate for the presidency, Kennedy had already personalized the conflict with Khrushchev. In a 1960 campaign speech Kennedy stated, "I want a world that looks to the United States for leadership. That does not always read what Mr. Khrushchev is doing or Mr. Castro is doing. I want them to read what the president of the United States is doing."[165]

Kennedy further personalized the conflict with Khrushchev once he was in office. In a televised address to the nation, after a 1961 summit meeting with Khrushchev, President Kennedy foreshadowed the coming confrontation over nuclear missiles in Cuba. He said in part:

> Only by such a discussion was it possible for me to be sure that Mr. Khrushchev knew how differently we view the present and the future. Our views contrasted sharply but at least we

knew better at the end where we both stood.

We believe in a system of national freedom and independence. He believes in an expanding dynamic concept of world communism; and the question is whether these two systems can ever hope to live in peace without permitting any loss of security or denial of freedom for our friends...

...Generally Mr. Khrushchev did not talk in terms of war. He believes the world will move his way without the resort to force. He spoke of his nation's achievements in space. He stressed his intention to undo us in industrial production, to out-trade us, to prove to the world the superiority of his system over ours. Most of all he predicted the triumph of communism in the new less developed countries...

...In the 1940s and early fifties, the great danger was from communist armies marching across free borders, which we saw in Korea. Our nuclear monopoly helped us to prevent this in other areas. Now we face a different threat. We no longer have a nuclear monopoly. Their missiles, they believe, will hold off our missiles; their troops can match our troops should we intervene in these so-called wars of national liberation.[166]

Crises Before the Crisis

Kennedy had given an accurate characterization of the Soviet view of the world. Cuba being a less developed nation, and one that had undergone a war of national liberation, was likely one of the countries Kennedy had in mind when he was speaking. The Soviets had theorized that former colonies, and nations which had been dominated by the West (as Cuba had been dominated by the US), would eventually try to free themselves in wars of national liberation.

Typically these conflicts involved a subversive communist guerrilla force, which sought to undermine a pro-western government. Khrushchev considered it legitimate to give any aid he could to these Marxist revolutionary movements, and to assist them in holding power once they were in control. In the coming confrontation, the Soviets were making clear their desire to protect socialism in Cuba. Soviet missiles in Cuba were intended to be a match for US bombers and a potential invasion force.

The missile crisis was one of an ongoing series of conflicts between the US and the Soviets. Three of these crises set the stage for the Kennedy-

Khrushchev show down over the nuclear weapons in Cuba. Some of these crises had a very direct relationship to the missile crisis (such as the Bay of Pigs invasion). Others had a less direct, but still important role in the missile crisis. These earlier crises had provided the two adversaries an opportunity to gauge each other's strengths and weaknesses. This was the case in regard to the situation in Laos.

On March 23, 1961, President Kennedy went on national television to explain the situation in Laos to the American people. His speech was also beamed into living rooms in France, Germany, and Great Britain by the Telstar satellite. Kennedy's speech was intended to express his concern over then communist advances in Laos. Kennedy stated in part:

> Laos is key to control of the whole of Southeast Asia. It adjoins free Thailand, free Cambodia, free Vietnam. Free Malaya is just to the south. Indonesia is only a short sea distance farther south. In the hands of the communists, Laos would be a pistol pointed at every free country.
>
> If in the past there has been any ground for misunderstanding our desire for a truly neutral Laos, there should be none now.
>
> My fellow Americans, Laos is far from America, but the world is small… The security of Southeast Asia will be endangered if Laos loses its independence. Its own safety runs with the safety of us all…[167]

Just a few days before sending this unequivocal message, Kennedy had turned down his military advisors' proposals for direct intervention in Laos. He opted for a strategy of negotiations. The president feared that the conflict in Laos might escalate into nuclear warfare. A year later Kennedy lost face in the negotiations. The settlement reached concerning Laos allowed the communists to keep control of much of the country and to maintain the supply of arms to their war effort in South Vietnam. One official in Kennedy's own administration, William Rostow, later referred to the settlement in Laos as "the greatest single error in American policy of the 1960s."[168]

The missile crisis was not the first confrontation the Kennedy administration experienced concerning Fidel Castro's Cuba. An earlier confrontation known as the Bay of Pigs invasion (called operation Zapata by the CIA) was to play a part in Khrushchev's decision to place nuclear missiles in Cuba.

On March 17, 1960, President Eisenhower authorized a plan to train and equip Cuban refugees to operate as a guerrilla force against Castro. In authorizing the plan Eisenhower was no doubt given confidence by his prior victory in the Latin American nation of Guatemala (with operation PB Success). The plan was to be fully developed and put into action by Allen Dulles at the CIA with the assistance of the Department of Defense (DOD). The initial plan was for a guerrilla-type operation; however, the plan grew into a full-scale invasion plan. The eventual plan called for a US trained brigade of about 1400 troops to land at the Bay of Pigs. It was thought that the invasion would spark a popular uprising in Cuba that would oust Fidel Castro.

Far from the initial concept of being organized to fight as guerrillas, the brigade was equipped with tanks, ships, and copious amounts of modern heavy weapons. They had been trained in Guatemala by 30 advisors from the US Army.[169] Also, the invasion force was promised the US Navy would protect them with air cover. The provision for US air cover was included in the original plan as it had been drawn up under Eisenhower. Being a veteran of the Normandy invasion, Eisenhower was fully aware of the need for a seaborne invasion force to be covered from the air.

In early 1961, after only a few days in office, Kennedy reviewed the invasion plan and authorized it to proceed. In addition to approving the plan, Kennedy decided to keep Allen Dulles on as head of the CIA. Kennedy was, however, wary that the invasion might lead to a full-scale conflict with Cuba's backer—the Soviet Union. He therefore stated that he retained the right to cancel the operation up to the last minute. The operation commenced on April 16, 1961 with the refugee's obsolete air force of WWII planes bombing Castro's air bases. On the 17th the seaborne invasion commenced. Khrushchev immediately sent an angry note to Kennedy about the invasion of his client. Khrushchev denounced the invasion and pledged "all necessary assistance" to Castro.[170]

The pre-invasion air strike on Castro's airfields had been necessary because Kennedy had decided to withhold protective US air cover from the invasion. In a news conference just two days prior to the invasion, Kennedy had said that he ruled out "under any condition, an intervention in Cuba by United States armed forces."[171] As a result of a lack of proper air support, two of Castro's jets, survivors of the air strikes the day before the invasion, shot down at least 6 of the refugees' propeller-driven aircraft, sank a critical invasion supply ship, and strafed the invaders on the beaches.

On April 20, 1961, the Bay of Pigs invasion was over. Kennedy had denied last minute requests made by his military staff for proper US air support to the refugee brigade. The Cuban Army captured most of the invasion force and the US was humiliated in the eyes of the world. This relatively minor operation had drastic consequences because Kennedy had taken such a strong position against Castro. Allen Dulles resigned from the CIA over the failure of operation Zapata.

In his State of the Union address only a few months before, Kennedy had stated:

> In Latin America, Communist agents seeking to exploit that region's peaceful revolution of hope have established a base on Cuba, only ninety miles from our shores. Our objection to Cuba is not for the people's desire for a better life. Our objection is their domination by foreign and domestic tyrannies.[172]

Kennedy had also strongly advocated direct US intervention in Cuba during the 1960 presidential campaign. He stated the Eisenhower and Nixon's actions in the region were "too little and too late."[173] As in the case of Laos, Kennedy had lost face in a struggle with Khrushchev. He has taken a strong anticommunist position in his initial rhetoric and backed down in the face of confrontation.

In a conversation with reporters that took place immediately following the Bay of Pigs fiasco, Kennedy remarked that unilateral intervention in Cuba would have violated America traditions. However, he added the somewhat vague warning, which reads as follows:

> Let the record show, that our restraint is not inexhaustible.... If the nations of this hemisphere should fail to meet their commitments against outside communist penetration—then I want it clearly understood that this government will not hesitate to meet its primary obligations, which are to the security of our nation.[174]

Considering the past invasion attempt, and this rhetoric, Khrushchev considered it a possibility that the US would act against Cuba in the future.

In light of these events, it is not surprising that Khrushchev began to consider a method to prevent an American invasion of Cuba. Years after the missile crisis, Khrushchev wrote in his memoirs:

> We were sure that the Americans would never reconcile themselves to the existence of Castro's Cuba. They feared, as much as we hoped that a socialist Cuba might become a magnet that would attract other Latin American countries to socialism.... It was clear to me that we might well lose Cuba if we didn't take some decisive steps in her defense.... It was during my visit to Bulgaria (May 14-20, 1962) that I had the idea of installing missiles with nuclear warheads without letting the United States find out they were there until it was too late to do anything about them.... In addition to protecting Cuba, our missiles would have equalized what the West likes to call the "balance of power".... We'd be doing nothing more than giving them a little of their own medicine.[175]

The taste of their own medicine that Khrushchev was referring to was the American stationing of missiles close to the Soviet union, in Turkey and other locations. We see then that Khrushchev's concerns were two-fold. First he was concerned with keeping Cuba in the Soviet orbit in the face of determined efforts by Kennedy to undermine Castro. Second, he was making an effort to equalize the balance of power on a strategic level (or the military aspects of the correlation of forces as the Soviets would put it). To accomplish these goals, Khrushchev would move some of his medium and intermediate-range missiles and long-range bombers to Cuba. From bases in Cuba, these weapons would be able to reach targets within the United States with ease.

In addition to the events in Laos, and the Bay of Pigs fiasco, one additional conflict had significant impact on shaping the missile crisis. The Berlin Crisis of 1961, sometimes called the Berlin Wall Crisis, had implications regarding the missile crisis. The reason being, Berlin was a potential flash point in the Cold War. In addition, Berlin was vulnerable to counter-reaction by the Soviets in response to US moves against Cuba. If the US were to have invaded Cuba during the crisis, it would have been a relatively simple matter for the Soviets to storm West Berlin.

Many of the officials in the Kennedy administration assumed that if there was to be a major showdown with the Soviets it would be over Berlin. Kennedy himself had minimized concern over Cuba in 1962 when he told one of his staff members, "If we solve the Berlin problem without war, Cuba will look pretty small. And if there is a war, Cuba won't matter either."[176] Berlin was indeed to become a major problem for the Kennedy administration. The Berlin crisis never developed as much intensity as the missile crisis, and it was not as significant a setback as the Laotian situation or the Bay of Pigs; nevertheless, Khrushchev may have been further emboldened by its outcome.

The Soviets' stated objective in regard to Berlin was to make it a "free" city inside East Germany. In reality it was Khrushchev's desire that NATO military forces should leave West Berlin and give the communists control of the city. The presence of NATO troops 110 miles inside East Germany was a thorn in the Soviet leader's side.

Kennedy made a public address in July of 1962 in order to state his determination to keep West Berlin out of Soviet hands. He said in part, "We cannot and will not permit the communists to drive us out of Berlin, either gradually or by force."[177] In his address, Kennedy also outlined a plan to discourage the Soviets from moving into West Berlin, as he and his staff expected they would. He mobilized a portion of the US military reserve forces, increased draft quotas, raised his defense spending proposal by $3.5 billion, and placed added emphasis on civil defense. Khrushchev responded in kind with a speech on August 7 in which he ordered the mobilization of part of his reserve forces.

Whether Khrushchev's attempts to get NATO out of Berlin were his genuine goal, or part of an elaborate deception, West Berlin remained in the hands of America and her allies. Khrushchev did, however, make one critical gain from the crisis. He was able to seal off the embarrassing flow of refugees from Communist East Germany into free West Berlin. The flow of these persons, daily, had long been a public relations problem for the Soviets and the East Germans. The crisis was to end with Khrushchev forcing NATO to accept the Berlin Wall or risk direct confrontation and possible nuclear war. Though Khrushchev was on the short end of the nuclear balance, he played his options over Berlin right to the brink, as he would in Cuba.

On August 13, 1962, Khrushchev presented Kennedy with a fate accompli, the East German military and police forces moved under cover of darkness to set up a barbed wire barricade separating East and West Berlin. On August 17, the East Germans began construction of the brick and concrete Berlin Wall. In spite of the fact that some in the administration had urged Kennedy to act, NATO did not intervene with the construction of the wall.

Throughout the Berlin Crisis, Kennedy's policies had been constructed to avoid the possibility of escalating to war with the Soviets. One Kennedy administration official noted that, "Berlin threatened a war that might destroy civilization."[178] The president wanted to avoid such a confrontation; his response to the building of the wall was to register a formal protest with the Soviets.

Further, in late August of 1962, Kennedy took steps to increase the strength of US forces in West Berlin. He dispatched a battle group from the 8th Infantry Division in West Germany to strengthen the western half of the city's garrison. When the reinforcements arrived in the city, Vice President Lyndon Johnson was there to greet them. No one in the Kennedy administration had considered initiating a war in response to the building of the wall, but prudent measures were taken in case one was sparked by the crisis.

Maximum tension in the Berlin Crisis had come in the middle of August when US and Soviet tanks found themselves face to face at Checkpoint Charlie. The checkpoint was one of the official crossing points established in the barrier system; only those individuals with Soviet approval could pass through the checkpoint. It was at this time that some US politicians suggested that Kennedy should have ordered US troops to take wire cutters and bulldozers to the barriers. Former President, Eisenhower, was one urging such bold action by the US. Kennedy took no such action, and though there were some shots fired along the construction line, the crisis did not escalate to war.

The significance of the Berlin Crisis in relation to the Cuban Missile Crisis is that Kennedy had been again forced to react to Soviet-backed Communist actions. In Laos he had reacted to Communist incursions into neutral territory by negotiating and leaving the Communists with the territory they had gained in order to avoid war. In the case of the Bay of Pigs, Kennedy was reacting to a Communist takeover of Cuba, and he prohibited the use of US airpower to avoid a wider conflict with Khrushchev.

Overall, Kennedy fared better in the Berlin situation than in Laos or the Bay of Pigs; however, Khrushchev may still have viewed his actions as signs of weakness. While Kennedy had managed to keep West Berlin out of Soviet hands, he had allowed the East Germans to build the wall. When viewing this series of crises and Kennedy's incomplete reactions to them, it becomes easy to understand why Khrushchev assumed he could place nuclear missiles in Cuba and believe that there would be a minimal US response.

US-Soviet Tensions Rise Over Cuba

As the Berlin Crisis was fading away in August of 1962, the events leading up to the Cuban Missile Crisis were coming into focus. US surveillance of Cuba had been stepped up in August and September of 1962. This was in response to indications that Cuba was receiving increasing amounts of military equipment from the Soviet Union. The shipments of weapons were becoming so frequent that many politicians in the US began calling for strong measures to stop the buildup. Republican Senator, Keating, criticized Kennedy for his "do nothing" policy on Cuba.[179] Former Vice President Nixon, with whom Kennedy had exchanged angry words over Cuba during the 1960 presidential campaign, urged Kennedy to institute an immediate blockade of Cuba.

In reality, concern over the shipment of Soviet weapons to Cuba went back to the time of the Bay of Pigs invasion. The possible use of Cuba as a Soviet military base had been one of Kennedy's reasons for proceeding with the action. Concern over Cuba continued after the fiasco. In February of 1962, the Senate Foreign Relations Committee secretly questioned Secretary of Defense, McNamara, over the issue of Soviet weapons in Cuba. The committee's concern was over the presence of advanced jet fighter aircraft and the possible placement of Soviet nuclear weapons in Cuba. In response to a direct question as to whether there were Soviet nuclear weapons in Cuba, McNamara answered, "We cannot say absolutely they have received none, but it is my firm belief that they have received none."[180]

Under this pressure from domestic critics, and in order to be ready in the case there was an anti-Castro uprising in Cuba, the Kennedy administration developed a series of secret invasion plans for Cuba. This time the forces would be US military, not Cuban exiles. These plans were developed to such an extent that actual rehearsals were conducted in April and May of 1962. These exercises were, in part, intended to rattle the saber before the Soviets, making clear US desires for no Soviet buildup on the island.

The first exercise was an amphibious landing called "Lantphibex 1-62." It consisted of a Marine air-ground task force landing on Vieques Island in the Caribbean. The second exercise, called "Operation Quick Kick," ran almost a full month from April 19 to May 11. Quick Kick involved 300 aircraft, 79 ships, and over 40,000 ground troops. At the time of the exercise the US public was not informed that they were rehearsals for an invasion on Cuba. However, the Soviets correctly assumed that Cuba was the target for the plans these rehearsals supported. The invasion plans were never more than contingency plans; Kennedy had made no actual decision to proceed with an invasion of Cuba. The rehearsals influenced Khrushchev in his decision to deploy the nuclear weapons to Cuba.

In addition to the contingency invasion plans, the president authorized a CIA operation against Castro himself. The operation was known by the code name "Mongoose." The operation Mongoose plan called for the infiltration of Cuba by US agents and operatives and even included direct CIA contacts with organized crime to get the job done. The plan unfolded beginning in November of 1961 and included sabotage and attempts to kill Castro. Operation Mongoose was intended to culminate in "a wide popular revolt in Cuba."[181] In the timetable for the operation it was stated that the revolt against Castro would peak in October 1962. Such a popular revolt (by now a recurring theme in US operations regarding Cuba) was in turn expected to justify direct American military intervention in Cuba (thus bringing into play the contingency invasion plans). As the sabotage and assassination attempts could not be kept a complete secret, the Cubans and Soviets were immediately aware of operation Mongoose, which caused increased fear for Cuba's sovereignty on the part of the Communists.

One item of interest is that the Soviet accounts of this time period, including what we call the Cuban Missile Crisis of October 1962, refer to the "Caribbean Crisis." This reflects how the Soviets viewed events in the region during the early 1960s. The Soviets saw the missile crisis, previous regional confrontations, and the US military maneuvers as one crisis. US historians tend to focus on the nuclear missiles and their removal in October 1962, thus the name "Cuban Missile Crisis."

In response to US threats to Cuba, and in a larger sense to make the correlation of forces favorable to the Soviets, Khrushchev ordered a massive military buildup in Cuba. He knew his nation was outnumbered in strategic missiles by over three to one. By covertly moving some of his shorter-range missiles to Cuba he was taking a short cut to equalize the military factors in the correlation of forces. It would have taken years to develop new long-range silo protected missiles that could reach the US from the USSR. This plan made use of the forces Khrushchev already had at his command. Further, the buildup of nuclear weapons on the island made it less likely that a US invasion would be successful, once the missiles were operational. Castro agreed with the plan.

The Soviets deployed 24 launchers for 48 medium-range ballistic missiles (abbreviated MRBMs). This would give the launch crew one spare missile for each launch site. This was necessary because the MRBMs were somewhat unreliable. In the event the first missile launched without problems, the launcher was reloadable. The MRBMs had an effective range of 1000-2000 miles.[182]

Khrushchev also ordered 12 launchers for intermediate-range ballistic missiles (abbreviated IRBMs) to be deployed to Cuba. They had a similar provision for a spare missile, for a total of 24 IRBMs deployed. The IRBMs had an effective range of up to 2200 miles, putting every major city in the continental United States within range except Seattle. While construction of their launchers was underway during the crisis, no actual IRBMs reached Cuba before all offensive weapons were ordered withdrawn.[183]

The MRBM and IRBM launchers were deployed around five major bases. Each base was divided further into sites supporting a total of 4 launchers and 8 missiles to each of the five major bases. Anti-aircraft missile batteries defended each of the missile sites. A total of 144 anti-aircraft missile launchers were deployed in 24 launch sites. Each launcher had up to three missile reloads available. The surface-to-air missiles (or SAMs as they were called) had a range to 30 miles and could shoot down aircraft flying at 80,000 feet.

In addition to the nuclear missiles, the Soviets deployed forty-two long-range IL-28 bombers (code named "Beagle"). The Beagles could reach targets up to 1200 miles from Cuba, with their round-trip range being 600 miles. The bombers were shipped to Cuba unassembled; only 7 of them were actually assembled before they were removed in December of 1962. To protect the bombers and missile sites the Soviets sent forty-two MIG-21 jet fighter interceptors to Cuba. The MIGs were some of the most advanced fighter aircraft of the time; they had a top speed of over 1000 miles per hour. The fighters were armed with air-to-air missiles designed to shoot down enemy fighters or bombers. In addition, Cuba possessed about 40 older jet fighters, which would have marginal effectiveness against an attacker.[184]

The missiles and bombers were protected from seaborne threats by a squadron of patrol boats and by the provision for shore missile batteries. The patrol boat squadron consisted of 12 fast attack Komar class boats. Each boat was armed with several twenty-foot-long cruise missiles. The cruise missiles had a range of up to 15 miles. The shore missile batteries consisted of launchers deployed at key beaches and harbors. The batteries were designed to protect against invasion and they had an effective range of up to 40 miles.

Over 40,000 Soviet soldiers and technicians protected the entire network of Soviet missiles and bombers. Of these personnel, 8,000 were divided into four combat infantry regiments stationed in close proximity to the nuclear missile bases. These troops were augmented by 40 medium tanks and by anti-tank guided missiles. In addition, each of the Soviet regiments was equipped with defensive nuclear rockets, which had a range of up to 25 miles. These rockets (called FROGs, which stands for Free Rocket Over Ground) were unguided once fired. They were to be aimed in the general direction of an attacking force and fired. It is presumable that the nuclear warhead would have compensated for any inaccuracy inherent in the weapons system.

This formidable force was in addition to the 200,000 troops that Castro had in his military. If one adds the total of Soviet forces to Castro's military, the total force available for defense from any invasion was about a quarter of a million men under arms. With that large a number of troops defending the island, in possession of modern weaponry, nothing short of a major D-Day type invasion could hope to succeed against them. Even considering the qualitative advantage US forces would have enjoyed, an invasion would need to have been proceeded by a major air attack in order to hope to succeed. The Soviets had turned Cuba into a fortress only 90 miles away from the United States.

Khrushchev's deployments had begun in July of 1962, just two months after the US practice maneuvers. Considering the size of the operation, the deployment of Soviet forces was rapid; it was kept as secret as possible. Most of the equipment was landed and moved only at night. Cuban residents living near the docks and the missile bases were moved out of the areas and high fences were erected and patrolled by Soviet soldiers.

In spite of their attempts at keeping the deployments a secret, US intelligence had discovered much of the equipment by September of 1962 (with the notable exception of the nuclear weapons). Much of this information on Soviet troop movements to Cuba reached the public domain in the US. The Republican Party made the buildup of Soviet forces on Cuba a major campaign issue in the congressional elections of that year. During this time, Kennedy administration officials, including the president himself, made repeated assertions to the public that only defensive weapons were being stationed in Cuba. Further, Kennedy assured his critics that if offensive weapons were delivered to Cuba, strong countermeasures would be taken. In one exchange with Khrushchev, the president stated that if Soviet offensive weapons were found in Cuba, "the gravest of consequences would arise."[185]

In late September, several Republican senators (Tower, Goldwater, and Keating) began calling for stronger measures against Cuba. Kennedy was initially opposed to such measures. However, when Congress passed a joint resolution authorizing the president to use force against Cuba if necessary, Kennedy did not oppose it. The resolution passed the Senate on September 20 and the House on September 26. It was at about this time that the White House ordered stepped-up reconnaissance flights over Cuba.

Initial discovery of the nuclear missiles in Cuba came on October 14. An Air Force U-2 spy plane on a photographic mission over western Cuba photographed what appeared to be an MRBM site in the San Cristobal area. By afternoon on Monday October 15, analysts at the CIA verified that the pictures were of an MRBM site under construction.

Since the Director of Central Intelligence was out of town on personal business, two of his deputies began notifying NSC members of the discovery. One of the Assistant Secretaries of State, Edwin Martin, received the notification call as he was delivering a speech at the National Press Club. The supreme irony of the timing was that he had just finished saying of the situation in Cuba, "this military buildup is basically defensive in character."[186]

The president's advisors decided not to give him the news until the next day; they felt it was better that he had a good night's sleep, as he was just returning from a campaign trip. According to presidential advisor, MacGeorge Bundy, who notified the president in his White House bedroom on the morning of Tuesday the 16th, Kennedy stated, "He can't do that to me."[187] The "he" being Khrushchev.

Immediately after receiving the news, the president called together the Executive Committee of the NSC (or EXCOM, as it was known). The EXCOM was made up of Kennedy's most trusted advisors from the military, diplomatic, intelligence, and policy communities. The exact membership at EXCOM committee meetings varied over the course of the crisis, but normally consisted of 12-15 members.

The EXCOM began immediate consideration of options. The initial list of 5 options included "do nothing." While this was favored by Secretary of Defense McNamara, in the beginning, it was ruled out in short order. The EXCOM reduced the options to three in the early stages of the crisis. The proposed options were:

1) Initiate a blockade or quarantine of Cuba to keep more

offensive weapons out and lift this only when the Soviets had agreed to remove the missiles.

2) Launch and immediate air strike against the Soviet missile bases without prior declaration of war against Cuba.

3) Begin quarantine and prepare for the air strike in the case the quarantine was unsuccessful.

The chief problem with the air strike option was that it would have to be conducted on a large scale. Most of the military capability in Cuba needed to be knocked out to prepare for the possibility of an invasion. An invasion was felt necessary as a follow-up to the air strike because the Air Force was unable to assure that the nuclear weapons capable of reaching the US could all be destroyed from the air. The president rejected an immediate air strike for two reasons: First, he felt that this would be the equivalent of the Japanese sneak attack at Pearl Harbor; he felt the option was un-American. Second, he felt the Russian casualties and Cuban civilian casualties caused by such a massive operation would be too great to justify. Kennedy believed that such high numbers of casualties, including Soviet soldiers, would cause a wider war.

The naval quarantine was considered the better option because it offered the chance to end the crisis without a major war. In addition, the quarantine would give both sides time to consider their options and negotiate a solution. Kennedy was able to "sell" the hawks on the EXCOM the quarantine option. He accomplished this by allowing the preparations for air strikes and invasion of Cuba to continue so as to be ready if the quarantine failed.

Invasion and air strike preparations had begun even before the president announced the crisis to the nation on the 22nd of October. Troops were moved to Panama and Florida, the contingency plans were updated, and operations orders were issued to field commanders. The invasion plan called for a parachute assault by the 82nd and 101st Airborne Divisions.

The plan also called for beach landings of up to a full division of Marines. The USMC landings were to be followed closely by the landing of the Army's 1st Armored and 2nd Infantry Divisions; each of the major ground force elements was to be backed up by at least one artillery group and on-call tactical air support. US casualties for the first ten days of the operation were expected to be in excess of 18,000 killed, wounded, or missing in action.[188]

Confrontation on the quarantine line came on Thursday, October 25. A Soviet tanker and an East German passenger ship contacted the quarantine line. Neither ship was boarded, but they were hailed and asked to identify their cargo by US destroyers. Since the cargo and passengers they declared were not prohibited, they were allowed to pass on to Cuba.

On Friday, the 26th of October, the first real boarding of a Soviet chartered ship occurred. The *Marcula,* a ship of Lebanese registry, was stopped 180 miles northeast of Nassau in the Bahamas. An unarmed boarding party examined the ship and found no weapons. The ship was allowed to pass on to Cuba.

Solving the Crisis

It was on that same day that a resolution to the crisis began to take shape. Alexander Fomin, of the Soviet embassy, got word to the Kennedy administration through a news reporter (John Scali of ABC News) that a certain approach might end the crisis. Fomin suggested a settlement that included the following parameters:

1) The Soviet nuclear weapons would be removed under UN supervision.
2) Castro would accept no further shipments of offensive weapons.
3) The US would pledge never to invade Cuba.

The offer seemed promising to Kennedy and the EXCOM.

On Saturday the 27th, the last full day of the crisis, one additional incident occurred that almost caused a disaster. A SAM missile shot down an American U-2 spy plane on a mission over Cuba. The pilot, Major Rudolph Anderson, was the same one who had piloted the October 14th flight, which discovered the missiles. Anderson was killed in the incident. The EXCOM's initial reaction was to consider retaliation. However, resolution of the crisis seemed so near that it was decided to wait and see what developed from the shoot down. It was believed that retaliation could always be ordered later if the incident proved to be part of a Soviet escalation of the crisis.

A settlement of the crisis was reached on October 28. Kennedy had added one more concession to the proposal in order to end the crisis. In addition to his promise of no invasion of Cuba in the future, he promised to withdraw a small number of US "Jupiter" model nuclear missiles from Turkey. This was not much of a concession because the Jupiters were obsolete and were scheduled for removal soon, anyway. Further, Kennedy would have the Jupiters removed only after all of the Soviet missiles were out of Cuba.

A major war had been avoided, though pressure had moved the spectrum of conflict through covert paramilitary action with the Bay of Pigs, to direct

US involvement (even US-Soviet conflict with the quarantine and shoot down of the U-2). The Soviet MRBMs, IRBMs, and long-range bombers were out of Cuba (under a UN inspection regime) in December of 1962. Kennedy had gone to great lengths to avoid war in Laos, Berlin, and the Bay of Pigs situation—for this reason Khrushchev thought he could get away with placement of the nukes in Cuba in the first place.

Further, it is a result of twin motivations that the Soviets placed offensive weapons in Cuba. The Soviets had a missile crisis of their own in 1962. Their problem was that they were outnumbered in strategic forces by greater than 3 to 1 (and US nuclear forces were of greater quality). This led Khrushchev to feel pressure in the face of US superiority. The Soviets felt they could break out of this vulnerability to US coercion in foreign affairs by moving some of their shorter range, yet plentiful, missiles to Cuba. The buildup of Soviet forces on Cuba also allowed Khrushchev to prevent an expected invasion of the island nation. The Soviets may never have intended to keep the missiles in Cuba after all. They may have intended them only for bargaining purposes, in the effort to save Cuba from invasion. Thus the Soviets were victors because the maintained Cuba in the Communist sphere; and the US was victorious in that Soviet missiles were removed from Cuba (and the US strategic nuclear edge was maintained). The crisis resulted in a win-win situation in that, nuclear war was avoided and civilization was not destroyed in October 1962.

Kennedy's Assassination

No book on the Cold War should side step the assassination of John F. Kennedy. This author deals with the relative nature of the subject in the following way: It is possible that the Soviets wanted Kennedy dead, he had directly challenged them with the rhetoric of his inauguration speech, and by his actions sought to prevent or reverse their gains in world affairs. It is also remotely possible that the president was a victim of "blow back" (or what in intelligence tradecraft are the unintended consequences of covert operations).

By the estimate of William Colby, a former Director of Central Intelligence, at the time of the Bay of Pigs about half of the CIA's operating budget was going to fund covert political and paramilitary operations. This trend in the CIA, of moving away from traditional intelligence functions and back to the OSS tradition of covert action, was troubling to some in the policy community. In December of 1963, former President Harry S. Truman wrote an article for *The Washington Post* entitled, "Limit CIA Role to Intelligence." In part he wrote:

> For some time I have been disturbed by the way the CIA has been diverted from its original assignment. It has become an operational and at times a policy making arm of the government. This has led to trouble and may have compounded our difficulties in several explosive areas.
>
> I never had any thought that when I set up the CIA that it would be injected into peacetime cloak and dagger operations. Some of the complications and embarrassment that I think we have experienced are in part attributable to the fact that this quiet intelligence arm of the president has been so removed from its intended role that it is being interpreted as a symbol of sinister and mysterious intrigue—and a subject for Cold War enemy propaganda.
>
> But there are now some searching questions that need to be answered. I, therefore, would like to see the CIA be restored to its original assignment as the intelligence arm of the president, and that whatever else it can properly perform in that special field—and its operational duties be terminated or properly used elsewhere.
>
> We have grown up as a free nation, respected for our free institutions and for our ability to maintain a free and open society. There is something about the way the CIA has been functioning that is casting a shadow over our historic position and I feel that we need to correct it.[189]

Truman was clearly backing away from the NSC memorandum 10/2 that he approved in June of 1948. 10/2 had been the memorandum allowing the CIA to conduct covert operations under the supervision of the NSC and therefore the president. Perhaps, in 1948, he did not foresee such vast paramilitary operations as operation PB Success in Guatemala or Operation Zapata at the Bay of Pigs. It may have been the scale of these operations that turned Truman off. Regardless of rationale, his view of such operations was now decidedly negative.

One question begged, intentionally or not, by the timing of Truman's rebuke of covert paramilitary operations is: Was the assassination of John F.

Kennedy in November of 1963 a direct result of these operations? Operation Zapata failed in April 1961, and there had been no large-scale public failure of the CIA between the time of Zapata and the publication of Truman's editorial in December 1963. This was a twenty-month lag. So, why then, exactly a month after Kennedy's somewhat mysterious murder, did Truman decide to write? Perhaps it was just coincidence, though Kennedy's assassin, Lee Harvey Oswald, spent time in the USSR as a defector and visited the Soviet and Cuban embassies in Mexico City in the months prior to the murder of the president.

Many books have been written about, and much money has been made on the murder of JFK in Dallas. Even Attorney Gerald Posner was able to do well with his rebuke of the various conspiracies entitled, *Case Closed: Lee Harvey Oswald and the Assassination of JFK*; even the debunkers get rich on this one. Posner's work does, however, confirm what this author found on his own investigation conducted on-site in Dallas, and no one has matched Posner's computerized ballistic analysis of the shots fired in Dealey Plaza that day.

It was possible for three shots to have been fired by Oswald and for one bullet to have produced multiple wounds on Kennedy and Governor Connely (with the exception of Kennedy's fatal head wound, which was produced by another shot by Oswald). This analysis invalidates the "magic bullet" criticism of Oswald as the lone assassin. The matter of hitting a target only 25 yards away with a telescopic sighted rifle would have been easy for the USMC trained Oswald. Anyone who doubts this should spend a few days practice firing a similar rifle with a scope at that short of a distance, then visit the museum in Dallas where one can look out the window from which Oswald fired. There can be only one conclusion, Oswald fired three shots that day and one of them killed Kennedy.

For there to be more gunmen in the plaza at that time would have involved a massive domestic conspiracy that would have become visible with credible evidence leaking out over time. The police would have had to be in on it, to prevent them from finding the other gunmen. Many of the spectators in the area would have had to be a part of the conspiracy as well. People would be on record of such a conspiracy, if it in fact existed.

The fact remains that Oswald had his own motivations for what he did, and these may have involved Kennedy's actions (or even lack there of) against Cuba. Oswald was known to have had both pro and anti-Castro sympathies. It is possible that while Oswald did all the shooting, he did not act entirely alone. It is even possible that Oswald was acting on behest of the Soviets, however, this seems unlikely because they had gone to so great lengths to avoid war with the US during the various crises of the Kennedy administration. (Why would they then risk war by assassinating the American president?) As with the massive domestic conspiracy possibility, any Soviet conspiracy would have left evidence, and with the opening of Soviet records at the end of the Cold War, there has been none forth coming. While the possibility that Kennedy was the victim of a Soviet plot has immense possible implications to the understanding of the Cold War, there is no convincing evidence to support this possibility.

A small, relatively low-level conspiracy is another possibility, and this idea that Oswald acted with the encouragement or aid of people on the fringe of the intelligence community is not new. It is different than the popularized Oliver Stone/Garrison hypothesis that there was a massive deliberate conspiracy involving the Vice President of the United States (Lyndon Johnson) and the heads of government agencies in Washington. Again, the massive deliberate conspiracy would have left credible evidence, and none exists to date.

Prior to the November 1963 meeting with destiny in Dallas, Oswald campaigned against US involvement in Cuba by handing out handbills in New Orleans attacking US policy toward Cuba as imperialistic. Some of the leaflets were stamped the address "544 Camp Street." According to Posner,

> that address was the office of Guy Banister, a highly decorated ex-FBI agent who maintained a relationship with Naval Intelligence.... Another frequent Camp Street visitor was David Ferrie, a rabid anti-Communist who worked with Banister, for some of the most rabid anti-Cuban groups....[190]

Posner states that Oswald pulled this Camp Street address out of relatively thin air and that, further, the assassin did not know either Banister or Ferrie. As Posner tells it,

> the issue of whether Oswald knew adventurer David Ferrie is equally important, since Ferrie has extensive anti-Castro Cuban contacts and also did some work for an attorney for Carlos Marcello, the New Orleans godfather.... The two most credible pieces of information linking Oswald and Ferrie are Oswald's

1955 Civil Air Patrol service, when Ferrie was allegedly the commanding officer, and an incident in Clinton, Louisiana, where six witnesses identified Ferrie, Oswald, and a third person, New Orleans businessman Clay Shaw...

...Ferrie was interviewed by the FBI on November 27, 1963 and denied ever knowing Oswald in the Civil Air Patrol. CAP records show he told the truth. Although he was a member through 1954, Ferrie was disciplined because he gave unauthorized political lectures to the cadets. When he submitted his 1955 renewal it was rejected. Ferrie was not reinstated until 1958. He was not even in the Civil Air Patrol when Oswald was a member in 1955.[191]

While the CAP may have disciplined Ferrie, there is credible hard evidence that he was associated with Oswald. In 1993, the year after Posner published his work, the Public Broadcasting System (WGBH - Frontline) proved at least a casual association between Oswald and Ferrie in its "Who Was Lee Harvey Oswald." The broadcast debunked Posner (who ironically is the ultimate debunker of all the assassination theories) when it produced a photograph of Oswald and Ferrie in the same small group at a CAP picnic in the 50s. From the transcript we can see the association:

NARRATOR: Frontline has uncovered the first hard evidence that places Oswald and Ferrie together: this photograph, taken in 1955 at a CAP barbecue. John Ciravolo and Tony Atzenhoffer were in the CAP with Oswald.

JOHN CIRAVOLO: This is several cadets, including Oswald on the end in the white T-shirt, myself standing in front of him. And over there in the white T-shirt and helmet is David Ferrie.

TONY ATZENHOFFER: Because of the publicity you can recognize Ferrie, you can recognize Oswald. They were both in the CAP at the same time. They were both wearing CAP uniforms.

NARRATOR: After the Kennedy assassination, David Ferrie denied that he ever knew Lee Oswald.[192]

Oswald may well have been connected to Ferrie, and through him to the shadowy underworld of Cuban politics and organized crime.

It is impossible to know with certainty what was in Oswald's mind when he killed Kennedy. It is even less likely that we will know for sure if any of his strange associations had any effect on his decisions.

Conclusions to Chapter 5

Cuba and its Cold War legacy are significant for several reasons: First, the CIA was handed its first public defeat at the Bay of Pigs. The failure of Operation Zapata resulted in a great loss of prestige for the agency, and in the macro view the totality of the struggle over Cuba amounted to a strategic stalemate between the US and USSR.

The second item of significance was that the CIA gained a major success in the missile crisis. The discovery of the missiles before they became operational gave Kennedy the chance to have them removed without a war through the use of the quarantine. Because of the failure of Operation Zapata and the success in detecting the missiles, the dichotomy between covert paramilitary action and pure intelligence gathering is never clearer than in the case of the Cuban Missile Crisis.

Third, while Lee Harvey Oswald fired all of the shots in Dallas on November 22, 1963, he was probably spurred on to his action by Kennedy's policy on Cuba. Oswald may have acted entirely alone. Or, he may have had encouragement from fringe actors like David Ferrie who was a reputed paramilitary soldier of fortune and also was associated with the mob and anti-Castro agitators who were on the right wing fringe (like Guy Banister, a detective and former FBI agent). This does not mean there necessarily had to have been a master plot against the president as some have said, but it does mean that Oswald may not have acted in a total void. Motive and any outside influences, in this case, are nearly impossible to establish, since Oswald was shot to death almost immediately after the assassination. It is entirely possible that Oswald was merely a vain and angry madman, who wanted to be remembered in history, and that he acted with no other motivation in his mind and no encouragement from others.

Fourth, and perhaps most important of the legacies of the situation in Cuba is the memory of what the Soviets did in building a fortress on Cuba, which stayed with America for a long time. One of the primary reasons for intervention in Nicaragua in the 1980s was to avoid their being "another Cuba" in the hemisphere. Before the Nicaraguan adventure took place, US policy on the use of covert paramilitary action went through many machinations as a result of the experience in Vietnam. This conflict and its significance are the topic of the next chapter.

Chapter 6

Vietnam: The Pentagon Papers, The Phoenix Program, and Differences That Persist Today

Basics: A Chronology

Vietnam was America's longest and most controversial war. US involvement in Vietnam's civil war came after the French colonial garrison at Dien Bien Phu (in far North Vietnam) fell to Communist forces in May 1954. The US had supported the French in their effort to hold their colony with $2.6 billion in military aid from 1950-54. After the French defeat they agreed to a division of Vietnam at the 17th parallel at the Geneva peace conference. The Communists would hold the north and forces friendly to the French would hold the south. The division was to be only temporary, with nationwide elections to be held in 1956.

With American backing, the South Vietnamese leader, No Dinh Diem, did not hold the unifying elections in 1956. Diem was afraid of the Communist leader, Ho Chi Minh, and his popularity as a nationalist in the more populous north. By the late 1950s there were 1,500 US civilian and military advisors in South Vietnam helping the Diem regime run that half of the country. In the years 1957-59 the North Vietnamese intensified their insurgency in the south. America responded by raising the number of military advisors in the country to 9,000 by the end of 1962.

Eventually America introduced ground troops and began large-scale bombing in Vietnam after the Gulf of Tonkin Incident of 1964. Vietnam became a full-scale proving ground for direct US military involvement used to support the policy of containment of Communism. All of the American ground troops introduced, and bombing conducted, did not break the Communist's will to continue fighting.

In January of 1973 a peace agreement was reached and the American military withdrew, leaving the country still divided. This was only a temporary halt in the fighting. In 1975, the North Vietnamese Communists resumed their offensive, this time with massive conventional army formations, and they soon gained control of South Vietnam. The US Congress prevented then President, Gerald Ford, from sending further aid to South Vietnam during these final stages of the war. The Pentagon Papers provide us with a convenient vehicle for examining the war and the policy of containment, and in many cases the use of covert means to formulate and implement policy.

The publication of the Pentagon Papers in June of 1971 was the most significant event in media-government relations during the Vietnam conflict. The very strength of the First Amendment to the Constitution would be tested by their release. In addition, through the paper's release, the American public would come to know much of the previously secret history of US involvement in the war for the first time. Early CIA operations in Vietnam would be revealed. Further, the CIA would support domestic spying as a result of their release (in contravention of the National Security Act of 1947).

The papers were released to the public and the world through *The New York Times* and *The Washington Post*. The press obtained the papers from a defense intellectual named Daniel Ellsberg. This master of the American national security apparatus was a complex man. Ellsberg was at once a creature of the system that was continuing the war in Southeast Asia and an individual alienated from that system. Only one who had been a trusted member of the system, and had walked in the corridors of power, would have had access to such information as was contained in the Pentagon Papers. Of equal importance is the fact that only one who had become disenchanted with the war effort, and the corridors of power, could have made such a release. Ellsberg was such an individual.

More than fifteen years before the release of the papers Ellsberg had been an officer in the United States Marine Corps. In addition, Ellsberg had degrees from Harvard and Cambridge. In the Marine Corps, Ellsberg had been, according to Peter Shrag in his work, *Test of Loyalty*, "well disciplined, organized, and systematic. He had commanded one of the best rifle companies in the First Marine Division."[193] It is difficult to imagine that such an individual would rise to the top of the White House "enemies list" in the 1970s.

Far from being the pinnacle of his career, his success as a Marine officer was only the beginning for Ellsberg. As a civilian consultant to various government agencies he was involved in some of the great events of the Cold War. He had, for example, been a consultant to the Departments of State and Defense during the Cuban Missile Crisis. In addition, Ellsberg had served in various projects calculating Soviet nuclear strength during the early days of the Kennedy administration.

In 1964, Ellsberg rose to the top of the Defense Department as a Special Assistant to Robert S. McNamara (then the Secretary of Defense). In 1965 he moved on to work on the staff of General Landsdale (who had been running covert operations in Vietnam since 1954) as a project manager. Later, in 1965, he went to work for the State Department studying pacification programs. During this time period he was photographed by *Life* magazine carrying an M-1 carbine in a Vietnamese village. This photo gave a graphic depiction of Ellsberg participating in the Vietnam conflict, as opposed to being a neutral spectator in Washington.

He later said of his gun toting in Vietnam that he,

> did go on a number of operations, one in particular with an Army battalion for ten days of significant combat in the Delta.... Well, I did a lot of shooting, because in the Delta we were under a lot of fire, some days every half-hour or so. I carried a weapon because the alternative was, if you did not carry a weapon, other people would have to take care of you.[194]

In the summer of 1967, on one of his stints in Vietnam, Ellsberg contracted hepatitis. He was sent back to the states to recover. It was then that he became involved in a study of American decision-making in regard to Vietnam that had been commissioned by Secretary McNamara. The study, officially known as, "US-Vietnam Relations: 1945-1967," would become known as the Pentagon Papers (when Ellsberg released them to the press).

The reason for the study was that McNamara had become concerned with the prospects for victory in Vietnam; he wanted to reassess past decision-making in order to develop a coherent policy for the conduct of the war. The study committee was a group of defense intellectuals put together by McNamara himself. The rules for the study were that no officials could be interviewed (because this would pose a security problem) and no material from the White House could be used (though some White House NSC documents made their way into the final product).

To some degree the study committee was limited to the use of Defense Department records; thus the name "Pentagon Papers." However, copious State Department records were also used, so in some ways the nickname Pentagon Papers was really just a convention of the media pundits. "US-Vietnam Relations 1945-1967" simply did not sell as many newspapers or television spots as "Pentagon Papers" and it took more copy space for both the press and TV.

History in the Papers: Secret Policy Making

The documents in the collection that make up the papers date back to the closing stages of World War II. They contain some interesting revelations that were not public knowledge until their release. For instance, the papers document that the OSS actually supported Ho Chi Minh and the Communist Viet Minh against the Japanese in 1945.

In addition, documents in the study show a US commitment to a non-Communist Vietnam even prior to the defeat of the colonial French forces in the 50s. This, of course, was a reversal of the policy of supporting the Viet Minh. In an NSC memorandum signed by President Truman in 1949, we find that American interest was beginning to focus on the Southeast Asia region. It stated that the US would,

> scrutinize closely the development of threats from communist aggression, direct or indirect, and prepare to help within our means to meet such threats by providing political, economic, and military assistance and advice where clearly needed to supplement the resistance of other governments in and out of the area which are more directly threatened [and] develop cooperative measures through multilateral or bilateral arrangements to combat Communist internal subversion.[195]

Thus we see that by the time of the Strategic Reassessment of 1950, the US was set on a course of involvement in Vietnam. Further, this had been done by secret means. The Congress had not been consulted, the American people had not been informed, and the documents outlining the policies themselves were classified "Top Secret."

Another set of revelations concerning even deeper American involvement in Vietnam is contained in documents dating to 1954-55. In these documents we see that a covert paramilitary organization known as the Saigon Military Mission (SMM) was formed by a Colonel Landsdale of the United States Air Force (the same person for whom Ellsberg would work a few years later when Landsdale had been promoted to General). From the documents we read:

> The Saigon Military Mission (SMM) was born in a Washington policy meeting in early 1954, when Dien Bien Phu was still holding out against the encircling Vietminh. The SMM was to enter Vietnam quietly and assist the Vietnamese, rather than the French, in unconventional warfare. The French were to be kept as friendly allies in this process, as far as possible.
>
> The broad mission for the team was to undertake paramilitary operations against the enemy and to wage political-psychological warfare. Later, after Geneva, the mission was modified to prepare means for undertaking paramilitary operations in Communist areas rather than to wage unconventional warfare.[196]

During the evacuation of Hanoi (as a part of the division of Vietnam) the SMM team performed several sabotage missions in violation of the Geneva accords—the contaminated fuel for the city bus line with compounds that would slowly wreck the engines of the busses. Military members of the SMM also sabotaged a railroad with assistance of a CIA team from Japan. The papers indicate that the team considered further operations such as the blowing up of bridges, a power plant, water supply facilities, and raiding a harbor. None of these operations was undertaken because it was felt they were too blatant a violation of the Geneva accords.[197]

We see then, that under President Truman there was a broad philosophical commitment to a non-Communist Vietnam and that this was taken a step further into action by Eisenhower when he assumed the presidency. In 1953, US personnel became directly involved in covert paramilitary actions which were, by their nature, acts of war. However, the Congress, which holds the power to declare war, was not even consulted; policy was being made by executive fiat with the intelligence community and military being the primary implements.

The next significant event covered by the papers was the overthrow of

South Vietnamese President No Dinh Diem in November of 1963. Diem had fallen into disfavor with the US when he allowed his brother, Nhu, to use the military in repressive attacks on the Buddhist minority in the country. Newspaper exposure of this section of the papers was explicit and to the point. In 1971, when the papers were released, Hedrick Smith of *The New York Times* wrote an entire section of the first article on the Diem affair. Smith led off with:

> The Pentagon's secret study of the Vietnam War discloses that President Kennedy knew of and approved the plans for the military coup d'etat that overthrew President No Dinh Diem in 1963.[198]

As the papers revealed, in August of 1963, the State Department sent the following message to its station in Saigon:

> We are prepared to accept the obvious implications that we can no longer support Diem. You may also tell appropriate military commanders we will give them direct support in any interim period of breakdown in the central government mechanism.... Ambassador and country team should urgently examine all possible alternative leadership and make detailed plans as to how we might bring about Diem's replacement if this should become necessary.[199]

In a cablegram from Ambassador Lodge to McGeorge Bundy dated October 25, 1963, the clear involvement of the CIA in the plot was outlined. According to this document, Lt. Colonel Lucien Conein, of the CIA, was involved in the coup observing directly the efforts of the South Vietnamese general staff. Conein, whose first trip to Vietnam was by parachute in 1944 while on assignment with the OSS, was at the general staff headquarters throughout the coup.[200] In addition, US intelligence sources provided the generals with vital intelligence sources on forces loyal to Diem. The president of South Vietnam was overthrown on November 1, 1963 and subsequently murdered in the back of a US supplied armored personnel carrier.

The Pentagon Papers contain some explosive material on the Gulf of Tonkin incidents (the naval actions that led to massive overt US military involvement in Vietnam almost a year after Diem was deposed). Material in the papers leads to the conclusion that there was a secret conspiracy to escalate the war in Vietnam long before incidents occurred. According to an article written by Neil Sheehan the June 13, 1971 issue of *The New York Times*, preparation for the escalation was far along when the incidents occurred. From Sheehan's article we read:

> The Pentagon Papers disclose that for six months before the Gulf of Tonkin Incident in August, 1964, the United States had been mounting clandestine military actions against North Vietnam while planning to obtain a Congressional resolution that the Administration regarded as equivalent to a declaration of war.
>
> Then the incident occurred, the Johnson Administration did not reveal the clandestine attacks and pushed the previously prepared resolution through both houses of Congress on August 7.[201]

In fact, the Johnson White House had prepared a draft resolution very similar to the eventual Gulf of Tonkin Resolution. This document, entitled "Draft Resolution for Congress on Actions in Southeast Asia," was completed on May 25, 1964 (almost 2 ½ months prior to the Gulf of Tonkin incidents). This directly begs the question of whether the Johnson administration provoked the incidents. The papers do not answer the question directly, however the evidence builds a strong circumstantial case for a conspiracy to escalate the conflict.

Here again, we see secrecy involved in the conduct of anti-Communist foreign policy (and the domestic politics involved in foreign affairs). This was secrecy concerned with policy, not just traditional military or diplomatic secrets. Democracy was not being allowed to function properly, it was being manipulated by an executive which was secretly drafting resolutions and waging war without Congressional approval (even prior to the Johnson administration). For years, until Daniel Ellsberg released the papers, not one of the thousands of individuals involved in this secret policy-making thought this was anything more than business as usual. In fact, it was business as usual according to the intent of the National Security Act of 1947. The intent of the act had been to remove congressional decision-making from the policy loop, and to use the CIA as the primary tool for this policy-making. By the time of the Gulf of Tonkin, the military was also being used as an implement for covert policy-making.

Based upon his reading of the papers, his personal experience in Vietnam, and his work at the upper echelons of the Defense Department, Ellsberg developed a theory about the conflict in Southeast Asia. He conceived the idea that the conflict had been a struggle by five successive presidents to avoid failure. If a president did not "lose Southeast Asia to the Communists," as China had been lost, he had, in fact, won a kind of victory. This was the force Ellsberg determined had been driving American policy in Vietnam. In his own words:

> It may be that five individuals, our presidents from Truman to Nixon ... aimed mainly to avoid a definitive failure ... during his tenure, so that renewed stalemate has been, for them, a kind of success.

The study behind the papers was born out of the utter frustration with this type of policy goal. It was an attempt to find a new way; Ellsberg thought this was an exercise in futility.

One final, and perhaps the most clear, example of this kind of policy-making, was the bombing of North Vietnam in the late 60s and early 70s. The papers revealed that US intelligence estimates stated the North Vietnamese would off-set any direct introduction of US ground combat troops with a corresponding increase of infiltration of guerrillas from the north. The same memo states that, "if worse comes to worst, the US could probably save its position in Vietnam by bombing the north."[202] Exactly this series of events took place. The US directly introduced large numbers of ground troops throughout the middle 60s and the North Vietnamese subsequently increased infiltration into the south. To avoid losing the Vietnam to the Communists, the US turned to increasing bombing of the north throughout the late 60s and early 70s. Ellsberg saw this as insane slaughter, with no chance for disengagement or victory.

Breaking the Barrier of Secrecy

The rules under which the Pentagon Papers were classified emanated from Executive Order #10501. The order set up a three-tiered system of classification. Under the order the levels of classification were: Confidential, Secret, and Top Secret. Top Secret information is the most potentially damaging in the case of unauthorized release; Confidential is the least. The Pentagon Papers were classified Top Secret. Each page was marked with a stamp reading: Top Secret-Sensitive.[203] The notation "Sensitive" had no foundation in law since it was not part of the classification system. This additional word may have been added to indicate that the material would prove embarrassing to the government if released to the public. Anyone releasing material classified under the Executive Order could be prosecuted for espionage.

With the real possibility of going to prison for his actions, why did Ellsberg release the Pentagon Papers? Ellsberg has never personally written about his experiences with the papers, at least not directly. However, we do get some explanation from his 1972 book on the conflict in Southeast Asia entitled, *Papers on the War*. From the introduction we read:

> For over seven years, I, like many other Americans have been preoccupied with our involvement in Vietnam. In that time I have viewed it first as a problem, then as a stalemate, and then as a crime.
>
> Each of these perspectives calls for a different mode of personal commitment: a problem, to help solve it; a stalemate, to help extricate ourselves with grace; a crime, to expose and resist it, to try to stop it immediately, to seek moral and political change.[204]

Only a properly informed public could determine policy through its elected leaders; Ellsberg was doubtlessly aware of this fact. With the papers in a Defense Department vault, this was impossible. So, we see Ellsberg as admittedly first a creature of the system with access to its secrets. As the carnage continued in Vietnam and no end appeared in sight, he gradually converted into being an agent for change.

By 1968-69 Ellsberg had become deeply concerned about what he had seen in Vietnam and read in the Pentagon Papers. The increasing cost of prolonged conflict in terms of Asian lives was particularly troubling to him.[205] The period was one of somewhat existential drifting, and in the summer of 1969 Ellsberg spent a great deal of time with friends at the beach in Malibu "smoking pot, listening to rock music, and engaging in a great deal of talk about ... Vietnam and sex."[206] In his own words he slept with "one girl after another ... trying to remind myself that I could have purposes or satisfactions entirely apart from politics."[207]

In the fall of 1969 Ellsberg read a story in *The Los Angeles Times* about the Army's decision to drop charges against some Green Berets accused of murder in Vietnam. This was the last straw. He contacted Anthony Russo, a friend from the Rand Corporation (where Ellsberg was then working), and the two decided to copy the papers. They located a copy machine at the advertising agency of another friend, Linda Sinay. The copy sessions took place on eight evenings over the course of several weeks in October and November of 1969.

An effort to provoke congressional hearings on the Vietnam conflict was unsuccessful when Ellsberg could not get Senators Fullbright and McGovern to accept that the papers were genuine. In September 1970 he left the Rand Corporation so he could more freely fight against the war. He had still not found a recipient for the papers that would do something with them.

Almost a year and a half after the copy sessions, he decided that the best thing to do was to go to the press. In March of 1971, Ellsberg contacted Neil Sheehan of *The New York Times*, whom he had met in Vietnam. He presented Sheehan with all but four volumes of the papers. Ellsberg withheld the volumes dealing with the secret negotiations to end the war, because he wanted to "get in the way of the bombing and the killing," not the peace efforts.[208]

It took reporters at the Times months to cull thorough the mountain of material. On Sunday June 13 the first story about the papers was published. US Attorney General, John Mitchell, immediately sent a telegram to the paper requesting they cease publishing on grounds of national security. The Times declined and on Tuesday morning a federal judge issued a restraining order against further publication by the Times until the case could be heard in court. Ellsberg countered this situation by giving another copy of the papers to *The Washington Post* and that paper published a story the next day. Ellsberg went into hiding and a restraining order was also issued against the Post.

Within a few more days the case was before the US Supreme Court. What was tested was the strength of the First Amendment to the Constitution. In the case the American Civil Liberties Union filed a brief on behalf of the newspapers, which stated that the only secrets that could properly be withheld from publication were those that pertained to future military operations, blueprints or designs of military equipment, or secret codes. The documents Ellsberg released to the newspapers contained none of these items.

On June 30th the court ruled 6 to 3 in favor of the newspapers being allowed to publish. The First Amendment had won out. This, however, was only the beginning of the court battle over the papers. Two days before the Supreme Court had rendered its decision, Daniel Ellsberg had been indicted for violations of the Espionage Act related to his 1969 copying of the papers.

Espionage Charges and the "Special Unit"

Ellsberg came out of hiding to face the charges. He and his partner in the copying, Anthony Russo, were charged with 15 counts of conspiracy, theft, and espionage. The key issues at the trial would be the classification system, secrecy, and free speech. If convicted on all counts Russo would go to jail for 35 years and Ellsberg for 115 years. In addition, a court verdict against Ellsberg and Russo would have meant that in the future the government could classify anything it wanted and the classification would have the full force of law.

Several events occurred prior to the trial, which would have a great impact on its outcome. The paranoid Nixon administration decided that the Department of Justice investigation of Ellsberg was insufficient. The president felt that Ellsberg was just the tip of the iceberg and that there was a vast New Left conspiracy against his administration and, in fact, favoring the Soviets in international affairs. Nixon empowered his assistant for domestic affairs, John D. Erlichman, with the creation of a "special unit" in order to gather information on the suspected conspirators. The unit consisted of Erlichman's deputy, Egil Krogh, David R. Young of the National Security Council staff, Howard Hunt (a recently retired 20-year veteran of the CIA), and G. Gordon Liddy (a former FBI agent). Only a handful of people at the White House knew of the existence of the unit.

One of the first actions of the unit was to obtain a psychiatric profile of Ellsberg from what was then known about him. Dr. Bernard Malloy, head of the CIA's psychiatric unit, was asked to develop a profile. This was the first time the CIA was used to develop a profile of a domestic individual and it was a violation of the National Security Act of 1947. The profile, when finished, showed Ellsberg to be sincere, patriotic, and intelligent. Nixon rejected this view of Ellsberg and a status report was sent to Erlichman, who recommended a domestic covert operation by the unit against Ellsberg.[209]

The physical target of the unit was at Dr. Fielding's office, because Fielding had performed psychoanalysis on Ellsberg as his private psychiatrist. The unit was to search for notes showing Ellsberg's connection to the pro-Communist conspiracy Nixon believed existed. Ellsberg later said of his reasons for being in analysis in the first place:

> It was in the '68-'69 period. So you know a lot was happening. I honestly did change in that period in a lot of ways, but it is hard to say exactly what was related to the analysis. I was against the war before I started analysis. I regard it is not possible for me to say why I did what I did.[210]

On August 25, 1971, the operation commenced. The break-in team consisting of Hunt, Liddy, and some Cuban veterans of the Bay of Pigs operation flew to Los Angeles. The CIA had supplied them with false identity papers, spy cameras, and other gadgets. They successfully broke into Fielding's office and escaped the scene, but found nothing useful. In addition to the break-in, Ellsberg was personally subjected to several rounds of secret FBI wiretappings that were done without a court order. The break-in had been another violation of the National Security act of 1947, since it was done with CIA assistance (in addition to violating Ellsberg's rights and other laws).

Police intercepted the same "special unit" when they botched a break-in of Democratic campaign headquarters at the Watergate on Saturday June 17, 1972. Again, the unit had been looking for a leftist, pro-Communist conspiracy in American politics. While they were never prosecuted for the raid against Ellsberg (in fact the occurrence of the earlier covert operation was not known at this time), the burglars were prosecuted for the Watergate break-in. As history has recorded they were found guilty and their ties to Nixon fully established. The resignation of Nixon, on August 9, 1974, was very much a result of the later actions of the "special unit," which had first operated against Ellsberg and with CIA assistance.

The trial of Ellsberg and Russo began after long delays on January 17, 1973. The defense argued that the Pentagon Papers were not properly classified in the first place. The Ellsberg/Russo defense team stated that the study did not contain material that could result in exceptionally grave damage to the national security (as required by Executive Order 10501 to be classified Top Secret). The government claimed that Ellsberg and Russo had unlawfully removed and copied material that was legally classified.

The government's case was hurt by several items. Most significant among them was a report commissioned by the Justice Department on the classification of the papers. The report stated that a large percentage of the material on which the case was based could not have helped a foreign government in 1969. The defense was able to produce the report in court, but the government countered, stating that this was not an official view—it was just the opinion of the report's author. On April 19, 1973, the defense rested its case; the trial was over except for motions yet to be filed. It should be noted that by this time other events had begun to eclipse the case in the news, among them the end of the Vietnam conflict and the building story of Watergate.

At the end of April the story of the "special unit" raid on Dr. Fielding's office broke in the headlines. With the trial not yet officially over, the defense made an immediate motion for the case to be dismissed. The defense stated that the government's illegal intrusions into Ellsberg's personal affairs made it impossible for him to get a fair trial.

On May 11, 1973, the judge in the case announced that he was ready to rule on the defense motion. Judge Byrne stated that, as a result of the extraordinary information disclosed about the government's actions, he was going to grant a motion to dismiss. From his lengthy statement one may read:

> The Central Intelligence Agency, presumably acting beyond its statutory authority, and at the request of the White House, had provided disguises, photographic equipment and other paraphernalia for covert operations. The government disclosure also revealed that the special unit requested and obtained from the CIA two psychological profiles of one of the defendants.
>
> FBI surveillance was conducted and records now have been removed from both the FBI and Justice Department.
>
> My duties and obligations relate to this case and what must be done to protect the right to a fair trial.
>
> I have decided to declare a mistrial and grant the motion to dismiss.[211]

Ellsberg got what he wanted from the trial. After the mistrial was declared, he said, "The issue of government misconduct is the issue of the Pentagon Papers."[212] What he meant was that the same trends of government misconduct that allowed the papers to be wrongfully classified in the first place had resulted in the illegal surveillance that caused the mistrial.

In September of 1999, Daniel Ellsberg consented to a brief interview with this author, the results of which shed a bit more light on the Pentagon Papers episode and Ellsberg himself. The following four questions and answers are provided from that interview:

Author: Why did you go into psychoanalysis in the first place?

Daniel Ellsberg: It's not terribly private, it wasn't a personal crisis, I had friends who urged me to do it, to understand why my first marriage failed and had a problem of publishing and letting go of material; I did not gain anything other than the trapping of Nixon.

Author: Do you feel vindicated by history?

Daniel Ellsberg: I never felt the need for vindication. Did I then feel that I did the right thing? I never really doubted that—it wasn't something I did for benefit. I thought it was the right thing to do. Had it lengthened the war I would have felt it was the wrong thing to do.... I'm gratified that they had the kind of effect that I'd hoped for.... I expected to be in prison for the rest of my life, it's not clear what the jury would have done.

Author: Before you decided to release the papers, did you bring your concerns to Secretary of Defense, McNamara, and others?

Daniel Ellsberg: Sure. Releasing the papers was just one thing I was doing; the other things did not subject me to legal risk. What I was mainly doing was talking to former and current officials trying to convince them of my view of what Nixon was doing; he was doing what his predecessors had done secretly—secret escalations—the papers did not prove that Nixon was doing this.... I was giving Kissinger the full benefit of my views in 1970.

Author: What have you done since the release of the papers?

Daniel Ellsberg: In May '73, the US was still bombing in Cambodia; I spent those two years trying to end it, and I reverted to antinuclear politics thereafter.

The Phoenix Program

Any discussion of the Vietnam conflict has to include mention of the Phoenix Program. The program, launched in 1967 and continued to 1971, was an example of a multi-agency covert counterintelligence operation. At its inception, an ambassadorial ranked diplomat, Robert Komer, designed the program as a means of destroying the Viet Cong Infrastructure (or VCI). The US Agency for International Development (AID) administered Phoenix. The man in charge of the Phoenix program was WWII OSS veteran, William Colby, who was on loan to AID from the CIA.

Under Colby, a program called ICEX (for Intelligence Coordination and Exploitation) was developed so that the CIA, military forces, and South Vietnamese police agencies could share information about suspected Viet Cong leaders. This led to the development of a database listing all of the VC leadership. Once an individual suspect was listed by three sources as being VC, that individual was placed on a hit list.

Police or military units rounded up these alleged members of the VCI. If they resisted, they were often killed on the spot. Those individuals who were captured alive in this way were offered amnesty if they would admit to being VC; if they would not cooperate, they were given prison sentences.

According to Colby in his memoirs, "17,000 had chosen amnesty, 28,000 had been captured, and some 20,000 killed" in these Phoenix Program operations.[213] The program did have its effect on lowering the level of VC activity in the South, and after the war several high ranking VC officers stated that the Phoenix Program had frustrated their efforts greatly.

The problem of the lack of due process of law in the Phoenix Program (when that is what the US was in Vietnam to defend in the first place) was never resolved. When reports of the program hit the news in the states it made the conflict even more unpopular. Colby himself admitted the captives were held in deplorable conditions—"There were shackled prisoners with paralyzed limbs, overcrowded cells, filthy surroundings and whispered cries for help" when he toured one of the Phoenix prisons.[214] It was questionable ventures like the Phoenix Program, and the atmosphere of Watergate, that caused the Congress to take its first serious look at CIA covert operations in the middle 70s.

Differences of Interpretation that Persist Today

The opinions expressed by this author are not the only ones on the topic of Vietnam. Many people saw Daniel Ellsberg as more a villain than a hero. Professional military men involved with the Vietnam Conflict did not have the luxury of hindsight that this writer has. For this reason, an interview with a 26-year US Navy veteran is included here for comparison, and to allow other voices to speak on the topic. Not only does the interview provide an alternative view of the Pentagon Papers episode, it provides background information on the classification system itself. The subject of the interview is Captain Nicholas Pacalo, father of the author of *Cold Warfare.* The interview was conducted in October of 1999 in Youngstown, Ohio.[215]

Question: Where did you work in the Pentagon?

Answer: I was in the Department of the Navy, in the Naval Aviation section, and I was responsible for aviation safety. I was an advisor to the senior staff on matters of aviation safety.

Question: In what capacities did you serve in Vietnam?

Answer: I was there from the middle of '65 to the latter part of '67. I was a Lieutenant Commander and a Naval Aviator. I was flying aircraft.

Question: How long did you work in the Pentagon?

Answer: From 1970 until I retired in 1979, but I changed jobs a couple of times. I did not do the same job the whole time.

Question: Did the military keep many secrets about the war then? If so, why?

Answer: Well, I don't know about many secrets. They kept things secret that they thought would hurt the war effort if it became public. I think a lot of people misconstrue what they mean by classified information. The military was not trying to keep secrets from the American public, we were trying to keep it from falling into the hands of unfriendly persons who would be detrimental to any type of military action that was going on in Vietnam, or anywhere for that matter.

Question: How did you find out about the release of the Pentagon Papers?

Answer: I read about it in the newspaper.

Question: Did you have any exposure to the material in the Pentagon Papers before its release?

Answer: Not directly, no.

Question: How often did you work with classified material related to the war in Vietnam?

Answer: Probably on a daily basis; being in the aviation business, we were concerned about our aircraft losses in Vietnam, both personnel and aircraft.

Question: What did you think of Daniel Ellsberg?

Answer: I don't know, that is kind of a hard question. I don't know the guy but I read about him. It was my personal opinion that he violated a trust. He was placed in charge of certain classified information with the understanding that it would not be divulged to unauthorized persons and he did exactly the opposite.

Question: What was the feeling of some of the more senior officers you worked with concerning Daniel Ellsberg and his release of classified material?

Answer: I think it's pretty much what I just said, that this person made unauthorized disclosure of classified material—he violated a trust. I don't have a problem with releasing classified material the way it's supposed to be released, but that is not the way it's supposed to be done.

Question: Were you in favor of the US involvement in Vietnam?

Answer: I don't know, I did not think about it much from a political standpoint when I was there. Being a professional military officer, I think at that time I had been on active duty for 10 or 11 years and decided to make the military my career. I did not give it much thought.

Question: Did the release of the Pentagon Papers have any effect on your opinion of the conduct of the war?

Answer: No, none.

Question: If you favored US policy at the time, why did you favor it?

Answer: Well I don't know if I favored it or disfavored it. I just did not think about it. I guess what I am trying to say is that as a military officer I don't make political decisions about some war being right or wrong. First of all, all war is wrong when we get into that situation, but I don't make those political decisions as to what is right or wrong. I approached it the way a dedicated military person does. For some reason there were some political failures that resulted in us becoming involved in Vietnam. And if I were opposed to that, then I would take that on at the ballot box, not by running off to Canada or something like that.

Question: What do you believe would have been a satisfactory outcome in Vietnam?

Answer: I guess if Vietnam had become a unified democratic country then I would have felt that any type of political ambitions we had that turned into the conflict would have been satisfied.

Question: What do you think of the argument that Daniel Ellsberg was morally bound to do what he did? If not, what should Ellsberg have done?

Answer: Well, I think there is a moral counter argument to that, too. If every person can make those types of decisions then we no longer have a democracy, we have chaos. The way you vote morally in this country, under the Constitution, is at the ballot box. If Ellsberg was not happy with the situation, in my opinion, he should have just resigned and taken another job.

Question: Was the release of the Pentagon Papers a true breach of security, or was it just a serious public relations problem for the Pentagon?

Answer: Well, it was a true breach of security. Second of all, it became a public relations problem for the Pentagon once it was released.

Question: Did you feel personally betrayed by the release of the Pentagon papers?

Answer: Not particularly.

Question: How do you feel toward *The Washington Post* and *The New York Times* for their part in the Pentagon papers? Should they have published the material?

Answer: I really don't know the answer to that. You know that our newspapers provide a great service to democracy. I guess I don't know the answer to that.

Question: From your point of view, did any good come of the release of the Pentagon Papers?

Answer: Not that I know of. I think it probably stirred up more emotion among the anti-war protesters.

Question: Doesn't a free society have the right to know what is going on in its military?

Answer: Absolutely, within certain confines; in other words the classification of material should be (and I am not saying it always is) based on the fact that if the material fell into unfriendly hands, then it could be detrimental to American security. Yes I do, but I think there are limitations, obviously.

Question: Do you think it was right to prosecute Ellsberg?

Answer: Well, I think the same rules should apply to everyone. If a member of the military had released classified information like that he would have been prosecuted. The prosecution of Ellsberg was unpopular in some circles, but it was the right thing to do.

Question: Do you have any additional comments, which you feel are necessary to understand the release of the Pentagon Papers?

Answer: Well, it might be good for people to understand that just because you have a security clearance doesn't mean you can walk into any office in the Pentagon and see top secret information. All clearances, whether they are military or on the civilian side of the fence, are based on what we call "the need to know" basis. If you had the clearance that does not mean that you could see any classified material. You had to have the need to know. I think that is important. Obviously, Ellsberg in this case had the need to know.

Question: So ... What you can see is based upon your clearance and if you have the need to know for your particular job?

Answer: That is correct. And I think it is important because I think some people have the impression that just because you have a Top Secret clearance you can walk into any office and see anything. That is not the case, nor would it be good from a security standpoint.

Conclusions to Chapter 6

Vietnam started for the US as a covert operation, first with the OSS assisting the Communists against the Japanese in the 40s and later with the US conducting anti-Communist raids in the North in 1954 (after the fall of the colonial French garrison at Dien Bien Phu). None of this involvement was ratified by the American people through their congressional representatives. If it was not for the release of the Pentagon Papers in 1971, our understanding of the conflict and covert operations in general would be decades behind where it is now. In bringing the secret study to the press, and exposing the truth about the long history of secret decision-making, Daniel Ellsberg did a service to democracy. For years, Americans did not have the facts they needed to make proper decisions about foreign policy; the release of the papers provided this much needed information.

The actions of the presidents from Truman to Nixon were the logical continuation of the policy of Containment of Communism, pursued by the secret means allowed under the National Security Act of 1947. In fact, involvement in Vietnam was a result of the base anti-Communism in American politics evident since 1918. No serious review of where these policies were leading America had ever been conducted and, with the Gulf of Tonkin resolution, the country's policy makers blundered into a trap from which they could not extricate themselves with any kind of grace. Instead of disengaging, those in control of US Vietnam policy cooked up vicious schemes like the Phoenix Program with its effective assassinations and lack of due process.

Differences on the history of US involvement in Vietnam and the issues surrounding that involvement persist today. There can be no doubt that the Soviets and their Communist ideology posed a global threat to US interests throughout the Cold War. Soviet Marxism called for global domination. The relevant question is whether a Communist regime in Vietnam was a significant part of this threat. It is indeed possible that the conflict in Vietnam bought the time countries like Thailand needed to remain democratic. The superpower stalemate over Cuba had not been enough to cause the dramatic rethinking of US foreign policy that the failure in Vietnam did.

Regardless of the lack of unanimity of views on the subject, the view that the government was guilty of a trend of misconduct and excesses in regard to the Vietnam conflict was bolstered by the Pentagon Papers publication and became the dominant view in the US. Serious reforms and restrictions on intelligence and military activities were enacted during the 70s, and simultaneously an era of "Détente" between the superpowers ensued. More on these reforms and the era of peaceful coexistence called Détente is contained in the next chapter.

Chapter 7

The 1970s

Kent State

The decade of the 70s began with shooting on American soil. The shooting was directly related to the course of the Cold War. The battle, not between the US and Soviets, produced a score of casualties, and was entirely between and among US citizens. Students of Ohio's Kent State University protested Nixon's incursion into Cambodia (a widening of the Vietnam War). Ohio's governor sent in the National Guard.

The report of the President's Commission on Campus Unrest summarized the events this way:

> Blanket Hill is a grassy knoll in the center of the campus of Kent State University, named by students who use it as a place to sun themselves in the day and to romance at night. From here, shortly after noon on a sunny spring day, a detachment of Ohio National Guardsmen, armed with World War II-vintage army rifles, fired a volley of at least 61 shots killing four college students and wounding nine.
>
> All of the young people who were shot that day were students in good standing at Kent State University.
>
> The National Guardsmen were under orders from both civilian and military authorities. Duty at Kent State had not been pleasant: they had been cursed and stoned, and some feared physical injury.
>
> Stones were thrown, then bullets were fired.[216]

The significance of Kent State to the study of the Cold War is that the riot and official reaction were cause for greater polarization in American politics. While it has never been proven that there were any foreign or significant subversive elements involved in the student demonstrations, many conservatives viewed the demonstrators as anti-American and deserving of what they got. Likewise, the events of May 1970 caused many students and others in the broad center of American politics to be forever radicalized and turned against the war effort.

It is worth going over the events that led up to the shootings at Kent State:

Friday, May 1, 1970: Students protest President Nixon's sending of US troops into Cambodia. The "dead" US Constitution is buried symbolically. At night a riot erupts on Water Street in the town of Kent and several businesses are damaged.

Saturday, May 2, 1970: At 8:45pm the ROTC building is burned. The Guard is sent in. At least one Guardsman is injured when a rock shatters the windshield of his Jeep.

Sunday, May 3, 1970: Ohio Governor, Rhodes, holds a press conference stating that "every force of law" will be used against the rioters. At 9pm the Ohio Riot Act is read to a crowd that is driven away from University President White's house by tear gas. In the general melee of that night, three Guardsmen are hurt and two students are bayoneted.

Monday, May 4, 1970: In 13 seconds of gunfire, Guardsmen on Blanket Hill kill Allison Krause, Jeffrey Glenn Miller, William Schroeder, Sandra Lee Scheuer, and wound 9 others.

Changing of the Guard

Public reaction to the events at Kent State in May 1970, while far from always sympathetic to the students, contributed to a trend. The trend had its beginnings in the reaction to the Tet Offensive of 1968; an increasingly large minority of Americans was opposing containment as it was being expressed on the battlefields of South East Asia. Rarely has foreign policy proved so divisive a factor on the American political landscape. The anti-war/anti-establishment sentiment developed during the Vietnam Conflict would have broad consequences for American foreign policy in the 70s, 80s, and beyond. When combined with revelations about executive branch wrong-doings, the sentiment became a potent political force for change. Containment remained the dominant US super-policy, but it became more participatory, open, and thus democratic.

Perhaps, in part due to increasing pressure from the domestic left and continued scrutiny in the media, the end of the conflict in Vietnam came gradually. In January 1973, after the devastating "Linebacker" B-52 raids, a truce was agreed to that left the Communists in control of much of South Vietnam. U.S. combat operations in the South ceased. In the meantime Nixon kept up the bombing of Cambodia. Congress finally turned the screw on July 31, by voting to cut off all funding for the bombing and further prohibiting any further U.S. military action in Indochina. Since Congress threatened to keep attaching the bill to crucial appropriations measures, Nixon signed the legislation and it became law.[217] The absolute end came in April 30, 1975, when invading forces from North Vietnam occupied Saigon and captured the just-evacuated U.S. embassy.

Legislative frustration over the long drawn out conflict fought largely via executive initiative became apparent in other ways prior to the final end in 1975. On October 10, 1973, the Congress sent the War Powers Resolution to President Nixon. The proposed law required that U.S. forces sent to foreign soil be withdrawn in 60 days unless: 1) Congress passed a resolution endorsing the deployment, or 2) Congress declared war, or 3) Congress was unable to meet due to invasion. The bill was an attempt to re-assert congressional prerogatives assigned by the Constitution as to war-making. Nixon promptly vetoed the measure and the Congress passed a resolution overriding the veto on November 7, 1973, making it law. The War Powers Act was never fully recognized by any president, Republican or Democrat, as constitutional. While calls for its implementation have been made in several cases since 1973, the act was never truly tested and now is seen as an anachronism on the historical ash heap.

Also, in the same vein as War Powers, the Hughes-Ryan Amendment of 1974 sought to limit executive prerogatives in the area of covert operations. The law stipulated that no funds could be expended in a foreign country by the intelligence community for other than intelligence gathering "unless and until the President finds that each operation is important to the national security of the United States and reports, in a timely fashion, a description and scope of such operations."[218] The law had the effect of requiring the president to report all covert actions by the Intelligence community to 8 separate committees of the House and Senate. Hughes-Ryan fared better than War Powers as a working law. On a number of occasions presidents reported to Congress under the law until the law was replaced by the Intelligence Oversight Act of 1980.

One facet of this trend toward democratization in American politics was the phenomenon of political investigative reporting. Polished as a genre during Vietnam and at zenith during Watergate (1972-74), journalistic investigation of government brought more people, the readers, into the mix. The Watergate break-ins occurred in May and June of 1972. They were a continuation of the Ellsberg covert operation of 1971 by the "special unit" also known as the "plumbers." Nixon himself was implicated in the subsequent cover-up. The resignation of Richard M. Nixon and the swearing in of Vice President Gerald R. Ford as president effective noon on August 9, 1974 was in large part due to the investigative reporting of Bob Woodward and Carl Bernstien of *The Washington Post*.

The Intelligence Investigations of 1975-76

Widespread publication of here-to-fore secret doings in government also served to be a motivating force behind policy makers. *The New York Times* writer, Seymour M. Hersh, blew the cover on intelligence community misdeeds in his December 22, 1974 story. The headline read "HUGE C.I.A. OPERATION REPORTED IN U.S. AGAINST ANTIWAR FORCES, OTHER DISSIDENTS IN NIXON YEARS." The story stated in part:

> The Central Intelligence Agency, directly violating its charter, conducted a massive, illegal, domestic intelligence operation during the Nixon administration against the antiwar movement and other dissident groups in the United States, according to well-placed government sources.
>
> A special unit of the C.I.A. conducted the activity and reported directly to then director, Richard Helms. In addition, the sources said, a check of the C.I.A.'s domestic files last year by Mr. Helms' successor, James R. Schlesinger, produced evidence of dozens of other activities by members of the C.I.A. inside the United States, beginning in the fifties, including break-ins, wiretapping, and surreptitious inspection of mail.[219]

On January 4, 1975 President Ford sought to stem criticism on the administration by forming "The Commission on C.I.A. Activities Within the United States," of which Ronald Reagan was a member, was chaired by Vice President, Nelson Rockefeller (known as the Rockefeller Commission). Also, in response to the Hersh disclosures, Senators moved to begin fact-finding. On January 27, they voted 82-4 to establish a special select committee to conduct a nine-month $750,000 investigation of American intelligence. The House of Representatives followed suit, forming its own investigative committee three weeks later.[220] The Senate investigation would last the longest of the three at 16 months.

The probes were the first significant attempt at oversight of the C.I.A. They were seen by some on Capitol Hill and long overdue. Until that point the Agency, with its thousands of employees and global reach, was the subject of less than 24 hours of legislative probing in any one year. Some, on the other side, believed them to be "an unwarranted exercise in self-flagellation, a witch-hunt leading to the destruction of the very capabilities designed to protect us from foreign and domestic threats."[221]

Senate Select Committee staffer, Loch K. Johnson, summarized the scope of domestic abuses by the intelligence community this way:

> The results were shocking. The C.I.A. program to open mail from or to selected American citizens produced a computer bank of 1.5 million names; the F.B.I. intelligence unit developed files on well over a million Americans, and carried out 500,000 investigations of "subversives" from 1960 to 1974 without a single court conviction; the N.S.A. (National Security Agency) computers were fed every single cable sent overseas by Americans from 1947 to 1975; Army intelligence units conducted investigations against 100,000 American citizens during the Vietnam War.[222]

In the summer of 1975, the Senate Select Committee dug into an area beyond the scope of the original Hersh article. The committee members and staffers uncovered the details of C.I.A. covert operations around the globe. The details of the investigation revealed that the Agency was involved in plotting the deaths of foreign leaders. In one form or another, there were plots at some level against the leaders of 5 nations (Congo, Cuba, the Dominican Republic, South Vietnam, and Chile). There were some implications of

Agency involvement in an additional two cases (Indonesia and Haiti). The "trail of evidence on assassination was at times easily traced, only to disappear completely or, at best, fray apart in a bewildering pattern like the ends of a shattered nerve."[223]

The Rockefeller Commission did not consider the area of covert operations; it considered only activity in the U.S. The commission report, dated June of 1975, is the first of the three major investigative documents to be published. From a passage in the report we can pick up a tone that attempts to soften the blow delivered to the Intelligence community, to apologize for the community's wrong actions, and to place the abuse in the context of violent unstable times. If looked at from the commission's perspective, perhaps the actions of the Intelligence community can be understood, though not excused. From the report:[224]

> The late 1960s and early 1970s were marked by widespread violence and civil disorders. Demonstrations, marches, and protest assemblies were frequent in a number of cities. Many universities and college campuses became places of disruption and unrest. Government facilities were picketed and sometimes invaded. Threats of bombing and bombing incidents occurred frequently. In Washington and other major cities, special security measures had to be instituted to control the access to public buildings...
>
> ...It was probably necessary for the C.I.A. to accumulate an information base on domestic dissident activities in order to assess fairly whether the activities had foreign connections. The F.B.I. would collect the information but not evaluate it. But the accumulation of domestic data in the Operation *exceeded what was reasonably required* to make such an assessment and was thus *improper*.
>
> The use of agents of the Operation on three occasions to gather information within the United States on strictly domestic maters was *beyond the C.I.A.'s authority*. In addition, the intelligence disseminations and portions of a major study prepared by the Agency which dealt with purely domestic matters was *improper*.
>
> The isolation of Operation CHAOS[225] within the C.I.A. and its independence from supervision from the regular chain of command within the clandestine service made it possible for

> the activities of the Operation to stray over the bounds of the Agency's authority *without the knowledge of senior officials*. The absence of any regular review of these activities prevented timely correction of such missteps as did occur.[226]

The House and Senate investigations continued long after the issuance of the Rockefeller Commission report. On January 19, 1976, in part of his State of the Union address, President Ford sought to undercut both the work still being done by the legislature and the influence of the press. He said in part:

> The crippling of our foreign intelligence services increases the danger of American involvement in direct armed conflict. Our adversaries are encouraged to attempt new adventures while our own ability to monitor events and influence events short of military action is undermined. Without effective intelligence capability, the United States stands blindfolded and hobbled.
>
> In the near future, I will take actions to reform and strengthen our intelligence community. I ask for your positive cooperation. It is time to go beyond sensationalism and ensure an effective, responsible, and responsive intelligence capability.[227]

In a February 17th news conference, Ford subsequently announced the issuance of Executive Order 11905, which was creating a new intelligence command structure under the National Security Council and Director of Central Intelligence (then George Bush, Sr.). The E.O. also created a new civilian board to watch over the Intelligence community (the independent Intelligence Oversight Board). Ford said further that, "I will not be a party to the dismantling of the C.I.A. or other intelligence agencies."[228] This action by the executive was an obvious attempt to head off the reform movement still brewing in the legislature.

In April of 1976, the Senate Select Committee to Study Governmental Operations With Regard to Intelligence Activity, called the "Church committee" after its chairman, published its final report and thus ended this "season of inquiry" into the Intelligence community. The report was six volumes in length. In the first volume we find extensive criticism on U.S. covert action programs. In part we read:

> The committee finds that covert action operations have not

> been an exceptional instrument used only in rare instances when the vital interests of the United States have been at stake. On the contrary, presidents and administrations have made excessive, and at times self-defeating, use of covert action. In addition, covert action has been a routine program with a bureaucratic momentum of its own. The long-term impact, at home and abroad, of repeated disclosure of U.S. covert actions has been increasingly costly to America's interests and reputation. The Committee believes that covert action must be employed only in the most extraordinary circumstances.[229]

In volume two we find criticism of domestic intelligence activity. We read in part:

> The findings which have emerged from our investigation convince us that the Government's domestic intelligence policies and practices require fundamental reform. We have attempted to set out the basic facts; now it is time for the Congress to turn its attention to legislating restraints upon intelligence activities that may endanger the constitutional rights of Americans.
>
> The Committee's fundamental conclusion is that intelligence activities have undermined the constitutional rights of citizens and they have done so primarily because checks and balances designed by the framers of the Constitution to assure accountability have not been applied.[230]

Both the House and Senate select committees on intelligence adopted several scores of recommendations to cure the ills of the Intelligence community. The key result of the investigations was that both chambers created permanent intelligence "oversight" committees (the Senate in 1976 and the House in 1977). The new committees would keep a watchful eye on the executive branch as it went about the day-to-day running of the intelligence community.

Arms Control and Détente

Arms control and détente were integral aspects of the Cold War in the 70s. To get an accurate picture of arms control and détente in the 70s, we must look back to the origin of the species earlier in the nuclear age. Both the

Truman and Eisenhower administrations paid modest lip service to some kind of purely notional arms control (and it is true that détente was more than just arms control). Nothing was done until the advent of the rise of the Kennedy administration in 1961.

The first significant event in relation to arms control in the nuclear age came after the Bay of Pigs fiasco and prior to the Cuban Missile Crisis. This was the formation of the US Arms Control and Disarmament Agency (ACDA). On September 28, 1961, President Kennedy signed bill H.R. 9118, giving the establishment of the agency force of law. At that time the president said in part:

> Our ultimate goal, as the act points out, is a world free from war and free from the dangers and burdens of armaments in which the use of force is subordinated to the rule of law, and in which international adjustments to a changing world are achieved peacefully. It is a complex and difficult task to reconcile through negotiation the many security interests of all nations to achieve disarmament, but the establishment of this agency will provide new and better tools for this effort.[231]

ACDA, whose purview extends into conventional as well as nuclear arms control, has served every president since JFK. It has provided expertise in negotiations and its staff has kept both Congress and the US military abreast of current arms control efforts.[232]

The next milestone, this one in 1963, was the negotiation and signing of the nuclear test ban treaty prohibiting nuclear testing in the atmosphere, in outer space, or underwater. President Kennedy said of the agreement before it was signed:

> I know there are some people who believe the very fact that if the Soviet Union signs it must mean that there is something ominous in it. There are occasions when interests of countries, even though they may be ideologically hostile, may coincide. I think the existence of a possibility of nuclear war, perhaps, does affect us both the same way.[233]

This way of thinking, that the US and Soviet societies could have shared interest, was expressed by every president after JFK through the end of the

Cold War and beyond (with respect to Russia). It was, however, a novel approach for the Kennedy administration.

The first arms control treaty of the nuclear age was signed on August 5th, in Moscow, by representatives of the US, UK, and USSR. On asking the Senate for ratification of the agreement, the president stated that it could be a trendsetter.

> There is hope that it may lead to further measures to arrest and control the dangerous competition for increasingly destructive weapons.[234]

The Senate ratified the limited nuclear test ban treaty in September 1963.

After Kennedy's assassination, that is, during the early phases of the Johnson administration, there were several mentions of warming relations with the Soviets through arms control, but nothing concrete came until the president sent a letter on arms control to Soviet chairman, Kosygin, on January 27, 1967. Kosygin responded to the letter first in the British media. He said:

> We are, as you know, in favor of an end to nuclear armaments and in favor of the total destruction of nuclear stockpiles, and you will, I trust, realize that we take this position not because we have few weapons, but rather, because we have many. We believe that mankind has no need for nuclear weapons.[235]

Near the top of his March 2 news conference, President Johnson announced he had gotten a response from the Soviets and took questions on the matter:

> I have a brief announcement to make. I have received a reply from Chairman Kosygin to my letter of January 27. This reply confirmed the willingness of the Soviet government to discuss means of limiting the arms race in offensive and defensive nuclear missiles.
>
> This exchange of views is expected to lead to further discussions of this subject in Moscow and with our allies. It is my hope that a means can be found to achieve constructive results.

I will be glad to take any questions in the time allotted to me.

Q. Mr. President, this applies, did I understand it correctly, to offensive weapons as well as the establishment of an antimissile system?

The President: Offensive and defensive.

Q. Mr. President, on what level will these discussions be?

The President: They will be in Moscow with Ambassador Thompson. Then we will see how they progress.

Q. Mr. President, will these Moscow discussions be concurrent with the ones going on in the Eighteen-Nation Disarmament Conference in Geneva?

The President: Not necessarily. They are not timed in connection with any other conferences.

As you know, I sent Chairman Kosygin a letter and asked him to consider the desirability of an exchange of views in this regard. He responded. We would assume that the discussions would be initiated with Ambassador Thompson. I wouldn't go further than that at this time.

Q. Mr. President, do you see an interconnection between Senate passage of the consular treaty, the space treaty, East-West trade, and the non-proliferation treaty? *Do you see these as kind of one movement?*[236]

The President: I think they are all very desirable moves in the national interest of the United States.

When I became president, one of the first steps I took in the first few weeks I was president was to communicate with Chairman Khrushchev and suggest that we explore together certain agreements that would be beneficial to both nations in promoting peace in the world.

Exchanges between our two countries resulted in: the signing of the civil air agreement; the signing of the consular agreement, which I devoutly hope will be ratified by the Senate, and about which I have had innumerable conversations with the leaders of the Congress of both parties; the progress that has been made in the non-proliferation agreement—although we have not come to a complete meeting of the minds with all of the individuals involved, we have made progress; the space agreement, which

> we hope the Senate will act favorably upon; and the East-West trade, which is being considered.
>
> We have recommended all of those. We hope that the Congress will confirm our judgment that they are in the best interests of the United States. They were not made as a package move. They were made as individual recommendations.
>
> But I do think that what your question implies is: Does that reflect a policy on the part of this government of attempting to find areas of agreement with the Soviet Union?
>
> *The answer is, yes. We are exploring, with every means at our command, every possible way of relieving tensions in the world and promoting peace in the world.*[237238]

Détente, the 70s policy or group of policies resulting in a relaxation in tensions between the superpowers, was beginning to coalesce, even though the term was not yet in general usage (most of the elements of Détente were mentioned by the president above). Raymond L. Garthoff, in his authoritative work "Détente and Confrontation" (Brookings Institution, 1994), states that Soviet leader Leonid I. Brezhnev first used the term publicly in 1966 and President Nixon in 1970. However, the term was in general usage in the CIA in its classified reports as early as 1963.[239]

Whether technically part of Détente or not, negotiations began on what would become the Strategic Arms Limitation Treaty (SALT I) and the Anti-Ballistic Missile (ABM) treaty. The efforts at agreement were stillborn when the Soviets invaded Czechoslovakia in 1968. It took another year and the entrance of the Nixon administration to begin negotiations again.

Negotiations for the SALT I and ABM treaties were begun in November 1969. President Nixon had said little about any such negotiations in his inaugural address. Even though the Kennedy-Johnson administrations had broken ground in this area, it is possible that Nixon's motive in being somewhat discrete was to allow the still infant policy of cooperation with Marxism to mature before it stood the public acid test. The only mention, and it was oblique, to the policies of cooperation with the Soviets that became a staple in the Nixon administration was:

> For the first time, because the people of the world want peace, and the leaders of the world are afraid of war, the times are on the side of peace.[240]

Six months after Nixon's inaugural and still five months before the start of the negotiations, First Secretary, Brezhnev, stated at the keynote speech at the International Meeting of Communist Workers Parties in Moscow:

> For us, peaceful coexistence is not a temporary tactical method, but an important principle underlying the consistently peace-loving foreign policy of socialism. Such a policy creates the most favorable conditions for building the new society in socialist countries, and for spreading the revolutionary and liberation movement."[241]

This statement was thinly veiled code stating that the Soviets would not stop their efforts at expansion of Marxism. What they had just finished doing by invading Czechoslovakia was "building the new society in socialist countries." Further, "spreading the revolutionary and liberation movement," meant that the Soviets would continue to expand at point of bayonet if necessary and would support Communist guerrilla insurgencies in non-Marxist countries.

This argument is a throw back to Marx and Lenin and speaks to the issue of the Soviet belief in the inevitability of world revolution and the duty of true Communists to support it by any means necessary. This rhetoric was both an expression of real determination by Brezhnev and necessary for internal consumption in the Communist world. Nixon had not wanted to seem to gung-ho on Détente with the Soviets in his inaugural, because of the potential for domestic criticism. Likewise, Brezhnev had the same problem in the Socialist world (the potential view that he was giving up on Marx and the revolution).

As the negotiations developed, the US intelligence community developed its estimation of how the Soviets would react in an atmosphere of cooperation. In February, 1970 a CIA "Special National Intelligence Estimate" looked at Soviet potential actions in this light:

> Actually, they will hope that as SALT develops they will have opportunities to exploit weakness and divisions in the US and between the US and its allies. They are *likely to exercise restraint*[242] in this respect, however, so long as they think they have a good chance of getting a satisfactory agreement."[243]

In this view, conflict would continue between the superpowers, but the operative factor dictating Soviet actions would be gaining an agreement. This assumption ignores the central fact the Marxism-Leninism was still the guiding light in Soviet politics. This view demonstrates a common misunderstanding in the history of US-Soviet relations, as we shall see when we look further down the road at Soviet actions in 1979 with respect to Afghanistan.

This view of Marxism as a motivator (not East-West diplomacy) is not a judgment made through purely hindsight; all of the elements of Détente were present in the Johnson overtures toward the Soviets in 1967—communications were open and agreements were in progress. Yet, when in their view socialism was threatened in Czechoslovakia, the Soviets invaded with armored divisions. It was the ghost of Karl Marx, not peaceful coexistence with America, that motivated Soviet foreign policy in 1968.

History would repeat itself in the 70s, in spite of the CIA's apparently wishful thinking and advising to the contrary. It could be that the pattern we were seeing develop was a result of an American conception that nobody in his or her right mind really believed in ideology (in particular, Marxism). Ideology was seen as a juvenile force; power politics and self-interest would motivate the Soviets, or so the theory went. In spite of the evidence to the contrary the Soviets were being depicted as pragmatists first. This misconception is still alive today, in the form of the substantial number of historians who discount ideology as a significant force in the course of Cold War.

Expectations were on the rise in the US intelligence community with regard to SALT. In a secret October 13, 1971 address to the National War College, Director of Central Intelligence (DCI) Richard Helms said:

> And may I remark that, as an old hand in an agency which is often accused of housing inveterate Cold Warriors, I will be extremely gratified when the day comes, as I think it will, when real limits can be placed on the arms race."

Helms gives us another possible explanation for his agency's soft-pedaling of the ideological motivators for Soviet actions in international relations. It is simply this, he was afraid that the team he led would continue to be viewed as "inveterate Cold Warriors" if they quoted Marx and Lenin in their estimates. Helms also states a clear preference for obtaining an agreement; all the more reason for him to estimate that Soviet action would be moderated in the event of an agreement (thus making an agreement palatable to the upper echelon consumers of his intelligence in the American government). Helms may not have been fully conscious of these biases as he went about the duties of the DCI. After nearly three years of negotiations, President Nixon and General Secretary Brezhnev signed the ABM treaty and "an interim agreement on the limitation of strategic arms" (SALT I) in a televised ceremony in the Kremlin on May 26, 1972. In a radio and television address to the people of the Soviet Union two days later, Nixon assured his listeners that:

> As great powers, we shall sometimes be competitors, but we need never be enemies.[244]

On May 29, 1972, in a continuation of the Moscow summit, Nixon and Brezhnev signed the "Basic Principles of Relations Between the United States of America and the Union of Soviet Socialist Republics." The document said in part that the USA and USSR would:

> The United States of America and the Union of Soviet Socialist Republics, guided by their obligations under the charter of the United Nations and by a desire to strengthen peaceful relations with each other and to place these relations on the firmest possible basis, aware of the need to make every effort to remove the threat of war and to create conditions which promote the reduction of tensions in the world and the strengthening of universal security and international cooperation, believing that the improvement of US-Soviet relations and their mutually advantageous development in such areas as economics, science, and culture, will meet these objectives and contribute to better mutual understanding and business-like cooperation, without in any way prejudicing the interests of third countries, conscious that these objectives reflect the interests of the peoples of both countries, have agreed as follows:
>
> First, they will proceed from the common determination that in the nuclear age there is no alternative to conducting their mutual relations on the basis of peaceful coexistence. Differences in ideology and social systems of the USA and the

> USSR are not obstacles to the bilateral development of normal relations based on the principles of sovereignty, equality, non-interference in the internal affairs and mutual advantage...[245]

Again we see that ideology was officially discounted as a factor in US-Soviet relations. It is interesting to note that the phrase committing the signatories to "non-interference in... internal affairs" was included at Soviet instance to protect their dictatorial Marxist-Leninist state apparatus from criticism and sanction of the United States. The US was officially giving up the right to seek change in the Soviet system of repression with those words. Accepting the brief period from 1941 to 1945 relations between the Soviet Union and the United States were never as good as they were after the 1972 Moscow summit. Détente was in full swing.

On June 13, the president sent the SALT I and ABM treaties up to Capitol Hill for the action of Congress. He stated in part:

> Besides enhancing our national security, these agreements open the opportunity for a new and more constructive US-Soviet relationship, characterized by a negotiated settlement of differences rather than by the hostility and confrontation of decades past.[246]
>
> The position that arms control actually strengthened American security was one often taken by presidents during Détente. This contention was necessary to combat right-wing criticism that arms control made America weak. Nixon was not the last to stress that arms control still allowed for US "strategic modernization."[247]

SALT I/ABM allowed the following limits in strategic arms: Antiballistic Missiles, Soviets 200, US 200; Intercontinental Ballistic Missiles, Soviets 1550, US 1054; MIRV independent warheads, Soviets 5700, US 5700; nuclear submarines, Soviets 41, US 42.

The US did not deploy any significant numbers of ABMs during the Cold War. The Soviets had one site defending Moscow at the time of the agreement and were, in fact, allowed to expand it slightly under the agreement. The actual number of US Multiple, Independently targeted, Reentry Vehicles was 5,700 where as the Soviets had deployed only 2,500 such warheads in 1972. The US also enjoyed a qualitative advantage in that its missiles were more accurate. The result was an offsetting of the Soviet advantage in ICBMs, however, the Soviets would be allowed, under SALT I, to build to the full 5,700 MIRV level of the US.[248]

Perhaps because of the radical change in the course of US-Soviet relations that SALT I/ABM represented, the unusual measure of considering the treaties in both houses of the Congress was undertaken.[249] The House and the Senate debated and voted favorably on the treaties. On September 30, 1972 President Nixon signed the joint resolution the Congress had generated, giving the treaties the force of US law.

As a result of another event in 1972, the break-in of Democratic Party Headquarters located at the Watergate complex; Nixon was ousted from office for abuse of power and conspiracy. His resignation was not unrelated to the Cold War, for the "special unit" that conducted the break-ins had been formed originally to target Daniel Ellsberg, the leftist foreign policy critic of the Pentagon Papers' case. The Watergate break-in itself may well have been motivated by an attempt to find the "holy grail" of ultra-conservative politics during Vietnam—evidence of the alleged connection between Communists in Hanoi or the Soviet Bloc and US anti-war demonstrators (or even the Democratic Party).

Gerald R. Ford assumed the office of President of the United States on August 9, 1974 in an air of uncertainty. Ford attempted to clear up this uncertainty in his August 12 address to a joint session of Congress. He said in part:

> We stand by our commitments and we will live up to our responsibilities in our formal alliances, in our friendships, and our improving relations with potential adversaries.
>
> On this, Americans are united and strong. Under my term of leadership, I hope we will become more united. I am certain we will remain strong.
>
> A strong defense is the surest way to peace. Strength makes détente attainable. Weakness invites war, as my generation—my generation—knows from four very bitter experiences.
>
> Just as America's will for peace is second to none, so will America's strength be second to none.

Further and more specifically Ford continued,

> To the Soviet Union, I pledge continuity in our commitment to the course of the past 3 years. To our two peoples, and to all mankind, we owe a continued effort to live and, where possible, to work together in peace, for in a thermonuclear age there can be no alternative to a positive and peaceful relationship between our nations.[250]

In one address Ford reassured twin constituencies about the course of his government's policies. In what was becoming a trend for presidents under Détente, the president struck on two themes. He told Americans the US would remain strong, and he told the Soviets that the course of Détente would be uninterrupted.

On November 24 of the same year, Ford and Brezhnev were meeting in Vladivostok, USSR. They released a joint communiqué on that date which outlined a program as follows:

> 1) Elements of the SALT I agreement would remain in force until 1977 and would be joined by a new agreement (SALT II).
> 2) SALT II would remain in force from October 1977 until December 31, 1985.
> 3) SALT II would include an aggregate number of delivery vehicles[251] for each side, and an aggregate number of ICBMs and SLBMs that each side could arm with MIRVs.
> 4) SALT II would be followed by SALT III. Negotiations on SALT III would begin no later than 1980-81 and concern the "question of further limitations and possible reductions of strategic arms in the period after 1985.
> 5) Continued talks on the as yet unfinished SALT II agreement would begin in January 1975 at Geneva.[252]

In addition to the communiqué, the two leaders signed what became known as the "Vladivostok Accord." This agreement pledged each side to maintain a level of 2,400 missiles and strategic bombers each, with no more than 1,320 of the missiles being MIRVed. One MIRVed missile might contain a half dozen or more independently targeted re-entry vehicles capable of destroying a target. So, in effect 1,320 MIRVed missiles could easily deploy around 8,000 nuclear bombs. With the Soviets being behind in MIRV development and deployment, the January 1977 ratio of warheads was

8,500 for the US and 4,000 for the Soviets (according to then Secretary of Defense, Donald Rumsfeld).[253]

In 1975, the CIA noted the arrival on the scene of a new mobile missile for use within a given theater of operation (a missile of less than intercontinental range that still had implications that may have required its inclusion in the SALT negotiations). This new weapon was the SS-20 mobile missile (also known as the SS-X-20). The CIA said of the missile:

> The SS-X-20 apparently consists of the first and second stages of the SS-X-16[254] with some modifications, and a similar post-boost vehicle.[255]

The SS-20 was MIRVed with three warheads per missile. The Soviets began deployment of the SS-20 in Europe while President Ford was still in office in 1976. They had 18 missiles in place by the end of 1977; this number rose steadily until it reached 378 total missiles deployed in 1983 (with around 250 within range of European targets). At this point, NATO began a long, planned counter-deployment of its own Intermediate Nuclear Forces (INF), which will be further discussed later in this chapter and in the next chapter.

For a short time, during Ford's failed election campaign of 1976, Détente was banished from mention in the administration. SALT II was also put on the back burner. These actions were the result of a somewhat bitter primary campaign in which Ford defeated his chief opponent, the man to be elected president in 1980, longtime conservative, Ronald Reagan.

Détente was high on the new president's international agenda on coming into office in January 1977. In his inaugural address, Jimmy Carter argued in favor of resuming arms control efforts. He said in part:

> The world is still engaged in a massive armaments race designed to ensure continuing equivalent strength among potential adversaries. We pledge perseverance and wisdom in our efforts to limit the world's armaments to those necessary for each nation's own domestic safety. And we will move this year a step toward our ultimate goal—the elimination of all nuclear weapons from this Earth. We urge all other people to join us, for success can mean life instead of death.[256]

In line with what previous presidents had done to maintain strength through the arms control process, President Carter committed the US fully to the new (and possibly mobile) MX (for Missile eXperimental) ICBM system on June 7, 1977. However, in somewhat of a retrenchment he canceled production of the B-1 manned strategic bomber in the same month (opting to modernize the aging fleet of B-52s with ALCMs).

National Security Advisor, Zbigniew Brzezinski, best explains the first storm that the new administration faced:

> The controversy over the enhanced radiation weapon (ERW), or neutron bomb, began when *The Washington Post* published, on June 7, 1977, an article describing the planned deployment of the battlefield nuclear weapon in Europe. Apparently, the reporter had noted the budgetary provision for the Lance missile version of the ERW in President Ford's 1978 budget. The Energy Research and Development Administration had neglected to delete the still-classified term "enhanced radiation" from publicly released congressional testimony. We were quite unprepared for the political storm that hit us only four and a half months after inauguration. Media portrayals of the ERW as the bomb that "destroys people and not property" sensationalized the debate then spread to Europe, where people had reason to be truly nervous about nuclear conflict on their own soil. Ultimately, Moscow used the material for a propaganda blitz that succeeded in obfuscating the issue of their own deployment of the huge 1,500 kiloton SS-20 missile.[257]

The CIA said of the controversy:

> Moscow has evidently seized upon the neutron bomb development and deployment issue to mount a major propaganda campaign against US defense policy and US positions on a number of issues in East-West relations.[258]

The neutron bomb was made necessary in the first place, in the minds of US defense planners, because the Soviets had a 3 to 1superiority in tanks in Europe.

The large Soviet armored force was a means of holding Europe hostage.

Only nuclear weapons, it was thought, could halt a Soviet Armored advance into Europe. The use of even small nuclear weapons on European soil was, however, problematic because of the dense population throughout the region. The neutron bomb was seen as a solution because it had a smaller blast radius and less fallout, but it produced intense radiation in the proximity of the detonation. This radiation would, in theory, kill the Soviet tank crews, and leave nearby towns and civilians unharmed.

The Soviets were successful in their campaign against the neutron bomb. In May 1978, after much fanfare in the media, President Carter decided not to deploy the weapon to Europe.

The Soviet SS-20 became and issue again in 1977. It was decided that the best course of action would be for NATO to counter-deploy to Europe Ground Launched Cruise Missiles (GLCMs with a range of 1,500 miles) and Pershing II ballistic missiles (with a range of more than 1,100 miles). In 1979, the exact figures were arrived at, with the plan for 464 GLCMs and 108 Pershing IIs for a total of 572 INF missiles. NSC Adviser Brzezinski, Secretary of State Cyrus Vance, Secretary of Defense Harold Brown, and JCS Chairman David C. Jones all agreed with this planned number (which was arrived at by NSC staffer David Aaron).

In July, President Carter approved the plan, under which the NATO counter-deployments would begin in 1983. By October a "two track" approach had evolved—NATO would go ahead with the deployments and at the same time pursue an arms control agreement on the INF missiles. The North Atlantic Council of foreign and defense ministers unanimously approved the two-track approach in a December meeting in Brussels.[259]

The pace of US-Soviet strategic arms control negotiations (SALT II) picked up in early 1979. From January 1 to May 9 senior representatives on both countries met some 25 times and subsequently announced that an agreement had been reached. It was decided that President Carter and General Secretary Brezhnev would meet at a summit to sign the agreement in June of that year.

In his remarks to the Annual Convention of the American Newspaper Publishers Association even before the negotiations were complete (April 25, 1979), President Carter laid out his reasons for supporting the treaty. He said:

> The strategic forces of the United States and the Soviet Union today are essentially equivalent. They have larger and more

> numerous land-based missiles. We have a larger number of warheads and, as you know, significant technological and geographical advantages.
>
> Each side has the will and the means to prevent the other from achieving superiority. Neither side is in a position to exploit its nuclear weapons for political purposes, nor to use strategic weapons without facing almost certain suicide.
>
> What causes us concern is not the current balance but the momentum of the Soviet strategic buildup. Over the past decade, the soviets have steadily increased their real defense spending, year by year, while our own defense spending over that decade has had a net decrease.
>
> In areas not limited by SALT I, they have launched ambitious programs to strengthen their strategic forces. At some future point, the Soviet Union could achieve a strategic advantage unless we alter these trends. That is exactly what I want to do—with the support of the American people and the bipartisan support of Congress.
>
> We must move on two fronts at the same time. First, within mutually accepted limits, we must modernize our own strategic forces. Along with the strengthening of NATO, that is a central purpose of the defense budget that I've submitted to Congress—improvements, which are necessary even in a time of fiscal restraint. And second, we must place more stringent limits on the arms race than are presently imposed by SALT I. That is the purpose of the SALT II treaty.
>
> The defense budget I've submitted will ensure that our nuclear force continues to be essentially equivalent to that of the Soviet Union.[260]

The president was moving over the well-worn ground of promising force modernization as an offset to arms control.

State Department public affairs documents of the same time frame also stressed that "we are now engaged in extensive modernization of our nuclear forces."[261] The State Department was also bold enough to state flatly that,

> first and foremost, SALT II will contribute to our security. By imposing important limits on the nuclear arms race between

> the United States and the Soviet Union, **SALT II will reduce the risk of nuclear war.**[250, 13]

This was political hard sell for arms control.

Also in its "SALT II: The Reasons Why," the State Department outlined a favorable argument for the limits agreed to in the negotiations:

> The initial ceiling for all ICBM launchers, SLBM launchers, heavy bombers, and ASBMs (Air-to-Surface Ballistic Missiles) is 2,400 [per side]. This ceiling will be reduced to 2,250 by December 31, 1981. Under these limits, the Soviet Union, now at a level of about 2,520, will be required to remove about 270 strategic nuclear delivery vehicles from its weapons inventory, while the United States, now at a level of about 2,060 operational systems, will be allowed to augment its strategic forces slightly under the terms of the overall ceiling.[264]

Conservatives were quick to oppose the SALT II treaty. Two of the best organized groups were the "Committee on the Present Danger" and the "American Security Council, a Coalition for Peace Through Strength." The latter enlisted the support of 175 congressmen and 89 special interest groups.[265] One of the points the conservative groups made about the treaty was that it would allow the Soviets to produce a new bomber that was not considered strategic or intercontinental by the treaty.

The bomber, with the NATO code name of "Backfire," was capable of carrying nuclear weapons and could make a one way [suicide] flight to the US from the Soviet Union. The State Department handled the Backfire issue this way:

> The Soviet Union has undertaken commitments not to increase the rate of production of the Backfire bomber above its current rate, and to limit upgrading of the capabilities of this aircraft. The freeze on the Backfire production rate at its current level means that the Soviets are committed not to produce more than 30 Backfires per year. The United States considers the obligations set forth on Backfire as essential to the integrity of the obligations of the treaty as a whole. The commitments by the Soviet Union regarding Backfire have the same legal force

> as the rest of the SALT II agreement. Thus, if the Soviet Union were to violate these commitments, the United States could withdraw from the treaty.[266]

In a summit between President Carter and General Secretary Brezhnev, June 15-18, the SALT II treaty was signed. On return from Vienna, President Carter stated to Congress:

> This is the 10th time since the end of World War II when the leader of the United States and the leader of the Soviet Union have met at a summit conference. During the past three days, we've moved closer to a goal of stability and security in Soviet-American relationships. That has been the purpose of American policy ever since the rivalry between the United States and the Soviet Union became a central fact in international relations more than a generation ago at the end of World War II.[267]

The president's address reveals much in terms of the conception of the Cold War, and perhaps illustrates why SALT II ultimately failed. As we saw in chapter 2, the rivalry between the US and USSR was a central fact from the birth of the latter nation. Woodrow Wilson made plain in 1917-18, his anti-Communist position in both rhetoric and action. The US refused to recognize the Communists as the government of the USSR until 1933. This rivalry was a fact then, as it was in 1979, because the legacy of Jeffersonian-Madisonian democracy and Marxism-Leninism were incompatible. Only the coming crucible of WWII forced a temporary alliance of the two forces.

These evident misinterpretations by President Carter, taking the approach that the two states were rivals locked in great state diplomacy—not ideological opposites bound to conflict regardless of circumstance—allowed for the commission of errors. Central among these errors was the assumption that the purpose of American policy up to June 1979 had been to establish "stability and security in Soviet-American relations." In reality, American policy in the post WWII era Carter was speaking of had at its core NSC Directive 10/2 of June 18, 1948 (see chapter 3). The directive took "cognizance of the vicious covert activities of the USSR" and allowed the CIA to engage in "sabotage, anti-sabotage, demolition ... subversion against hostile states, including underground resistance movements," etc. ...Rightly or wrongly, this decree was hardly the centerpiece of a foreign policy whose primary aim was "stability and security."

Backfire, ideology, and other issues impacting the treaty aside, the anti-SALT forces were handed a plum with the next major disclosure in Soviet-American relations. On August 30, it became public knowledge that a brigade of some 3,000 Soviet troops, equipped with approximately 40 tanks, 60 armored personnel carriers and field artillery had been discovered in Cuba. Though the troops were referred to in Washington and in the media as a "combat brigade," the Soviet Chargé d'Affairs, Vladilen Vasev stated that the troops did not constitute "combat units."[268] President Carter had no choice but to address the issue on September 7, and later on October 1 in a formal address to the nation. The president stated:

> Recently, we obtained evidence that a Soviet combat brigade has been in Cuba for some years. The presence of Soviet combat troops is of serious concern to us.
>
> I want to reassure you at the outset that we do not face any immediate, concrete threat that could escalate into war or a major confrontation—but we do face a challenge. It is a challenge to our wisdom, a challenge to our ability to act in a firm, decisive way without destroying the basis for cooperation that helps to maintain world peace and control nuclear weapons. It's a challenge to our determination to give a measured and effective response to Soviet competition and to Cuban military activities around the world...
>
> ...This is not a large force, nor an assault force. It presents no direct threat to us. It has no airborne or seaborne capability. In contrast to the 1962 crisis, no nuclear threat to the United States is involved ... Nevertheless, this Soviet brigade in Cuba is a serious matter.[269]

President Carter was taking a dichotomous position; the brigade was a serious matter requiring a response, but he desired there be no hindrance to East-West cooperation. Jimmy Carter did not want the presence of the brigade to sidetrack the SALT II treaty. As a result, his administration did not do much about the brigade. On October 17, 1800 Marines were landed as reinforcements to the sole US base on Cuba, Guantánamo Bay. After the much-publicized landings, the issue of the brigade was left to quietly languish on the back pages of the media. The brigade did not kill SALT II.

The end of SALT II would come from other causes. On December 12, 1979, Soviet General Secretary Brezhnev and his closest advisors, without consulting the full politburo, decided to invade Afghanistan to replace a friendly Socialist government on the USSR's southern border. The government of Hafizullah Amin could not control an insurgency and was about to get the brotherly assistance of the larger socialist state. Starting December 25 and continuing through the 27th and after, Soviet Spetznaz (Special Forces) and airborne troops began landing at the Kabul Airport. By the 27th Amin was dead and Soviet puppet Babrak Karmal was in his place in the presidency. At the same time Soviet Army ground troops crossed the Soviet-Afghan border and headed for the major cities. Within weeks there were 75,000 soviet troops in Afghanistan (that number would increase to a maximum of 108,800 by 1985).[270]

On January 8, 1980, in remarks to members of Congress and the media, President Carter stated:

> In my opinion, shared by many of the world's leaders with whom I have discussed this matter, the Soviet invasion of Afghanistan is the greatest threat to world peace since the Second World War. It's a sharp escalation in the aggressive history of the Soviet Union…
>
> …Politically, we joined with 50 other nations to take to the [UN] Security Council two propositions: one, to condemn the Soviet Union for the invasion and therefore the threat to world peace; and secondly, to call upon the Soviets to withdraw their troops. The vote was cast after the debates were concluded. The only nations voting against these two positions were East Germany—again, a Soviet puppet nation—and the Soviets themselves. The permanent members, as you know, have a veto right. And now a move is underway, which I think will be realized, to take this vote to the [UN] General Assembly for further condemnation of the Soviet Union.
>
> It is difficult to understand why the Soviets took this action. I think they probably underestimated the adverse reaction from around the world.[271]

President Carter's wish to see the Soviets condemned in the UN General Assembly happened in January 1980. As well other, both unilateral and cooperative, measures against the Soviets were taken. Soviet fishing rights were revoked for US territorial waters, high technology equipment was embargoed, grain sales were suspended, and the Olympics scheduled for Moscow in the summer of 1980 were boycotted. Sixty-four countries did not attend the Olympics including the US, Japan, West Germany, and China. The net results of all this was that US-Soviet trade fell 60% in 1980 (but Soviet trade with West Germany, France, Italy, and Japan, who did not share US foreign policy goals, correspondingly increased).[272]

Official Soviet reaction to the move for sanctions on the part of the Carter administration was predictively negative. The Soviet government line as expressed in "Pravda" was that the sanctions showed "disregard for the fundamental long-term interests of peace, relaxation of international tension, and constructive development of Soviet-American relations."[273] Détente was rapidly dying.

On January 21, 1980, in his "State of the Union" President Carter withdrew SALT from Senate consideration. He said:

> I firmly believe that SALT II is in our Nation's security interest and that it will add significantly to the control of nuclear weapons. But because of the Soviet invasion of Afghanistan, I do not believe it is advisable to have the Senate consider the Treaty now.[274]

While the president probably fully intended to re-introduce the treaty at a later date, this never happened. SALT II and Détente itself were dead.

Détente failed because the Soviets never gave up on the ends of spreading Marxist-Leninist ideology. They may have temporarily suspended violent means to continue their advances, but as we have seen with Czechoslovakia and Afghanistan—some 11 years distant from each other—the ends dictated a departure from peaceful means. The ends dictated, and the Soviets used whatever means at their disposal, regardless of the consequences for Détente and arms control.

The 1980 election brought Ronald Reagan to the Presidency. Long-term frustration with US foreign policy failures dating back to Vietnam, the seeming rise of the Soviet Union in international affairs and military strength, US diplomatic hostages in Iran, and a dismal economy combined to defeat Jimmy Carter's re-election bid. Ronald Reagan brought with him a whole new set of policies and objectives, as outlined in the next chapter.

Chapter 8

The Reagan Era

Nicaragua: The Rise of the FSLN

In confronting the Nicaragua of the 1980s, policy makers were faced with a complicated and, as yet, incomplete revolution that was being interpreted from conflicting perspectives. These conflicting perspectives were largely a result of the issues facing Nicaragua at the time not fitting easily into the East vs. West dichotomy. There was no overt Soviet (or even surrogate) military occupation of Nicaragua, and it suffered from serious problems of poverty and inequality within its society. Under these conditions, America's constitutionally-mandated fragmentation of power (between the executive and legislature) and the controversial, if not illegal, actions of some in the executive branch caused the organs of democracy to work at cross-purposes. Over the broad course of US Nicaragua policy from 1981-1990 the solutions arrived at may appear to have been the result of perseverance toward well-defined goals. It would be a mistake, however, not to realize, as we shall see, that there were many points of uncertainty, and many fits and starts to US policy toward Nicaragua in the 80s.

In historical terms, the US often intervened in the countries of Central America and the Caribbean. Prior to 1949, intervention typically took the form of overt US military presence. US Marines occupied Nicaragua for most of the years from 1912 to 1933, leaving in their wake a government that fell under control of the autocratic Somoza family. From 1949-1979, various economic, political, and military assistance programs were implemented with varying degrees of intensity of effort and few results in terms of long-term success. The stated goals of these programs: a) to foster private enterprise that would give rise to a middle class with a vested interest in democracy, and b) to build professional military establishments in the region that would be apolitical and responsive to civilian authority, were not achieved. American efforts of the time were permeated by,

> the idea that our country has been successful and Central America has not; the notion that we are more developed than they in a moral, political, and psychological sense as well as an economic one.[275]

Furthering the problem was the fact that North Americans tended to assume that change and development are easy, and that democratic political systems would spring from economic development. The idea that all Central America needed was something akin to the Marshall Plan motivated Truman's "Point Four" and Kennedy's "Alliance for Progress." Contrary to the assumption that change would be easy were the facts that the problems faced in Central America were those of initial development rather than the rebuilding of bombed-out factories. If that were not enough to hinder the development process, the economies of Central America were, at the time, competitive producing many of the same export commodities (fruit, beef, and coffee).

Of the two programs mentioned, the "Alliance for Progress" produced more of an economic benefit in the region. With an investment of $20 billion the US spurred economic growth south of the border. During the period the Alliance was in place, the Nicaraguan economy prospered. From 1961 to 1970, the country's GNP grew 23%. Manufacturing, which made-up 10% of Nicaragua's GNP prior to the Alliance, increased to over 23% of GNP by the early 70s.[276] To shield this historic infusion of development capital, US military advisors were sent to the region.

In spite of impressive overall economic growth, a large viable middle class did not develop in Nicaragua in the 60s and 70s, nor did a professional and apolitical military. While a small and successful middle class did exist by the late 60s, its influence remained strictly limited. Increased wealth and the benefits of development remained largely in the hands of Somoza-owned firms and their patrons. In the early 70s, only $2 per $100 of the increase in per capita GNP actually made its way to the poorest ¼ of Nicaraguan society. One counter-productive facet of the Alliance programs was that high-visibility improvement in communications and infrastructure, such as road building, caused rising expectations among the poor and the middle class.

It is out of this climate of rising expectations that the Sandinista Front (FSLN) insurgency arose to oppose Somoza and began to expand and mature. In 1967 the CIA in its "SECRET" Special National Intelligence Estimate #83.3-67, entitled "The Political Prospects for Nicaragua in the Next Year or So," stated of the still then infant group:

> There is a Castro-oriented organization, the Sandinista Front of National Liberation (FSLN), which has from time to time fielded guerrilla bands and had some success in carrying out individual terrorist acts and robberies. FSLN membership is small, probably fewer than 100. These include some members trained in insurgency in Cuba and Guatemala. **Although the Castro government has proclaimed its support for armed revolution in Nicaragua, there is no tangible evidence of present direct Cuban support for the movement**.[277] The FSLN's present capabilities for conducting armed insurrection appear to be small. In August 1967, National Guard patrols killed some members of an FSLN band encountered in the mountainous north-central area. Other guerrillas, under FSLN leader, Carlos Fonseca Amador, are being sought by the Guard.[278]

In 1969 the FSLN issued a letter of intent to the Nicaraguan people. "The Historic Program of the FSLN" contained statements about everything from religious beliefs to foreign policy. It was a rather militant document; it rang of Marxist influences but was not decidedly Marxist in content. On the topic of civil war in Nicaragua the document stated:

> We have concluded that the triumph of the Sandinista people's revolution and the overthrow of the regime that is the enemy of the people will take place through the development of a hard-fought and prolonged people's war.[279]

This is, perhaps, a statement that the Sandinistas believed in the Maoist theory of protracted war over time. The Historic program also stated a belief that both the proletarians and the peasants would fight the war for liberation. Perhaps another statement of Maoist intent for the FSLN, because Soviet Marxist doctrine usually only included the industrial workforce, not the agrarian peasants as the target class for their revolutionary pronouncements.

With the occurrence of a devastating earthquake in 1972, the Nicaraguan economy began to falter. Rising oil prices, a sharp increase in interest rates, and the devaluation of the dollar (to which the Nicaraguan Cordoba was pegged) further accelerated the decline. Disaffection with Somoza's handling of international earthquake relief funds (the lion's share of the money went to the dictator's family firms) helped the FSLN to garner more broad-based support in the effort to overthrow Somoza. The Nicaraguan Roman Catholic Church, while never fully embracing the FSLN, proved to be a valuable partner in the building of anti-Somoza coalition.

The FSLN grew bolder. On December 27, 1974 Contreras Escobar and a number of FSLN members seized Los Robles, the home of a former cabinet minister, where a reception was being given for the US ambassador. The ambassador had departed before the attack. In exchange for several important hostages, the Nicaraguan government agreed to free jailed guerrillas, pay ransom, and provide safe passage to Cuba for the terrorists and freed prisoners.

In a 1976 "Intelligence Information Cable," the unknown CIA analyst/writer displayed a reversal of the view held by the authors of Special National Intelligence Estimate #83.3-67 (above). The cable dated 4 May 1976 stated in part:

> Nicaragua's only active terrorist organization is the Sandinist National Liberation Front (FSLN) which is Cuban oriented and dependent on Cuba for foreign training assistance. The FSLN, however, has representatives throughout Central America and Mexico and has traditionally tried to maintain contact with terrorist organizations in neighboring countries.[280]

This change of viewpoint could have represented the discovery of new information proving Cuban support of the FSLN, or it could have represented the winning of a power struggle within the CIA by those holding the view that the Sandinistas were Cuban surrogates. It could have been circumstance or politics. Whatever the case, the cable represents a significant watershed, because after this time the FSLN is often, though not always, referred to in CIA literature as Cuban sponsored.

This statement of FSLN dependency on Cuba represents a somewhat conservative view of the situation in Nicaragua and it pervades the CIA writing of the 70s and the 80s. There are, however, numerous exceptional notes in the documents about Castro's hesitancy in fully embracing the Sandinistas. Also, a lack of Cuban overseas and military support for the FSLN is noted in numerous places (particularly in the 70s). Clearly some in the CIA were drawing stark boundaries with the FSLN, and this was years before the advent of the Reagan administration, which was oft criticized for harsh Central America policy.

On October 13, 1977 the guerrillas struck at National Guard units in two widely separated areas (near the Costa Rican boarder and the boarder with Honduras). Four days later the Sandinistas hit Guard units around the Capitol City of Managua and at the town of Masaya. Fifteen soldiers and 14 guerrillas were killed in the skirmishes, which were the first significant attacks since the operation against Los Robles.[281]

In January of 1978, in the capital city of Managua, unidentified gunmen assassinated Pedro Joaquin Chamorro. Chamorro was the prominent owner-publisher of *La Prensa*, the only opposition newspaper in Nicaragua. He had owned *La Prensa* since 1952 and it has never been determined who killed him. It was widely assumed at the time that the killing was linked to the Somoza dictatorship and his death added fuel to the Sandinista cause. His wife, Violetta Barrios de Chamorro, remained a leading figure in Nicaraguan politics. For a time she worked with the Sandinistas on the five-person junta that ruled the country after Somoza's defeat. Remaining on the junta until being forced out by the FSLN, Chamorro began to side with the Contras in diametric opposition to the FSLN. In 1990 she became the democratically elected president of Nicaragua following 11 years of Sandinista rule.

On August 22, another milestone along the path to FSLN victory over Somoza was achieved. A band of about 40 guerrillas under the command of Eden Pastora "Commander Zero" captured the Nicaraguan National Palace and some 1,500 hostages. The band of raiders held the palace until the 24th when they were granted their demands of release of political prisoners, a cash ransom, and free passage to Panama. The departure of the Sandinista force from Nicaragua was jubilant, according to *The Washington Post*:

> Thousands lined the route to the airport cheering the guerrillas as they drove past. The crowds chanted "Down with Somoza!" and "Somoza to the gallows."[282]

CIA documents from this time frame demonstrate the general increasing intensity of FSLN operations. From a 1978 summary we read:

> FSLN recruitment is, if anything, intensifying ... new adherents are being taken on board in Costa Rica so quickly that they are being incorporated directly into FSLN urban and rural units without training. Indicative of decreased emphasis on ideology by the leading FSLN faction, the new recruits are given little screening other than to determine that they are anti-Somoza.[283]

The Sandinistas were finally able to garner broad-based support, outside of traditional Marxist-Leninist circles. The governments of Panama and Venezuela both offered some support in terms of money and arms to the Sandinistas. Also in 1978, in its classified literature, the CIA said of support to the FSLN from within the Nicaraguan political scene:

> The Sandinistas' chief link to other anti-Somoza organizations has been through the Group of 12, a collection of prominent professionals formed in Costa Rica last year but now openly campaigning against Somoza in Nicaragua. Members of the group have lobbied for acceptance of the Sandinistas as a legitimate element in the overall opposition movement. At least two of the group of 12 have been members of the FSLN, and others have sons who are Sandinistas. While in Costa Rica, members of the Terciario faction [of the FSLN] worked closely with the Group of 12 in planning guerrilla operations as well as propaganda and fund-raising activities.[284]

The description of the situation and its details continued in the same CIA document:

> Resistance is spreading in the sense that more towns have been sites of serious anti-government attacks and violence...
> ...Since their formation in the early 1960s, the Sandinistas have looked to Cuba for ideological inspiration, strategic guidance, tactical training, material support, and sanctuary. In the last few years, however, Cuba appears to have declined repeated Sandinista appeals for money, arms, and increased training outside Cuba. Havana has apparently concentrated its

> material support on training in Cuba and related expenses, including transportation and documentation. The bulk of our reliable evidence to date points to a role, but we believe it would stop short of a direct military participation.
>
> The Cubans were cautious in their dealings with the FSLN because they have been skeptical about the group's capabilities and sensitive to international opinion. Havana has insisted that the FSLN first purge itself of factionalism, establish a unified leadership base, and prove itself under fire.
>
> The Cubans have, however, apparently increased their contacts with Central American groups. At least three times this year, a high-level Cuban representative has tried to meet in Costa Rica with FSLN leaders to help iron out their factional differences, but there are no indications that he succeeded in bringing all three groups together... More recently, a member of the Guatemalan Communist Party related that Havana intends to hold a meeting at the end of the year of all the Communist parties of Central America to plan a coordinated campaign against Somoza, but the details of the campaign were not spelled out.[285]

We see then, that by 1978, the FSLN had mustered considerable support from within Nicaragua, and perhaps some on-again, off-again support from Cuba. It was beginning to become clear that the Somoza dictatorship would not last. The battle for Nicaragua was developing into a full-blown insurgency. At this juncture, the Carter administration acted to put further distance between the US and Somoza.

President Carter and US Ambassador to Nicaragua, Lawrence Pezzulla, made several abortive attempts to bring the Organization of American States (OAS) to implement a solution that would bring forces more moderate than the FSLN to power in Nicaragua. Unilateral American action was considered out of the question in the post-Vietnam policy environment of the late 70s. Direct American efforts to prop-up Somoza would only have been seen as evil and neo-colonial in nature. On the other end of the spectrum, forceful action to remove Somoza, on the part of the US, would have met strong opposition from conservatives in the Congress.

In the background, so the declassified CIA records state, Castro put on a full-court-press to unify the three divergent factions of the FSLN under his leadership. According to a classified intelligence memorandum of 2 May 79:

> The Castro regime apparently concluded by at least last fall that prospects for revolutionary upheaval in Central America over the next decade or so had markedly improved largely because of the weakened position of Nicaragua's Somoza and the ripple effect his removal would have on other countries in Central America. As a result, Cuba has intensified its attempts to unify insurgent groups not only in Nicaragua—where Cuba has concentrated its efforts—but in Guatemala and El Salvador as well.[286]

The document continued under the subtitle "promoting FSLN Unity":

> Fidel Castro's recent discussions with FSLN leaders may lead to more active Cuban support to the FSLN. In early March, leaders of the three major FSLN factions traveled to Cuba to meet with Castro. The Cuban leader is said to have spent nearly 48 hours over a four day period helping to hammer out a basis for cooperation. As a result of the meeting a unified FSLN directorate was established containing three members from each faction.[287]

By June of 1979, the end of Somoza rule was visible. On the 26th of that month Assistant Secretary of State Viron P. Vaky said, "too much blood, too much hate, too much polarization have occurred for"[288] reconciliation between Somoza and the opposition to be possible. An abortive attempt had already been made on the part of the Carter Administration to head off an FSLN rise to power through the use of OAS peacekeepers. This did not come to pass and the Sandinistas routed the National Guard in extensive combat operations.

On July 20, 1979, the Sandinistas were in power in Managua. Somoza and his National Guard had been routed. Upon assuming control, the FSLN included members of moderate factions in the new government. These forces had helped bring about the revolution. This coalition included business leaders and figures from the Roman Catholic Church as well as members of non-socialist political factions. The government expropriated some newspapers and radio stations and others continued to operate under various degrees of censorship. In spite of the non-Sandinist trimmings on the government in Managua, the nine-man Sandinista directorate, as established with Castro's aid, held the real power. In the post revolutionary structure of government set up by the FSLN, non-Sandinist factions could only make recommendations to the "Commandantes" on the directorate.

On the right of American politics, anything to do with the Sandinistas was suspect. The media covered this angle of the story, sometimes on the front pages, as in the August 12 issue of *The Washington Post*, which carried the following lead:

> **Quito, Ecuador, Aug. 11**—The revolutionary government of Nicaragua warned today that if it does not receive financial assistance from Western countries to buy arms, it will seek military aid "from the socialist bloc or elsewhere."

As a result of these accusations against the Sandinistas, and perhaps also because of past feelings of goodwill toward the Somoza dictatorship, foreign policy critics like Georgetown University professor, Jeane Kirkpatrick,[289] dealt with the FSLN and the Carter Administration in stark and harsh terms. In a November 1979 article in *Commentary* magazine Kirkpatrick stated:

> The failure of the Carter administration's foreign policy is now clear to everyone except its architects, and even they must entertain private doubts, from time to time....[290]

She defended the bygone Somoza autocracy by saying further that, "decades, if not centuries, are normally required for people to acquire the necessary disciplines and habits"[291] (required for democratic government to take root in a given society). The professor continued that "although there is no instance of a revolutionary 'socialist' or Communist society being democratized, right-wing autocracies do sometimes evolve into democracies."[292] The key for Kirkpatrick was in the liberalization of autocracy, not its replacement by revolution.

According to the CIA documents written at this time, the Sandinistas welcomed "Cuban economic and military technicians"[293] into Nicaragua "after the coup" and in October. At roughly the same time, the roots of a force that would clash with the Sandinistas over most of a decade were taking shape. On 5 December 1979 the CIA noted the establishment of "counterrevolutionary activities of former members of the Nicaraguan

National Guard in (neighboring) Honduras."[294] From the term counterrevolutionary came the name of the "Contras." From the CIA's own documents we see this Contra army in its infancy and that it had firm roots in the Somoza Guard.

While the CIA tracked the forming Contras, it also followed Cuban (and once removed, Soviet) designs on Latin America. In December 1979, a CIA employee (whose name is still classified) stated:

> El Salvador and Guatemala appear to head the list of countries where Cuba thinks the Nicaraguan experience might be repeated. While continuing to offer paramilitary training and other forms of support to revolutionary groups, the Cubans will urge the opposition factions in these two countries to join forces.[295]

In the meantime, President Carter and the Congress created and enacted foreign aid legislation that sent over $100 million dollars to rebuild Nicaragua. US supporters of the aid package hoped that the infusion of capital would make-up for recent neglect of Nicaragua and would prevent the Sandinista's already anti-North American views from becoming pro-Soviet. Money was flowing within weeks of the July 20, 1979 ascendancy of the FSLN. In comparison, aid to other countries in the region averaged between 4-10 times less per capita, per year.

In 1980 a revision to the 1974 Hughes-Ryan amendment (which required the president to notify 8 full committees of the House and Senate of any covert operation) was enacted. This reform of post-Vietnam era policy came in the form of the Intelligence Oversight Act of 1980. Key provisions of the law were as follows:

> 1) The president would keep the House and Senate select committees informed of all intelligence activities. This provision required notification of Congress, not permission. Under certain conditions, in the case of sensitive operations, as few as 8 key legislators would have to be informed. This provision required the president to issue a "finding" determining that covert operations were in the interest of national security.
>
> 2) The president would furnish any information requested by the Select Committees.
>
> 3) The president would report any illegal activity conducted

> by the intelligence community in a timely manner to the Select Committees.

Under this more workable relationship the president would again have the ability to launch covert operations. It would come into play most forcefully during the Reagan administration.

In the meantime, the attempts at reconciling differences with the Sandinistas did not work out for the Carter Administration. Prior to leaving office in January 1981, President Carter suspended economic aid to the Nicaraguan government. Evidence of Nicaraguan support for the Marxist revolutionaries in El Salvador, in the form of weapons shipments gave him no other choice.[296] Further, the Sandinistas allowed the Salvadoran Marxists (the FMLN) to maintain a headquarters in the Capitol City of Managua. In addition there was evidence of thousands of Cuban teachers and hundreds of Cuban/East European advisors in the country helping the Sandinista Party to consolidate power. At this time the Carter administration approved a program of covert political action in Nicaragua. Under the program the CIA would channel moneys to pro-democratic political, labor, and religious groups inside Nicaragua.[297]

The New President's Mindset

The transition from Reagan to Carter Administration was abrupt. Détente was not just bruised and bleeding, but dead. Ronald Reagan came into office with a brave new agenda for radical change in American domestic and foreign policy. In his inaugural we can see the thoughts of the president on such issues as inflation and the evils of government. Mixed in with his remarks on this topic was the somewhat vague statement that "we as Americans have the capacity now, as we've had in the past, to do whatever needs to be done,[298] to preserve this last and greatest bastion of freedom."[299] To Reagan, America was isolated and besieged on all sides by inflation, unemployment, big government, and the Soviets (and their allies).

He continued more with somewhat more elaboration in the area of foreign affairs that,

> as for the enemies of freedom, those who are potential adversaries, they will be reminded that peace is the highest aspiration of the American people. We will negotiate for it, sacrifice for it; we will not surrender for it, now or ever.

> Our reluctance for conflict should not be misjudged as a failure of will. When action is required to preserve our national security, we will act. We will maintain sufficient strength to prevail if need be, knowing that if we do so we have the best chance of never having to use that strength.
>
> Above all, we must realize that no arsenal or no weapon in the arsenals of the world is so formidable as the will and moral courage of free men and women. It is a weapon our adversaries in today's world do not have. Let that be understood by those who practice terrorism and prey upon their neighbors.[300]

A little more than two years later, perhaps because of being hardened through his dealings with the Soviets, President Reagan said:

> As good Marxist-Leninists, the Soviets have openly and publicly declared that the only morality they recognize is that which will further their cause, which is world revolution ... Morality is entirely subordinate to the interests of class war. And everything is moral that is necessary for the annihilation of the old, exploiting social order and for uniting the proletariat.[301]

To Reagan, and to many others, the Cold War with the Soviets was ideological war, based upon the tenets of Marxism-Leninism as expressed by Marx in the 1800s and Lenin during the Russian Civil War—long before the end of WWII.

The administration would use a new tool in the ideological Cold War against the Soviets and their allies. This tool would be the "Reagan doctrine." Support for anti-Communist insurgencies, guerrilla armies fighting Communist governments, would be the cornerstone of this new policy. The doctrine would be applied most notably in Nicaragua and Afghanistan, but would also see utilization in Angola.

The Reagan Administration Organizes for Conflict

Upon taking office, the Reagan administration was faced with three possible courses of action in Nicaragua:

A) Peaceful coexistence with the Sandinistas—take no action.

B) Bring pressure on Nicaragua until the FSLN agreed to expel Cuban/Soviet military personnel and stop its support of regional insurgent movements.

C) Intervene and overthrow the Sandinista government, or force such a change in its nature that pluralistic democracy develops and Nicaragua moves out of the Cuban/Soviet orbit.

It was the Reagan administration position that Nicaragua under the FSLN was developing along the lines of Castro's Cuba, and further that a Cuba model state on the American mainland was an unacceptable threat to US national security. The presence of Cuban and East European security advisors, 2,000 Cuban teachers conducting a "literacy crusade," and a sizable infusion of Soviet military equipment to the FSLN party's army all pointed toward a totalitarian Cubanization being the future for Nicaragua. Considering these trends in FSLN policies, it was considered by the administration unlikely that diplomatic initiatives such as negotiations alone could succeed (without the application of economic, paramilitary, and military pressures).[302]

Secretary of State, and former US Army General, Alexander Haig, tended to support the argument for direct American intervention. Three times, between June 1981 and January 1982, he put forward proposals that went so far as to call for a US naval blockade of Cuba and "go to the source."[303] Officials within the State Department and the Joint Chiefs of Staff opposed Haig's ideas on the grounds that they would destroy American credibility as a force for reform in Central America and because of the fear of being drawn into a protracted conflict that the American public would not support.[304]

President Reagan eventually adopted a policy that encompassed options B and C above. Initially, the administration offered the Sandinistas a deal, stating that expulsion of Cuban/Soviet advisors and withdrawal of Sandinista support for regional insurgencies would have been acceptable. In return the US would agree to non-intervention in Nicaragua's internal affairs, strict enforcement of US neutrality laws, and the renewal of economic aid to Nicaragua. When the Sandinistas twice rejected this offer, a policy of pressure to gain Sandinista concessions was initiated.[305] On December 1, 1981, President Reagan signed a finding authorizing the CIA "to support and conduct paramilitary operations against the Cuban presence and Cuban-Sandinista support infrastructure in Nicaragua and elsewhere in Central America."[306] In conjunction with these covert operations in the region the president ordered the "Big Pine" military maneuvers to apply overt pressure.

At this time, a Restricted Interagency Group (RIG) directed Reagan administration policy. This group, which met at the State Department, included representatives from the departments of State, Defense, and Justice, as well as the CIA, NSC, and Joint Chiefs of Staff. Initially headed by National Security Advisor Robert Mcfarland, later by Assistant Secretary of State for Inter-American Affairs Thomas O. Enders and his successor Langhorne Motley, the RIG provided options to the National Security Planning Group from which President Reagan chose. The RIG also served to coordinate policy in the region among the various agencies and departments of the US government. However, most of the RIGs fell into disuse in favor of more informal associations among administration officials.[307]

Reagan and the Sandinistas Clash

Patience with the Sandinistas began to wear thin, when their promise of free elections did not materialize. Elections were delayed at first for six moths, then they were further put off until "sometime in 1985." Allies from business and the press, who had joined the FSLN in its fight against Somoza, began to flee the revolution when it did not deliver on its promise of democracy. Some of these former anti-Somoza coalition members even joined hands with the former Somoza National Guard members organizing in Honduras and Miami. Others formed independent anti-Sandinista organizations like the Revolutionary Democratic Front (ARDE) under Eden Pastora.

In April 1981, the CIA outlined the case against the FSLN in its major report entitled "The Sandinistas and the Creation of a One-Party State." The report remains heavily redacted, that is to say there are portions of it that are still classified. From its largely unclassified introduction it reads:

> Since seizing power, the Sandinista National Liberation Front (FSLN) has transformed a national triumph into a partisan victory, strengthened the belief of Castro that armed struggle is the only route to power for the left, and put Nicaragua well on the road to becoming the first authoritarian Marxist state in Central America. The Sandinistas move toward total dominance has nonetheless been restrained by three factors: a desire to prevent international condemnation, a need for major private-sector participation in rebuilding the economy, and a reliance

> on Western financial assistance.
>
> The Sandinistas have avoided a complete crackdown on opposition elements, choosing instead to circumscribe the activities of moderate forces through tactics ranging from harassment to concerted violence. This strategy has given the Sandinistas time to consolidate their control through the application of a Cuban-inspired institutional framework designed to protect against foreign and domestic threats and eventually to eradicate all democratic forces.
>
> The cornerstone of FSLN power is a comprehensive security apparatus boasting an Army of at least 20,000, a fledgling Air Force, a Militia exceeding 50,000, and a Ministry of Interior that has assumed the role of national intimidator. Mass organizations based on the Cuban model compliment the security forces and serve as propaganda vehicles and as shock troops to intimidate opposition elements.
>
> The Sandinistas have also taken over most of the news media and control 48 of 59 radio stations, two of its three daily newspapers, and both television channels. In addition they are attempting systematically to mold the younger generation in the Sandinista image.[308]

Sandinista justice was another area opponents criticized. Interior Minister, Commandante Tomas Borge, developed formal procedures for the annihilation of opponents to the FSLN. Under Borge, the Ministry of Interior was far from a bureau of national parks; it controlled the FSLN secret police and other organs of state security. From a summary written in 1985, we can see what was going on in Nicaragua in 1981 with regard to prisoners of war:

> In 1981, admitting privately that the indiscriminate executions had been wide spread since the Sandinista triumph of 1979, Borge issued a directive reserving to himself and his second in command, Deputy Interior Minister Luis Carrion, the authority to apply "special measures"—a euphemism for execution. Borge and Carrion have sanctioned the killing of prisoners, dissidents, suspected insurgent collaborators, and Indians and peasants who resisted Sandinista policies. They have also protected government officials involved in such abuses, even when the

perpetrators had not received proper authorization.[309]

Further complicating the situation for the Reagan administration was the fact that the Communist Bloc was sending increasing amounts of aid to Nicaragua in 1981. The total of aid from the USSR, Bulgaria, East Germany, Czechoslovakia, and Cuba for that year was a staggering $171 million. This aid came in the form of merchandise and currency credits.[310]

In addition to receiving aid from the Communist Bloc, the FSLN served to pass along portions of this aid to Marxist guerrillas in the region. According to the CIA,

> in early January 1981, Honduran police intercepted a shipment of arms concealed in a large truck en route from Nicaragua. The police caught six individuals unloading weapons, who identified themselves as Salvadorans and members of the International Support Commission of the Salvadoran Popular Liberation Forces (FPL). They had in their possession a large number of altered and forged Honduran, Costa Rican, and Salvadoran passports and other documents. This one truck contained over 100 M-16 automatic rifles, fifty 81 mm mortar rounds, approximately 100,000 rounds of 5.56 mm ammunition, machine gun belts, field packs, and first aid kits. Over 50 of these M-16 rifles have been traced to US stocks in Vietnam.[311]

The presence of captured US M-16s, whose source was the then Communist nation of Vietnam being exported from FSLN-dominated Nicaragua to support Marxist guerrillas in El Salvador, shows a high degree of coordination among various pro-Marxist parties involved. Finds like this one tended to prove the Reagan administration thesis that there was an international Communist conspiracy operating, and that it was a force behind events in Central America.

Faced with a building case against the Sandinistas, Ronald Reagan acted on 1 December 1981 to issue a finding under the intelligence oversight requirements then in place. The finding authorized "the Agency (CIA) to support and conduct … paramilitary operations against the Cuban presence in Nicaragua and Cuban-Sandinista support infrastructure in Nicaragua and elsewhere in Central America."[312] From the heavily redacted documentation of the matter we read that the finding further outlined that the Reagan administration, through the CIA, would,

> provide paramilitary support, equipment, and training assistance to Nicaraguan resistance groups as a means to (induce) the Sandinistas and Cubans and their allies to cease support for insurgencies (in the region); to hamper Cuban/Nicaraguan arms trafficking; to divert Nicaragua's resources and energies from support to Central American guerrilla movements; and to bring the Sandinistas into meaningful negotiations and constructive agreements...[313]

Until around the time of this finding, there were never more than 600-1000 resistance troops in armed opposition to the Sandinistas; most of these were former Somoza National Guard members organized under the banner of the Legion of the 15th of September (the anniversary day of Nicaragua's independence from Spain).[314] The chief activity of these troops had centered on training to convert their dubious counter-insurgency experience into the skills of a guerrilla army. Only occasionally did they foray into Nicaragua from their operational bases in Honduras.

At the outset of the finding, the CIA estimated that it would take from 6-18 months before the Contras[315] became an effective fighting force. To bridge this gap, a force referred to in the press as Unilaterally Controlled Latino Assets (UCLAs) were recruited from the Honduran military and from other Latin-American countries. Some of the missions conducted by the UCLA forces included US personnel. The purpose of these forces was to hit Cuban and other strategic targets in Nicaragua that were contributing to the flow of arms to the Marxist revolutionaries in El Salvador.

Simultaneously with the undertaking of the UCLA missions, the CIA began funding and training the small Nicaraguan Resistance groups already in place in Honduras. The former connection of many of the resistance leaders with Somoza and his brutal tactics would be a continuing liability for US policy in the region. It was at this point, in late 1981 and early 1982, that three significant watersheds occurred in the development of the Contra force.

First, internal strife increased the flow of refugees from Nicaragua to Honduras. In early 1982, observers indicated that as many as 1000 Nicaraguans were joining the resistance movements monthly. Most of these new recruits had nothing to do with the Somoza Guard and, in fact, many of them wanted nothing to do with the former Guard members.

Second, a substantial number of former Sandinista officials began to align themselves with the resistance. Most notable of the early defectors were Ferdanando Chomoro and Alfonso Robelo. Chomoro, who had fought against Somoza during the revolution of 1979, now commanded a small but effective group of anti-Sandinista guerrillas known as FARN. Robelo had been a member of the post Somoza ruling junta in cooperation with the Sandinistas immediately following the revolution. He aligned himself with the groups then training in Honduras.

Third, on recommendation of the CIA, the resistance groups formed the FDN (Nicaraguan Democratic Front). The political leadership of the front included many former officials of the Sandinista coalition government. During this time, three former Somoza Guard members who occupied senior positions in the resistance (the Chief of Staff, the Chief of Intelligence, and a senior field commander) were executed for war crimes, abuse of their own troops, and theft. This change of command was the start of a significant and sweeping trend; by 1984 only 13 (23%) of the regional commanders of the FDN were former Guard members; 27 (48%) were former Sandinistas.[316] Over the years the FDN typically consisted of 10-20,000 troops under arms at any one time.

While the number of armed resistance groups and the various coalitions formed are too numerous to name, two non-FDN resistance groups began active military operations against the Sandinistas at this time. Misura, a group of Native Indian resistance fighters, was made up of refugees from Nicaragua's geographically and culturally isolated Atlantic coast population. The Indians resented the presence of Cuban teachers and Sandinistas in the traditionally semi-autonomous region. While never fielding more than 1000 troops at any one time, Misura did pursue intermittent alliances with the FDN and received some American aid.

The second non-FDN resistance group of note was Eden Pastora's ARDE. Pastora, a Sandinista hero of the revolution, broke with the FSLN in 1982 and took up arms in southern Nicaragua. ARDE was headquartered in Costa Rica and was composed of up to 6000 troops at its height. ARDE received some US aid through third parties. Reportedly, larger sums of aid were initially denied to ARDE because of Pastora's refusal to align with the FDN. In May of 1986, after several attempts on Pastora's life, he went into retirement. Six of the 8 ARDE commanders then joined the FDN in an organization known as the UNO (United Nicaraguan Opposition).[317]

By late 1982, about a year after President Reagan's finding,

Congressional opposition to US support for the resistance had grown. The opponents of Reagan's policies stated concern that US policy would push Honduras and Nicaragua into a war. Further, critics pointed out that the US still officially recognized the FSLN as the governing party in Nicaragua and still allowed unrestricted trade with the regime. The administration was accused of waging an "illegal war" on a country whose government the US still recognized. The goals of Reagan administration policy in the region were also questioned.

At this point, a paradox that would plague US policy in the coming years became apparent. In March 1982, in an attempt to elicit public support and congressional consensus behind US measures against the Sandinistas, Reagan administration officials (Admiral Bobby Inman, Deputy Director of the CIA, and John Hughes, a senior DIA analyst) briefed the press on the military buildup then taking place in Nicaragua. The presence of Cuban and Warsaw Pact military advisors and the increasing flow of Soviet military equipment into Nicaragua were stressed.

According to the briefing, the Sandinista military, which was larger than any other force in the region, posed a direct threat to regional stability and thus American interests. It was stated that the Sandinistas also posed an indirect threat. The Sandinistas using their superior military to protect Nicaragua while using the homeland as a base for covert support of Marxist insurgents in other countries created this indirect threat. The clear implication in the briefing was that the situation in Nicaragua was unacceptable and contrary to American interests, the means by which such activity could be stopped were not mentioned.

From a CIA briefing paper that dates to the same month as the press briefing we can read some of the highlights of the case against the FSLN:

> Nicaragua's armor and artillery have been greatly expanded, giving it a distinct advantage in both over any of its neighbors. This new equipment includes Soviet-made 57 mm antitank guns and 152 mm howitzers, East German military trucks, Soviet-made T-55 tanks with 100 mm guns, and armored personnel carriers, river crossing equipment for the tanks, which gives Nicaragua an offensive capability. In addition to the land force buildup, the Sandinistas have acquired ZPU-4 and ZU-23 antiaircraft guns and SA-7 surface-to-air missiles. There are Nicaraguan pilots training on MIGs in Cuba and Bulgaria, and

> they will probably return to their country this year. In addition, four airfields—Sandino International Airport, Puerto Cabezas, Monteliner, and Bluefields—currently are being expanded and improved to handle sophisticated fighter aircraft.[318]

Some six months after the Reagan finding, press reports of the UCLA missions were common. It is likely that these missions were the unmentioned "stick" seen as necessary to correct the problems outlined in the Inman/Hughes briefing. In the press, the CIA had been tied to the dynamiting of several strategic bridges inside Nicaragua. These missions were the subject of testimony by Director of the CIA, William Casey, in December 1982. Reportedly, in secret testimony, Casey admitted to the CIA connection and characterized the UCLA missions as "harassment" designed to cut the flow of arms to the Marxist revolutionaries in El Salvador.[319]

In this atmosphere of conflict, some members of Congress became fearful that the administration was actually trying to bring down the Sandinista regime and the goal of cutting the flow of arms to El Salvador was being used as a cover. The wounds to the executive-legislative branch relationship suffered during the Vietnam era were not yet healed. In December of 1982, Congress passed the first in a series of legislative measures that restricted the use of US aid to the resistance movements. Known as the Boland amendment, the legislation prevented the Department of Defense and the CIA from "overthrowing the government of Nicaragua or provoking a military exchange between Nicaragua and Honduras."[320]

The congressional debate on the issue of aid to the Contras brought out into the open the paradoxical nature of the reasons behind the Boland amendment. Some members of Congress stated that the resistance could never "win"; thus support for them only delayed a regional negotiated settlement. Yet, it was congressional alarm over press reports that the resistance force had grown to over 4000 men under arms (and the success of the UCLA missions) that caused Congress to enact the Boland amendment.

Further, if the resistance did have a chance to win, the Boland amendment only made it more difficult and a protracted stalemate more likely. Congress escaped responsibility for its actions by purposely leaving the term "overthrow" undefined. DOD and CIA could still conduct operations and support the Contras, at the direction of the president, as long as the stated goal did not include overthrowing the Sandinistas. Thus, the Congress had it both ways, escaping the blame for cutting off the resistance totally, and escaping the guilt of being part of the overthrow of the FSLN government.

By 1983, paramilitary assistance to the Contras remained covert in name only. While elements of the program remained secret until the Iran-Contra Affair Hearings of 1987 (and in fact some of the documentation remains secret to date), the media was, in 1983, carrying regular stories of US support to the resistance. As early as November 1982, *Newsweek* reported the existence of a 4000 man resistance army staging in Honduras with US support. According to the report the force in Honduras received training and equipment from the CIA and its goal was the overthrow of the Sandinistas.[321]

In spite of a stated concern for regional security that Congress was not convinced that the administration was pursuing the proper policy in the region, some members were becoming concerned the administration was attempting to circumvent congressional authority by skirting the Boland amendment. A visit to the region by Senator Patrick Leahy (D-VT) of the Senate Select Committee on Intelligence in January 1983 resulted in the conclusions that,

> the Nicaraguan program was growing beyond that which the (Select) Committee had initially understood to be its parameters, and there was uncertainty in the Executive Branch about United States objectives in Nicaragua, particularly in view of the goals avowed by some of the forces receiving United States support. In addition to raising questions about compliance with the Boland amendment, there seemed to be a lack of coordination between United States diplomatic initiatives, with the program appearing to precede policy, rather than follow it.[322]

These conclusions on the part of the Select Committee had serious implications in regard to the executive gaining support for its Nicaragua policies. One of two key legislative bodies that was required to be notified of covert action, had just expressed that it felt left out in the cold by executive policy. The president appeared to be deceiving the committee as to the goals and scope of the programs involved. Further, the observation that executive policy seemed to be uncoordinated was correct. This lack of coordination was evidenced by the fact that the US still recognized the FSLN as the legitimate government of Nicaragua and normal trade relations were still in effect with that country. Thus, critics of the covert action programs were able to successfully accuse the administration of seeking a solution through hard military means alone and of not making full use of all of the policy tools available.

On August 3 of 1983, DCI William Casey appeared before the Senate Select Committee to outline the latest presidential finding authorizing covert action in Nicaragua. During the same time period, the CIA-backed UCLAs undertook missions to mine several Nicaraguan harbors. In conflict with the requirements for oversight, no mention of the mining was made by the DCI until after the operation became public. In the words of the committee report, the lack of notification "fractured" the fragile consensus that had approved limited aid to the Nicaraguan resistance.

The resulting impasse between the DCI and the 2 congressional committees responsible for oversight lasted until June of 1984 and it stalled efforts of the administration to gain funding for the resistance. A resolution to the standoff came only when Director Casey "apologized profoundly"[323] before the committee and signed a written agreement to abide by the Intelligence Oversight Act of 1980 for the reporting of covert operations.[324] The mining operation also cost the US support overseas. The Sandinistas won an international propaganda victory when they took the case to the World Court at The Hague.

In March 1984, the administration attempted to gain approval for $21 million in supplemental funding for the Contras from the Senate Appropriations Committee. This was done before the Select Committee was notified of a continuing covert operation. The attempt to obtain the funding failed and subsequent securing of approval only happened after Secretary of State, George Shultz, apologized to the Select Committee for the irregular procedure.[325]

Also, as a result of an October 14, 1984 Associated Press piece appearing in *The New York Times*, a low-grade scandal erupted in the press over the CIA sponsorship of a manual for the Contras entitled "Psychological Operations in Guerrilla Warfare" and published under the pseudonym "Tayacan." The manual was loosely referred to as an "assassinations manual" because of its vagueness and anti-democratic overtones that seemed to imply assassination of political figures and infiltration of democratic institutions were to be conducted as a matter of course. From the preface of the manual we can get the overall tone of the manual:

> In effect, the human being must be considered as the priority objective in political war. And viewed as the military target of

> guerrilla warfare, the most critical point of the human being is the mind. Once the mind has been reached, the "political animal" has been vanquished, without necessarily having received any shots.[326]

From chapter 1, section 6 "Control of Meetings and Mass Assemblies" we read a passage that particularly angered some in the American labor movement:

> When the cadres are placed in or recruited from organizations such as labor unions, youth groups, agricultural organizations or professional associations, they will begin to manipulate the groups' objectives. The psychological apparatus of our movement, by means of these internal cadres, will prepare a mental attitude which, at the crucial moment, could become involved in a fury of justified violence.[327]

Also in chapter 1, and in violation of the Boland amendments the manual advocated "overthrow" of the Sandinistas:

> This is the moment in which an overthrow may be achieved and our revolution can come out in the open, requiring the close collaboration of the entire population of the country, and requiring contacts who are rooted in reality.[328]

Some of the most damning of all material came from chapter 3, section five, which reads in part:

> *We could neutralize carefully selected and planned-for targets, such as court judges, cattle judges [jueces de mesta], police or state security officers*, CDS chiefs, etc. For purposes of the psychological effect, it is necessary to take extreme precautions, and it is essential to gather the affected population to attend, take part in the act, and formulate accusations against the oppressor.[329]

In the version of the manual provided to this author by the CIA (under the Freedom Of Information Act, FOIA) the above italicized had been added to the original (I received a photocopy) by hand and the words "translation error" are written in the margin. Further, above the word "neutralize" is written in the word "remove."[330] If we are to believe the anonymous CIA editor, the implication that select officials should be killed was not the result of deliberate vagueness but was the product of a mistake. The CIA, we are to believe, did not want these people "neutralized," but peacefully "removed."

In chapter six comes the suggestion that, "If possible, professional criminals will be hired to carry out specific selective jobs." Thus we see a series of unpalatable, if not illegal in the case of the violations of the Boland amendments, suggestions made by the manual, "Psychological Operations in Guerrilla Warfare." Whatever position one takes on the Nicaraguan revolution and its aftermath, publication of this manual clearly did not represent the "high road" in American foreign policy.

This was not the only manual produced by the CIA for use by the Contras. In 1983 the agency produced the "Human Resource Exploitation Training Manual." It was revised after the disclosure of "Psychological Operations in Guerrilla Warfare" in the press. According to Tom Blanton of the National Security Archive:

> The 1983 manual as declassified included numerous revisions made by CIA apparently in July 1984 in the wake of public revelations about a CIA "assassination" manual ["Psychological Operations in Guerrilla Warfare"] used by the Nicaraguan contras. The revisions added a full page following the table of contents labeled, "Prohibition against the use of force," and overwrote in hand-printed letters most of the manual's references to "coercive techniques." For example, the 1983 sentence on the second page of the introduction read, "While we do not stress the use of coercive techniques, we do want to make you aware of them and the proper way to use them." The 1984 revision overwrote "do not stress" with the word "deplore" and replaced the phrase "the proper way to use them" with the phrase "so that you may avoid them."[331]

There was a low-key CIA inquiry into the matter with some congressional oversight. Only two relatively low-level officers were disciplined over the matter. The agency somehow avoided a major disaster over the gaff. A real firestorm over the Contras was yet to come.

Congress Cuts Off Aid: Private Funds Sought

The net result of these disputes was a congressional suspension of aid to the Nicaraguan resistance. In October 1984, the House prohibited funding to the resistance while the Senate had approved funds. In order to resolve the dispute the legislators conferenced and agreed to terminate funding until February 28, 1985. Further funding would only be reinstated if the executive branch met the following conditions:

> 1) The president submits to Congress a report,
>
> a). Stating that the government of Nicaragua is providing material or monetary support to anti-government forces engage in military or paramilitary operations in El Salvador or other Central American countries;
>
> b) Analyzing the military significance of such support.
>
> c) Stating the president has determined that assistance for military or paramilitary operations prohibited by (the legislation) is necessary.
>
> d) Explaining the goals of United States policy for the Central America region and how the proposed assistance would further such goals, including the achievement of peace and security in Central America through a comprehensive, verifiable and enforceable agreement...
>
> 2) A joint resolution approving assistance for military or paramilitary operations in Nicaragua is enacted.[332]

The legislators further stipulated that:

> During the fiscal year 1985, no funds available to the Central Intelligence Agency, the Department of Defense, or any other agency or entity of the United States Government involved in intelligence activities may be obligated or expended for the purpose of which could have the effect of supporting directly, or indirectly, military or paramilitary operations in Nicaragua by any nation group or organization, movement, or individual.[333]

As a result of these restrictions, CIA headquarters sent instructions to its field stations in the region, "to cease and desist with actions that can be construed to be providing any type of support, either direct or indirect" to the

Nicaraguan resistance.

As 1984 wore on and relations with the Congress deteriorated, it became apparent to members of the National Security Council staff that funding for the resistance would not be forthcoming. This posed the possibility that the then 12,000-man army in the filed would be abandoned and left without food, medical support, or munitions. NSC staff member, Lieutenant Colonel Oliver North, was particularly concerned with the implications of "a Contra wipeout and an American walk away and write off."[334] North, a United States Marine Officer detailed to the National Security Council staff, sought to find means to keep the Contras viable when congressional support expired. During the August 1984 Republican National Convention in Dallas, North met with people who would direct efforts to fund the resistance over the next two years.

They were Robert Owen, resistance leader Aldofo Calero, and retired General Jack Singlaub. Owen was a Stanford University graduate and had worked for Senator Dan Quale from 1982-83. Prior to that he had worked in the US refugee assistance program in Thailand "long enough to be dangerous, yet not long enough to become an expert in what went on over there" (in his own words). After leaving the employ of Senator Quale, Owen worked for the public relations firm Gray and Company until 1984, when he was approached by the FDN to represent the Nicaraguan resistance.[335]

Calero, a former supporter of the Sandinista revolution, then served as the director of the FDN. He served as a contact between the FDN, Congress, and the Reagan administration in the efforts to gain support for the resistance.

General Singlaub, retired from the US Army, served as the Chairman of the World Anti-Communist League (WACL) and the United States Council for World Freedom. These ultra-conservative groups were active in support to the resistance and other anti-Marxist groups worldwide. Singlaub would use his international contacts to provide money and arms to the Contras.

While according to North, he never solicited donations, he did serve to coordinate donors from third countries and private sources with the needs of the resistance. While not ordered to engage in these activities, North kept his superiors (National Security Advisor Bud McFarland—and later Admiral John Poindexter, and DCI William Casey) informed of his actions.[336] Under the questioning of the Joint Select Committee investigating Iran Contra North revealed how the network functioned:

Mr. Neilds: (referring to a document from North to McFarland dated November 1984, entered into evidence in the hearings) And you see at the top it said, "The FDN is in urgent need of near-term financing; approximately $2 million—"

Lt. Col. North: Right—

Mr. Neilds: "For the purpose of our files, ammunitions and boots for new volunteers." And then lower it says, "Singlaub will be here tomorrow. With your permission I will ask him to approach ______ embassy urging that they proceed with their offer."[337]

Lt. Col. North: Yes, I would point out that it says, "proceed with the offer," it does not say, "proceed with what I asked for."

Mr. Neilds: But you asked General Singlaub, did you not, to go back and proceed with their offer?

Lt. Col. North: Yes, but…[338]

Further testimony illuminated North's role in coordinating support from private citizens.

Mr. Neilds: Well, you asked Joseph Coors for $65,000—

Lt. Col. North: Wrong.

Mr. Neilds: And a Maul airplane, didn't you?

Lt. Col. North: Not so. He offered the money, and I told him where he could send it. And a plane was bought with it, and it flies today in support of the resistance, unless the Sandinistas have shot it down.[339]

The money to which North referred was deposited into a Swiss bank account set up by retired US Air Force Major General Richard Secord. He had served in the first term of the Reagan administration, maintained the accounts from which the resistance drew to purchase arms, medicine, and other supplies.

Lt. Col. North also served to provide advice and intelligence vital to the conduct of the FDN's operations. Robert Owen served to carry messages between North in Washington and the resistance leaders in Honduras and Costa Rica. These messages included intelligence information that North obtained from the CIA and/or DOD:[340]

Mr. Egglston: Do you know why the mission was not

undertaken?

Mr. Owen: It was felt it was probably too risky.

Mr. Egglston: Was the decision not to undertake the mission made after the maps were received, reviewed?

Mr. Owen: I believe so, yes.

Mr. Egglston: Let me ask you, did you have any idea or did you know at the time where Col. North obtained the maps?

Mr. Owen: I don't know specifically, but I think he said something like he got them across the river.

Mr. Egglston: And is that an expression Colonel North used on occasion?

Mr. Owen: Occasionally.

Mr. Egglston: And where did you—when he used those expressions—where did you understand him to be referring to?

Mr. Owen: Either the Pentagon or to Langley.

Mr. Egglston: and Langley is the location of the CIA?

Mr. Owen: Yes it is.

Mr. Egglston: To whom did you take the maps on that occasion.

Mr. Owen: I flew to Honduras and met with Adolfo Colero at Tegucigalpa.

Mr. Egglston: You provided him with the maps?

Mr. Owen: Yes, I did.

In mid-1985 the Reagan administration continued efforts to obtain congressional funding for support of the Contras. Members of the administration submitted reports required under the stipulations for the resumption of aid. The president also sought to allay fears that the paramilitary operations were preceding policy.

On May 1, 1985, President Reagan signed an Executive Order stating "that the policies of the government of Nicaragua constitute an extraordinary and unusual threat to the National Security and foreign policy of the United States, and hereby declare a National Emergency to deal with the threat."[341] This action instituted a full embargo of trade between the United States and Nicaragua, as well as psychologically put the backing of the US government behind the Contras. This order, which was preceded by covert paramilitary action programs for over three years, was also designed to show the Congress that assistance to the resistance was part of a larger overall policy aimed at preserving US interests in Central America.

At this time the administration, which seemed better able to coordinate the skirting and massaging of congressional intent than to make regional foreign policy, switched tactics in its approach to Congress. The administration asked for "humanitarian" or non-lethal assistance for the Contras. On August 15, 1985, the Congress approved $27 million in humanitarian assistance to be administered by the State Department. The prohibitions on DOD and CIA activity remained in place.

The Iran-Contra Diversion

By January 1986 the $27 million of humanitarian aid appropriated in 1985 was running out. The NSC staff was faced with the problem of keeping the insurgency alive while the Congress debated the status of funding. It was during this time (November 1985 – February 1986) that the diversion of funds known as the Iran-Contra Affair began. In short, the US sold weapons to Iran through Israel to affect the release of American hostages held by Muslim radicals in Lebanon. The profits from these weapons' sales were transferred to Swiss bank accounts maintained by retired General Richard Secord. The surplus money was then used to purchase arms and supplies for the Nicaraguan resistance.[342]

The exposure of the Iran-Contra Affair in October-November of 1986 resulted in the transfer of Lt. Col. North and NSC advisor, Admiral Poindexter, out of the White House staff. The resulting investigations and disclosures further polarized debate over support for the Nicaraguan resistance and temporarily paralyzed the Reagan administration. Instead of concentrating efforts on policy formulation and execution, administration officials were pre-occupied with the three major investigations (the inquiry by Congress, the Tower Commission, and the Justice Department criminal investigation).

It is significant to note that the principles involved in the diversion (North, Poindexter, Secord, Singlaub, etc.) did not view it as a clear change of direction and possibly did not comprehend the implications of these actions taken in secret. General Secord, Lt. Col. North, and the others had been involved in facilitating "private" funding for the resistance since 1984. In the climate established by the Reagan White House, it was simple to assume that the president would have approved of the diversion. (Reagan denied knowledge of the diversion and there has never been conclusive proof that he knew of it.)

Further testimony by Lt. Col. North, responding to the questioning of congressional counsel, Mr. Neilds, reveals the casual nature with which the diversion was approached:

> **Lt. Col. North:** What I am saying to you is that over a protracted period of time, he (General Secord) had been spending large sums of money in that country for the purposes of supporting the Nicaraguan resistance, and that at some point in time, I told him he ought to go ahead and use the profits of the weapons' sales to support the Nicaraguan resistance…
>
> …General Secord had a number of accounts set up in Europe by which the Nicaraguan resistance was being supported, yes. Certainly by November 1985. And that those accounts were in one fashion or another supporting this covert operation.[343]

The congressional committees investigating the Iran-Contra Affair concluded their activity and issued a final report in November of 1987. In chapter 24, entitled, "Covert Action in a Democratic Society," the committees asked some questions; they said in part:

> The Iran-Contra Affair raises fundamental and troublesome questions about the secret intelligence operations of the US Government. Can such operations, and particularly covert action, be authorized and conducted in a manner compatible with the American system of democratic government and the rule of law? Is it possible for an open society such as the United States to conduct such secret activities effectively? And if so, by what means can these operations be controlled so as to meet the requirements of accountability in a democratic society?[344]

The report gives no clear-cut answers to these questions.

After a brief discussion of the intelligence oversight battle of the 1970s, the report continues with a modest condemnation of Reagan administration officials without slighting the president directly. The report reads in part:

> The Director of the Central Intelligence Agency, William J. Casey, and other government officials showed contempt for the democratic process by withholding information that Congress

> was seeking and by misrepresenting intelligence to support policies advocated by Casey.[345]

In the same chapter, under the heading of "Misuse of Findings," the report condemned further the actions of the Reagan administration, and perhaps by implication of the president himself, without singling the president out as an individual. The report reads:

> The findings process was circumvented. Covert actions were undertaken outside the specific authorizations of Presidential Findings. At other times, covert actions were undertaken without a Presidential Finding altogether. Actions were undertaken through entities other than the CIA, including foreign governments and private parties. There were claims that the Findings could be used to override provisions of the law. The statutory option for prior notice to eight key congressional leaders was disregarded throughout, along with the legal requirement to notify the Intelligence Committees in a "timely fashion."[346]

The report concluded with general statements that covert actions were necessary and unlike the controversy of the 1970s, without recommendations for any sweeping reforms (or any reforms for that matter). From the conclusions of Chapter 24 we read:

> The United States of America, as a great power with worldwide interests, will continue to have to deal with nations that have different hopes, values, and ambitions. These differences will inevitably lead to conflicts. History reflects that the prospects for peaceful settlement are greater if this country has adequate means for its own defense, including effective intelligence and the means to influence developments abroad.
>
> Organized and structured secret intelligence activities are one of the realities of the world we live in, and this is not likely to change. Like the military, intelligence services are fully compatible with democratic government when their actions are conducted in an accountable manner and in accordance with the law.[347]

The third and final investigation into Iran-Contra was the Justice Department's special prosecutor investigation. On December 19, 1986 Lawrence E. Walsh was appointed to conduct the prosecutors' investigation by the Special Division of the United States Court of Appeals for the District of Columbia Circuit. When the Walsh investigation was concluded in August of 1993, there had been 14 individuals prosecuted. The results were as follows:

1) Robert C. McFarlane, President Reagan's National Security Advisor: pleaded guilty to four counts of withholding information from Congress, pardoned in 1992 by President Bush.

2) US Marine Corps Lieutenant, Colonel Oliver L. North, of the National Security Council Staff: convicted of altering and destroying documents, accepting an illegal gratuity, and aiding in the obstruction of Congress; conviction reversed on appeal.

3) US Navy Admiral, John M. Poindexter: convicted of conspiracy, false statements, destruction and removal of records, and obstruction of Congress; conviction reversed on appeal.

4) Richard V. Secord, retired US Army general: pleaded guilty to making false statements to Congress.

5) Albert Hakim: pleaded guilty to supplementing the salary of Oliver North.

6) Thomas G. Clines: convicted of four counts of tax-related offenses for failing to report income from the operations.

7) Carl R. Channell: pleaded guilty to conspiracy to defraud the United States.

8) Richard R. Miller: pleaded guilty to conspiracy to defraud the United States.

9) Clair E. George, the retired chief of the CIA's covert operations division: convicted of false statements and perjury before Congress, pardoned by President Bush in 1992.

10) Duane R. "Dewey" Clarridge: indicted on seven counts of perjury and false statements, pardoned before trial by President Bush in 1992.

11) Alan D. Fiers, Jr., retired chief of the CIA's Central America task force: pleaded guilty to withholding information from Congress, pardoned by President Bush in 1992.

12) Joseph F. Fernandez: indicted on four counts of obstruction and false statements; the case was dismissed when Attorney General, Richard L.

Thornburgh, refused to declassify information needed for his defense.

13) Elliott Abrams, appointed in 1985 to head the State Department's Latin American bureau: pleaded guilty to withholding information from Congress, pardoned by President Bush in 1992.

14) Caspar W. Weinberger, President Reagan's Secretary of Defense during Iran-Contra: charged with four counts of false statements and perjury; pardoned before trial in 1992 by President Bush.[348]

Lawrence Walsh not only prosecuted individuals in a figurative sense, he indicted the whole "system" including the president and Congress. His final report said in part:

> The underlying facts of Iran/Contra are that, regardless of criminality, President Reagan, the secretary of state, the secretary of defense, and the director of central intelligence and their necessary assistants committed themselves, however reluctantly, to two programs contrary to congressional policy and contrary to national policy. They skirted the law, and most all of them tried to cover up the President's willful activities...
>
> The disrespect for Congress by a popular and powerful President and his appointees was obscured when Congress accepted the tendered concept of a runaway conspiracy of subordinate officers and avoided the unpleasant confrontation with a powerful President and his cabinet... Congress destroyed the most effective lines of inquiry by giving immunity to Oliver L. North and John M. Poindexter so that they could exculpate and eliminate the need for the testimony of President Reagan and Vice President Bush.[349]

With the issuance of the Walsh report, the last of the investigations into Iran-Contra had played itself out some six and a half years after the exposure of the scandal.

Conclusions on Nicaragua

Efforts aimed at achieving peace in Nicaragua began as early as January 1983 at a meeting of foreign ministers from Columbia, Mexico, Panama, and Venezuela on Contadora Island in the Gulf of Panama. This meeting turned into a process of ongoing negotiations known as "the Contadora process."

Nicaragua, under the Sandinistas, signed on to the process in September 1984. There was some involvement of El Salvador, Honduras, and Costa Rica, who signed the Act of Tegucigalpa in October 1984 emphasizing "their commitment to the establishment of pluralistic democratic systems and their belief that simultaneous and verifiable arms reductions were a necessary component of the process."[350]

The talks bogged down in 1985 as the war in Nicaragua and El Salvador continued unabated. In July 1985, the governments of Argentina, Brazil, Peru, and Uruguay announced they were joining the Contadora Process as a "support group." The process came to a halt in June of 1986 when progress at the negotiating table became impossible. In that same month the US Congress approved $100 million in non-lethal aid to the Contras. More non-lethal aid was forthcoming in early 1988.[351]

Progress on the negotiating front again continued when Costa Rican President, Oscar Arias, organized a summit meeting of the Presidents of Costa Rica, El Salvador, Guatemala, Honduras, and Nicaragua. Nicaraguan President, Daniel Ortega, subsequently agreed to a lifting of the state of emergency within his country and face-to-face talks with the contra leadership. As the process progressed, political prisoners were released and detailed peace negotiations took place. In February 1989, a crucial summit of the Central American presidents was held in El Salvador and Ortega agreed to free and open elections in Nicaragua in February 1990.

Owner of La Prensa, and widow of Pedro Joaquin Chamorro, Violetta Barrios de Chamorro ended 11 years of Sandinista rule by winning the elections held on February 25, 1990. The new administration inherited a country in ruins.

It is a fact that by the dawn of the 1980s Nicaragua was a potential Soviet-Cuban beachhead on the mainland of the Americas. There were thousands of tons of Soviet equipment and scores of Cuban advisors to prove it. However, we must ask and answer this question: In their heart of hearts were the Sandinistas Marxist-Leninist? By 1980 they clearly were, but what about earlier? Could the clearly revolutionary Sandinistas of, say, 1967 been co-opted by US interests if the US had, at the same time, backed away from the Somoza dictatorship? It is possible, but unlikely; even early Sandinista writings ring of a Marxist-Leninist tone or at least push for the kind of redistribution of wealth and power that the United States of 1960s and 1970s would not support under any terms.

We must also ask a question that some would rather avoid: Did US actions push them closer to the Cubans and Soviets? This is probable. Tracing the documentary CIA evidence of FSLN ties to Cuba and the Soviets tends to indicate that, as time went on, ties to the Communist bloc grew stronger. At the same time, US pressure on the FSLN was growing. I believe, that once the Sandinistas were in power, had they not had the necessity of fighting of US backed insurgents, the Sandinistas would have pursued a foreign policy more independent of the traditional Communist bloc, and more oriented toward uniting all of Central America under their revolutionary banner. This course of action on the part of the FSLN may have been equally unacceptable to the Reagan administration. So, we see that there are no clear and easy answers on Nicaragua.

We must ask and answer this question: What about the existence and effectiveness of the Contras themselves? Were they an effective measure? On one hand we can say yes. Marxism-Leninism, as it developed within the Sandinista party and elsewhere in the hemisphere throughout the 70s and 80s, never got more than a toehold in Central America, and this is due in large part to the standing army the Contras provided. The Contra force was an army that acted to forestall the need of the US army in combat in Central America. US forces only became involved in combat in the Caribbean Basin in late 1983 in Grenada and as advisors in El Salvador.

The Contras failed in that they brought so much negative press to American foreign policy. Though there seems to be some credible evidence that some of the Contra forces had human rights problems (not uncommon to all sides in the conflict) much of the negative publicity on the subject of the Contras comes through no fault of their own. It is almost a truism in some quarters that the Contras were financed with funds raised through the sale of drugs in US cities. "Oliver North sold crack" is the conclusion drawn by many of the web sites on the topic. Just enter "Contra" into many of the search engines on the web and you will see that these sites proliferate on the drug conspiracy theory, not on the Nicaraguan civil war.

The fact remains that there is not one shred of hard, credible evidence that the Contras were, to any large measure, funded by drug money. The Contra army was funded by nearly half a billion dollars in US taxpayer money and through the efforts of the private financing scheme of the Iran-Contra scandal. Even if this fact of the conventional nature of Contra funding is accepted, when the Iran-Contra scandal and the drug accusations that seem to have stuck are taken together, the Contra army was a public relations nightmare.

Afghanistan Before the Soviet Invasion

As stated in the previous chapter, an insurgency in Afghanistan was the cause of a massive Soviet direct military intervention in that country in December 1979. The insurgency was flowering and enjoying foreign support even before the time of the Soviet invasion. In late 1978 the "Afghan National Liberation Front," led by Sibghatullah Mojaddei, opened an office in Jidda, Saudi Arabia.[352] The Saudis were not the only ones aiding the guerrillas prior to the invasion; the US was soon to get into the act. According to a former CIA director, aid from the US began to flow to the anti-communist guerrillas when President Carter signed a finding authorizing it on July 3, 1979, a full six months before the Soviet invasion.[353]

The relationship between the Saudis and the Afghan insurgents was being monitored by the CIA in November 1979—if not before. From the "Near East and South Asia Review" dated November 23, 1979 (which remains heavily redacted for reasons of national security) we may read:

> The rebel effort will continue to be impeded by the failure of the various independent insurgent groups to coordinate operations. Additionally, unless the rebels receive more meaningful military support (redacted). than it has thus far—particularly antitank and antiaircraft weapons—and more financial backing from Saudi Arabia, their effort to bring the Soviet-equipped Army to the point of collapse may lose momentum.[354]

More than the glance provided above, the agency's "Soviet Options in Afghanistan" (an "Interagency Intelligence Memorandum" classified "Top Secret") dated 28 September, 1979, shows that the CIA was taking great pains to observe, in detail, the developments in Afghanistan prior to the Soviet invasion. On the subject of Soviet military involvement the memorandum said,

> 10) (redacted). there are Soviet advisers attached to every major Afghan Army command, as well as to at least some regiment and battalion-level units. They appear to be heavily involved in guiding Afghan combat operations, as well as Afghan Army logistics and administration.
> (redacted).

> 11) In addition, there are some reports which are not confirmed, but which we regard as fairly credible, alleging that Soviets have piloted helicopters together with Afghan pilots in strikes against insurgent positions, and have, on occasion, furnished tank personnel for combat operations.
>
> 12) If these latter reports are accurate, the Soviets, in addition to guiding Afghan combat operations, are themselves already participating in combat on a small scale and in certain limited ways. In general, however, they are not organized in cohesive combat units intended to conduct unilateral operations.[355]

The memorandum goes on to discuss the various possibilities of further Soviet intervention in Afghanistan. It postulates the possibility of an increase in equipment and advisers, or the "Introduction of Combat Support and Combat Service Support Units." Presumably the introduction of Soviet non-combat troops in a support role would bolster Afghan government forces resolve. In the paragraphs following, the memorandum looks at direct Soviet intervention as follows:

> 26) **Limited Intervention with Soviet Combat Units**. The Soviets might consider deploying a limited number of their own units to provide security or operate in combat as separate entities. The Soviets would have to weigh whether their increased combat presence would alienate rather than bolster the Afghan forces that are now loyal to the regime. Because of this uncertainty the introduction of Soviet combat units probably would be accomplished incrementally. It might begin, for example, with a few battalions up to and including an airborne division or two to help stiffen Afghan Army resolve or provide security for key cities or critical points. As noted earlier, we believe one such battalion has already been introduced to provide security for Bagram airfield since early July.
>
> 27) The most likely airborne division to be called in is the one nearest Afghanistan, located at Fergana in the Turkestan Military District (MD). It could be brought up to its operational strength of some 7,900 men in a few hours.
>
> 28) The airlift of an airborne division into Afghanistan could be accomplished within a day or so if the transport and airborne

> forces were previously alerted and prepared.[356]

The above passages would prove both correct and incorrect when the Soviet invasion came in December 1979. They were incorrect in that soviet intervention was not incremental; it was a massive surge, from a status quo of military advisers to a full-fledged invasion. It was correct however in its focus on the importance of the airborne divisions. It was Soviet airborne forces that seized key points in Kabul, while the ground troops crossed the Afghan-Soviet frontier.

However, far from ruling out the possibility of a massive invasion the memorandum spends a full page discussing the possibility. The existence of this discussion in the intelligence community record makes President Carter's declaration that he was "shocked" by the invasion difficult, at best, to understand. From the memorandum.

> 31) **Massive Soviet Military Intervention**. Anything beyond securing Kabul or some other key city and a few critical points would require the commitment of large numbers of regular ground forces in a potentially open-ended operation. An overland move to Kabul—particularly with the possibility of Afghan Army and insurgent opposition—would be a multi-divisional operation exhausting the resources of the Turkestan MD. An operation of this magnitude would therefore require the redeployment of forces—and their supporting elements—from western and central military districts, in addition to those near the Soviet-Afghan border.
>
> 32) Soviet ground forces closest to Afghanistan are located in the Turkestan MD—some 45,000 men in four cadre-level motorized rifle divisions, an artillery brigade, and various MD-level support units. All of these forces are manned considerably below their intended wartime strengths. In about a week some 50,000 reservists could be mobilized to fill out the Turkestan units and an additional division could be moved from the Central Asian MD.
>
> 33) Six other Central Asian Military district divisions would also be available for operations but would require a few weeks or longer to mobilize reservists and move to the Afghan border. The Soviets probably would be reluctant to move any substantial

> portion of their Central Asian forces into Afghanistan, however, for fear of weakening their position opposite China.
>
> 34) The Soviets have 12 other divisions located well over 1,000 miles from Afghanistan in the Volga, Ural, and North Caucasus MDs from which they could draw intervention forces. These units are also manned at low levels in peacetime and would require a few weeks to fill out and move to the Afghan border.
>
> 35) The terrain and lack of modern transportation network in Afghanistan are hampering the Afghan Government's military effort against the insurgents and would seriously complicate large-scale Soviet military operations. Most of the country is hilly or mountainous—terrain that would limit the use of transport and logistic vehicles. In addition to controlling the mountainous areas, the insurgents could disrupt Soviet movement by cutting roadways that lead from the border area to several key cities, as well as those roads between major urban areas.[357]

As is self evident from the above, a great deal of thought on the part of the Intelligence Community had gone into Afghanistan prior to the invasion. Yet we are often led to believe that the Soviet move was a complete surprise to the Carter administration.

The next section of the memorandum is a throw back to the discussion of "balance of power" and "correlation of forces" from chapter 5. It may ultimately explain why the Soviet undoing in Afghanistan contributed to the downfall of the USSR. Under the heading of "Prospects" we may read:

> 36) The prospect of a successful Communist government in Afghanistan is important to Moscow for ideological reasons: such a government would provide substance to determinist claims that world "socialism" will eventually emerge victorious. The Soviets feel obligated to support such revolutions and embarrassed when they fail. The outcome assumes an added importance when the revolution occurs in a country on the USSR's border. In addition, it is conceivable that some Soviet planners have welcomed the advent of such a revolution in Afghanistan on strategic grounds, arguing that if this revolutionary regime could be consolidated in power at

> acceptable cost, it could open the way for the eventual expansion of Soviet influence southward.[358]

In the concluding paragraphs the memorandum stated that further Soviet intervention in Afghanistan would probably be incremental in nature and "would be primarily intended to buy time."[359] Under an annex entitled, "Warning Considerations," the unknown CIA analysts identified what would happen in three months time:

> Even the largest intervention, which would take weeks to fully prepare if undertaken as a coordinated assault, could be undertaken piecemeal, beginning with airborne or ground forces near the border. Such an operation could be initiated in a day or so, with little or no warning, as follow-on forces were being mobilized.[360]

Thus we can see perhaps why the White House was tactically surprised, and still wonder how the strategic surprise was achieved given all the intelligence available.

Reagan's Position

Ronald Reagan was almost silent on Afghanistan for most of his first year in office. There was cursory mention of the subject early on, but hardly more than that. One mention of the subject, four months into his administration, came in a joint statement with Chancellor Helmut Schmidt of the Federal Republic of Germany on May 22, 1981. The statement read in part:

> The President and the Federal Chancellor reaffirmed their view that the Soviet occupation of Afghanistan is unacceptable. They demanded the withdrawal of Soviet troops from Afghanistan and respect for the country's right to return to independence and nonalignment. The destabilizing effects which the Soviet intervention of Afghanistan has on the entire region must be countered.[361]

A stronger, more direct and comprehensive statement of policy had to wait until December 27, 1981 when Reagan released his "Statement on the Situation in Afghanistan." In the conclusion of this statement the president unequivocally promised support for the Afghan resistance as long as it was necessary. The entire text of the statement follows:

> Our current concern regarding Poland should not cause us to forget that 2 years ago today, massive Soviet military forces invaded the sovereign country of Afghanistan and began an attempt to subjugate one of the most fiercely independent peoples of the world. Despite the presence of 90,000 Soviet combat troops, a recent increase of some 5,000, the courageous people of Afghanistan have fought back.* Today they effectively deny Soviet forces control of most of Afghanistan. Efforts by the Soviets to establish a puppet government in the Soviet image, which could govern a conquered land, have failed. Soviet control extends little beyond the major cities, and even there the Afghan freedom fighters often hold sway by night and sometimes even by day. The battle for Afghan independence continues.
>
> But the gallant efforts of the people of Afghanistan to regain their independence have come at great cost. Almost 3 million Afghan refugees, a fifth of the pre-invasion population of Afghanistan, have fled their homes and taken refuge across the border, largely in Pakistan. Those who have remained at home have become unfortunate victims not only of the dislocations of war but also of indiscriminate Soviet attacks on civilians. So, while we express our admiration for those who fight for the freedom we all cherish, we must also express our deep sympathy for those innocent victims of Soviet imperialism who, because of the love of freedom of their countrymen, have been forced to flee for their lives.
>
> On three separate occasions, most recently on November 18, 1981, the United Nations General Assembly passed by overwhelming margins resolutions aimed at Soviet aggression in Afghanistan. The U.S. Government and the American people join in the broad international condemnation of the Soviet invasion and occupation of Afghanistan. Just as in Poland we see the use of intimidation and indirect use of power to subjugate

*Soviet forces grew in strength in numbers to around 300,000 troops before the war ended.

a neighboring people; in Afghanistan we see direct aggression in violation of the United Nations Charter and other principles governing the conduct of nations.

While extending our admiration and sympathy to the people of Afghanistan, we also call upon the Soviet Union to avail itself of proposals set forth by the community of nations for the withdrawal of Soviet forces from Afghanistan so that an independent and nonaligned nation can be reestablished with a government responsive to the desires of the people, so that millions of Afghans who have sought refuge in other countries can return with honor to their homes. *As long as the Soviet Union occupies Afghanistan in defiance of the international community, the heroic Afghan resistance will continue, and the United States will support the cause of a free Afghanistan.* [18, 345]

Soviet Use of Chemical and Biological Weapons

Reports Soviet use of chemical and biological weapons against the Afghan resistance (the Mujahideen) began to leak out of Afghanistan shortly after the invasion in 1979. Afghanistan was not the only place the Soviets were accused of having a hand in the use of these weapons. In 1982 the CIA published a Top Secret and rather comprehensive two-volume report on the topic entitled "Use of Toxins and Other Lethal Chemicals in Southeast Asia and Afghanistan."

From the report we can read:

Soviet forces in Afghanistan have used lethal casualty-producing agents on Mujahideen resistance forces and Afghan villages since the December 1979 invasion. There is some evidence that Afghan Government forces may have used chemical weapons provided by the USSR against the Mujahideen even before the invasion. No agents have been identified through sample analysis, but we conclude from analysis of all the evidence that attacks have been conducted with irritants,incapacitants, nerve agents, phosgene oxime[364], and trichothecene toxins[365], mustard[366], lewisite[367], and perhaps unidentified smokes.

(redacted).

Implications:

> Our review of the chemical warfare evidence has yielded three findings with serious implications that need to be reflected in future threat estimates: (1) The Soviet Union has a well-developed program for the employment of chemical and toxin weapons. (2) The Soviet military consider the employment of chemical weapons by their forces and those of their allies to be an acceptable and effective means of suppressing resistance in even local wars. (3) There is a growing sense of alarm in countries like Thailand, Pakistan, and China in contemplating conflict with Soviet client states, and there is international concern that lethal chemical weapons may become an accepted method of warfare in limited conflicts throughout the Third World.[368]

Toward the end of the report the observation is made that:

> Evidence accumulated since World War II clearly shows that the Soviets have been extensively involved in preparations for large-scale offensive and defensive chemical warfare.[369]

In reaction to this Soviet willingness to use chemical weapons, the US Army requested funding for, and received from Congress and the president, an expansion of chemical training facilities at Fort McClellan, Alabama and new safer "binary" nerve agent artillery rounds as the 80s came to a close.

The Resistance Unifies

A heavily redacted CIA document dated May 18, 1985 declares that the Afghan resistance has unified seven different groups into a common council or alliance. The document stated:

> The new alliance of seven Afghan resistance parties based in Pakistan will aid efforts to publicize the Afghan cause, but deep-seated differences are likely to hamper military cooperation.
>
> The alliance spokesman, Guibuddin Hekmatyar, says a council will direct joint military operations. The first council chairman is to be chosen by a congress of guerrilla leaders; the post will be held by each party in turn.
>
> (redacted).

> Comment:
> Naming a single chairman will help the resistance influence opinion and obtain diplomatic, financial, and military support. A council, however, will have little success directing military operations. Most insurgent leaders inside Afghanistan will not accept orders from the exiled leaders, despite the insurgents' dependence on exiles for arms and supplies.[370]

The table on the next page describes the various groups that were part of the alliance:

Table 8-1[349]

Group	Leader	Ethnicity	Ideology	Geography
Islamic Union for the Liberation of Fundamentalist Afghanistan	Abdul Rasul Sayyaf	Pushtun	Islamic	Eastern Afghanistan
Hizbi Islami (Islamic Party) (Gulbuddin)	Gulbuddin Hikmatyar	Pushtun	Islamic Fundamentalist	Eastern Afghanistan
Jamiat-I-islami (Islamic Society) Fundamentalist Afghanistan	Burhanuddin Rabbani	Tajik	Islamic	North & West
Hizbi Islami (Islamic Party) (Yunus Khalis)	Muhammad Yunus Khalis	Pushtun	Islamic Fundamentalist	Nangarhar & Paktia Provinces
Jabha-I-Najat-I-Milli Afghanistan	Sibghatullah Mojadedi	Pushtun	Moderate	Eastern
(Afghanistan National Liberation Front) Harakat-I-Inqilab-I-Islami (Islamic Revolutionary Movement)	Muhammad Nabi Muhammadi	Pushtun	Islamic Traditionalist	Eastern Afghanistan
Mahaz-I-Milli-Islami (National Islamic Front)	Sayyid Ahmad Gailani	Pushtun	Moderate Islamic	Eastern Afghanistan

Clearly, from the table one can see that the alliance was dominated by Islamic Fundamentalists. One faction, the Hizbi Islami (Islamic Party) (Gulbuddin) led by Gulbuddin Hikmatyar was known to have executed fighters from other factions and to have support from Saddam Hussein and Muammar Qaddafi. In terms of US aid this faction is said to have received $600 million dollars. Hekmatyar is important to the understanding of present events because he worked closely with the now notorious Usama bin Laden.[372] The resistance received the bulk of US aid dollars through Pakistan over the course of the war. US aid to the Mujahideen peaked at $630 million dollars in 1987 and reached a total of $3 billion by war's end.[373]

Usama bin Laden

Not included in the alliance were the Afghan Arabs—Arab nationals who came to Afghanistan to fight for the Mujahideen. The most famous, or infamous, of these Afghan Arabs is one of their leaders, Usama bin Laden. Some estimates put the number of Afghan Arabs fighting in Afghanistan at between 20,000-50,000.[374] This number represents a small but significant portion of the total Mujahideen strength of between 170,000 and 350,000 troops.[375] There seems to be conflicting evidence as to if the Afghan Arabs received direct support from the CIA (including the possibility of support for bin Laden's Al-Qaeda organization). Peter L. Bergen in his Holy War, Inc. states that, "While charges that the CIA was responsible for the rise of the Afghan Arabs might make good copy, they don't make good history."[376]

Whether bin laden and the Afghan Arabs got help from the CIA or not may remain a matter of controversy for a generation. This is because the documentary paper train from within the agency may not be declassified for that long. One document declassified by the CIA in 1996 is entitled "Usama bin Laden: Islamic Extremist Financier." From the document we may read:

> Usama bin Muhammad bin Awad Bin Laden is one of the most significant financial sponsors of Islamic extremist activities in the world today. One of some 20 sons of wealthy Saudi construction magnate Muhammad Bin Laden—founder of the Kingdom's Bin Laden Group business empire—Usama joined the Afghan resistance movement following the 26 December, 1979 Soviet invasion of Afghanistan. "I was enraged and went there at once," he claimed in a 1993 interview. "I arrived within days, before the end of 1979."

> Bin Laden gained prominence during the Afghan war for his role in financing the recruitment, transportation, and training of Arab nationals who volunteered to fight alongside the Afghan Mujahedeen. By 1985, Bin Laden had drawn on his family's wealth, plus donations received from sympathetic merchant families in the Gulf region, to organize the Islamic Salvation Foundation, or al-Qaeda, for this purpose.[377]

Bin Laden's backing of the 9-11-01 attack in the World Trade Center, and other prior targets including the USS Cole are now well known. They also go beyond the scope of this book, which is the Cold War. It is sufficient to say here that bin Laden got his start in the anti-Soviet war in Afghanistan; he fought alongside US allies, and may have even gotten some indirect support from the US through third parties like Gulbuddin Hikmatyar. Anything further than this picture will be difficult to discern for, perhaps, a generation.

1986: New Afghan Leadership and the Entry of Anti-Air Weapons

Dr. Najibullah Ahmadzai became the General Secretary of the People's Democratic Party of Afghanistan in May 1986, succeeding Babrak Karmal with Soviet backing. He had been head of the Soviet-supported Afghan version of the KGB since after the invasion in 1979. Najibullah was a member of the same Parcham faction of the PDPA as Karmal. In line with Gorbachev's reform movement in the Soviet Union, he allowed the existence of some opposition parties in Afghan politics. The Mujahideen steadfastly boycotted this process, preferring to fight on for a total Soviet pullout.

Najibullah remained president for 6 years. He maintained himself in power from the time the Soviets eventually withdrew in 1989 until his eventual defeat by the Mujahideen in 1992. From 1992 until 1996 he took refuge in a UN compound in Kabul. In September 1996, when radical fundamentalist Taliban troops swept into power throughout much of Afghanistan and entered the city, they captured and hung the former president.

Perhaps more significant than the change of leadership in Afghanistan was another event that occurred in 1986. This landmark was the September introduction of the American "Stinger" and British "Blowpipe" man-portable, heat-seeking, anti-aircraft missiles into the packages of support for the resistance. Some of the documentation concerning this introduction has been declassified, though it is heavily redacted. One document, a cable entitled "Impact of the Stinger Missile on Soviet Resistance Tactics," is found in the collection of the National Security Archive. Written in February of 1987, the report was classified "Secret." From the document we may read:

> Summary: The introduction of the Stinger Antiaircraft missile system into AF[378] in September 1986 has had significant and extensive impact on Soviet close air support tactics.
> (redacted).
> (redacted).General impact has favored the Mujahidin and altered the application of air power and the conduct of close air support by the Soviet and ◇◇Afghan◇◇ armed forces. More tactical and air support changes occurred in the last quarter of 1986 and the first quarter of 1987 than in the previous seven years of the conflict. (redacted).
> 2. Reduction and change in close air support role The quantity of direct close air support to ◇◇Soviet/Afghan◇◇ ground operations has been reduced significantly, and the application of all forms of close air support have been modified. (redacted). By January 1987 the changes in response to the increased Mujahidin air defense capability were uniform and obvious the low altitude circling aircraft were absent from most ground movements. On call air strikes are still available, but less responsive than was possible previously.
> 3. (redacted). Casualties among the supported ◇◇Soviet/Afghan◇◇ troops are still common and probably outnumber Mujahidin casualties in applications of close air support.
> 4. (redacted).[379] An additional cable from the same time frame, also "Secret," gives the following details:
> 5. (redacted). More jets have been shot down with heavy machine guns since January 1987 than in any similar previous period. The Mujahidin also attribute this to the Stinger presence, which is credited with causing the low-level approaches.
> 6. Convoy air support changes Convoy air cover has similarly changed, and the low level circling helicopter gunships accompanying ground transport convoys have disappeared: (redacted).
> 7. (redacted). ◇◇Soviet/Afghan◇◇ armed forces' lines of communications (LOC's) have (sic) been radically diminished

> since late 1986. The primary factors in motivating the change are: the increase in the effectiveness of the Mujahidin air defense weapons inventory: (redacted).[380]

The Soviet/Afghan air forces lost in the neighborhood of between 54 and 62 aircraft due to Stinger hits in the first quarter of 1987. These casualties were the result of a total of 69 Stingers being fired in combat during that time.[381] Clearly the introduction of the Stinger was increasing the costs of occupying Afghanistan to the Soviets.

The Soviet/Afghan air forces extracted their revenge for lost comrades due to the new missiles. As another cable from early 1987 concludes, one of the end results of the introduction of advanced air defense weapons into Afghanistan was that, "the use of air power against all types of civilian targets as retaliatory or punishment strikes has also increased significantly since late 1986."[382]

Soviet Domestic Discontentment and Subsequent Withdrawal

The Foreign Broadcast Information Service (FBIS) is an organ of both the Department of State and the CIA. Its small army of technicians and translators intercept and translate radio and television broadcasts around the globe. They then compile both unclassified and classified reports of broadcast activity, which are made available to other US government agencies and, in the case of the unclassified reports, the general public. Many types of unclassified FBIS reports can be found in many of the larger libraries throughout the country; subscriptions to them are for sale through the CIA's unclassified publications catalog.

On April 8, 1987 a publication called *FBIS Trends* issued the following report (classified "Confidential") on the USSR and Afghanistan:

> *Moscow Airs Domestic Frustration Over Afghan Involvement*
>
> Moscow has begun giving greater publicity to adverse remarks by the Soviet populace on Soviet involvement in Afghanistan, possibly heralding more frequent and more detailed discussion of the sensitive Afghan issue in the Soviet media. The Gorbachev regime is apparently convinced that greater candor in portraying popular attitudes toward the Soviet role in Afghanistan will strengthen its credibility and build support for whatever course the regime chooses.

Soviet media in recent weeks have shown greater willingness to deal directly with popular disquiet over the war in Afghanistan, including some frankly critical views of the Soviet role in the conflict. On three occasions in the last two months, Moscow radio's *International Situation*, a weekly question and answer program intended for the domestic audience that has generally not aired controversial material in the past, carried remarkably candid inquiries concerning the Afghan war:

> On 6 February the program aired several questions posed to a guest military commentator dealing with sensitive subjects related to the war. Three listeners asked about the "losses" sustained by Soviet troops. Although the commentator declined to answer on grounds that the figures were classified information, permitting the broadcast of the questions is unusual. The same listeners also asked, "why did we go into Afghanistan" since "no one has attacked us," and "is it worth our getting involved in this business when our people are dying over there?"
>
> Panelists on the *International Situation* program—prominent media commentators do not usually participate in this program—generally attempted to answer the queries about Afghanistan with standard arguments justifying Soviet involvement. However, in commenting on the difficulty in defeating the insurgency, panelist Vladimir Fadeyev made several telling admissions about the Afghan regime's inability to stand on its own. At one point in the 27 March program he intimated that the regime depended for its survival on Soviet support by admitting that "our internationalist air" is the "chief, if not the only, guarantee" of the regime's "integrity and sovereignty." On the 3 April program he painted a disquieting picture of the Afghan border troops whom he described them as "still very young and few in number" and as relying on the help of inexperienced youths from local tribes.

Ambartsumov's complaint:

> Concern over the impact of Moscow's involvement in Afghanistan on one recent occasion even led to a published call

for Soviet troop withdrawal, although in a vehicle far less available to the Soviet public than *International Situation. Moscow News* carried in its 8-15 February (No. 5) issue and article by commentator Yevgenly Ambartsumov that openly argued for withdrawal of Soviet troops without the preconditions that are invariably included in the official Soviet position. Such a withdrawal, Ambartsumov wrote, would mean that the death notifications "would no longer bring untold grief to Soviet families" and that the country "would be able to release the additional forces and means that are so needed."

To the blunt question: "Do we pull out of Afghanistan?" Ambartsumov surprisingly answered unequivocally in the affirmative. He denied that this would be "playing into the hands of our adversaries," and presented the contrary argument: that continued Soviet involvement in Afghanistan undermines Moscow's "international prestige" and works to the advantage of the United States which, in any case, could not fill any "vacuum" left by departing Soviet troops. Ambartsumov concluded that continued Soviet engagement in Afghanistan is "pernicious" because it entails continued "bloodshed," maintenance of a "seat of tension" in the area, and a "slowing down of our reconstruction."[383]

In fact, negotiations aimed at the withdrawal of foreign troops from Afghanistan had been going on since April 1982, when talks between the Karmal government and Pakistan opened in Geneva. A breakthrough occurred on February 8, 1988, when in light of aircraft losses in Afghanistan and criticism at home, Mikhail Gorbachev announced that a Soviet pullout would begin on May 15.

A "Secret" CIA estimate of March 88 then observed that:

> We believe Moscow has made a firm decision to withdraw from Afghanistan. This decision stems from the war's effect of the Soviet regime's ability to carry out its agenda at home and abroad, and its pessimism about the military and political prospects for creating a viable client regime...
>
> ...In our view, the Soviets will begin withdrawal this year even if the Geneva talks are deadlocked...

> We judge that the Najibullah regime will not long survive the completion of Soviet withdrawal even with Soviet assistance. The regime may fall before withdrawal is complete.
>
> Despite infighting, we believe the resistance will retain sufficient supplies and military strength to ensure the demise of the Communist government. We cannot confidently predict the composition of the new regime, but we believe it initially will be an unstable coalition of traditionalist and fundamentalist groups whose writ will not extend far beyond Kabul and the leaders' home areas. It will be Islamic—possibly strongly fundamentalist, but not as extreme as Iran.[384]

Under the concluding section, "Implications for the United States," the report had this to say about possible consequences for the withdrawal:

> There is a chance that withdrawal will yield more negative consequences than Gorbachev has led the leadership to expect—contributing to nationality unrest in the USSR, destabilization in Eastern Europe, or what Moscow would see as more assertive US efforts to challenge Soviet global interests. In that event, a foreign policy backlash that produces a more conservative, defense-minded leadership in Moscow—and a tougher policy toward Washington—cannot be ruled out.
>
> We believe it is more likely, however, that the benefits of withdrawal for Moscow will, on balance, outweigh the costs, giving impetus to the rethinking of traditional policies already under way and improving the prospects for more innovative Soviet approaches toward issues of concern to the United States and the Western alliance.[385]

The first part of the conclusion would seem to be accurate in that a right wing coup would eventually rise up against Gorbachev in 1991. The perceived loss of Soviet prestige on the part of the coup plotters was doubtless a cause for their action and with withdrawal from Afghanistan likely a contributing event to this perception.

On April 14, 1988 the Soviets signed and agreement which allowed for the withdrawal of their forces from Afghanistan. The agreement included Afghan and Pakistani promises not to interfere in each other's affairs. It also included guarantees of neutrality for Afghanistan from the US and USSR. A UN monitoring force was also established as part of the agreement.

On May 15, as scheduled, the withdrawal began with the departure of 1,200 Soviet troops from Jalalabad, with the city being totally evacuated by May 22. During the course of the withdrawal (in November 1988) the CIA predicted that, "the Afghan regime will probably collapse within six to 12 months following the departure of Soviet forces...[386] Also during the course of the withdrawal, the US closed its embassy in Kabul. US Chargé d'Affairs, Jon Glassman, stated at the time that, "after the Soviets leave we have doubts about the ability of the regime to protect diplomats."[387]

Soviet withdrawal was completed on schedule with the last of the troops out by February 1989. Najibullah managed to beat the CIA estimate of 12 months or less post-Soviet longevity and survived until 1992. Part of the reason Najibullah lasted that long was because he continued to receive Soviet aid until January 1, 1992. Aid was cut off after agreement on the part of the US and Soviets to quit aiding rival factions inside the country.

In that same year Mujahedin forces, Ahmed Shah Massoud, took power in Kabul. As mentioned Najibullah took refuge on a UN compound. The factions of fighters agreed on the appointment of Burhanuddin Rabbani (see table 8-1) as president. A state of near anarchy ensued. This lawlessness continued until the Taliban took over in 1996, executing Najibullah and establishing an iron-handed Islamic fundamentalist rule.

Karl F. Inderfurth, Assistant Secretary of State before the Senate Foreign Relations Committee, said of the Taliban in July 2000 (well before 9-11-02):

> I must emphasize that, contrary to some false and damaging allegations, the US does not now support and has never supported the Taliban. When they took over the capital of Kabul in 1996, we told them we would look at what they did, and react accordingly. Well, what they have done, in a word, is horrendous. They have chosen to prolong their country's agonizing civil war, while oppressing its numerous ethnic and religious minorities. They have trampled on the human rights of all Afghans, especially women and girls. They have condoned and indeed profited from the deadly trade in narcotics and they have condoned that other scourge of civilized society, namely terrorism, by providing, among other things, safe haven for Usama bin Laden and his network. This is the murderer directly

responsible for the loss of a dozen American and hundreds of other innocent lives in the East Africa embassy bombing 2 years ago. We believe Usama bin Laden continues to this day to plan further acts of international terrorism.[388]

Conclusions on Afghanistan

By invading Afghanistan, the Soviets helped sow the seeds of their own undoing. US aid to the resistance, while it dated to before the invasion, turned out to be a key factor in the Soviet demise. This downhill slide began in late 1986 with the introduction of advanced anti-aircraft weapons from America and Great Britain. The toll of Soviet losses served to exacerbate the internal criticism over the war. Rising casualty figures combined with the public disillusionment to pressure Gorbachev to seek withdrawal at any cost. The end result of the conflict was that Afghanistan fell into anarchy and adopted a reactionary government. The cold war had provided a rich media, on which the Taliban and al-Qaeda could grow and flourish.

The War College in the Early 80s: Personal Experience

In 1983, I was allowed access into the inner sanctum of official Army political thought. As an intern at the Army's Strategic Studies Institute (SSI) I got a view of the Cold War. I gained other insights on the Cold War during the 14 total years I served in the reserve components of the Army. My view from SSI included exploration of nuclear warfighting issues, conventional war in Europe, and unconventional warfare in Central America.

Carlisle Barracks, just outside the city of Carlisle, Pennsylvania is where the US Army War College is housed. The post was not an imposing piece of real estate in August of 1983, when I piloted my 5-speed, silver, 4-door Renault Alliance of the same year through the front gate. Though I was in the dress green uniform of a Second Lieutenant of Armor, from the Pennsylvania Army National Guard's 28th Infantry Division, and a white plate bearing black "airborne wings" adorned the front of the car, I had no official military business on this post. The uniformed Military Policeman in the guardhouse did not make any attempt to stop my car, though it was devoid of an official decal. It was not his duty to do so; "Carlisle," as the officially named Carlisle Barracks was known in the vernacular, was an open post with a ceremonial guard at only the front gate. Even less secure, the back gate was totally unguarded.

As I write this, 17 plus years after the events, I am not too sure of exactly what order the events of that first day happened. I recall going to the post housing office, that I had prior contact with over the phone. They had some "substandard" housing available. It consisted of two-story wooden open bay barracks from the Second World War era. Over the years some improvements to the barracks were made, chiefly that they were subdivided into individual bedrooms with a locking door on them. I don't think the housing officer charged me anything for the quarters. He said some Colonels that commuted from Washington stayed there during the week.

** [389]

On checking out my room I found a serviceable metal spring cot with a mattress on it and a dresser. The floor was bare wood and painted battleship gray. The walls were white, and the sole light fixture in the room was a bare bulb attached to the ceiling. It would serve as my place to crash during the week, but I would return home to Indiana, PA each weekend.

After a few minutes of familiarization with my new digs, I headed over to the War College to report in. In those days most of the activity was housed in one building of about 5 stories. It was fairly large, with an auditorium that could seat the entire class of Lieutenant Colonels at one end, on the ground floor. I was to report in to the Director of the Strategic Studies Institute (SSI) in the institute's offices on one of the upper floors of the East wing of the building. As I did not yet have a security badge, I stopped first at the security desk manned by uniformed MPs. They called up to SSI and my prearranged escort, the Director's assistant, came down to meet me. Security here was a bit more serious than at the main gate; no one without a badge was permitted past the desk without an escort, and there were TV monitors behind the desk linked to security cameras on every floor.

I was ushered in to see the Director in his office. He was a full Colonel, but, like the majority of the officers I had seen so far, was in civilian business attire. There was some initial confusion over the fact that I was a commissioned Lieutenant and not an ROTC Cadet. The Interns who had come from Indiana University of Pennsylvania (IUP) in the past had all been cadets. I explained that the confusion might have come about because I was in the Early Commissioning Program. Because of my prior enlisted service in the National Guard I was only required to take two years of ROTC before receiving my gold bar. Thus, at the end of my sophomore year in college I was a commissioned officer in the Guard. My Political Science advisor, Dr. Ed

Platt, suggested I undertake the assistantship, and helped coordinate it with Carlisle and the IUP campus internship office. Somewhere in the process it was lost on the Director of SSI that he would be getting a Lieutenant not a Cadet. The only negative consequence to me was that I was told I would not be able to eat in the enlisted mess and would have to fend for my self for meals—which was of no consequence to me.

The Director, Colonel Keith Barlow, asked me what I wanted to work on. I told him I thought there was a connection between national strategy and procurement—that the weapons we bought determined the strategy we could adopt. He sat back in his high-backed chair, looked me straight in the eyes, and said, "I am not so sure." I had struck out right off the bat. He told me to come up with something else and suggested I look over some of SSI's previous work for ideas. Colonel Barlow also stated that I would be working with Colonel Staudenmaier on a project during my time at SSI. I was given a stack of booklets on various defense topics that SSI had produced in the past and shown to a desk in an office I would share with a Colonel. I found none of the 30 or so booklets of any interest. This selection of a topic to study was important because it was a requirement of the internship that I complete an independent study. The internship director back at IUP, not the staff of SSI, would grade this, but it would be prepared under the tutelage of the SSI staff.

Before I could get a good start in looking over the booklets, or accomplish anything else for that matter, the director's assistant (Karen Bailey) came into the office in which I was situated. She told me I would need to get down to the security office to get my ID badge. Karen gave me directions, and I made my way back down to the first floor and to an office staffed by a Major who was in uniform. He asked me some questions and was writing down the answers, when he got to date of birth, I told him September 4, 1963. He said, "that means you're 19 … I don't believe it." He continued with the interview asking to see my military ID. He then asked my security clearance. "Secret," I said.

The levels of security clearance were 1) Top Secret, 2) Secret, and the lowest was 3) Confidential. When I enlisted in 1980, they were granting everybody a Secret based upon a check with the FBI and other "National Agencies." I never had a formal background investigation, as that was usually only required to get a Top Secret and for the "compartmented" levels above that. The major stated that he would need proof of my security clearance before he could issue me a Secret level badge. After retrieving some papers from my car I produced an official document, which listed me as having the

Secret I claimed. This was backed up by a telephone call to the ROTC department back at IUP and I was issued the badge.

I met Colonel William "Bill" Staudenmaier and Dr. Keith Dunn, the two people I would be working closest with, shortly after getting my badge. Staudenmaier was a graying Air Defense Artillery officer and Dunn was a 40ish active Army veteran (then serving in the Army Reserve) with a Ph.D. in Political Science. The two were presently working on a volume of papers presented at a conference at the War College in early 1983. The volume of papers was to be published, and it would be one of the projects I would be working on. Dunn and Staudenmaier seemed very "laid back" as did most of the people at Carlisle. At about this time, one of the secretaries took me on a walk-around tour of most of the offices at the War College. I met about 50 different people, most of whom I did not see much again; there were experts on many conceivable areas with broad backgrounds. Most of the people I met were Colonels, Lieutenant Colonels, or civilians; there was an occasional Captain or two in the mix, but no other Lieutenants. I would be alone at the bottom of the totem poll.

I think it important to note here that many of the day-to-day events at the War College were somewhat routine and therefore not worth much space here. That being said, there was always an air of excitement to me underneath it all. I was, after all, working at a level far above my military or academic rank. What I am saying, though, is that from here forward, I will take the liberty of only recounting those incidents and facets of my internship that may prove most interesting and relevant to the reader. I was at Carlisle for about four months; if done in sufficient detail a whole book could be written about that experience, but that is not the purpose here.

My first contact with classified information came in some of the War College classes. Part of my program of study there at Carlisle was to sit in on the classes being taught for the class of Lieutenant Colonels and Colonels making up the student body. At the beginning of each week I got, in my mailbox on the first floor, a schedule of classes for the week. Many of these classes were annotated as "Secret." I intended to attend all of the Secret classes. Some of these classified classes were more interesting than others, but none were what I would call mundane. I recall one classified discussion on Soviet "Operational Maneuver Group (OMG)" tactics. An OMG was an armored unit comprising about 15,000 troops and 350 tanks. Its mission was to penetrate behind the lines and capture or destroy important political or military targets (such as the NATO nuclear deterrent force). Being a reservist in the armor, with a mission of reinforcing Europe in the event to war, this class was of particular interest.

In one such class things got particularly interesting when the instructor dropped a bomb.

***[390]

Another source of exposure to classified information at Carlisle was the project I began work on for Dr. Dunn and Col. Staudenmaier. (Though most people at Carlisle went on a first name basis, I was so junior I never took up the practice.) The book, *Competing Strategies for the 80s*, was a collection of papers presented at a spring 1983 conference held at the Strategic Studies Institute. In one of the essays that was to make up the book the author put forward the idea that a conventional (non-nuclear) ground counter attack (aimed at liberating Eastern Europe from the Soviet Bloc) would be an easy possibility for NATO (in the event of a massive Soviet land attack to capture Western Europe). The paper's author, Dr. Samuel P. Huntington, called tactic a "counter-retaliatory offensive." My assignment was to graphically depict Huntington's thesis on a map of Europe. This map would be one of the major factors in my grade for the 4-month internship.

The classified work involving the map came in the form of some documents provided by Dr. Dunn. To produce the map for the book, I laid a map of central Europe across two desks in Dunn and Staudenmaier's large office. Over the top of the map was placed a clear plastic overlay that could be drawn on with grease pencils. I then took the classified map provided by Dr. Dunn (that showed Soviet deployments) and drew the position of the major soviet Armies, Corps, and Divisions onto the clear plastic with the grease pencils. The final step in the process was to draw in the counter-retaliatory thrusts proposed by Huntington in his paper. The whole process took several months of working several hours a day on the project. When the finished product was viewed, it was clear Huntington's plan had some problems.

The primary problem with the Huntington thesis that the map made so apparent was that there were more Soviet units in position to deflect Huntington's thrusts than the author accounted for. In particular Huntington stated a thrust could be made in the area of Pilsen, Czechoslovakia where there was only one lone Soviet Division. In reality there was a whole group of Soviet Divisions in the area. Staudenmaier and Dunn made much of this in their critique of Huntington's paper. What they did not say was that their conclusions were drawn from using classified sources that Huntington had no access to. Dunn and Staudenmaier, with my assistance, had declassified material to prove Huntington wrong. The large map that I produced was eventually taken to the reprographics department and shrunk down to book size and included in the final product.

In addition to the assignment to work on the map, I began work on my independent study shortly after settling in at Carlisle. Colonel Barlow had canned my idea of doing something on strategy related to procurement. For some reason I picked the topic of Nicaragua. At this time, 1983, there was a great deal of controversy in the news about US involvement in the war against the Sandanistas (who were then in power in Nicaragua). The Sandanistas had come to power in 1979, after defeating the US-backed dictatorship of Anistasio Somoza. Even before they were in control in the capital city of Managua, there were those saying that the Sandanistas were the stooges of the Cubans, and once removed the Soviets. Some voices cried that the Sandanistas were turning Nicaragua into "another Cuba." Voices on the left cried that Central America would become "another Vietnam." With the apparent stakes so high, I could not resist the idea of studying this conflict with the resources I had at hand.

The first, and very obvious resource, available for the study of Nicaragua was the press. Every day at the security desk on the way in to my office I picked up a copy of *The Wall Street Journal*, *The New York Times,* and *The Washington Post*. It was from articles in these papers that my interest in Central America was sparked. I don't recall any further meetings with Colonel Barlow on the subject of my independent study; I simply told Col. Staudenmaier and Dr. Dunn what I wanted to work on and commenced work.

One of the first places I searched for information was in the unclassified portion of the War College Library. The staff of very professional librarians was very helpful in locating items. I dug into the back issues of *The Washington Post* on microfilm, going back to the 70s when the Sandanistas were fighting for their existence against Somoza. I delved into the congressional record, where the morality of aiding dictators like Somoza in the name of US national security was being debated. Further, I looked into the Foreign Broadcast Information Service (FBIS) daily reports on Central America.

FBIS reports are translations of TV and Radio broadcasts (and some newspaper articles) from foreign areas. They are a joint project of the State

Department and the Central Intelligence Agency and are unclassified. At the present, anybody can subscribe to FBIS reports (provided they are prepared to pay the hefty subscription rates). The Central America reports I focused on came in a pastel pink cover. They contained such things as translations of clandestine rebel radio broadcasts. Sometimes I would see items in the FBIS reports that would appear a day or so later in the mainstream press (without attribution to the FBIS).

In terms of using classified information for my research project I took my cues mostly from the full Colonel with whom I shared an office. John Morin was an Infantry officer, a Vietnam veteran, and a graduate of West Point. He had just come from an Infantry Division in Germany and was assigned to the War College as an academic fellow for one year. He was doing a study on the use of civil airliners for military transport (as would happen a number of years later during the Gulf Conflict).

When Colonel Morin found out I was doing a study involving guerrilla warfare he put on the black board in the office an illustration of the Maoist theory of war. First there was a "latent and incipient phase" where the guerrillas began to come together; then there would follow a "cadre phase" where identifiable leaders arose within the movement; then would follow an "unconventional phase" where small units would ceaselessly engage the enemy; finally would follow a "conventional phase" where large regular military units would engage and destroy the enemy. This is how it happened in Vietnam. Colonel Morin left his depiction of this theory on the board for months. When I would bring up the topic of unconventional warfare, he would refer to it.

We had a cordial relationship. We answered each other's phone calls when one was out of the office and passed messages where appropriate. Even though it was the practice to go by first names at the War College, I always called him Colonel or Sir; I just could not see doing it any other way. When I had questions of procedure I often took them to him (and this included the proper handling of classified material).

I was not formally instructed in the use of classified, and most of what I learned I got from Colonel Morin. Each member of the SSI staff, including myself, had a combination safe near his (there were no women in SSI except secretaries in 1983) desk for holding classified documents. I did not use mine, initially, but I asked around about the procedures. Colonel Morin explained to me that I could use the classified library and even check documents out from there up to my security clearance of Secret. Documents I checked out from the classified library were to be stored in my safe for the period I was using them. I could take notes from the documents, but then I had to classify my notes and keep them locked up. Further, Dr. Dunn cautioned me about using classified when I brought the subject up. He said I should be able to tie every fact in my report to an unclassified source, and to only use classified information as background material (a gauge to evaluate other sources).

I went down into the basement of the library, where the classified documents were located behind security cages, saw the librarian there, and checked out about a dozen secret documents on Nicaragua. I read them over in the basement and took them up to my office and stored them in my safe for use as references. I only recall two things about these documents, some 17 years later. One contained a statement that on such and such a date 8 FSLN (The abbreviated name of the Sandanista political party) officials visited Moscow, the same information was available in unclassified sources. I also recall one statement that the wife of a certain Sandanista official did not like to entertain officially. I thought it odd, and was a bit perturbed by the fact that the mighty US government should be collecting and propagating information on the social habits of a Nicaraguan government official's spouse.

Before I could call my research on the topic of Nicaragua complete, I had to interview one member of the SSI staff. Colonel John D. Wagelstien, a Research Fellow at the Institute, was a cowboy-boot-wearing Vietnam veteran and green beret. His assignment before coming to SSI was that of commander of the U.S. Special Forces in El Salvador who were assisting the pro-US government resist, a pro-Communist guerrilla force. The tie-in to my work on Nicaragua was that the Communist Salvadoran guerrillas were allegedly receiving support from the Soviet-Cuban leaning Sandanistas in Nicaragua.

The one hurdle to the interview was the War College policy of strict "non-attribution" of statements made by officers assigned there. What this meant in practice was that one could use or repeat information another member of the staff said, but one could not attribute the statement to an individual. It was thought that this level of anonymity led to a free flow of information within the academic institution of the War College. Colonel Wagelstien agreed to go on the record, I would be able to quote him.

The interview with the Colonel started almost comically. I asked the colonel flat out if he thought the action the Reagan administration was taking in Central America was adequate to meet the threat. He responded with a raised voice in the form of a question, "what are you looking for Lieutenant, room at the top?" I laughed appropriately and moved on to my next question. I gained nothing earth shattering from the interview. In some ways Wagelstien was not just a follower of the party line. He stated that the Salvadoran guerrillas had three possible sources of weapons and war material: "they can steal it from the enemy (the Salvadoran army), they can make it themselves, or they can import it." The official Reagan administration line was that the most significant support for the guerrillas was being imported from Nicaragua. More along the lines of the administration rhetoric, Wagelstien also stated that the presence of a sympathetic government in Nicaragua gave the Salvadoran rebels a "sanctuary" where they could go if "things got really bad."

Here I will mention one item about the War College that may be of interest to the reader. On many of my trips to the library I took the stairs instead of the elevator. On my route I would pass a poster advertising a "secret" video on Soviet bridging techniques. The poster stated that the film could be seen on request in an office one level below the library. Passing that sign day after day, curiosity got the better of me and I followed the stairs one flight further down than usual.

I knocked at the door I came to and a 30ish man in a civilian sports jacket answered. He seemed surprised when I asked about the bridging video (I don't guess too many people took the poster seriously). He said, "just a minute" and closed the door in my face. He came back a minute or two later, blocking the entranceway with his body when he opened the door, and said, "we're sanitizing." Evidently they were hiding material that was above the "secret" level for which my badge said I was cleared. After a few minutes the man led me in through a large office in which two others were working. The office was lined with computer terminals and teletypes on either side and at the far end, our destination, was a room that contained a conference table and a VCR/TV set-up.

He put the video in and asked me what I was working on. "Nicaragua" I said. He left and let the video play. Other than the fact that it was classified "secret," and the general conclusion that rivers were not to be considered obstacles to Soviet armored movement because of the speed at which they could bridge, I do not remember much about the ½ hour video. When it was over the man in the sports coat returned with a sheaf of papers in his hand. He said, "Here are some of our messages on Europe, we don't have anything on Nicaragua right now." He left again, giving me a few minutes to look over the messages he had just handed me. I noticed, with one exception, they were up to the minute "secret" messages dealing with Soviet troop movements behind the Iron Curtain. The exception was a message marked, "Top Secret," which I was not supposed to see. It was coincidentally on the subject of the location of Soviet bridging units.

I got nervous, scared even, thinking I had been left alone with the message to see if I would try and steal it. In retrospect, no doubt it was a simple error on the message handler's part. When the man in the sports coat returned I handed him all of the messages without saying anything. He said they could keep a file for me on Nicaragua. Not wanting any trouble, I said, "no thank you," and found my way out. Though the incident with the "Top Secret" message was probably nothing, I never returned to that office again. Nor did I mention my visit there to anybody else at Carlisle. I have often wondered what the exact purpose of that office was.

When I began to mold all of this information into the ideas that would form the paper, I was intellectually taken in by the work of one of the sharpest Colonels at Carlisle. Shortly after I reported in and found my desk, I was sent to the library to pick up the basic issue of books for War College students, there were two or three brown grocery bags full of them. Among the books was a manual covered in green construction paper. It was written by one of the SSI staff, Colonel Harry Summers. The book was entitled, *On Strategy: A Critical Analysis of the Vietnam War*. I met Colonel Summers only once; we talked briefly in his office about the failed hostage rescue attempt that was executed during the Iranian hostage crisis. The influence of his work on me was, however, significant.

I gathered from my reading of *On Strategy* two conclusions. The first of these conclusions was that if President Lyndon Johnson had asked the Congress (and indirectly the American people) for a declaration of war, instead of the Gulf of Tonkin Resolution, America might have triumphed in Vietnam. In short, if American political will had been fully mobilized we would have applied the measures necessary to win the conflict. The second conclusion from *On Strategy* that fell hard on me was that it was not "dialectical materialism," but four North Vietnamese Army Corps that brought the war to a conclusion in 1975. Summers made the point that US policy failed because it reacted to a Communist insurgency in South Vietnam and ignored the army of their protector in North Vietnam. I believed both of these conclusions were relevant to Central America in the 1980s and I argued this in my paper. My views on the subject of Vietnam and Central America have changed somewhat over time.

Afterthoughts

Cold Warfare: A Compact History was written to foster the all-too-illusive understanding of some of the ideas at work and events of the Cold War. Without compromising the ethics surrounding the security clearance once held by its author, we have taken a tour of the covert nature of the Cold War and some of the many mistakes made along the treacherous path to victory in December 1991. One major mistake that prolonged the struggle was that the Russian Communists, who became the leaders of the Soviet state in 1917-18, were never able to find themselves with the stomach for varying much from the Marxist-Leninist paths in the world of internal and external affairs.

A fact that made defeating the Soviets of primary importance is that Communism, in particular Marxism-Leninism, was (is) almost universally genocidal in its result. One only needs look at the USSR in 1918 and Pol Pot in the 70s and 80s. Also present in the history of the Cold War was China's litany of partisan genocide. Likewise, from the beginning of the titanic struggle we saw the use of Russian military power maintain and expand the empire. Specifically we see the Soviets crushing civil disputes in Hungary, and invading Afghanistan.

The major mistake being made by American historians now is the underestimation of the WWI period, where this writer says it all started (records are available in the National Archives). The genocidal nature built into Marxism-Leninism is perhaps oft ignored because so many American academics lean toward the left. We see the flaws of the disciples of Marx and Marx himself hidden by a quiet conspiracy that says, "looking in this direction is forbidden, for it shall yield nothing." Looking at the speeches and writings of the Marxists demonstrates the strength of the Soviet state for most of a century, and its weaknesses. The Soviets were often able to dig deep into the gut filled with Marxist platitudes to staunch the flow of blood from their hemorrhaging state. The Soviets, from 1917 to 1991, were more or less in a genocidal fight to keep power from both within and without. They were evil—nature took its course and the west won the protracted conflict with the dissolution of the USSR. Seeing this we have asked, where did this struggle begin, and what were the means employed?

We see in the first section that George Washington, while engaging the British in North America, put the wheels of covert action into motion over 50 years before Marx wrote the *Manifesto*. The intent here is not to blame the US for the origin of the Cold War, far from it. The intent was to show the origins of the American means of covert warfighting and how they predate the Cold War. When Washington heard the war he wanted between France and England was nearly under way he said, "God send it." Without French involvement the US chances for victory in her revolution would have been much slimmer.

What evolved some one hundred years after Marx's writing was a CIA capable of clandestine and covert military/paramilitary operations. In one breath George Kennan stated that what was wanted was not a "department of dirty tricks," but then stated that the CIA would operate in peacetime with operations including sabotage and guerilla war.

The means for this action was National Security Council memorandum 10/2—which is now in the public realm.

The first attempt to really rationalize American intelligence policy came in the 1970s under the direction of Senator Frank Church of Idaho. The end result was to make the agency more responsive to the Congress through permanent committees on oversight. Reaction to these strict limitations, which required a full 8 committees of the House and Senate, and in many cases their staffs, to be informed of any proposed covert actions. The Reagan administration, and the later part of the Carter administration's reign were subject to a re-organization and reduction of the number or people to be involved in reviewing operations down to as few as 8 members of the entire Congressional body politic. Some confusion comes about in the 60s, though the 80s led many in the world community to conclude that America had done great wrong during this time period. The help the US provided to the Afghani freedom fighters was, at the time it took place, never very controversial because Afghanistan was directly invaded by Soviet forces in 1979 (and harassed much earlier).

In the case of Nicaragua the CIA first doubted, in 1967, that the Communists were involved in the fight against the dictator. Eventually the agency was to see both Cuban and Soviet involvement as clear and dangerous. This switch of opinion is clear when looking at the document trail. Perhaps some would view this change as a form of treachery on the part of the CIA. More likely it was as a result of new evidence that caused the picture to become clearer.

Three areas are left out of this history to any substantial extent. They are all from the 50s. These items were McCarthyism, China, and the Korean Conflict. Also left out were some more significant statistics from that decade, like for instance in 1958, long after the Korean War was over, the US military aircraft production companies were employing more people than were employed in WWII (according to the Air Transport Association yearbooks).

McCarthyism was nothing more than political grandstanding by an unethical politician. The light of day finally caught up with him. The phenomenon of McCarthyism did not result in higher defense spending (it was already astronomical as a part of GNP). Nor did it result in a more aggressive foreign policy. The witch hunts were, in effect, much ado about nothing.

China is another area this author left almost entirely untouched. In fact, one could say that the Cold War is not truly over, with the lineage of the regime that perpetrated the Tiananmen massacres in 1989 in power to date. Further it is a Communist regime. In the beginning the Chinese adopted Maoist versions of that genocidal ideology. These temperaments were more favorable toward the agricultural peasantry than the Russian variants of Marxism (and Leninism).

A whole book could easily be written about Chinese Communism (and Maoism), and many have been. As the threat from Chinese and their growing strategic nuclear arsenal, combined with their provision of some level of support of terrorist countries like Iran and North Korea continues to become evident, it is possible that the end of the Cold War will be fixed at the end of Chinese communism in some future date, not the fall of the Soviet state in 1991. This would be similar to the idea that war with Germany ended in May 1945, but the end of the Second World War did not come till Japan was likewise defeated some months later. I leave it to future historians to decide what the case of the end of the Cold War is in regard to China.

For the purposes of this writing, Korea was (is) part of the overall regional struggle for the eastern environs of Asia. While over 50,000 US soldiers died, and threatened escalation occurred on the part of the US, it remained a strictly regional conflict. There were few consequences at home (the Vietnam controversy started to echo through political culture a full 10 years before the war ended), and no vertical, or even true horizontal escalations. Korea (1950-53) remained primarily a ground and air with few impacts beyond the peninsula. There simply was not space for Korea and China, except in the macro view, in this condensed history.

In the end game, this author hopes that at least two main ideas are discernable by the reader. First, the Cold War was ideological at its base. Without the ideologies described early on in the work, and in reality throughout *Cold Warfare,* there would have been no Cold War. The Russo-Soviet state (looking somewhat like the old Russian Empire) may not have been fast friends with the West; in fact, it may have been a chief competitor. The competitive actions of a non-totalitarian and hostile state would likely have been much less violent and polarizing without ideology fanning the flames. Ideology simply means ideas that are to rule over a group or class and provide for their aspirations to be achieved. Marxist-Leninist doctrines in action are some of the most developed form of following a set of ideas.

The second main idea is that the Cold War had, in effect, begun in 1918. President Wilson allowed himself, and the US troops in question, to be lured into the fighting against the upstart Red Army in North Russia. The British had promised Wilson that US troops sent in under British command would only be used to protect military supplies already presented to the Russian government before the revolution from falling into the Reds' hands. As it turned out the US troops were sent directly into combat against the reds on their arrival in north Russia under British General Poole. The facts surround this deployment were somewhat acknowledged by America, but many of the official records of the mission remained classified until the 1970s.

Likewise, on the second main idea and the start of the Cold War, was the fact that a red scare and subsequent spate of deportations occurred in the US. It was non-citizen aliens that were sent out from the US, as citizens are not subject to deportation. This series of actions, and the fact that the foreign Reds were a danger, occurred in the early 1920s.

Lastly, on the start of the Cold War in 1918, was the fact that Wilson engaged the State Department to urge the global community to rebuke the new leaders of the Soviet state over the murder campaign launched by Lenin. Apologists for Lenin oft state that the killing spree he launched came only after an attempt on his life.

Two points show that terror was within Soviet plans well before that event. First, the secret police had been created to be called on when the need for terror arose. Second, Lenin had advocated the future us of terror as a tool as early as 1905 in his speeches and writings. When in power he launched the "red terror" at the first opportunity in 1917-22. This included not only the traditional use of the secret police and secret trials, with executions often the outcome, it also led to the forced starvation of 2-3 million Russians (well before the Stalinist "great terror)." With the beginning of red terror in the post World War I period, the US did not recognize the Communist leadership of the new Soviet state until 1933. This is further proof a near warlike state between America and the Soviets was in effect well before the end of WWII.

I cannot say loudly enough in this conclusion, that is to say it is my conclusion, that the forms of Communism practiced in the 20th century are almost universally genocidal and therefore evil and without excuse. Accommodation of this heinous evil without a doubt would have been equally evil; taking on the Soviets was worth the risks for the many millions or even billions of souls that would have perished under the global reign of terror that would have ensued.

Webster tells us that genocide is the systematic and planned extermination of a given group of people. The French revolution could be considered genocidal. It is left to the prognosticators to determine that whether the US had simply walked out of that conflict, the Soviets would have gotten a positive boost in their moral by way of the calculation of the correlation of forces. This author thinks that outcome would have been likely. We are only left to consider, was prevention of a global reign of terror—or its legitimate possibility—evil enough to do what was done? I say the answer is a resounding note that the Soviets had to be stopped.

One area not examined to any degree in putting this history together was the Soviet Archives. Two former Soviet officers were interviewed in numerous occasions for deep background information. One served in Afghanistan, the other had no combat experience. Both live in the US under asylum. Even if the Soviet archives could be examined, the accuracy of them would be in even greater question than US archives. An experienced writer's account always suffers under the pain of knowing that some day what they have written is subject to be read. Also, the various Soviet official papers in their archives have been opened and closed several times since the fall of the Soviet state. It is possible that this on-again-off-again access given to researchers may be taking place in order to sanitize unfavorable items on file.

Cold Warfare

Here is a brief note on my tangential time in the reserve components of the US Army. I served in the Pennsylvania Army National Guard from 1980 to 1990. I was in an infantry unit for two and a half years, then in an armor battalion from 1983-89, and then for a short time I served as the nuclear, biological, and chemical center director in the division headquarters. After that I served as the intelligence officer for a chemical brigade in 1990-92. In that final assignment of my short career I was assigned to keep tabs on the Foreign Broadcast Information Service reports from around the world—I was to pay close attention to any report dealing with terrorism. We were packed and ready but not called. After almost two years of service with that brigade I again requested and was granted discharge in 1992. My discharge became fully final in July 1994.

Not to confuse anyone, I never heard a shot fired in anger. My highest award was the basic parachutist's badge (Airborne wings) after completing jump school in 1981. This trip to jump school was made on my senior year spring break at high school in Indiana, Pennsylvania. I was part of the Indiana University of Pennsylvania ROTC in anticipation of being there for an early commissioning program between the University and the National Guard to begin in the fall of 1981. I will match that spring break story with any beach bum any day!

Bibliography

Documents Received Under the Freedom Of Information Act (FOIA)[391]

Central Intelligence Agency (CIA), Patrick J. Pacalo, collector, documents received pursuant to FOIA requests, 1994-2002.

Central Intelligence Group (CIG), Patrick J. Pacalo, collector, documents received pursuant to FOIA requests, 1994-2000.

Cohen, Edmund. Letter to Patrick J. Pacalo. Central Intelligence Agency, February 16, 2000.

Office of Strategic Services (OSS), Patrick J. Pacalo, collector, documents received pursuant to FOIA requests 1994-2000.

Interviews

Pacalo, Patrick J. *Interview with Daniel Ellsberg*. September 1999. Telephonic.

Pacalo, Patrick J. *Interview with Captain Nicholas Pacalo, USN Retired.* October 1992, Boardman, Ohio.

Congressional Documents

(Primary Sources)

Joint Hearings before the House /Senate Committees Investigating the Iran Contra Affair, May 11, 12, 13, 14 and 19, 1987. "Testimony of R.C. McFarland, Gaston J. Sigure, Jr. and R.W. Owen." Washington, DC: GPO, 1987.

Senate Select Committee to Study Governmental Operations With Respect to Intelligence Activities. *Final Report of the Select Committee to Study Governmental Operations With Respect to Intelligence Activities.* Washington, DC: GPO, 1976.

US House of Representatives Select Committee to Investigate Covert Arms Transactions with Iran and US Senate Select Committee On Secret Military Assistance to Iran and the Nicaraguan Opposition. *Report of the Congressional Committees Investigating the Iran-Contra Affair with Supplemental, Minority, and Additional Views, November 1987.* Washington, DC: GPO, 1987

US Senate. *Executive Sessions of the Senate Foreign Relations Committee: 1962.* Washington, DC: GPO, 1986.

US Senate. *Report of the Select Committee on Intelligence, January 1, 1983 to December 31, 1984.* Washington, DC: GPO, 1984.

Miscellaneous Government Documents

The Commission on C.I.A. Activities Within the United States. *Report to the President by the Commission on C.I.A. Activities Within the United States*. Washington, DC: GPO, 1975

Leighton, Richard M. *The Cuban Missile Crisis of 1962: A Case in National Security Management*. Washington, DC: GPO, 1978.

The President's Commission on Campus Unrest. *Report of the President's Commission on Campus Unrest*. Washington, DC: GPO, 1970.

US Department of State. *Salt II: The Reasons Why*. Washington, DC: GPO, May 1979.

US Department of State. "President Carter's Address to Congress June 18." *Vienna Summit: June 15-18, 1979*. Washington, DC: GPO, June 1979.

Young, Maj. John (USMCR). *When the Russians Blinked: The US Maritime Response to the Cuban Missile Crisis*. Washington, DC: USMC, 1990.

Collections of Papers, Documents, Letters, Speeches, Statements, Reports, or Writings (Primary Sources)

Borge, Tomás, et. al. *Sandinistas Speak.* New York: Pathfinder Press, 1986.

Carter, Jimmy. *Public Papers of the Presidents of the United States, Jimmy Carter.* Washington, DC: GPO, 1977-81.

Eisenhower, Dwight David. "Text of General Eisenhower's Address to the American Legion Convention." *The New York Times.* August 26, 1952, p. 12.

Etzold Thomas H., and John Lewis Gaddis, editors. *Containment: Documents on American Policy and Strategy, 1945-1950.* New York: Columbia University Press, 1978.

Ford, Gerald R. *Public Papers of the Presidents of the United States, Gerald R. Ford.* Washington, DC: GPO, 1975, 1979.

Galster, Steven R. editor. *Afghanistan: The Making of US Policy, 1973-1990.* Washington, DC: The National Security Archive, 1990.

Historical Files of the American Expeditionary Force, North Russia, 1918-1919. Washington, DC: National Archives and Records Service, 1973.

Jefferson, Thomas and James Madison. James Morton Smith, editor. *The Republic of Letters: The Correspondence Between Thomas Jefferson and James Madison, 1776-1826.* New York, London: WW Norton and Co., 1995.

Johnson, Lyndon B. *Public Papers of the Presidents of the United States, Lyndon B. Johnson.* Washington, DC: GPO, 1968.

Kennedy, John F. *Public Papers of the Presidents of the United States, John F. Kennedy.* Washington, DC: GPO,1962, 1963.

Kennedy, John F. Theodore Sorensen, editor. *"Let the Word Go Forth:" The Speeches, Statements, and Writings of John F. Kennedy, 1947 to 1963.* New York: Dell, 1988.

Leary, William M., editor. *The Central Intelligence Agency: History and Documents.* University, Alabama: The University of Alabama Press, 1984.

Lenin, V.I. Stefan T. Possony, editor. *The Lenin Reader: The Outstanding Works of V.I. Lenin.* Chicago: Henry Regnery Company, 1966.

Marx, Karl. Frederic L. Bender, editor. *Karl Marx: The Essential Writings.* New York: Harper and Row, 1972.

Nixon, Richard. *Public Papers of the Presidents of the United States, Richard Nixon.* Washington, DC: GPO, 1971, 1974.

Reagan, Ronald. *Public Papers of the Presidents of the United States, Ronald Reagan.* Washington, DC: GPO, 1982, 1984.

Tower, John, Chairman. *The Tower Commission Report.* New York: Times/Bantam, 1987.

Truman, Harry S. "Limit CIA Role to Intelligence." *The Washington Post.* December 22, 1963, p. A11.

Truman, Harry S. *Public Papers of the Presidents of the United States, Harry S. Truman.* Washington, DC: GPO, 1963.

Truman, Harry S. "Text of President Truman's Foreign Policy Speech at Parkersburg." *The New York Times.* September 3, 1952, p. 20.

US Department of State. *Soviet World Outlook: A Handbook of Communist Statements.* Washington, DC: GPO, 1959.

Washington, George. *The Writings of George Washington from the Original Manuscript Sources, 1745-1799.* Washington, DC: Government Printing Office, 1933.

Wilson, Woodrow, Arthur S. Link, editor. *The Papers of Woodrow Wilson*. Princeton: Princeton University Press, 1985.

Books

(Primary Sources or Firsthand Accounts)

Agee. *Inside the Company: CIA Diary*. New York: Stonehill, 1975.

Brzezinski, Zbigniew. *Power and Principle, Memoirs of the National Security Adviser 1977-1981*. New York: Farrar, Straus, Giroux, 1983.

Colby, William. *Honorable Men: My Life in the CIA*. New York: Simon and Schuster, 1978.

Eisenhower, Dwight David. *Mandate for Change*. Garden City: Doubleday, 1963.

Ellsberg, Daniel. *Papers on the War*. New York: Simon and Schuster, 1972.

Gates, Robert M. *From the Shadows*. New York: Touchstone, 1997.

Hoover, Herbert. *The Memoirs of Herbert Hoover, 1920-1933, The Cabinet and the Presidency*. New York: The Macmillan Company, 1952.

Johnson, Loch K. *A Season of Inquiry: The Senate Intelligence Investigation*. Lexington, KY: The University Press of Kentucky, 1985.

Kennan, George F. *Memoirs: 1950-1963*. Boston: Little, Brown, and Co., 1972.

Khrushchev, Nikita, Strobe Talbot, translator. *Khrushchev Remembers: The Last Will and Testament*. Boston: Little, Brown. 1974.

The Pentagon Papers: The Defense Department History of US Involvement in Vietnam. The Senator Gravel Edition. Boston: Beacon Press, 1971.

Phillips, David Atlee. *The Night Watch*. New York: Ballentine, 1977.

Roosevelt, Kermit. *Countercoup: The Struggle for Control of Iran*. New York: McGraw-Hill, 1979.

Shorr, Daniel, introduction. *Taking the Stand: The Testimony of Oliver L. North*. New York: Simon and Schuster, 1987.

Snepp, Frank. *Decent Interval, An Insider's Account of Saigon's Indecent End*. New York: Random House, 1977.

Books

(Secondary Sources)

Armstrong, Scott, editor. *The Chronology*. New York: The Fund For Peace/National Security Archive, 1987.

Augur, Helen. *The Secret War for Independence*. Boston, Toronto: Little, Brown and Co., 1955.

Bergen, Peter L. *Holy War, Inc.* New York: The Free Press, 2001.

Binney, Horace. *An Inquiry Into the Formation of Washington's Farewell Address*. New York: Da Capo Press, 1969.

Corsen, William R. *The Armies of Ignorance*. New York: Dial Press, 1977.

Daniels, Robert V. *Russia: The Roots of Confrontation*. Cambridge: Harvard University Press, 1985.

De Tocqueville, Alexis. John C. Spencer, translator. *The Republic of the United States of America, and Its Political Institutions, Reviewed and Examined*. New York: A.S. Barnes and Co., 1851.

Divine, Robert A. *The Cuban Missile Crisis*. Chicago: Quadrangle Books, 1971.

Fisher, Louis. *Presidential War Power*. Lawrence: University Press of Kansas, 1995.

Flemming, D.F. *The Cold War and Its Origins*. New York: Doubleday, 1961.

Fried, Jonathan L. Marvin E. Gettleman, Debora T. Levenson, and Nancy Peckenham, editors. *Guatemala in Rebellion: Unfinished History*. New York: Grove Press, 1983.

Gaddis, John Lewis. *Strategies of containment: a critical appraisal of postwar American national security policy*. New York: Oxford University Press, 1982.

Gaddis, John Lewis, *The United States and the origins of the cold war, 1941-1947*. New York: Columbia University Press, 1972.

Garthoff, Raymond L. *Détente and Confrontation*. Washington, DC: The Brookings Institution, 1994.

Garthoff, Raymond. *Reflections on the Cuban Missile Crisis*. Washington, DC: The Brookings Institution, 1989.

Giglio, James N. *The Presidency of John F. Kennedy*. Lawrence, Kansas: University of Kansas Press, 1991.

Jonas, Susan. *The Battle for Guatemala: Rebels, Death Squads, and US Power*. Bolder: Westview, 1991.

Leiken, Robert S. *Central America: Anatomy of Conflict*. New York: Pergamon Press, 1984.

Miller, Nathan. *Spying for America: The Hidden History of US Intelligence*. New York: Paragon House, 1989.

Oye, Kenneth. *Eagle Resurgent?* Boston: Little, Brown, and Company, 1987.

Posner, Gerald. *Case Closed: Lee Harvey Oswald and the Assassination of JFK*. New York: Random House, 1993.

Schlesinger, Arthur M. *A Thousand Days: John F. Kennedy in the White House*. Boston: Houghton Mifflin, 1965.

Schlesinger, Stephen and Stephen Kinzer. *Bitter Fruit: The Untold Story of the American Coup in Guatemala*. Garden City: Doubleday, 1982.

Shrag, Peter. Test of Loyalty: Daniel Ellsberg and the Rituals of Secret Government. New York: Simon and Schuster, 1974.

Smith, Malcolm E. *Kennedy's 13 Great Mistakes in the White House*. New York: The National Forum, 1968.

Sorensen, Theodore. *Kennedy*. New York: Harper & Row, 1965.

Troy, Thomas F. *Donovan and the CIA: A History of the Establishment of the Central Intelligence Agency*. Washington, DC: The Center for the Study of Intelligence, 1981.

Unterberger, Betty M. *American Intervention in the Russian Civil War*. Lexington: D.C. Heath, 1969.

Various Authors. *The Pentagon Papers, As Published in the New York Times*. New York: Quadrangle Books, 1971.

Periodicals

"America's Secret War." *Newsweek*. November 1982.

"Arms Control, Agreement Enough." *Time*. May 15, 1972, p. 36.

Churchill, Winston. *Vital Speeches of the Day*, XII (March 15, 1946): 392-396.

Dulles, John Foster. "The New Phase of Struggle with International Communism." *Department of State Bulletin*. December 19, 1955, p. 1004.

Eisenhower, Dwight David. "Communist Imperialism in the Satellite World." *Department of State Bulletin*. November 5, 1956, p. 703.

Kirkpatrick, Jeane. "Dictatorships and Double Standards." *Commentary*. November 1979, p. 34.

Lodge, Henry Cabot. "The Hungarian Question Before the General Assembly on November 4." *Department of State Bulletin*. November 19, 1956, p. 800.

Lodge, Henry Cabot. "Statement by Ambassador Lodge, November 19." *Department of State Bulletin*. December 3, 1956, p. 867.

Moskin, Robert J. "Ellsberg Talks." *Look*. October 5, 1971, pp. 33-34.

Radu, Michael. "The Origins and Evolution of the Nicaraguan Insurgencies: 1979-1985." *Orbis*, winter 1986, p. 32.

"Resolution Adopted By the General Assembly on November 4." *Department of State Bulletin*. November 19, 1956, p. 803.

"Resolutions Adopted by the General Assembly on November 9." *Department of State Bulletin*. November 19, 1956, p. 807.

"We Tell Russia Too Much." *US News and World Report*. March 19, 1954, p. 63.

"X" (George Kennan). "The Sources of Soviet Conduct." *Foreign Affairs*. 25, no. 4 (1947).

Newspaper Articles

"General for Peaceful Drive to Let Captive Nations Determine Their Own Rule." *The New York Times*. August 14, 1952, p. 1.

"Group Set to Aid 'Slaves' of Reds." *The New York Times*. August 23,1952, p. 4.

Hersh, Seymour M. "Huge C.I.A. Operation Reported in U.S. Against Antiwar Forces, Other Dissidents in Nixon Years." *The New York Times*. 22 December 1974, p. 1.

"House Members Call US Strategy Parley." *The New York Times*. February 5, 1952, p. 14.

Kissinger, Henry. "America's Contra Muddle." *The Washington Post*. August 28, 1987, p. A19.

"New Fight on Reds Urged, Donovan Suggests Guerrilla Tactics in Communist Lands." *The New York Times*. December 10, 1952, p. 3.

Porter, Russel. *"Dulles Gives Plan to Free Red Lands*." The New York Times. August 28, 1952, p. A12.

"Rebels Are Flown From Nicaragua; Hostages Released." *The*

Washington Post. August 25, 1978, p. A1.

"US Making Use of 'Escapee' Fund." *The New York Times*. January 18, 1952, p. 3.

"US Says Somoza's Ouster Needed for Nicaragua Peace." *The Washington Post*. June 27, 1979.

Television Transcripts

Public Broadcasting System. *Frontline*, show #1205. "Who Was Lee Harvey Oswald." Boston: WGBH, November 16, 1993.

Web Resources

Blanton, Tom. "The CIA in Latin America." *The National Security Archive Electronic Briefing Book no. 27.* http://www.gwu.edu/~nsarchiv/NSAEBB/NSAEBB27/index.html posted March 14, 2000.

Central Intelligence Agency, "Usama bin Laden: Islamic Extremist Financier." Released 1996 and found on the web at the site of the National Security Archive at: http://www.gwu.edu/~nsarchiv/NSAEBB/NSAEBB55/index1.html#1

Inderfurth, Karl F. US State Department. "The Taliban: Engagement or Confrontation." Testimony before the Senate Foreign Relations Committee, US Congress. Washington, DC: July 20, 2000. Found on the official State Department web site at: http://www.state.gov/www/policy remarks/2000/000720 inderfurth afgha.html

"Iran Contra, Independent Counsel, Summary of Report." Found at: http://www.webcom.com/pinknoiz/covert/icsummary.html

"The Men in the Shadows: Biographies of six men pardoned by George Bush for their role in the Iran-Contra Scandal." Found at: http://do-oh.juma.com/fishrap/classic/pardon/cast.html

Unpublished Papers

Pacalo, Patrick J. "Democracy Divided: The Case of Covert Paramilitary Assistance to the Nicaraguan Resistance." Indiana University of Pennsylvania, spring 1988

Endnotes

[1]*The American Mind*, by Henry Steele Commager, New Haven, Yale University Press, 1950.

[2]Alexis de Tocqueville, John C. Spencer trans., *The Republic of the United States of America,and Its Political Institutions, Reviewed and Examined.* (New York: A.S. Barnes and Co., 1851), p. 254.

[3] Helen Augur, *The Secret War of Independence* (Boston, Toronto: Little, Brown and Co., 1955), pp. 67-68.

[4] George Washington, *The Writings of George Washington from the Original Manuscript Sources, 1745-1799.* (Washington, DC: Government Printing Office, 1933), Volume 8, p. 98.

[5] *Ibid.* p. 100.

[6] *Ibid.* p. 182.

[7] Washington, *op. cit., Writings*, volume 10, p. 61.

[8] Washington's farewell address, as reprinted in Horace Binney *An Inquiry Into the Formation of Washington's Farewell Address* (New York: Da Capo Press, 1969), p 214.

[9] *Ibid.* p. 218.

[10] Thomas Jefferson and James Madison, James Morton Smith ed., *The Republic of Letters: The Correspondence Between Thomas Jefferson and*

James Madison, 1776-1826 (New York, London: WW Norton and Co., 1995), p. 1327.

[11] Jefferson was the key architect of the Declaration of Independence and Madison the primary author of the Constitution—together they are responsible for a large portion of American political thought.

[12] Karl Marx, Frederic L. Bender, ed., *Karl Marx: The Essential Writings* (New York: Harper and Row, 1972), 241.

[13] *Ibid.*, 247.

[14] *Ibid.*, 252.

[15] *Ibid.*, 254.

[16] *Ibid.*, 267.

[17] *Ibid.*, 268.

[18] V.I. Lenin, Stefan T. Possony, ed., *The Lenin Reader: The Outstanding Works of V.I. Lenin* (Chicago: Henry Regnery Company, 1966), pp. 468-469.

[19] D.F. Flemming, *The Cold War and Its Origins* (New York: Doubleday, 1961), p.22.

[20] Robert V. Daniels, *Russia: The Roots of Confrontation* (Cambridge: Harvard University Press, 1985), p. 140.

[21] Betty M. Unterberger, *American Intervention in the Russian Civil War* (Lexington: D.C. Heath, 1969), p. 41.

[22] Woodrow Wilson, Arthur S. Link, ed., *The Papers of Woodrow Wilson* (Princeton: Princeton University Press, 1985), Volume 51, p. 78n2.

[23] *Historical Files of the American Expeditionary Force, North Russia, 1918-1919* (Washington, DC: National Archives and Records Service, 1973), document #87.

[24] Flemming, *op. cit.*, pp. 39-40.

[25] *Ibid.*, p. 41.

[26] U.S. Department of State, *Soviet World Outlook: A Handbook of Communist Statements* (Washington, DC, 1959), p. 66.

[27] *Ibid.*, p. 80.

[28] *Ibid.*, p. 66.

[29] Flemming, *op. cit.* P. 43.

[30] Herbert Hoover, *The Memoirs of Herbert Hoover, 1920-1933, The Cabinet and the Presidency* (New York: The Macmillan Company, 1952), p. 182.

[31] Thomas H. Etzold and John Lewis Gaddis, eds., *Containment: Documents on American Policy and Strategy, 1945-1950* (New York: Columbia University Press, 1978), p. 51.

[32] John Lewis Gaddis, *Strategies of Containment: A Critical Appraisal of Post War American National Security Policy* (Oxford: Oxford University Press, 1982), p. 3.

[33] Wilson, *op. cit.*, volume 68, p. 201.

[34] Thomas F. Troy, *Donovan and the CIA: A History of the Establishment of the Central Intelligence Agency* (Washington, DC: The Center for the Study of Intelligence, 1981), p. 24.

[35] *Ibid.*, pp. 31-32.

[36] William Colby, *Honorable Men: My Life in the CIA* (New York: Simon and Schuster, 1978), p. 26.

[37] *Ibid.*, p. 205.

[38] *Ibid.*, pp. 124-125.

[39] William R. Corsen, *The Armies of Ignorance* (New York: Dial Press, 1977), p. 239.

[40] Colby, *op. cit.*, pp. 58-59.

[41] *Ibid.*, pp. 60-62.

[42] Gaddis, *Strategies of Containment*, p. 266.

[43] William M. Leary, ed., *The Central Intelligence Agency: History and Documents* (University, Alabama: The University of Alabama Press, 1984), p. 126.

[44] *Ibid.*, p. 127.

[45] Thomas H. Etzold and John Lewis Gaddis, eds., *Containment: Documents on American Policy and Strategy, 1945-1950* (New York: Columbia University Press, 1978), pp. 51-61.

[46] *Ibid.*, p. 62.

[47] Gaddis, *The United States and the Origins of the Cold War, op. cit.*, p. 348.

[48] Gaddis, *Strategies of Containment*, pp. 21-22.

[49] *Ibid.*, p. 23.

[50] Winston Churchill, *Vital Speeches of the Day*, XII (March 15, 1946), pp. 392-396.

[51] Harry S. Truman, *Public Papers of the Presidents of the United States, Harry S. Truman, 1947* (Washington, DC: GPO, 1963), pp. 176-180.

[52] "Mr. X" (George Kennan), "The Sources of Soviet Conduct," *Foreign Affairs*, July 1947, volume 25, number 4.

[53] Colby, *op. cit.*, p. 71.

[54] Etzold and Gaddis, *op. cit.*, pp. 121-122.

[55] *Ibid.*

[56] George F. Kennan, *Memoirs: 1950-1963* (Boston: Little, Brown, and Co., 1972), pp. 202-203.

[57] *Ibid.*

[58] Leary, *op. cit.*, p. 131.

[59] Colby, *op. cit.*, p. 71.

[60] Leary, *op. cit.*, p. 133.

[61] *Ibid.*, p. 132.

[62] Central Intelligence Group, *Soviet Foreign and Military Policy* (23 July 1946). Originally classified Top Secret, approved for release June 1988.

[63] Nathan Miller, *Spying for America: The Hidden History of US Intelligence* (New York: Paragon House, 1989), p. 322.

[64] Etzold and Gaddis, *op. cit.*, pp. 385-442.

[65] CIA, "The Tudeh Party: Vehicle of Communism in Iran," published 18 July 1949, p. 5.

[66] Kermit Roosevelt, *Countercoup: The Struggle for Control of Iran* (New York: Mcgraw-Hill, 1979), p. 75.

[67] *Ibid.*, p. 91.

[68] *Ibid.*

[69] *Ibid.*, pp. 99-101.

[70] *Ibid.*, pp. 102-107.

[71] CIA, "Probable Developments in Iran in the Absence of an Oil Settlement," *National Intelligence Estimate*, published February 4, 1952, p. 2.

[72] *Ibid.*, pp. 2-3.

[73] Roosevelt, *op. cit.*, pp. 107-115.

[74] CIA, "Probable Developments in Iran Through 1953," *National Intelligence Estimate*, published January 9, 1953, p. 1.

[75] *Ibid.*, p. 2.

[76] *Ibid.*, p. 3.

[77] Roosevelt, *op. cit.*, pp. 116-117.

[78] *Ibid.*, pp. 172-173.

[79] *Ibid.*, pp. 174-178.

[80] *Ibid.*, p. 191.

[81] *Ibid.*, p. 215.

[82] CIA, "Probable Developments in Iran Through 1954," *National Intelligence Estimate*, published November 16, 1953, p. 2.

[83] Nikita Khrushchev, Strobe Talbot, translator, *Khrushchev Remembers: The Last Testament* (Boston: Little Brown, 1974), p. 297.

[84] Jonathan L. Fried, Marvin E. Gettleman, Debora T. Levenson, and Nancy Peckenham, editors, *Guatemala in Rebellion: Unfinished History* (New York: Grove Press, 1983), pp. 48-49.

[85] Susan Jonas, *The Battle for Guatemala: Rebels, Death Squads, and US Power* (Bolder: Westview, 1991), p. 23.

[86] *Ibid.*

[87] Fried, *op. cit.*, pp. 49-50.

[88] Jonas, *op. cit.*, p. 25.

[89] *Ibid.*, pp. 25-26.

[90] *Ibid.*

[91] *Ibid.*, p. 31.

[92] *Ibid.*, p. 27.

[93] *Ibid.*, pp. 27-28.

[94] *Ibid.*, p. 32. Fried, *op. cit.*, p. 55.

[95] Dwight David Eisenhower, *Mandate for Change* (Garden City, New York: Doubleday, 1963), p. 3.

[96] Stephen Schlesinger and Stephen Kinzer, *Bitter Fruit: The Untold Story of the American Coup in Guatemala* (Garden City, New York: Doubleday, 1982), p. 108.

[97] *Ibid.*, p. 185.

[98] *Ibid.*, pp. 110-111.

[99] CIA, "classified message to Director from code name Lincoln." July 5, 1954.

[100] *Ibid.*, p. 115.

[101] CIA, Letter to Thomas Farmer re: PB Success, October 15, 1979, declassified in October 1999.

[102] Fried, *op. cit.*, p. 79.

[103] David Atlee Phillips, *The Night Watch* (New York: Ballentine, 1977), p.

42-43.

[104] *Ibid.*

[105] *Ibid.*, pp. 50-54.

[106] *Ibid.*, p. 55.

[107] Eisenhower, *op. cit.*, p. 424.

[108] *Ibid.*, p. 424.

[109] Phillips, *op. cit.*, p. 58.

[110] *Ibid.*, p. 59.

[111] Schlesinger, *op. cit.*, pp. 183-184 and Phillips, op. cit., pp. 60-61.

[112] *Ibid.*, p. 200.

[113] *Ibid.*, p. 209.

[114] Jonas, *op. cit.*, p. 41.

[115] *Ibid.*, p. 41-42.

[116] Fried, *op. cit.*, p. 79 and Eisenhower, op. cit., p. 427.

[117] *Ibid.*, p. 72-77.

[118] Eisenhower, *op. cit.*, pp. 425-426.

[119] *Ibid.*, p. 427.

[120] Jonas, *op. cit.*, pp. 59-60 and 149-199.

[121] CIA, *Current Intelligence Digest*, October 24-29, 1956.

[122] OSS, 2677th Regiment Headquarters, "Orders to Lieut. J. Holt Green," dated 16 September 1944 (Released 11 January 1980), and "Rumania Team," dated 10 August 1944 (Released in August 1990).

[123] OSS, "Final Report of OSS Sofia Unit 15 November to 25 December 44," dated 30 December 1944.

[124] OSS, Robert P. Joyce, "Analysis of OSS activities in the Balkans and Central Europe," dated 3 January 1945, released December 1990, page 1.

[125] *Ibid.*, p. 4.

[126] *Ibid.*, p. 3.

[127] *Ibid.*, p. 5.

[128] OSS, William J. Donovan, Director of the OSS, "Memorandum for the President," dated 20 June 1945, approved for release 6 January 1993, p. 1.

[129] *Ibid.*, p. 2.

[130] Nikita Khrushchev, Strobe Talbot, trans., *Khrushchev Remembers: The Last Testament* (Boston: Little, Brown, and Co., 1974), p. 175.

[131] CIA, Arthur Bliss Lane, Letter to Allen Welsh Dulles, July 16, 1948. Released October 1992.

[132] *Ibid.*

[133] *Ibid.*

[134] Philip Agee, *Inside the Company: CIA Diary* (New York: Stonehill, 1975), p. 72.

[135] CIA, William J. Donovan, Letter to Allen Dulles at Sullivan and Cromwell. November 6th, 1950. MORI DocID: 30227. Released October 1992.

[136] CIA, Allen W. Dulles from [street address redacted], Washington DC, to William J. Donovan, Two Wall Street New York. 8 January 1951. MORI DocID: 30243. Released October 1992 with redaction.

[137] "New Fight on Reds Urged, Donovan Suggests Guerrilla Tactics in Communist Lands," *The New York Times.* December 10, 1952, p. 3.

[138] CIA, Allen Dulles, Memorandum draft dated 22 December 1950, MORI DocID: 31941, Released October 1992.

[139] CIA, Author Redacted, Letter to Allen Dulles at Sullivan and Cromwell, January 19, 1951. MORI DocID: 30246, Released October 1992.

[140] "U.S. Making Use of 'Escapee' Fund," *The New York Times*. January 18, 1952, p. 3.

[141] "House Members Call U.S. Strategy Parley," *The New York Times*. February 5, 1952, p. 14.

[142] "General For Peaceful Drive to Let Captive Nations Determine Their Own Rule," *The New York Times.* August 14, 1952, p. 1.

[143] "Group Set to Aid 'Slaves' of Reds," *The New York Times*. August 23, 1952, p. 4.

[144] "Text of General Eisenhower's Address to the American Legion Convention," *The New York Times.* August 26, 1952, p. 12.

[145] Russel Porter, "Dulles Gives Plan to Free Red Lands," *The New York Times*. August 28, 1952, p. A12.

[146] "Text of President Truman's Foreign Policy Speech at Parkersburg," *The New York Times*. September 3, 1952, p. 20.

[147] CIA, "Notes from the Foreign Language Press," Hungarian, September 13-19, 1952.

[148] "We Tell Russia Too Much," *US News and World Report*. March 19,

1954, p. 63.

[149] John Foster Dulles, "The New Phase of Struggle with International Communism," *Department of State Bulletin*, December 19, 1955, p. 1004.

[150] President Dwight D. Eisenhower, "Communist Imperialism in the Satellite World," *Department of State Bulletin*, November 5, 1956, p. 703.

[151] Henry Cabot Lodge, "The Hungarian Question Before the General Assembly," *Department of State Bulletin*, November 19, 1956, p. 800.

[152] "Resolution Adopted by the General Assembly on November 4," *Department of State Bulletin*, November 19, 1956, p. 803.

[153] "Resolutions Adopted by the General Assembly on November 9," *department of State Bulletin*, November 19, 1956, p. 807.

[154] "Statement by Ambassador Lodge, November 19," *Department of State Bulletin*, December 3, 1956, p. 867.

[155] Letter to Patrick J. Pacalo, from Edmund Cohen (CIA), dated February 16, 2000.

[156] John F. Kennedy, Theodore Sorensen ed., *"Let the Word Go Forth": The Speeches, Statements, and Writings of John F. Kennedy, 1947 to 1963* (New York: Dell, 1988), p. 272.

[157] Robert A. Divine, *The Cuban Missile Crisis* (Chicago: Quadrangle Books, 1971), p. 4.

[158] US Senate, *Executive Sessions of the Senate Foreign Relations Committee: 1962* (Washington, DC: GPO, 1986), pp. 145-147.

[159] *Ibid.*, pp. 144-146.

[160] *Ibid.*

[161] Divine, *op. cit.*, p. 119.

[162] State Department, *op. cit.*, p. 98.

[163] Nikita Khrushchev, Strobe Talbot, ed., *Khrushchev Remembers: The Last Testament* (Boston: Little, Brown, and Co., 1974), pp. 530-531.

[164] Kennedy, Sorensen ed., *op. cit., Let the Word Go Forth*, p. 14.

[165] Theodore Sorensen, *Kennedy* (New York: Harper & Row, 1965), p. 183.

[166] Kennedy, Sorensen ed., *op. cit., Let the Word Go Forth*, pp. 249-252.

[167] Malcolm E. Smith, *Kennedy's 13 Great Mistakes in the White House* (New York: The National Forum, 1968), pp. 2-8.

[168] James N. Giglio, *The Presidency of John F. Kennedy* (Lawrence, Kansas: University of Kansas Press, 1991), p. 96.

[169] Smith, *op. cit.*, p. 55.

[170] Arthur M. Schlesinger, *A Thousand Days: John F. Kennedy in the White House* (Boston: Houghton Mifflin, 1965), p. 275.

[171] Smith, *op. cit.*, p. 62.

[172] Kennedy, Sorensen ed., *op. cit., Let the Word Go Forth*, p. 220.

[173] Smith, *op. cit.*, 52.

[174] Schlesinger, *op. cit.*, pp. 287-288.

[175] Raymond Garthoff, *Reflections on the Cuban Missile Crisis* (Washington, DC: Brookings Institution, 1989), p. 10.

[176] Sorensen, *op. cit., Kennedy*, p. 669.

[177] Schlesinger, *op. cit.*, p. 391.

[178] *Ibid.*, p. 390.

[179] Richard M. Leighton, *The Cuban Missile Crisis of 1962: A Case in National Security Management* (Washington, DC: GPO, 1978), p. 6.

[180] US Senate, *op. cit., Executive Sessions (1962)*, p. 162.

[181] Garthoff, *op. cit.*, pp. 6-7.

[182] Major John Young (USMCR), *When the Russians Blinked: The US Maritime Response to the Cuban Missile Crisis* (Washington, DC: USMC, 1990), pp. 21-24.

[183] *Ibid.*, pp. 23-24.

[184] *Ibid.*

[185] Leighton, *op. cit.*, p. 5.

[186] *Ibid.*, p. 9.

[187] *Ibid.*

[188] Young, *op. cit.*, pp. 70-71.

[189] Harry S. Truman, "Limit CIA Role to Intelligence," *The Washington Post*, December 22, 1963, p. A11.

[190] Gerald Posner, *Case Closed: Lee Harvey Oswald and the Assassination of JFK* (New York: Random House, 1993), p. 137.

[191] *Ibid.*, pp. 142-143.

[192] Public Broadcasting System, Frontline, Show #1205 - "Who Was Lee Harvey Oswald" (Boston: WGBH, Air Date: November 16, 1993), Transcript page 13.

[193] Shrag, *Test of Loyalty: Daniel Ellsberg and the Rituals of Secret Government* (New York: Simon and Schuster, 1974), p. 26.

[194] Robert J. Moskin, "Ellsberg Talks," *Look* magazine, October 5, 1971, pp. 33-34

[195] *The Pentagon Papers: The Defense Department History of US Involvement in Vietnam*, The Senator Gravel Edition (Boston: Beacon Press, 1971), Volume I, p. 39.

[196] Various authors, *The Pentagon Papers, As Published in the New York Times*, (New York: Quadrangle Books, 1971), pp. 54-55.

[197] *Ibid.*, p. 61.

[198] *Ibid.*, p. 166.

[199] Colby, *op. cit.*, p. 209.

[200] *Ibid.*, pp. 223-224.

[201] *Ibid.*, p. 224.

[202] *Ibid.*, pp. 109-110.

[203] Shrag, *op. cit.,* p. 12.

[204] Daniel Ellsberg, *Papers on the War* (New York: Simon and Schuster, 1972), p. 9.

[205] Shrag, *op. cit.*, p. 40.

[206] *Ibid.*, p. 43.

[207] *Ibid.*, p. 42.

[208] *Ibid.*, p. 54.

[209] *Ibid.*, pp. 111-112.

[210] Moskin, *op. cit.*, p. 40.

[211] *Ibid.*, pp. 354-355

[212] *Ibid.*, p. 356.

[213] Colby, *op. cit.*, p. 272.

[214] *Ibid.*, p. 277.

[215] Patrick J. Pacalo, "Interview With Captain Nicholas Pacalo (USN-Retired)," October 1999, Boardman, Ohio.

[216] The President's Commission on Campus Unrest, *Report of the President's Commission on Campus Unrest* (Washington, D.C.: GPO, 1970), p. 233.

[217] Frank Snepp, *Decent Interval, An Insider's Account of Saigon's Indecent End* (New York: Random House, 1977), p. 64.

[218] Louis Fisher, *Presidential War Power* (Lawrence: University Press of Kansas, 1995), p. 172.

[219] Seymour M. Hersh, "Huge C.I.A. Operation Reported in U.S. Against Antiwar Forces, Other Dissidents in the Nixon Years," *The New York Times*, 22 December 1974, p. 1.

[220] Loch K. Johnson, *A Season of Inquiry: The Senate Intelligence Investigation* (Lexington, KY: The University Press of Kentucky, 1985), p. 11.

[221] *Ibid.*, p. 2.

[222] *Ibid.*, p. 223.

[223] *Ibid.*, p. 49.

[224] Emphasis added.

[225] The name of the C.I.A.'s secret operation to monitor and evaluate the antiwar movement in the United States. The C.I.A., and, in fact, the Nixon

administration, had the long-standing goal of proving the antiwar movement was tied to the Soviet Bloc or the North Vietnamese. No such connection has ever been proven.

[226] The Commission on C.I.A. Activities Within the United States, *Report to the President by the Commission on C.I.A. Activities Within the United States* (Washington, D.C.: GPO, 1975), pp. 23,25.

[227] Gerald R. Ford, *Public Papers of the Presidents of the United States*, Book I, January 1to April 9, 1976, Document 19 – "Address Before a Joint Session of the Congress Reporting on the State of the Union," January 19, 1976" (Washington, D.C.: GPO, 1979), pp. 41-42.

[228] Ibid., Document 107, "The President's News Conference of February 17, 1976," pp. 106-107.

[229] Senate Select Committee to Study Government Operations with Respect to Intelligence Activities, *Foreign and Military Intelligence, Book I, Final Report of the Select Committee to Study Governmental Operations With Respect to Intelligence Activities* (Washington, D.C.: GPO, 1976), p. 425.

[230] Ibid., *Intelligence Activities and the Rights of Americans, Book II,* p. 289.

[231] John F. Kennedy, *Public Papers of the Presidents of the United States*, January 20 to December 31, 1961, Document #388 "Remarks in New York City Upon Signing Bill Establishing the U.S. Arms Control and Disarmament Agency" (Washington, D.C.: GPO, 1962), p. 626.

[232] In 1988, the author of this volume was part of a class of First Lieutenants and Captains at the Army "Chemical Officer Advanced Course" at Fort McClellan, Alabama. The school saw fit to have a full Colonel from ACDA who was stationed in Washington (at the State Department) come in and talk to us about the progress of the chemical weapons ban and the Intermediate Nuclear Forces treaty negotiations then going on. Several of the class members grumbled privately about having to be involved with such a thing as arms control.

[233] *Ibid.*, January 1 to November 22, 1963, Document 319a "The President's

Interview with Robert Stein," August 1, 1963, p. 609.

[234] *Ibid.*, Document 324 "Special Message to the Senate on the Nuclear Test Ban Treaty," August 8, 1963, p. 622.

[235] CIA, *Intelligence Report*, "Soviet Public and Private Statements on SALT and MIRVs," Document marked SECRET, document dated July 1969, statement dated 9 Feb 67.

[236] Emphasis added.

[237] Emphasis added.

[238] Lyndon B. Johnson, *Public Papers of the Presidents of the United States*, 1967, book 1 January 1 to June 30, Document #80 "The President's News Conference of March 2, 1967," (Washington, D.C.: GPO, 1968), pp. 259-260.

[239] In the CIA's "Special National Intelligence Estimate #13-4-63 of 31 July 1963," marked "SECRET CONTROLLED DISSEM," and entitled "Possibilities of Greater Militancy by the Chinese Communists," the unknown author or authors stated on page 1, "It is clear that the leadership of Communist China resents the turn of events which has seen the USSR move toward *detente with the West* at the very moment when the Sino-Soviet quarrel has reached a new peak of vindictiveness."

[240] Richard Nixon, *Public Papers of the Presidents of the United States*, 1969, Document #1 "Inaugural Address, January 20, 1969," (Washington, D.C.: 1971), p. 1.

[241] CIA, *Intelligence Report*, "Soviet Public and Private Statements on SALT and MIRVs," Document marked SECRET, document dated July 1969, statement dated 9 Feb 67.

[242] Emphasis added.

[243] CIA, *Special National Intelligence Estimate*, "Soviet Attitudes and SALT," 19 Feb 1970, marked "Top Secret Sensitive Limited Distribution,"

p.10.

[244] Richard Nixon, *Public Papers of the Presidents of the United States*, 1972, Document 176 "Radio and Television Address to the People of the Soviet Union, May 28, 1972," (Washington, D.C.: GPO, 1974), p. 629.

[245] *Ibid.*, Document #177 "Text of the 'Basic Principles of Relations Between the United States of America and the Union of Soviet Socialist Republics,' May 29, 1972," (Washington, D.C.: GPO, 1974), p. 633.

[246] *Ibid.*, Document #197 "Message to the Senate Transmitting the Antiballistic Missile Treaty and the Interim Agreement on Strategic Offensive Arms. June 13, 1972," p. 674-675.

[247] *Ibid.*

[248] *Time*, "Arms Control, Agreement Enough," May 15, 1972, p. 36. (no author given).

[249] Usually only the advice and consent of the Senate is required for treaties. This is laid out in the Constitution, which gives the House no role in the process of treaty making.

[250] Gerald R. Ford, *Public Papers of the Presidents of the United States*, 1974, Document 6 "Address to a Joint Session of the Congress, August 12, 1974," (Washington, D.C.: GPO, 1975), pp. 11-12.

[251] Delivery vehicles include ICBMs, SLBMs, and manned strategic bombers.

[252] *Ibid.*, Document 257 "Joint United States-Soviet Statement on the Limitation of Strategic Arms," pp. 657-658.

[253] Raymond L. Garthoff, *Détente and Confrontation*, (Washington, D.C.: The Brookings Institution, 1994), p. 878.

[254] The SS-X-16 was a new ICBM system in 1975. It was being tested in both mobile and silo-based versions then.

[255] CIA, *Mobile Missile Verification Issues*, 1 April 1975, marked "TOP SECRET."

[256] Jimmy Carter, *Public Papers of the Presidents of the United States,* 1977, Book I, "Inaugural Address of President Jimmy Carter, January 20, 1977," (Washington, D.C.: GPO, 1977), p. 3.

[257] Zbigniew Brzezinski, *Power and Principle*, Memoirs of the National Security Adviser 1977-1981, (New York: Farrar, Straus, Giroux, 1983), p. 3011.

[258] CIA, *The USSR: Regional and Political Analysis*, 4 August 1977, marked "SECRET."

[259] Garthoff, *Détente and Confrontation*, op. cit., p. 953.

[260] Jimmy Carter, *Public Papers of the Presidents of the United States*, 1979, Book I, "Remarks at the Annual Convention of the American Newspaper Publishers Association, April 25, 1979," (Washington, D.C.: GPO, 1980), p. 695.

[261] US Department of State, *SALT II: The Reasons Why* (Washington, D.C.: GPO, May 1979), p. 1.

[262] *Ibid.*

[263] Emphasis added.

[264] *Ibid.*, p. 3.

[265] Garthoff, *Détente and Confrontation*, op. cit., p. 800.

[266] US Department of State, *SALT II: The Reasons Why, op. cit.*, p. 12.

[267] US Department of State, Vienna Summit: June 15-18, 1979, "President Carter's Address to Congress June 18," (Washington, D.C.: GPO, June 1979), p. 9.

[268] Garthoff, *Détente and Confrontation*, op. cit., p. 923.

[269] Jimmy Carter, *Public Papers of the Presidents of the United States*, 1979, Book II, "Address to the Nation on Soviet Combat Troops in Cuba and on the Strategic Arms Limitation Treaty, October 1, 1979," (Washington, D.C.: GPO, 1980), p. 1802-1803.

[270] Garthoff, *Détente and Confrontation*, op. cit., p. 1018-1021.

[271] Jimmy Carter, *Public Papers of the Presidents of the United States*, 1980-81, Book I, "Remarks at a White House Briefing for Members of Congress. January 8, 1980," (Washington, D.C.: GPO, 1981), p. 40-41.

[272] Garthoff, *Détente and Confrontation*, op. cit., p. 1082-1088.

[273] *Ibid*., p. 1102.

[274] Jimmy Carter, *Public Papers of the Presidents of the United States*, 1980-81, Book I, op. cit., "Annual Message to the Congress, January 21, 1980," pp. 119-120.

[275] Robert S. Leiken, *Central America: Anatomy of Conflict* (New York: Pergamon Press, 1984), p. 663.

[276] *Ibid*., p. 195.

[277] Emphasis added.

[278] CIA, Special National Intelligence Estimate Number 83.3-67, 12 October 1967, "The Prospects in Nicaragua Over the Next Year or So," marked "SECRET CONTROLED DISSEM", p. 6.

[279] Tomás Borge, et al., *Sandinistas Speak* (New York: Pathfinder Press, 1986), p.13.

[280] CIA, Directorate of Operations, "Intelligence Information Cable," 4 May 76, p.2.

[281] CIA, Weekly Summary, 21 October 1977, p. 8.

[282] *The Washington Post*, "Rebels Are Flown From Nicaragua; Hostages Released," August 25, 1978, p. A1.

[283] CIA, Director of Central Intelligence, "Situation in Nicaragua," 1978, p.3.

[284] *Ibid.*, p. 4.

[285] *Ibid.*, p. 5-6.

[286] CIA, Memorandum, "Subject: Cuban Support for Central American Guerrilla Groups," May 2, 1979, p.1.

[287] *Ibid.*, p. 5.

[288] Associated Press, *The Washington Post*, "US Says Somoza's Ouster Needed for Nicaragua Peace," June 27, 1979.

[289] Kirkpatrick would later become the US ambassador to the United Nations under President Reagan.

[290] Jeane Kirkpatrick, "Dictatorship and Double Standards," *Commentary,* November 1979, p. 34.

[291] *Ibid.*, p. 37.

[292] *Ibid.*

[293] CIA, "Cuban and Soviet Influence in the Caribbean and Central America," 2 November 1979, p.6.

[294] CIA, National Foreign Assessment Center, Memorandum of 5 December 1979, p.1.

[295] CIA, Special Analysis, "Policy Toward Latin America," 27 December 1979, p2-3.

[296] Scott Armstrong, et. al. *The Chronology* (New York: The Fund For Peace/ National Security Archive, 1987), p. 8.

[297] Patrick J. Pacalo, "Democracy Divided: The Case of Covert Paramilitary Assistance to the Nicaraguan Resistance," (Indiana University of Pennsylvania, Spring 1988), p. 8.

[298] Emphasis added.

[299] Ronald Reagan, "Inaugural Address," *The Public Papers of the Presidents of the United States,* Book 1 January 20 to December 31, 1981 (Washington D.C., GPO, 1982), p. 1.

[300] *Ibid.*, p.3.

[301] *Ibid.,* "Remarks at the Annual Convention of the National Association of Evangelicals in Orlando, Florida, March 8, 1983," Book 1, January 1 to July 1, 1983 (Washington D.C., GPO, 1984), p. 362.

[302] *Ibid.*, p. 9.

[303] Kenneth Oye, *Eagle Resurgent?* (Boston: Little, Brown and Company, 1987), p. 363.

[304] Pacalo, "Democracy Divided," op. cit., p. 10.

[305] Oye, *Eagle Resurgent?,* op. cit.

[306] CIA, Heavily redacted document "MORI DocID: 28938."

[307] John Tower, Chairman, *The Tower Commission Report* (New York: Times/Bantam, 1987), p. 14.

[308] CIA, *The Sandinistas and the Creation of a One-Party State*, An Intelligence Assessment, April 1981, p.2.

[309] CIA, *The Organized Subversion of Human Rights in Nicaragua*, September 18, 1985, p. 1.

[310] CIA, "Nicaragua: Economy in Crisis," 12 January 1982, p. 7.

[311] CIA, "Nicaraguan Military Buildup," 22 March 1982, p. 5-6.

[312] CIA, Unidentifiable document on 1981 finding, MORI DocID: 28939.

[313] CIA, Unidentifiable document on finding, MORI DocID: 28954.

[314] Michael Radu, "The Origins and Evolution of the Nicaraguan Insurgencies: 1979-1985," Orbis, winter 1986, p. 32.

[315] The Sandinistas hanged this name, from the Spanish for "counterrevolutionaries" on the Nicaraguan Resistance—when Sandinista usage of the term "Contra" was picked up in the world press, it stuck. The resistance fighters, who saw themselves as true revolutionaries, not "counterrevolutionaries," did not view it as a favorable term.

[316] Radu, "The Origins and Evolution of the Nicaraguan Insurgencies: 1979-1985," op. cit., p. 38.

[317] *Ibid.*, p. 40.

[318] CIA, "Nicaraguan Military Buildup," 22 March 1982, p. 2.

[319] Armstrong, et. al. *The Chronology*, op. cit., p. 70.

[320] Henry Kissinger, "America's Contra Muddle, *The Washington Post*, August 28, 1987, p. A19.

[321] "America's Secret War," *Newsweek*, November 1982.

[322] United States Senate, Report of the Select Committee on Intelligence, January 1, 1983 to December 31, 1984 (Washington DC: GPO, 1984), p. 23.

[323] *Ibid.*

[324] *Ibid.*, p. 25.

[325] *Ibid.*

[326] CIA/"Tayacan," *Psychological Operations in Guerrilla Warfare*, page 1.

[327] *Ibid.*, p. 6.

[328] *Ibid.*, p. 7.

[329] *Ibid.*, p. 26.

[330] *Ibid.*

[331] Tom Blanton, "The CIA in Latin America," The National Security Archive (electronic briefing book no. 27), http://www.gwu.edu/~nsarchiv/NSAEBB/NSAEBB27/index.html – posted March 14, 2000.

[332] United States Senate, Report of the Select Committee on Intelligence, January 1, 1983 to December 31, 1984 (Washington DC: GPO, 1984), p. 24.

[333] *Ibid.*

[334] *Joint Hearings before the House/Senate Select Committees Investigating the Iran Contra Affair, May 11, 12, 13, 14 and 19, 1987*, "Testimony of R.C. McFarland, Gaston J. Sigure, Jr. and R.W. Owen," p. 325.

[335] *Ibid.*, p. 328.

[336] Lt. Colonel North repeatedly claimed that he kept his superiors informed of his actions in regard to private sources of funds for the resistance. See Daniel Shorr, *Taking the Stand: The Testimony of Oliver L. North* (New York: Simon and Schuster, 1987), pp. 104, 105, 114, 115.

[337] *Ibid.*, pp. 106-108.

[338] *Ibid.*

[339] *Ibid.*, p. 127.

[340] *Joint Hearings before the House/Senate Select Committees Investigating the Iran Contra Affair, May 11, 12, 13, 14 and 19, 1987*, "Testimony of R.C. McFarland, Gaston J. Sigure, Jr. and R.W. Owen," p. 341.

[341] Oye, *Eagle Resurgent?*, op. cit., p. 360.

[342] Shorr, *Taking the Stand: The Testimony of Oliver L. North*, op. cit., pp. 79, 81-82.

[343] *Ibid.*

[344] US House of Representatives Select Committee to Investigate Covert Arms Transactions with Iran and US Senate Select Committee On Secret Military Assistance to Iran and the Nicaraguan Opposition, *Report of the Congressional Committees Investigating the Iran-Contra Affair with Supplemental, Minority and Additional Views, November 1978* (Washington, DC: GPO, 1987), p.375.

[345] *Ibid.*

[346] *Ibid.*, pp. 378-379.

[347] *Ibid.*, p. 384.

[348] "Iran/Contra, Independent Counsel, Summary of Report," found at: http://www.webcom.com/pinknoiz/covert/icsummary.html and "The Men in the Shadows: Biographies of six men pardoned by George Bush for their role in the Iran-Contra Scandal," found at: http://do-oh.iuma.com/fishrap/classic/pardon/cast.html

[349] Lawrence E. Walsh, United States Court of Appeals for the District of Columbia, *Final Report of the Independent Counsel for Iran/Contra Matters, Volume 1: Investigation and Prosecutions* (Washington, DC: August 4, 1993), p. 561.

[350] US Library of Congress, "El Salvador, The Contadora Process," located at: http://lcweb2.loc.gov/cgi-bin/query/r?frd/cstdy:@field(DOCID+sv0105)

[351] *Ibid.*

[352] Steven R. Galster, editor, *Afghanistan: The Making of US Policy, 1973-1990* (Washington, DC: The National Security Archive, 1990), p. 73.

[353] Peter L. Bergen, *Holy War, Inc.* (New York: The Free Press, 2001), p. 68 and Robert M. Gates, *From the Shadows* (New York: Touchstone, 1997), p. 146.

[354] CIA, "Near East and South Asia Review, 23 November 1979," approved for release August 1997, p. 4.

[355] CIA, "Soviet Options in Afghanistan," Interagency Intelligence Memorandum, Top Secret, September 28, 1979, p.6-7.

[356] *Ibid.*, p. 11.

[357] *Ibid.*, pp. 12-13.

[358] *Ibid.*, pp. 13-14.

[359] *Ibid.*, p. 17.

[360] *Ibid.*, p. 18.

[361] Ronald Reagan, *Public Papers of the Presidents of the United States, Ronald Reagan, 1981, January 20 to December 31, 1981* (Washington, DC: GPO, 1982), "Joint Statement Following Discussions With Chancellor Helmut Schmidt of the Federal Republic of Germany," p. 455.

[362] Emphasis added.

[363] *Ibid.*, "Statement on the Situation in Afghanistan, December 27, 1981," pp. 1199-1200.

[364] Phosgene oxime attacks the lungs.

[365] Trichothecene toxins are highly poisonous chemical substances extracted

from biological material (specifically molds). They attack the nervous system in a manner similar to nerve agents.

[366] Mustard agent, often incorrectly called "mustard gas," is an oily liquid that attacks the skin, lungs, and eyes. Victims can suffer blisters, blindness, and suffocation.

[367] Lewisite attacks exposed skin, producing large sores called "wheels."

[368] CIA, "Use of Toxins and Other Lethal Chemicals in Southeast Asia and Afghanistan, Special National Intelligence Estimate, Volume 1—Key Judgments," Top Secret, February 2, 1982, pp. 3-4.

[369] *Ibid.*, p. 19.

[370] CIA, "Afghanistan: Resistance Alliance," 19 May 1985, 1 page document.

[371] CIA, "Developments in Afghanistan," May 2, 1985, p. 5 and CIA, "USSR: Withdrawal From Afghanistan," Special National Intelligence Estimate, Secret, March 1988, p. 6.

[372] Bergen, *op. cit.,* pp. 68-71.

[373] *Ibid.*, p. 68.

[374] *Ibid.*, p. 55.

[375] CIA, "Near East and South Asia," November 1988, p. 7.

[376] *Ibid.*, pp. 64-68.

[377] CIA, Usama Bin Ladin: Islamic Extremist Financier, released 1996, found on the web site of the National Security Archive at: http://www.gwu.edu/~nsarchiv/NSAEBB/NSAEBB55/index1.html#I

[378] Abbreviation for Afghanistan.

[379] Department of Defense, cable with the subject – "Impact of the Stinger

Missile on Soviet and Resistance Tactics in AF," 03/1987, in the collection of the National Security Archive *(Afghanistan: the making of US policy, 1973-1990).*

[380] US government, Cable 03/1987, title redacted, classified Secret, in the collection of the National Security Archive *(Afghanistan: the making of US policy, 1973-1990).*

[381] Department of Defense, cable with the subject – "Aircraft losses in AF, Jan – Mar 87," 03/1987, in the collection of the National Security Archive *(Afghanistan: the making of US policy, 1973-1990).*

[382] US government, Cable 03/1987, title redacted, classified Secret, in the collection of the National Security Archive (Afghanistan: the making of US policy, 1973-1990).

[383] CIA/Foreign Broadcast Information Service, *FBIS Trends,* "Moscow Airs Domestic Frustration Over Afghan Involvement," April 8, 1987, classified confidential.

[384] CIA, "USSR: Withdrawal from Afghanistan," Special National Intelligence Estimate,' Classified "Secret," March 1988, p. 1.

[385] *Ibid.*, p. 12.

[386] CIA, "Near East and South Asia," November 1988, p. 7.

[387] Galster, *op. cit.*, p. 201.

[388] Karl F. Inderfurth, US State Department, Testimony before the Senate Foreign Relations Committee, US Congress, Washington, DC, July 20, 2000, "The Taliban: Engagement or Confrontation," found on the official US State Department web site – http://www.state.gov/www/policy_remarks/2000/000720_inderfurth_afgha.html

[389] Indicates classified material redacted – review of this material is still in progress at the Pentagon. When it becomes properly declassified this section will be revised.

[390] Indicates classified material redacted – review of this material is still in progress at the Pentagon. When it becomes properly declassified, this section will be revised.

[391] The formerly classified documents have been donated to the Cold War Museum.

Printed in the United States
128702LV00006B/247/A

9 781413 719253